I had already begun to
swell.
I had the bad gene,
    as I had already
On a Bed of Rice suspected

Edited

by

Geraldine

Kudaka

With a Foreword by

Russell Leong

Anchor Books

Doubleday

New York

London

Toronto

Sydney   Auckland

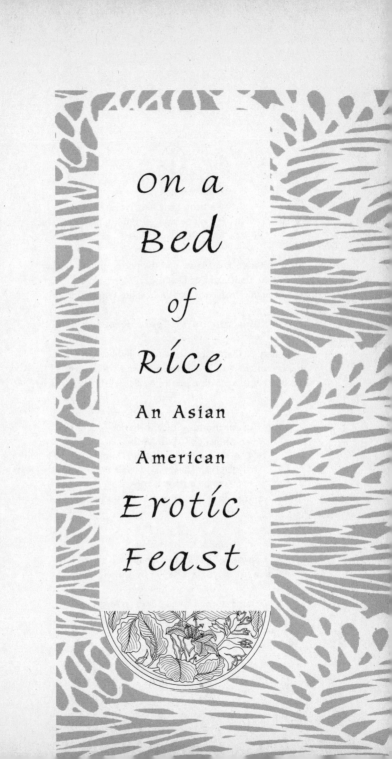

On a
Bed
of
Rice

An Asian

American

Erotic
Feast

AN ANCHOR BOOK
PUBLISHED BY DOUBLEDAY
a division of Bantam Doubleday Dell Publishing Group, Inc.
1540 Broadway, New York, New York 10036

ANCHOR BOOKS, DOUBLEDAY, and the portrayal of an anchor
are trademarks of Doubleday, a division of
Bantam Doubleday Dell Publishing Group, Inc.

BOOK DESIGN BY TERRY KARYDES

Library of Congress Cataloging-in-Publication Data
On a bed of rice : an Asian American erotic feast / edited by
Geraldine Kudaka ; with a preface by Russell Leong.—1st ed.
          p.   cm.
          1. Erotic stories, American.
     2. Asian Americans—Sexual behavior—Fiction.
     3. American fiction—Asian American authors.
          4. American fiction—20th century.
          I. Kudaka, Geraldine, 1951–   .
               PS648.E705   1995
     813′.01083538—dc20   95-15723
                    CIP

ISBN 0-385-47640-X
Copyright © 1995 by Geraldine Kudaka
Foreword copyright © 1995 by Russell Leong
All Rights Reserved
Printed in the United States of America

November 1995

10 9 8 7 6 5 4 3 2

Contents

Part V   Mating

Part VI   Colors of Love

Part VII   Betrayal and Infidelities

Part VIII   Mind Sex

Acknowledgments

I would like to thank the many people who made this book possible, including Garrett Hongo, who taught me that by pushing to find the truth, a writer becomes a better person. For an editor to do any less is a waste of time. I am thankful to Shawn Wong, who generously gave of his time and expertise and kept me on track. Shawn's comments and the input from Frank Chin, Julie Shigekuni, Ginu Kamani, Allan deSouza, Jana Monji, and Lily Pond helped concentrate my thoughts on a complex subject. Thanks also go to my agent, Barbara Lowenstein, and Bobby Ward; my editor, Charlie Conrad, and his assistants, Jon Furay and Jennie Guilfoyle, without whom this book would not have been possible. And to the many supporters of this project, including Eugene Ahn, Estelle Akamine, Shirley Ancheta, Susie Bright, Wilma Butler, Eric Chock, Jean D'Armpit, Glenn Hayashi, Howard Jonathon Hong, Ellen Krout-Hasegawa, Robert Kuwada, Kiran Lalloo, Shirley Geok-lin Lim, Ofun Milayo Makarah, Laureen Mar, Carlos Mayr, Hazel Nakamura, Chin Chin Ning, Bernadette Padilla, Arthur Sze, and Amy Uyematsu, and to my assistants, Chris Cabana, Alberta Lee, and Judy Weng. I am also grateful to Randolph Pitts and Lila Cazès of Lumière Films for their belief in my taste and aesthetics. Last, my deepest appreciation to the many writers and artists without whom this book would not have been possible. Thank you for giving me this opportunity to work with you.

This book is dedicated to the voice of Asian American desire.

Foreword

Unfurling Pleasure, Embracing Race

RUSSELL LEONG

*A*s an Asian American, I have found my sexuality entangled with race. In America, sex and race were my siblings—as close as sister and brother—full of love and hate, familiar and forbidden at the same time. Within the family, images of sex and race were one thing, but once outside the family, another thing altogether.

Some forty-odd years ago I discovered the connection between sex and race in San Francisco's Chinatown. My mother, father, brother, and I lived in a fourth-floor walkup facing an interior light well and our neighbors' windows. At eight years old, I could see across the light well into my neighbors' crowded rooms as they cooked, wrung clothes, or beat their children behind half-drawn window shades. Of lovemaking, of sexual desire or sensual pleasure beyond creating or maintaining the family, I do not remember seeing or hearing a thing.

It was 1958, only three years after Rosa Parks had refused to step to the back of the bus in Montgomery, Alabama, thereby starting the movement for civil rights. My neighborhood elementary school was segregated in those days—all of the eight hundred or so students were Chinese. Not until I took the bus outside Chinatown to junior high school several years later did I meet people of other races and colors—black, white, Latino. Taking a shower after gym class one day I saw that my naked body was colored differently from the other boys'. My hue was neither "white" nor "black" but brown in the arcs of my jaw, armpit, and soles of my feet. I kept the discovery of that color to myself. Armed with curiosity, I looked and listened more keenly to every person and conversation around me. From this period, I remember three experiences that hinted at the relationship between race and sexuality—all outside my family.

The ground floor of my apartment building had small stores—a dressmaker shop, a watch shop, and a magazine store that sold Chinese and English magazines and papers, along with school supplies. At the back of the store older men were always standing in front of the magazine rack. They were taller than I; I could only reach their shoulders and see their hands with sports or auto magazines. They would never shift their bodies to make room for me. One day, I wedged myself between two of them and began to reach for *Popular Mechanics.* Craning my neck, I could see other magazines pressed between the folds of pages that the men were holding, like hidden layers of a cake. The images were not of automobiles, however, but of nude women, with light hair and rosy breasts. One magazine displayed only photographs of muscular men wearing bikinis. I noticed that the highest rack above my head contained more erotic magazines. I couldn't wait to grow taller so that I could stand shoulder to shoulder with these other men, our fingers turning the printed pages surreptitiously. (Thirty years later—whether in New York, Taipei, Hong Kong, or Nanjing—I see naked Asian women on the covers of magazines or books on the street stands. The same kinds of older men flip through the books or magazines. Only now, no one cares or hides his voyeurism. It's not much different from the women several feet away who are picking through persimmons or oranges.)

The second image I remember—from the same period—is a twenty-inch-tall porcelain vase, cracked at its lip, but with a surface design of a peony in enameled colors. I found the vase lying by the hallway garbage chute when I opened the wooden door to throw away the daily trash. I brought the treasure home, and my mother asked where I got it. I said in the chute.

"Oh, that must have been thrown away by Miss Yen, the mistress of the department store boss," my mother said. "She's from Shanghai, you know, and her lover keeps her in that apartment there. She can afford to waste things, but we'll save it for New Year's flowers."

I vaguely knew what a mistress was, and remembered the businessman with dark spectacles, who did not live in our building but ambled weekly toward Miss Yen's door. I have often wondered whether, when Miss Yen met her lover, she took out the pins that held her dyed hair pulled back into a tight chignon, and they drank whiskey in small glasses. All I knew then was that theirs was a fascinating relationship outside family and marriage and the working-class people that I knew. Here, race was not the only issue, but how women and men related to power and desire within a traditional society.

By the time I was sixteen I would return to the apartment well after ten P.M. Rushing through alleys, I passed brick tenement buildings inhabited by older males: Chinese and Filipino men—retired cooks, laborers, sailors, and an occasional widower. White women would flit about those dark apartment entrances and then enter. To my eyes they were glowing creatures, with their orange lipstick and fair skin. One time, a young woman asked me whether I wanted a date tonight, and laughed before I could reply. I was tall enough by then, but my pockets were empty, I lived with my parents, and she probably knew it. Sex across racial lines was available but illicit.

These fleeting images have stayed with me because they took place in the barrio where I was born and grew up, before I had ever experienced any of the emotion, pleasure, or pain of sex. What little I saw as a youngster hinted at sexuality outside marriage and home, and across racial and generational lines.

Whether we are Vietnamese, Cambodian, Hmong, Lao, or Sri Lankan who arrived by ship or plane after 1965, or whether our grandparents were born to turn the soil of America, our lives, including our sexuality, were tested by our experience of race and racism in the United States. From the earliest Filipinos and Chinese sailors who settled in Louisiana in the eighteenth century to the Japanese, Asian Indians, and Koreans who came to Hawaii and the continental United States in greater numbers later—we confronted racial, economic, and social discrimination. Asians were barred from naturalization until 1952. As a result, we learned how to survive and resist: we struck for equal pay in sugar cane fields and in sweatshops, for the right to unionize when unions excluded us, and for our day in court to challenge ordinances and laws that discriminated solely against Asians. In the face of segregated American schools, housing, and public institutions, we sent our children to Asian-language schools, temples, and churches, established newspapers and magazines, and founded poetry and musical societies. The sheer energy we expended on survival and the building of our communities did not always find its way into sexuality or experiments with erotic pleasure.

Where did we place our physical and emotional energies? Both Ronald Takaki's *Strangers from a Different Shore* and Sucheng Chan's *Asian Americans: An Interpretive History* trace the energy of our migration and settlement as we struggled for a place and position in this society. Yet both books, as timely as they are, ignore our sexual lives and erotic impulses. Why? Most Asian immigrants who came to America in the nineteenth century were single workingmen, due to exclusion laws from 1882 onward that prohibited the bringing of spouses and kinfolk. Many had relationships with white, black, Latina, or Indian women, despite local miscegenation laws in many states that prohibited their marrying white women. These men were unlikely to write about their sexual experiences, especially if they crossed the lines of race and the law.

At the same time, some nineteenth-century Asian women—Japanese and Chinese—who were forced into prostitution in America did write about their experience of sexual and labor exploitation. The UCLA historian Yuji Ichioka documents the arrival of the first Japanese prostitutes, whom he calls *Ameyuki-san,* in the late 1880s in San Francisco. The procurers were Japanese immigrant men, including merchants and seamen. One prostitute referred to the male procurers as "Whores without human feelings (*ninjo*) . . . And people at large, in apparent glee, respect male whores who have power."

I remember my father telling me that in the 1920s and thirties he used to be a drugstore delivery boy in Northern California's Pajaro Valley, the farmland where he was born. He made deliveries to bordellos segregated by clientele—some houses permitted white men only, while others were reserved for Asians or Mexicans. Most Asian men who frequented prostitutes were laborers who worked up and down the West Coast. The exclusion laws were not repealed until after World War II. Later amendments to the 1965 Immigration and Nationality Act permitted more Asians to enter the United States, changing the bachelor society. Increasingly, Asians used the family reunification category to bring their kin to the United States. From the 1960s onward, Filipinos, Asian Indians, Koreans, and others reunited their families. Today, over seven million Asian and Pacific Americans live here. Understandably, for first-generation immigrants or refugees who had left their countries —often during war—the pursuit of erotic sexuality and the individual enjoyment of it took second place to the urgency of family survival.

Native-born Asian Americans who are second, third, fourth, or fifth generation here may find themselves in another situation. Like others, we have felt pressure to conform to American culture and society, sometimes at the expense of our own culture and consciousness. The term "model minority" has been applied to us as a group since the 1960s in relation to assimilation: to not bucking the status quo, getting good grades and working hard, and not questioning the American system. The Protestant work ethic, the traditional nuclear family, and heterosexuality within marriage were the norms. Those of us who experienced sexuality outside marriage, who chose partners outside our race, or who preferred to love members of our own sex were somehow suspect, as the writings in this anthology reveal. To conform, we kept our mouths shut and hardly wrote about sexual differences across race and gender, or sexual pleasure outside the family, until now.

When I said that sexuality and race for me were as close as siblings —I meant that to apply to what I had experienced within my own family or barrio. To non-Asians, we were another matter. To others, we were usually the *objects, rather than the subjects,* of attitudes toward exotic Asian sexuality that go back decades in my memory. The underlying reasons go farther back—to the European and American invasions of Asia and of the Pacific in the eighteenth, nineteenth, and twentieth centuries—including China, Japan, India, the Philippines, Malaysia, Vietnam, Indonesia, the Hawaiian Islands, and the Pacific. The devastating wars of the twentieth century, including World War II, the Korean War, and the debacle of Vietnam, added fuel to the fire. Simply put, throughout this history of Western subjugation and colonization Asians were seen by whites as both threatening and desirable—the men as dangerous and threatening, and the women as sexually available and desirable. Racial and sexual depictions converged, forming a distorted lens through which we—Asians and Asian Americans—were viewed by non-Asians.

Popular images that tie Asian and Asian American sexuality to our most visible racial features—eyes, skin, hair, and height—persist today. A recent article in a trendy Los Angeles magazine, entitled: "Asian Women/L.A. Men," with the subcaption "Why Do So Many Hollywood Types Go Looking for Love in Bangkok, Hong Kong, and Tokyo?" reports that the new passion and fetish of fortyish white Hollywood movie industry males are Asian women as lovers or wives. One white cinematographer ended up bringing a Thai wife to Hollywood:

> He saw women. Lithe, coy women with eyes that either hid or smiled at themselves in his own eyes; women who endured men's flaws and giggled in the hollow of men's shoulders; women of waist-high embraces; women with flawless skin wearing gloves and shoulderless dresses; women who loved-hated the erotic dance and eternally kept men guessing; laugh-bringing, praying good-bye, trusting the heavens with every human mystery.

The combination of Asians and sex, especially female, is the hot commodity on the sexual marketplace. Fantasies of Asian and Oriental women are conflated by male journalists, reinforced by the pornography industry, affirmed by American pop and popular culture, and colored by Hollywood. The same article found that, for males, "the new trophy dates at screenings are all Asian." The energy of Asian women is seen as "unfiltered and uninhibited, from very much the same place that sex comes from." The poet Janice Mirikitani resists being reduced to a childlike object of racial fantasy. This excerpt is from her poem "American Geisha."

> American white actress
> plays the role

of white American Geisha
filmed on location
in Japan.

It was sooooo hard
says she
because American women walk
in strides
shaking it baby.

Over there,
no hips, no shaking,
point the toes inward and . . .
don't speak
unless spoken to.

Japanese women,
says she
don't walk
They place themselves
like art objects.

While we have had to defend our kin and communities against
the cultural, aesthetic, and political "sexploitation" of women,
Asian American men have had to confront different issues around
the image of our sexuality—mainly the lack of it. Racist myths and
assumptions about smaller stature, smaller penises, smaller eyes—
and less sexual and erotic drive—have stymied the development
and acceptance of Asian American men as full erotic beings. The
emphasis of American media and movies has been on Asian male
martial prowess, on our kicks and punches rather than on our
passions. Michael Cimino's film *Year of the Dragon* (1985) is about
an Asian American female journalist, played by Ariane, who falls
for the white cop, played by Mickey Rourke, and eventually is
raped by Asian "thugs." The Asian males in the movie are either

cold-hearted thugs who forgo sex for power—as the protagonist, played by John Lone, does—or nerds like the Asian sidekick, played by Dennis Dun, who eventually sacrifices his life in the line of duty to the police force. These narrow images reinforce either the exotic, perverse, and threatening—or emasculated aspect of Asian and Asian American men—while upholding the sexual desirability and passivity of Asian and Asian American women.

As popular ideas about "Oriental sexuality" limit the range of our emotional response and sexual expression, we tend to avoid the topic. Traditional images or ideas—from the *Kama Sutra,* the ancient Hindu treatise on love and social conduct, the eighteenth- and nineteenth-century Japanese *shunga* manuals that contain printed images of sexual acts, or traditional Chinese Taoist yoga texts—hardly appear in our writing. Nor does Asian American writing on sexuality tap Buddhist treatises where sexual desire and attachment are sources of suffering and rebirth. Exceptions are in the brilliant stories by the Japanese American writer Hisaye Yamamoto that pit sexual desire against Buddhist or Catholic precepts, and in some stories of Toshio Mori that employ Zen and Indian philosophical ideas.

Despite our struggles in America, some individuals did take the time, risk, and effort to write about sexuality. Few works in the immigrant language dealt directly with the subject. Most works that addressed sexuality had to wait until families took hold and the second generation began to write in English.

Many writings were found or reclaimed by Asian American scholars or writers during the last twenty-five years. Following are some examples—out of thousands of Asian American literary works —from the turn of the century to about 1980. (During the 1970s Asian American writers began consciously to use and define themselves as "Asian American" and sought each other out as friends, as writers, editors, and publishers. The 1974 publication of the landmark *Aiiieeeee! An Anthology of Asian American Writers* gathered contemporary writers and placed them squarely on the literary map.

In the 1970s, 1980s, and 1990s, more Asian American novels, poetry, and drama were published. Current anthologies may contain some works of an erotic or sexual nature, but not as their major focus.)

When I first began to research this foreword, I sought voices that reflected my own particular background and biases—having been born and raised in a barrio that was patriarchal and heterosexual. My small community had a rigid division between sex for procreation and sex for pleasure. It had divided thoughts about sexuality outside marriage, though much took place that was unspoken. In Marlon K. Hom's translation and introduction to *Songs of Gold Mountain: Cantonese Rhymes from San Francisco Chinatown 1911–1915,* I found material that reflected an approach to my past. At the same time, Hom's materials shed light on what I had always deemed to be a lack of emotion in the Asian men of my father's generation.

In *Songs* Hom has culled and translated works from the over a thousand colloquial Cantonese poems written around the turn of the twentieth century, rhymes that are "folksy, somewhat vulgar, and at times erotic." The songs reflect the experiences of the massive immigration of Cantonese natives from Guangdong, China, beginning in the 1850s. The immigrant experience, according to Hom, created a new content—and context—for the oral literature of folk songs and other rhymes. Many pieces, though written by men, were from the persona of a wife, revealing affection for her spouse in America. Other poems dealt with women, prostitutes, and sex. After reading these poems, I realized that the Chinatown bachelor men who were a part of my youth had found voice in these songs.

The following poem, written in the persona of a young wife to her husband in America, was written by a man:

We had been wed for only a few nights;
Then you left me for Gold Mountain.
For twenty long years you haven't returned.
For this, I embrace only resentment in my bedroom;
Heaving a sigh
For the faraway sojourner who hasn't come home.
Everything brings me sorrow; I no longer care about my
     appearance,
Endless longing for you leads only to streams of falling tears.

Around the same time, Edith Eaton, a Eurasian writer with the nom de plume Sui Sin Far, published a collection of short stories, *Mrs. Spring fragrance,* in 1912. Her stories chronicled family and social life in Chinatown during the late 1800s and early 1900s. "The Story of One White Woman Who Married a Chinese," for example, examined an early interracial relationship. Eaton penned her stories at a time when books and films from the same period cast Asians in a dimmer light. Sax Rohmer was creating his invidious Dr. Fu Manchu, and William Hearst was fanning his newspaper's vehement anti-Asian bias with editorials. In Hollywood, Cecil B. DeMille was editing *The Cheat* (1915), and D. W. Griffith was promoting his *Broken Blossoms* (1919). Both films dealt with interracial sex and miscegenation, and in both scripts Asian males— played by the actors Sessue Hayakawa and Richard Barthelmess— were sinister, exotic figures who lusted after white women.

Contemporary Asian American writing reveals the complexity of sexuality within and outside Asian communities. In *Clay Walls,* the Korean American writer Kim Ronyoung places her story in the first two decades of the twentieth century. In the novel, Chun, an immigrant from a poor farming family, "forces his wife to have sex," all the while belittling her and enjoying the downfall of her noble (*yangban*) status as the wife of a common American immigrant.

In *Picture Bride,* Yoshiko Uchida introduces Hana Omiya, who, married to a first-generation Issei through an arranged betrothal in 1917, eventually falls in love with someone outside their conjugal bed. Under the gentlemen's agreement of 1907, Japan had voluntarily restricted the migration of laborers to the United States, leading to the arrival of young Japanese women who married men they had never before met. In both novels, the Asian wives of traditional immigrant men did not enjoy sex. Indeed, sexuality was but a bleak condition of marriage.

Until the 1920s, the second generation of Asian American women and men was almost nonexistent because of the exclusion laws that denied entry to women and therefore worked against the establishment of families. After the Great Depression, Asian American women of the second generation began to question their traditional roles in relation to their families, to men, and to their work. The historian Valerie Matsumoto examines how women of the 1930s sought advice about emotional, sexual, and interpersonal relationships from the columns of local English-language Japanese American papers. A newspaper advice column called "The Rendezvous Club" first appeared in 1933, before World War II. Second-generation women saw love and sexuality in different ways from their mothers. Later, during the unjust internment of 120,000 Japanese Americans in World War II concentration camps, inmates did write discreetly about love. The noted playwright Wakako Yamauchi translates this *haiku:*

> *Senta no*
> *jimusho no ko o*
> *sasayite.*
> —Bosai

> In an office
> at the Center, love
> is whispered.

Besides the Japanese, Chinese, Indians, and Koreans, Filipinos migrated to Hawaii and to the mainland United States—but as nationals of the U.S. government—beginning in the 1920s. One popular image of the times is a photograph of a well-dressed young man standing in front of a shining roadster with, more likely than not, a white woman. Filipino workers were prohibited from bringing in their wives or families, yet the desire for love and companionship persisted. Carlos Bulosan's semi-autobiographical *America Is in the Heart* depicts part of the first-generation Filipino saga in America prior to 1950. (During this period anti-Filipino race riots occurred in 1928 and 1930 in Washington, in California, and elsewhere. Riots in Watsonville, California, were incited by press coverage of the arrest of a Filipino man for walking with his fiancée, a white woman.) Throughout Bulosan's novel, the Filipino protagonist falls in love with women, usually white, and female icons figure prominently in his account. Here again, racism and racial exclusion steer the direction of romantic and sexual ties between men and women.

Such ties are also found in Asian American stories, novels, and poetry from Hawaii during the 1920s to the 1970s about interracial marriage, race relations, and romance. Milton Murayama's *All I asking for is my body* is an earthy novel about Japanese, Filipino, and Asian Maui sugar plantation workers in Hawaii during the 1930s. You can almost smell the soil and hear the lives of workers as they speak in Hawaiian Creole English. What follows is one description of courtship, plantation-style:

Guys would sneak behind hibiscus and meow like cats for the girls to come out. But even then in no time the whole camp knew about it, and everybody waited; it was just a matter of time before the girl got pregnant. Whenever anybody got married, the old ladies would size up the new bride in the bathhouse where she was stark naked and had only a wash rag the size of a hand towel to shield her pregnancy.

Other important postwar works include *Eat a Bowl of Tea.* Louis Chu's classic novel takes place in New York's Chinatown. Ben Loy, the husband of Mei Oi, becomes impotent; in the meantime, his new wife is seduced by another man. Both Murayama and Chu in their novels dealt with sexuality within predominantly Asian communities, though the possibility of crossing racial lines was always present.

During 1947–1948 twenty-three short stories from a New York Chinese-language literary magazine, *The Bud,* were published, but they are now out of print. In a few of his stories, the writer Bai Fei focuses on sexuality. "An Afternoon in Late Autumn" is about Ziming, a forty-two-year-old Chinese American man working the fields of Mexico, Cuba, and the United States. Obsessed by sex, he succumbs to a black prostitute whom he had earlier resisted.

After World War II, Hisaye Yamamoto was one of the first Asian American writers to gain national recognition for her stories. Some of her best-known stories, collected in *Seventeen Syllables and Other Stories,* explore themes of sexuality. They include "Seventeen Syllables," "The High-Heeled Shoes, A Memoir," "Epithalamium," and "The Legend of Miss Sasagawara." "Seventeen Syllables" depicts the romantic and physical liaison between two adolescents, Japanese American Rosie and the Latino fieldworker Jesus, set against the backdrop of the disturbing marriage of Rosie's mother and father. By the story's end we learn about the mother's own artistic and sexual attachments and how they affected Rosie. "High-Heeled Shoes" may be the earliest Asian American work that deals with transgender and transvestite issues, the main character being a man who wears a woman's high-heeled shoes, perhaps nothing new today, but in 1948 certainly startling. In "Epithalamium," alcohol, religious faith, and guilt drive the interracial romance between a "tall Italian seaman from Worchester, Massachusetts," and a "plain-faced Japanese girl." "The Legend of Miss Sasagawara" is about a lonely spinster confined behind the barbed-wired fence and guard towers of Poston, an internment camp in

Arizona, "an unlikely place of wind, sand, and heat." Yamamoto sets the repressed sexuality of Miss Sasagawara, a former ballet dancer and the daughter of a Buddhist priest, against her father's Buddhist beliefs and nonattachment to desire.

The post–World War II writers who grew up in the late 1960s and seventies, including myself, were most influenced by the liberalization of American sexual attitudes and mores and the widening of political frontiers. We were the baby boomers and the inheritors of the social revolutions of the late 1960s. Our political models were the Black Power movement in the United States and, internationally, in the post–World War II liberation and anticolonial struggles of Cuba, China, Vietnam, Kampuchea, Algeria, and other Third World countries. As writers and artists, we supported low-income affordable housing, making college education relevant to Asian, Chicano, black, and Native American students, and the principle of self-determination for our predominantly working-class neighborhoods.

We were seduced by liberation politics and the sexual revolution. We moved toward the feminist and gay movements, and became prey to the flourishing drug and pornography industries.

The dynamics generated by the political and sexual revolutions were reflected in writing by Asian American women. Women asked political questions about sexuality and their sexual status and did not separate the personal and the political as readily as we men did. Geraldine Kudaka, in her poem from that period "i was born . . ." places her birth in multiple contexts of the personal and the political—"i was born from the seed of a ford motor co. lineman / nakedly given with love to my mother . . . i died and was born again in the streets of chinatown / in the rising sun The East is Red . . . i was born seven hundred and twenty-four days before the / thundering fall of b-52s . . ." The East is her "fetal cord," yet she dies many times in the "schizophrenia of the West."

From the 1970s, an unsigned essay in *Third World Women* touches upon linkages between race and sexuality. In "Pomegranate Breasts," a young Asian woman has been through the job mill, selling encyclopedias for $1.65 an hour, applying for jobs as a cashier. She ends up as a topless dancer. "I, a daughter of the third world, was brought up to believe that topless dancers were the same as prostitutes." The experience changed the dancer's perspective: on the white women with whom she worked, on the customers, mainly white and Asian, and on the ex-Vietnam servicemen who either loved or hated Asian women.

By the 1970s, sexuality became fused with politics. This trend continued in the writing of Asian American women to the 1990s. The writing in this book asserts the right of a woman to love in her own way within or without marriage, to pursue her object of desire whether Asian or non-Asian, man or woman, and to be free of the "uninterpretable chattering, pidgin English, giggling or silence" that have characterized the Hollywood stereotypes of Asian women. Marilyn Chin puts forth a manifesto on "the right to be happy" that transcends political correctness, race, and academic notions of eroticism. Kimiko Hahn's essay, "The Hemisphere: Kuchuk Hanem," excerpted here, subverts notions of Orientalism and "Oriental sexuality" as they have served to exoticize and limit the humanity of Asian and Asian American women. Meena Alexander's protagonist risks the fast life—abortion in the age of love and AIDS —in her "Poet's Café." Other nationally known writers have their short stories, poetry, or excerpted works here, including Bharati Mukherjee, Diana Chang, Chitra Divakaruni, and Lois Ann Yamanaka.

For me, eroticism is the fruit born of the delicate tension between the repression and the expression of sexual desire. A male friend recently asked me, "If you're a Buddhist, why are you writing about Desire?" A woman friend accused me of hypocrisy in my obsession with sexuality most of the time while quoting religious homilies at other times. My friends had a point—that contradiction and conflict are also part of my being an Asian American and of living as a sensual and spiritual being. I told them that I was working through my states of Desire and would be doing so through future rebirths. Nonetheless, reading the varied selections in this anthology helped to extend my perception of what Desire could contain and how far it could go, from the sections on "Sexual Awakening" and "Blood Links" to "Embracing the Female Body" and "The Size of It" to "Betrayal and Infidelities" and "Mind Sex."

I paid particular attention to writers whose work I had not read before. Three accounts—two stories and a poem—by writers relatively unknown on the Asian American literary scene come to mind. Each of these writers managed to capture that tension between repression and expression through a different strategy of writing: narrative description, journalistic reportage, or lyric poetry. Their verbal strategies were linked to the premium they placed upon their sexuality and sexual expression. In other words, it cost them dearly to write honestly about what they saw, felt, and desired. Thus, their struggles spoke to me in a personal way: whether they adhered to or fought against social tradition, or whether their sexuality in some sense conflicted with sexual mores, as mine did.

"Defection," by Christina Yao (a pseudonym), is about a female medical doctor, Ping Wu, from the People's Republic of China whose marriage to a Chinese medical student has gone sour after fifteen years of living in the United States. She lives without passion, "as if living was a habit." At a medical conference she attends in Paris, she has an affair with a man who is not Asian. She recalls the bleak conditions of her own mother's marriage and the absence of marital bliss and sexual pleasure. Ping Wu must confront her sexual identity as an immigrant, as a lover, and as a wife and mother.

"Defection" raised questions about sexual choice in a way that reminded me of Miss Yen, the neighborhood woman whom I had known as a teenager. She, like Yao's Dr. Ping Wu, had to make a choice in life—to love outside the bounds of family and codes of a tightly bound community. While life for women within the traditional confines of an Asian family and neighborhood might offer warmth and security, that very life might be robbed of its passion by locks on sexual expression.

For women as well as men, our choices were often demarcated by images, verbal texts, and scripts of stories we did not write ourselves. Asian American men have been usually scripted as neutered objects in the media or as mindless kung fu artists in Hollywood. In contrast, the writing by males in this collection takes on the bold, transmuted, or transfixed "colors of Desire," to paraphrase David Mura. Asian American male writers depict themselves as the subjects—and objects—of representation, discourse, and diverse sexual drives in their accounts, essays, stories, and poems. As with the women writers, well-known names abound here: Frank Chin, Shawn Wong, John Yau, David Henry Hwang, S. P. Somtow, David Wong Louie. But I choose here instead to touch upon the work of two other male writers because of the verbal freshness and insights they bring to their subjects: homosexuality and the convolutions of intimate family love, both taboo subjects in everyday Asian American lives.

In "Potato Eater," Eulalio Yerro Ibarra describes a gay Filipino man's obsession with white Western men. The protagonist moves from the hustling bars of Manila, Chicago, and New Orleans to New York. At the same time, Ibarra gives us vignettes of growing up as a youth colonized by the Americans and oppressed by home-grown dictatorships. Public sex in sauna massage clubs is juxtaposed against soldiers under the Marcos regime arresting his father. What is the relationship between power and ideology, or between sexual and political liberation? The story questions our assumptions about same-sex desire, cross-racial attraction, and the linkage between sexual positioning and "political correctness."

Eulalio Yerro Ibarra is also a nom de plume. Are these writers who wish to remain anonymous like the immigrant Gold Mountain writers of a hundred years ago, who could express their emotions only under cover? Are women writers such as Christina Yao linked, by virtue of their relative isolation and unrequited feelings, to thousands of anonymous Asian wives left behind in the old country? The choice of anonymity reveals the ambivalence that Asian Americans may have toward disclosing the nature of their sexual drives in a society that confounds racial and sexual characteristics.

No matter what topic a writer may choose, however, it is through verbal strategy that subtlety, lyricism, and wit are conveyed, as in the poetry of Pulitzer-prize nominee G. S. Sharat Chandra. His poem "Moths" both filters and amplifies the eroticism found in intimate relationships among a South Asian husband, wife, and father, as these passages from the first section of the poem attest to:

> She moved out quickly,
> I let her go,
>
> tore her dress
> to the outer world
>
> then spun my body
> with all my spit
>
> to rise in my chest
> the chant of moths,
>
> my father waking
> somewhere in a dream,

> my brother turning
> in the belly of the bulb.

Torn or entangled, asleep or arising, these Asian American images and voices are most erotic when they link or cross both race and sexuality, as the stories and accounts, poems, and essays in this book do. As we release race from the stranglehold of prejudice and discrimination, we unfurl new pleasures and embrace our sexuality once more.

NOTE

I would like to thank Geraldine Kudaka and Frank Chin, Jinqi Ling, Michael Laurence, James Lee, Valerie Matsumoto, Yuji Ichioka, and Jean Pang Yip for their readings of earlier drafts of this essay. Steven Masami Ropp and Marjorie Lee at the UCLA Asian American Studies Reading Room shared their resources, for which I am grateful.

Sexual Awakening

I

What People Knew

Diana Chang

$\mathcal{M}$y education in the mysteries of sex happened in four distinct phases. The first one was so long ago, I don't remember exactly where I was that day with Tamara and my best friend, Mimi. They were horsing around under me—Mimi, who was the spitting image of Merle Oberon as a girl, but bold as brass, as my mother said, and Tamara, who was half-Russian and brawny. We were often at one another's houses, and nothing about that afternoon suggested it would turn out to be an unsettling one for me.

I didn't care for tree-climbing, not being a roughneck, Mother said approvingly, but had to prove myself to my friends, so I was standing balanced on a forked limb while they talked below.

Perhaps I missed the beginning of their conversation, but suddenly Tamara announced, "I know what boys do to girls."

In recognition of her superior knowing, a weighty pause followed, broken by Mimi, whose Merle Oberon voice was always hoarse. *"You* won't believe it."

"Try me," I retorted with a snort, hoping to be as tough as she was.

"You're the *only* one who doesn't know."

Were they one-up on me? But the time to admit it hadn't arrived.

"You tell," Tamara said.

"You tell," Mimi echoed.

Tamara said, "They stick their thing—you know, that thing— into girls."

I didn't actually hear what she said, didn't grasp the words. What I felt was thunder in my head, a roar of my being. My left foot slipped, and I struggled, scratching my hands against bark. I found my balance without knowing I'd lost it, without knowing I'd regained it.

How can one be thrown by something one doesn't understand? I didn't fall out of the tree but dropped to the ground, weak and stiff at the same time. At eight years of age, I didn't know the word "apocalyptic." But I'd been in an accident, a cleaver of reality splitting the day.

I remembered the cleaving but forgot the first question that came to mind. *If* boys did do that to girls—why? Whatever for?

"I did too know," I declared, while Mimi and Tamara laughed loud and hard.

That same year my mother, who didn't have a sister or a close friend to talk to, told me something quite baffling. She pointed out to me that a certain woman living in the same hotel with us had a husband who was oversexed.

I don't remember the accommodations we had—my mother and myself. My father was always working back home in Nanking. But I immediately imagined that the room or suite Mrs. Albrecht was in was a dim place, maybe windowless. Its atmosphere was furry and had a smell like leftover soup. Did I understand more than I could grasp?

I never met Mr. Albrecht, which was just as well, for I would have fixed my eyes on him, staring and trying to decide if I was supposed to hate him or admire him. Sex was an idea with me then, like geography or decimal points, the way it probably is with ninety-year-olds for whom it's a memory but no longer a drive. Although Mr. Albrecht might not agree yet, even if he's a hundred and ten now.

As if to herself, my mother commented, "Three times a day she has to douche. No wonder she's so anemic-looking."

Anemic Mrs. Albrecht wore thin sweaters of no particular color and linen skirts over her lank frame. By her side, Mother looked vigorous from playing tennis and swimming every day. At tea time, she and Mrs. A, as we called her, sat on the wraparound veranda and ordered triangular sandwiches and cupcakes. This was in Chefoo, a Chinese port and resort town, but the guests and the waiters spoke English.

"Imagine having to dress and undress that often," Mother muttered, her head going from left to right, from right to left.

I struggled to understand. "She must have an awful lot of clothes."

"He even comes home for lunch to do it. I call that going too far, going much too far."

"Where?" I asked. "Where's he going?"

"Never mind. You don't understand."

"Maybe we'll meet him in the dining room," I said, hopefully.

"Not a chance, it's room service for them." She also threw in, "That kid of theirs is a mangy-looking thing, if you ask me."

"Mangy," I repeated. "What's mangy?"

"Moth-eaten, sort of."

When my father was around one weekend, Mother brought up Mrs. A, said she would be joining them for tea on the veranda. "A new friend?" he asked, while we waited for her. "Chinese or Western?"

"Three times a day," I put in brightly, happy to inform him. "She has to keep changing her clothes and that's why she's so anemic." He looked at me and then at Mother.

"Eurasian," she answered, "but he's something else, to put it mildly."

"And he always wants to play with me—that moth-eaten kid of theirs."

"What's going on here?" my father asked.

"Say no more," Mother ordered me sharply. She spelled out some long words, and then abruptly changed the expression on her face as Mrs. A approached our table waveringly. She was so thin, the wicker chair didn't even creak when she settled down opposite Daddy.

After deferring to one another about pastries versus an English trifle and ordering an ice-cream sundae for me, everyone smiled all around.

As we ate, Daddy said to Mrs. A, "I don't need all this, but you should build yourself up."

I could tell she found him a nice man. "It's rest I need, actually," she said.

"Now, you," Mother said, trying not point a finger at me. "Seen but not heard, remember?"

Suddenly demoted, I'm sure I looked betrayed. When there were just the two of us, I was her friend, wasn't I? When we were alone, I was her sister, wasn't I?

My mother was as old as every adult then, and every adult was her age—twenty-nine. I must have been in a coma not to know if she was attractive or plain, special or ordinary. Years later, when I came to, I found out a lot, but that was a long while after I knew what sex was. Sex is simpler than other things, including love, including parents and most other people, what they are and why, in China or over here, wherever we are.

My parents couldn't help having non-Chinese friends. Like Mrs. Albrecht, Mother was Eurasian, and had been brought up in the

States. And the average Chinese, tending to be as cosmopolitan as citizens of Grand Rapids, Michigan, found her an oddity—intriguing but not relaxing to be with.

"Mr. Hayward," she told me, "gets in his car and drives around a bit, returns to this hotel, but uses the back entrance."

I was so puzzled, it took me a moment to say, "That doesn't make any sense."

"His mistress is not doing too well." She nodded her head and lapsed into silence.

A day later, out of the blue again, she continued, "Mr. Hayward and his wife are on the second floor of the opposite wing. Valerie, who has been his mistress for fourteen years, is in this wing. She's quite ill, so Mr. Hayward took the risk of having her near, not halfway across town. She waits for two things—for him and to get well."

Mother sighed and went on, "Daddy and I have known all three of them from before you were born. A long sad story."

I had seen Valerie once as in a dream. She had on a long gown called a negligée, something I was looking forward to wearing someday. It picked up the light and shone as if parts of it were metal and polished. It was tied with ribbons all the way from the V-neckline to the floor. To walk in it, she had to hitch it up or trip over her feet.

"I might as well tell you, though your father wouldn't approve, that Mr. Hayward and his wife are husband and wife in name only, except his wife doesn't seem to know it. It's been that way for years —in name only. For years, he's been madly in love with Valerie, but he's too much of a gentleman to ask for a divorce. That's the situation in a nutshell. There's no point going into more detail, because you're too young to understand."

I had other things on my mind, but I did hope to see Mr. Hayward getting out of his car and coming into the hotel by the freight elevators, past the kitchen and garbage pails. I could imag-

ine the consternation of the Chinese hotel staff, and the way our
amah, who never missed a trick, would react—disapproving and
tight-lipped.

Older than my father, Mr. Hayward was the special friend who
offered Daddy cigars that he said were the mellowest he'd ever
smoked. I think they were Balkan, but I can't remember for sure.
My mother was sporting cigarillos in those days.

The hotel we were in was in Tsingtao, another Chinese port and
resort. My father actually spent a whole week with us that vacation.
During it, he and Mother got dressed up and disappeared for an
afternoon, Mother in a tea-dance frock and a flowered hat. When
they returned, she was holding a bouquet of roses and kept burying
her nose in it. Daddy was very quiet.

That whole week they visited Valerie every day, sometimes
twice a day. One evening I heard Mother say, "She keeps turning
the wedding ring on her finger. It kills me. Keeps turning and
turning it. Did you notice?"

"Of course," Daddy said and, after a pause, added, "She's
waited long enough for it."

"She's so happy, it kills me. So happy."

He nodded. "Finally."

"He's good, he's really good."

"We mustn't say anything about this, you know."

"It's not that serious," Mother said. "Besides, foreigners can get
away with anything in this country. You Chinese should put a stop
to it." Later on, after China went communist, I remembered her
words.

He jerked his head in my direction. "We must keep it to
ourselves." Almost whispering, he added, "Bigamy is still bigamy."

"Her happiness is what he was thinking of." My mother's voice
rose and then broke.

Daddy patted her gently. "He did the right thing. Yes. Not the
legal thing, but the right thing."

"She looked so ethereal today."

"What's ethereal?" I asked.

"Almost not there, or something. Spiritual. Want to visit Valerie?" Mother asked me. "Before—"

"Sh-sh," Daddy put in.

She was sitting up in bed in a different negligée, had lipstick on, and her right hand turned her gold ring around and around. She seemed younger or smaller than the only other time I'd seen her.

"Come over here," Mother told me, "and kiss Valerie."

I did, feeling how cool her cheek was. She kissed me back, and said, "You know I was once your age."

How could that be? She was a lady, a grownup who'd inhabited a world that was complete before I came on the scene. I looked at my father.

"Really?" I asked, nonplussed. They laughed, seemed glad to laugh.

Daddy was standing with the window behind him, so I couldn't see his face when he commented blandly, "Most everyone's been nine once."

Then Valerie said something peculiar. "A good thing one can't see around corners." The remark stayed with me a long time, like the perfume she wore, a scent of lavender.

I found out later my parents had been her witnesses in the marriage ceremony held at a consulate office. There was cake and champagne, and lots of roses.

Mr. Hayward's wife never knew. In any case, he was a bigamist for less than five weeks. My parents went to Valerie's funeral, too, and her ashes were sent back to Budapest in an urn.

My father declared, "The important thing was that he loved her enough to do it, to take the risk. She needed to know that."

Perhaps Mr. Hayward's solution is not unusual. I suppose people do what is necessary. He no longer had a reason to stay, so Mr. and Mrs. Hayward left China soon after, not leaving a trace, except in me, and in my thinking kindly of bigamy, that is, for people who know how to love.

---

*F*our years later, in Manhattan, we visited Mme. Wang, who was French. In China we laughed behind her back because she never walked on a rug of hers, skirting it at an angle like a sailboat tacking in the wind.

"Not used to much," was my mother's verdict. "Rugs are for walking on. They can take punishment, especially Chinese ones of any quality, their naps are so deep."

I was thirteen, and I don't know how I knew right away that Mme. Wang's daughter was pregnant, perhaps three months gone. Our lunch had been *sandwiches de jambon, salade de tomates,* and *thé citron*—delicious and sophisticated, even if Mme. Wang was *petit bourgeois* about rugs. I envied half-Chinese, half-French Claudette with the hazel eyes.

Our visit ending, my mother went into a bedroom to put on her hat. Mme. Wang placed her hand on my shoulder and smiled conspiratorially. "We know you know," she declared.

I was frightened, but Mme. Wang seemed proud of me. *"You* know," she said, pointedly.

Claudette was only fifteen, but the family seemed to take everything in stride. The French are different, I thought for the first time —they'd been around, were so worldly.

"We also know that you will not tell," Mme. Wang said. True, I had planned to say nothing to Mother.

I nodded, strangely content. I realized I was understanding something, and was being understood, seen.

Mme. Wang said, "We know what people are ready to know, *n'est çe pas?* There's no necessity for gossiping, speculating. Very soon we will see what to do."

I nodded and nodded, beset with realizations, suddenly no longer as young as—as Mother; suddenly recognized for myself by Mme. Wang and Claudette, to whom gender, sex, and love and its consequences were all in a day's living.

The Great Depression

Hiroshi Kashiwagi

sitting atop
the billboard that said
"I'd walk a mile for a Camel"
behind the sign
I saw
a man and woman
peeing
then standing up
they began
to fuck
it was the Great Depression
there were no beds and such
not even food
only love on the run
watched by a bug-eyed kid
who got so tense
he nearly
fell through the olive branch
to join
the festivity

The Mother "i"

FRANK CHIN

ULYSSES

My last year in high school I meet Fat Jack, the fat cocky China-man who teaches me how to draw, downstairs in the brick under-ground nightclub, the Mother "i," across Kearney Street from Chinatown, Frisco. Mr. Tucci, wearing a red beret that day, likes my drawings and tells me to come back tonight and see "Fat" Jack Fat.

Fat Jack makes all the decisions about the art that hangs on the walls, on consignment, and takes a cut of the sale price, when it sells. I'll recognize him because he's Chinese like me and looks like his name. He's short. He has a perfectly round head and face. He looks like the Pillsbury Doughboy with slanty eyes, tweed jacket, brown slacks, sandals and no socks. He stands behind a table covered with rings and bracelets, brooches and pins all blobular and fungoid shaped in silver, and gold, inlaid with wood and stone that looks like junk sifted from the ashes to me. He hates my drawings, laughs at me because I'm Chinese and wear glasses. "How old are you? You can never tell how old Chinese are, man. So tell me, how old are you?" he asks.

"Seventeen," I tell him.

He takes a pair of glasses out of his pocket and laughs. "All Chinese wear glasses," he shouts. His glasses have big lenses and big frames. "Humph!" he snorts and sneers, pokes a cigarette between his little guppy lips, glancing at me and bouncing with the burning cigarette in his mouth and his hands in his pockets. "You look older than seventeen. It's the acne scars. My mother took care of my face. Russian and Japanese. High-class Japanese, you can see it in my eyes. High-class amber eyes, man. She taught me art. Took me to galleries. Played music in the house. Not like the other Chinese kids, huh? Ha ha ha! I'm not quiet and reserved like other Chinese, right? You tell her. How many Chinese friends do you have? Tell her," he says as he stands, wagging his cigarette at the hair of the tall blond woman sitting almost as tall as he stands in the chair next to him. "I have a few," comes chickening out of my mouth at a crawl.

"A few! Ha!" he says. "Just a few, right? Like *none!* Am I right? Because you're a freak! You're an artist, like me." He scowls, the ash falls off his cigarette, crashes on his table. He wags his head at the blonde, who doesn't look happy. "But I never had acne, like you, man! My mother never let me. A zit never had a chance. She gave me facials. How about that! Facials! You don't believe me? That's you. Turn your head that way. Yeah, you look younger than seventeen too. That's okay. You have time to get serious about art! Ha ha ha!" he laughs. "I bet you've never seen a Chinaman like me before! Ha ha ha."

He laughs his every "ha" as separate words, and shouts them one by one, reminding me of a toy wooden machine gun that cracks a hard click sound as I turn a crank, in the country, in the middle of the war. I live here but am afraid of the big lumbering slobbery-lipped crunching cows, and the clicking of the machine gun, made from non-strategic materials and approved for sale in the Woolworth's in Placerville, is not scaring the cows. It seems to be attracting the cows. When a cow shoves its head into the doorway and knocks my machine gun over, I pick up the toy and use it like a stick on the cow and chase it away, and chase all the cows till someone yells, Stop. I'm running the fat off them, and I bask in my fading anger and the sun shines on me. I like Fat's laugh. A middle-aged woman holds up a ring and whispers, "How much?"

"Lady, you are too stupid and offensive to wear any of my jewelry, if you're going to begin a relationship with me with a stupid question like that!" he yelps without moving. His fat is rock.

She recoils as if bitten by a snake. He's more like a frog. Skin smooth as rubber. Whiskey-brown eyes like a frog. And he doesn't move very much. Like a frog. "I design and shape and choose the medium of the jewelry for the whole body and the personality of who is going to wear it. If you wear my stuff, you wear it because you know art, you can see! You don't pick something up, and ask how much. You look at it, you ask if you can try it on, to see how it looks on your finger, or wherever you personally would wear something like that." He introduces the tall blond woman sitting with him behind the table as his apprentice.

She says she hates him and he's a genius. "But he's lousy salesman!" she says and hits him on his shoulder. "That's not true!" he says, "I am a great salesman. I know people. I have the instinct for public relations. But I don't have time for bullshit. I'm sorry, no bullshit for Fat Jack. That's me! Just me, that's all!" Fat Jack laughs that stupid laugh I start to like. He says he doesn't take many apprentices. He's not like other artists who take anybody with money and giggly society brides looking for a little depth. He only takes talented people for apprentices. He likes talent. He asks me about my teachers. Teachers used to notice him in high school. Do they notice me? I tell him about the social studies teacher who says she's scared of me and dodges my eye when I'm sketching in class now. "Mrs. Mitten? Mary Mitten! She was my social studies teacher at Fremont!" he says, and his Mary Mitten is the same as mine. So he can't be too much older than me, and he lives by making his jewelry. He has a shop in Berkeley where professors with international reputations and Nobel Prizes are his clients. He lives in an old Victorian house on the edge of Chinatown near the

Nimitz freeway in Oakland where his Japanese wife comes to spend the night with him in very tight dresses till their divorce becomes final.

"Why shouldn't she? I'm good in bed," he says, "Ask her! She loves the way I ball her. That's it. But I'm me. That's all." He is the last word on art. "What's Jimmy Dean's problem?" he asks. "He has his own car. Natalie Wood lives down the street. What's his problem?"

He teaches me to practice drawing with a stick, with a twig, with a rock, with my finger dipped in ink on wet paper. I find I enjoy drawing with a Chinese writing brush, a bamboo stick, and fine steel pen. I sell my drawings to two Spanish teachers, a social studies teacher, and the Girls' Vice Principal for ten dollars apiece. Though I never took an art class in high school, the art teacher invites me to her room after school to rifle her supplies. Paper, paint, pastel crayon, bottles and bottles of black India ink that smells almost like something to eat. Brushes and penpoints. I get my bamboo stick and Chinese brushes in a bookstore in Chinatown that smells of dusty shelves, brass inkboxes going strange, polished glass and India ink. She enters me in competition for a scholarship to an art college in Oakland, and asks me to put together a portfolio. I don't know what a portfolio is. She has one of her art classes make me a portfolio to hold my drawings, as a crafts project.

She meets me after school to pose for me, in her studio in the back of her house, with northern light. I sketch her as she undresses. The brush and ink. A steel pen ready too. Fat Jack says I have a problem with hands, elbows, hips, knees. I don't know how to foreshorten. I can't draw a finger pointing straight at me, see the folding of shadow and flesh. She poses and I draw how the thighs fall round bone, and spread to one side of the chair. I draw the toes of a foot pressed against glass. I draw the flow of musculature and soft bulges from the neck, shoulders, elbows resting on the knees down the thighs to her buttocks. I throw shadow and light on her to show up her shapes.

One day I'm surprised when the art teacher barefoots down off the modeling platform and unbuttons my shirt. "You have been sketching me in the nude for a while now. It's only fair you return the favor," she says and pulls my T-shirt up off my chest and licks my left nipple, then my right, with my head inside the bag of my T-shirt and my arms straight up. "I have never emphasized it, but I want you to know, I'm an artist too. I want to show you my work," she says.

We sketch each other naked and our fingers and our bodies are dirty with charcoal and India ink, when she sits cross-legged right in front of me and starts scratching up a sketch of my dong in charcoal. And the thing changes shape, goes straight and throbs as she sketches across more and more paper, and it hurts, and I'm a little scared, just when she puts her tongue on the tip and slips her mouth over the whole thing. She lifts her lips, showing her teeth in a smile around my dick and looks in my eyes and inside she's licking. I try not to act surprised, say nothing to say nothing stupid, and let it feel good though I have no idea what's going to happen next. I hear my dick being gurgled and gagged and growled on like a bone in a happy dog's mouth, and come to know white girls are girls too.

My drawings win a state art contest, a prize at a county fair, and a scholarship to the art college. My drawings sell at the Mother "i," I'm passed into the showroom as a friend of the house pianist. I'm not out of high school and am a regular, a kind of fixture at the Mother "i," smoking dope on weekends under Fat Jack's table with his apprentice and the house pianist.

All Chinamen think no other Chinaman has seen a Chinaman like them, all the Chinamen I know, all the Chinaman in my family, Pop, Charlie Chan's Number Four Son; my Uncle Morton Chu, the electronics whiz turned guitarmaker; my older brother, Longman, Jr., Benedict Han, are dead certain, that they and only they are so much more deeply and tangibly but inexplicably *American* than every other Chinaman who has ever lived, that all Chinamen who meet them run hot and cold with jealousy and terror. And that day with the art teacher: me too.

But Fat Jack really is different. Fat Jack is right. I have never met a Chinaman like him. It is in his shop that I first hear Dylan Thomas reading elaborately worded children's stories and the poetry of W. H. Auden riffing Shakespeare's *The Tempest,* in a loping cadence fit to be sung as a country song, and today Kenneth Patchen's deep tubercular egg-shaped rumblings, to jazz about somebody's ducks on somebody's pond bounce off the black walls and clobber me, too loud for Fat to hear anyone step in from the street and shout his name, and sticks in my memory.

"You don't care about them being homosexuals, right? Or do you? Yes or no?" Fat Jack asks, looks up from his hands on the worktable, lifts his magnifying goggles and laughs at me.

"Who're what? Who're you talking about?" I ask.

Fat jerks his goggles off his head. "You're cherry!" he says. "You are a good Chinese boy after all! Seventeen and still a virgin. Ha! Ha! Ha! I see it, man. Am I sensitive, or what! You have never done it with a woman. But you've heard about it. You have heard about it, haven't you? You can talk to me." Patchen's voice fills the black walls of the shop like loud warm messy soup. The boyish-looking girl working next to him looks up. She doesn't smile or look as if she cares what's happening. "Come on, Fat," I say.

"So of course you haven't thought about men who might want sex with you, because you haven't found a woman who wants sex with you," Fat says. "Or is it something else? Don't be afraid of me, Chinese boy, I don't swing that way. Some people say I do, but that's them. If they want to think that way about me, that's them. I'm me. And I like Kenneth Patchen's poetry and listening to him read it, man, no matter what he is, okay?" His voice has the birdy nasal resonance of a banjo and cuts through Patchen's rumbling groaning boom, about somebody once drowning in the water under the ducks, like a barking electric saw.

"Well, in theory," I say, knowing it sounds especially stupid because I have to shout it to be heard. I know he'll say, "Ha! Ha! Ha! Just like a Chinese boy!"

"Ha! Ha! Ha! Just like a Chinese boy!" he barks. And his short-haired apprentice, who wears no makeup and has the sad eyes of a baby seal, smiles and spits up a little laugh. She wipes it off her lips with her fingers and makes a face. "My fingers taste awful," she says.

"So wash your fingers before I eat them," I say.

"I don't suggest you eat them raw," she says and stops me.

He introduces me to the sound of Spanish Gypsy flamenco guitar and singing I don't stop to listen to, out of little clubs under the apartments where the Chinese live all over North Beach. Fat Jack takes me to the Old Spaghetti Factory to see the Flamencos de la Bodega for the first time and hear Adonis El Filipino, a kid no older than me, play the smoked dry moans of beat-up boozy old men who've seen it all, out of a guitar he Frankensteined himself together from old parts in the guitarmaker's shop he works in as an apprentice, instead of going to high school.

Fat Jack talks about his short-haired apprentice that night, for the first time, riding with her in the back seat of Ma's two-tone green-on-green '53 Chevy. She is the fifteen-year-old daughter of a professor at Cal, he's happy to say. I drive them to his house in Oakland, on the edge of Chinatown, and he sends me home without inviting me in.

"This is my dog-faced boy," he says, nodding his chin at her. "Fuck you, Jack!" she says in a voice sounding older, worn deeper than fifteen. She turns and walks out of the Mother "i." Fat bounces on his heels with his hands in his pocket and ash falling off the cigaratte poked between his little Tweety Bird lips. I go after her for Fat. He doesn't ask me to go after her, but I do. She's on the corner angry, looking across Kearney Street up Jackson, into China-town, and across Jackson to Columbus and the espresso bars and pizza parlors of North Beach. I ask her if she feels like something to eat in Chinatown. "I know Chinatown. And it's just across the street," I say.

She's afraid of everything on the menu. She sounds like a kid, the way she talks about food.

"Are you going to make a big fucking deal about what I eat with you?" she asks.

"No."

"I want something plain. Something not too strange, you know what I mean? Something I shouldn't regret putting in my mouth. Something meat and potatoes, like that."

"How about beef stew with potatoes?" I ask her.

"No rice?"

"You can have it on rice. You can have it with potatoes and rice, if you like."

"Really? In a Chinese restaurant?"

"It's Chinese beef stew," I say.

She tells me Fat showed her my poetry, "I think it's pretty childish, but I like it, because I'm a child too."

Her voice and look curl my toes and clear my asthma. There's nothing I can do next. There is no next but eating, and walking back to the "i."

I'm not in the wacky Buddhist church anymore, but Sharon still calls me. I haven't seen her since I was thirteen or fourteen. First she asks me out to her sophomore dance, a sock hop, or Sadie Hawkins, and it's too sad. I know her folks won't let her go with me, but she has a plan. I have to ask her before she will ask her folks. If she tells them I asked, maybe they won't want to hurt my feelings.

Nothing stopped them before. Why should they not want to hurt my feelings now? But I ask her, the way she wants, and sure enough she comes back to the phone saying they won't let her go out with me. Now is when it would be nice to talk on, and arrange to casually meet by accident someplace, like the San Francisco Zoo, or at City Lights Books, and I'll take her to see my drawings at the Mother "i," just across the street from her sewing factory, and a million miles away. She likes me when I talk that way. I hear her sigh, like Mom at the movies, reconsidering the sight of a dream come true.

Then a year later she phones asking me to ask her out to her junior prom, and it is a ritual chant now, a primitive, children's ceremony. I ask her out, so she can say I phoned to ask her out, and they may not want to hurt my feelings. I have heard it before. I know what is coming, and she comes back to the phone saying her parents won't let her go out with me. And a year older, it's sadder this time.

Minutes later, she calls saying she has arranged a date to her junior prom with her best friend, a Chinese Catholic who wants to have a pre-prom date with me to see if we get along. It's okay, I don't want to go to your prom if I'm not going out with you, unless we're going to switch dates at the prom. No, she can't lie to her parents. Yeah, I know she can't lie to her parents. She likes making me do things over the phone. I agree to take her friend out this next weekend, and take her to the prom if she likes me. Why is she arranging dates for me with other girls? I go feeling, hoping, she is just beyond her friend. After this she'll owe me.

Sharon's friend has never met a Chinaman like me or been inside the Mother "i." She can't keep her hands off me while I'm driving her home out to the foggy Sunset District, where all the houses are the same height, have the same tile roofs and are painted the colors of faded swimming-pool bottoms. After making out awhile, in the front seat of Ma's Chevy, under the streetlight gone milky in the fog around the car, I tell her I don't want to go to her junior prom. My thing is with Sharon, and you're nice, but I really don't want to go to the prom. She cries. She puts her hand on my crotch. She won't go all the way, but she will help me out, she says into my neck, as she begs me to take her to her junior prom. Her tears run down my neck under my shirt and down my chest and ribs. It's a long drive from the Sunset in Frisco to Bancroft Way in Berkeley and my apartment across the street from Fat Jack Fat's jewelry shop.

The whole Saturday night feels awful, and I climb the stairs home to sleep it off but hear groaning and a girl's voice inside, and the record player, playing the label, and smell burning pot and incense smoking up the insides of my apartment. Fat Jack Fat grunts the way he laughs. I recognize the low voice of his short-haired apprentice in her groans and sighs, and don't open the door. Round and round I go. Back into Ma's old Chevy and drive back through the empty streets of Berkeley, and over the empty Bay Bridge to Frisco again, into Chinatown. The restaurants are closing. The garbage is out on the street. The only place open is the little Chinese and American food and suey next door to the Times Theater where the whores socialize all night long and do their office work. Boiled noodles and a piece of custard pie are on my mind as I open the door into the high-ceilinged steam of the cafe, and all I see is Ron in a white T-shirt, with his hands on his hips, a mass of keys on a huge key ring, looking like a weapon of some kind on one hip. "What are you doing here?" he asks.

"I'm getting something to eat," I say.

"Uhh, yeah? Okay," he says, and nods me past him. I sit at the counter and see the way whores always pat Ron on the ass, and say something to him on the way in or on the way out, and see the old strange white-skinned brother of Sharon the princess of the Buddhist church, some kind of bodyguard here. I stay, order doughnuts and coffee, and watch, till it begins to get light out, and I can see the traffic begin to flow on Broadway, to and from the Broadway tunnel just behind the movie house. I think of sleeping a couple of hours in the Times Theater, like everyone else, instead watching the movies for once. But, no, Fat Jack and his apprentice have had my apartment long enough.

One day Fat Jack asks me if I've eaten yet, if I'm hungry, just like the Chinese, and makes me a raw spinach omelette with sour cream, like I'd never seen made in Ma's restaurant. "French," he says. "A rolled omelette, not that airy, puffy, dried-up mess most Americans call an omelette."

It's delicious.

"You dig the different textures, man? The egg, and the cool sour cream and crunchy spinach? What a trip, huh? French!" he says, and fixes himself a bowl of corn flakes and milk. "Corn flakes and milk!" he says, amazed at himself. "How Zen of me! Ha. Ha. Ha. My therapist is amazed, she says. I don't see things the way other people see them. I have insights, and artistic understanding, dig. She says she has never had a client like me. I'm a fucking genius, that's all! Ha! Ha! Ha!"

"There's this art teacher who thinks I'm a genius," I say, and Fat Jack jumps on me with "No, *I'm* a genius. You're just very bright." He stops and makes a face all the way into his scalp, and says, *"Maybe* brilliant. My dog-faced boy apprentice is brilliant. I validated her brilliance. I began to culture her genius. They all say I was the one who taught her discipline. I helped her find her art, that's all," Fat Jack says, off hand, urgent, intimate. "That's all, I turned on the artist in a fucked-up kid. That's all."

I don't ask Fat Jack for a knife and try not to be awkward cutting and shoveling up pieces of the omelette with a fork.

"What happened is this," he says. "I became her lover, but I'm too much to just make love to her like that, I mean, I *mean* too much to her to just make love to her. I am her teacher. I could have. She wants to. She says she wants to. She's not a virgin. She has a beautiful young body, but I do not take her body, she can do that with anybody, but I am special. I am an artist. She's an artist. We are. I see it in her work. Her sense of design. It's a gas the way we communicate, like without talking, just working together at the table together in the sour smell of pickling and polishing solutions, and carving our lost wax, we are digging each other, man, grooving on each other's creativity, you know what I mean? Making real love, real communication. I never went looking for her. She came to me. Our eyes glommed when she came in with her father the famous professor up for the Nobel Prize in his field, or I'd tell you who he is, and her mother, very classy from up on the North Side to pick up a pair of rings they commissioned me to create for their wedding anniversary. Gold rings. Long muscular fingers. Her mother's too. And one day she came into the shop by herself interested in making jewelry."

He says, "I could have had her then if I wanted. I knew it. I felt it. She wanted to. I could tell. She was experienced. I could tell. She didn't have to tell me. Her father was my friend, after all. In for fittings before, he had talked about her, and even then I knew he didn't understand her, he didn't communicate with her. But I understand, man. He's a genius, and deep into his bag, man. He works out.

"So she was fifteen and experienced. It happens. My father took me to a Chinese whorehouse in San Francisco on my twelfth birthday, but like everything about me, my father was not like other Chinese boys' fathers," he says, and laughs. "Wow, I haven't thought of that in years. My father was a hero in Chinatown! He was the best-dressed gambler Chinatown ever saw. A gassy Robin Hood hero kind, who looked like Errol Flynn to my mother. She thought he was low class, and a criminal, but he worshiped her, and we had money. If we did not have money, my mother was going to take me and split.

"So, we had money. Everyone else was poor around where we lived, but we had money. We had a radio in every room but the dining room, where she kept the record player. We had a baby grand piano. We had French food. I tell you, I am not like other Chinese boys. I am not isolated in that cramped, guilt-tripping Chinesey thing, man. She knew Louis Armstrong, and Billie Holiday, and Trotsky. She was something else. Until I was three years old my hair was long, and she kept it in curls, you know, and dressed me in these little Lord Fauntleroy suits and buckles on my shoes. See, there's no Chinese boys like me.

"I grew up with culture and art with the nearsighted, Chinesey Chinese, poor and stupid all around me. And my dad was their hero. Every Chinese New Year's he used to leave a hundred-pound sack of rice at every door in Oakland Chinatown. My mother knocked him for being a pagan anti-Christ to humiliate her, in front of her parents. She's a Christian, of course, and the last couple years before he died, he passed out sacks of rice on Christmas Eve and Chinese New Year to make her happy. I understand people, man. I understand people because I *am* so many people! Wow! Wiggy thought! You don't have to believe me, you can ask her father.

"He says I'm a genius. I have insight. See? Lots of my clientele from Cal says that, not me. You smoke a little grass, right, you get high, you buzz with sensitivity, right? You can get turned on to things in your ears, in your eyes, in your mind and buzz into them into close-up, man. Am I right? I know. I'm like that all the time. No one had to tell me the Egyptians were great artists but had no three dimensions, man. I see the Greeks invented eyebags and the kind of painting that goes for the real of the look only, and the camera came and photographs were the real look of the real, and cats like Monet, and Touslouse Lautrec and Van Gogh said *enough of that noise, if I want to paint a face green because I feel the face is green, I will.* And they did, and that's the fucking history of art, man, and why today, I am me, just who I want to be, and not fucked up with guilt because I'm not somebody else. *So when I smoke, man!* Wow! Yeah, you know, what you're like when *you* smoke, so think of that supersensitive you, as me just normal blowing me, wigging through the art experiences of the day, man, and *then smoking!* Whew! These professors who hang out here can't believe the things I say, man. It's like my thoughts are out there with Einstein and Aristotle, and I don't know them. That's just me!"

He smiles and looks like he's laughing, but doesn't. "You know she smokes some herself. I thought she could handle it. I told her father. I thought we were friends, man, but I can't beat him up to make him believe me, man. She doesn't say I did anything but make her an artist, man. So, it's him, not her, and not me, man. No problem." Fat Jack says, "I didn't *fuck* her. And if I had I wouldn't feel guilty. No guilt. No guilt. Guilt is bourgeois."

Buying Shoes

SANDRA MIZUMOTO POSEY

*A*s I stood at the
entrance of the Kick Up Your Heels Folk Dance and Music Festival
on Saturday at 9 A.M., the heat was already oppressive. The sounds
of fiddles and flutes and panpipes traveled across green lawns like a
chorus of crickets. I scanned the tent-speckled grounds with my
eyes. In the distance, I could hear the shuffle-tap stomping of
people dancing to Cajun music, and with each tap of those multitu-
dinous feet I thought about one thing: shoes.

Most mothers tell their daughters that if they give away the
milk for free, no one will buy the cow. My mother, on the other
hand, always asks me, "Would you buy a pair of shoes without
trying them on first?" So when I'm single, I become Imelda Marcos.
All I see are shoes arrayed before me in every color and size: sexy
slingbacks, strappy sandals, and lace-up thigh-high boots; stiletto
heels, penny loafers, mules, and sneakers.

I knew who it would be too; I'd met him the year before.
Aaron. Aaron spelled with a double *a* as if you were about to write
"aah" but changed your mind at the last minute. Maybe I should
have read that as a clue; I didn't.

My strategy was simple. I conveniently placed myself near a
performance venue where I knew he and his friends would congre-
gate. When I spotted him, I pretended not to notice but made sure

I was in his direct line of vision. Eventually, he said, "Hello." I bestowed upon him a perhaps overly fervent hug. "What events are you gonna go to today?" I asked, intending to have identical plans. Very subtle.

When he replied, however, that the first event on his calendar was a workshop on Jewish songs, I hit a sort of snag. Being tone deaf, half Irish and half Japanese, raised a combination of Buddhist, Shinto, and Holy Roller Pentecostal, there wasn't a particularly good way to justify my sudden interest. Never, however, underestimate a woman with a mission. Especially never underestimate a woman who was trained at five on the take-home board game version of TV's "Dating Game." I went to Jewish Songs.

By five o'clock that evening, however, it was becoming apparent that the subtle approach was not working. In the car, on our way to dinner, I sought the advice of my friend Michael. "Michael," I said, "should I be more direct? More forthright?"

"You know," he said wearily, "I am not going to give you any advice."

I took that as a clear indicator that I should be more direct. I sat myself directly across from my target. I shot out carefully calculated bashful glances. Everyone but Aaron seemed to be reading my signals. Michael seemed to find the whole situation very amusing. "Just what is your type?" he asked me as the table fell to an attentive silence, knowing full well what it was. I described it anyway. "Thin," I said, "but not too thin. Kind of lanky. Dark hair, dark eyes." I basically described Aaron. Aaron was clueless.

When dinner was over, Aaron began to walk to his car and was about to disappear. I ran up to him. I draped my arm across his waist. "Come with us," I said. "It'll be so much fun . . ." Just then, as Michael approached a vanload of people heading for the hotel, he called out to us, "You guys coming, or what?"

"I don't know," Aaron replied. "I have tickets to a concert tonight, but she has her arm around me and it's kind of convincing."

"Is that all it takes?" I asked, and wrapped the other arm around him. "Come," I whispered in his ear.

"Okay," he replied, as we walked toward my car. I leaned him up against the door; I let my nose trail across his cheek; I let my lips graze his, then bit his lower lip.

He never made it to the concert. We never made it back to the hotel room I was sharing with three other people. We never left that car or that parking lot. I obeyed impulses to stroke the wave of his hair where the brown softened into gold and framed his face and I kissed what and where I wanted to kiss.

I have never quite figured out how to make love in a bucket seat gracefully, but when you consider making love never looks really graceful, how different is it? Our arms and elbows bumped and entangled with everything imaginable. I kicked the shoes off his feet, placed them on my own. His shoes hung lopsided on my toes for a moment, then fell with a clunk to the floor. I pushed his jeans down his legs and up toward the ceiling. My panties disappeared somewhere. I never found them again. I ran my hand along his side, down the curve of his hip, and pulled his thigh over and across mine. My mouth found his ear and traveled down, gently biting into his neck. I found his teeth sinking into me in impossible places; I still cannot fathom how they got there in that confined space. It was, maybe, our whole bodies biting into one another. The sharp pains of bodies merging where they should and where they should not. Our legs entwined; the sole of my shoeless foot pushed at the windshield as I collapsed into him; the sound out of my mouth began as a sigh, progressed into a hiccup, then became a full rolling laugh as I realized that the gearshift in my back really hurt. I heard an inauspicious snap, and looked up to see the pressure from my foot creating an ever-expanding crack in the windshield.

And then it was all over. And then it was time again for me to realize that the process of getting to know someone can be complicated and messy in more ways than one. I looked into his deep-set eyes rather sheepishly and handed him a Kleenex. With my heart I take risks: I jump out of buildings and wait for the sidewalk to race up to me, hoping my air-cushioned soles will live up to all their advertised promises. But my body is another story entirely.

"I'll just say goodbye," he said smiling back at me. "Okay," I said, and watched him leave, rolling over me as he made his way out the door.

The next day, I don't know what exactly I expected to happen, but in the end it didn't matter because nothing did. The sun was as hot as ever, but whenever I wanted to cool down, all I had to do was find Aaron. The air around him was downright chilly. When I first caught sight of him, I ran up to give him a quick hug. He stiffened and whispered politely in my ear, "I'm not comfortable with public displays of affection." He pulled away slightly. He tried to smile, his eyes looking down. "Oh, there's my friend Joe," he said. "I need to go talk to him. Then there's this workshop I have to take."

I may be dense, but I am not stupid. I gave him another quick hug, so quick it was virtually imperceptible, and scampered off. The day eventually passed of its own accord. I watched performances I didn't remember as I obsessed about the situation. Aaron appeared now and again in the far peripheries of my vision. Tears tried to invade my eyes. I brushed them away as if they were mosquitoes. I tried to act cool on a day that was unbearably hot.

As I was leaving, I heard steps racing up behind me on the grass. I didn't look back. Aaron pulled up alongside me and walked with me the rest of the way to my car. We were silent. He gave me a hug, then kissed me, his tongue tracing the outline of my mouth. I felt nauseous. My stomach turned as I looked down. I saw my left foot slip out of my shoe and hover near his.

"What's going on?" I asked. "You're sending mixed signals." He was just getting out of a relationship, he said. He was moving into a new apartment. He said, well, all the things you say to someone in a situation like this.

I turned away with what I hoped was a smile and got into my car. Through the soft smog-dense haze of L.A. I made my way home.

"Maybe I'm just too easy," I thought to myself. "In an age of computers and cars that go yet faster and faster, you would think that speed would be appreciated. I'm not easy. I'm improved technology."

As I traveled south, traffic eased to a halt. I realized that advanced technology means nothing when everyone around you wants to go slower and slower: There are people who watch accidents. They are the same people who window-shop without ever buying a thing.

I realized I'm not really like Imelda Marcos. I don't want a million pairs of shoes. All I want is one good pair of Birkenstocks. Something that you love more with each passing year as it begins to meld with your sole. Something that seems more beautiful to you the older it gets, even when it just looks worn and tired to everyone else. So when I meet someone, they don't have to be fancy or fit just exactly right away. Something just has to tell me that I could love them and they could love me and I will walk with them and walk with them with the hope that we will grow together and eventually the fit will be perfect. But you have to buy the shoes before that will happen. You can't just try them on forever.

The Chocolatier

Tina Koyama

Find a special spot on your body
and use it, he tells us, like *this,* and he touches
chocolate to his lip again and again,
closing his eyes. Spurning all
thermometers, he waits for the perfect moment
to slide truffle centers deep
into a bowl of cooling chocolate.
It's all a matter of patience, he says,
for while the science of chocolate
is the altered crystalline structure
of sugar, the art
is treating it with love.
I nod along with the class and pretend
to take notes, all the while

melting in his arms, falling
for his every tempered word: my hair
is a riverful of dark couverture,
my eyes the color of ephemere truffles.
I could learn to love

a man like this, his hands at first cool
then warming the way a square
of chocolate takes after the tongue.

I could learn to wait
for a man like this, but he no longer
waits for me: the chocolatier dips truffles now, one
by one, by hand, holding each
not as he might the breast of a woman
he loves but perhaps of a woman he once loved, then slowly
let go. Chocolate, treated right, will love you
back, he says. Look at that shine,
as if the light belonged there
in the dark.

Two Rooms

Eric C. Wat

I

*F*or only that moment, Eric feels a sense of satisfaction. For only that moment, he isn't thinking about the constant arguments and the future—it is not appropriate to speak of "their" future—that, he knows deep down inside, would be doomed. Sergio's thigh makes him forget all that. It leans against Eric's own and attaches itself there. Without the lights, they have become inseparable, each giving the other warmth, as if the heat had found a tunnel from pore to pore, traveling through sweat that, like glue, binds one thigh to the other. Eric pretends to watch the television screen, but out of the corner of his right eye he watches Sergio intensely, as if he would disappear into thin air. He wishes their stillness, even with all its uncertainties, would last awhile, like that morning when he awoke to find the two of them in exactly the same position they had been before they closed their eyes, each pursuing his separate dreams. That morning he felt the warmth from the lower part of his body, for Sergio was still in him, having found that perfect place that stroked sweet, wakeless slumber. Sergio's head hanging over his shoulder from behind, Eric could feel on the back of his neck the soft corner of Sergio's mouth, the curve of his smile.

There is no expression on his face now, and Eric's eyes grow sleepy, weak and tired from seeing. He closes them. In the darkness of his mind, he sees molecules—impressions pressed upon his eyes—colliding into each other, changing shapes like making love, then exploding. In the darkness of his mind, even then, he hears Sergio's fingers making noises with his stubbles as he scratches his face. The molecules slow. Sergio removes his thigh. Eric opens his eyes, feeling his lover taking the stickiness from him, the stickiness carrying part of him. It—the sweat and everything else torn apart—feels exactly like a bandage peeled away from an unhealed wound. Without taking his eyes off the screen, Sergio wipes the sweat off his thigh; Eric's heart sinks.

II

It is as innocent and uncomplicated as we were in the beginning. My thigh moves toward his for no particular reason, and when they touch, it feels good. But the goodness is too much to bear. I loved him from the very beginning, but I was not supposed to. Things are not simple anymore, as hard as I try to pretend they are, watching the screen as if life goes on only on it. I can never forget how he made kissing so easy and free of delusions, lips pressed against mine, his breath sending ripples across my field of stubbles. How his mouth travels and massages places that have not yet hurt. And how he nestles his nose in the curvature of my brown face like a small child running through an overgrown wheatfield, chasing the wind. I can never forget the few nights we shared, kept warm by the heat of our touch, sustained by each other's soiled perspiration. Our bodies knew no boundaries, no laws, and we had touched each other as quietly and as intensely as my thigh touches his now. But I cannot even gather up the strength to whisper his name. Not now. Not ever. For I know he would use that as evidence. Sometimes I wake from a dream saying his name aloud, then becoming afraid that others in the house might have heard. But I have imagined my life differently, imagined my thigh distinct and separate from his. I look straight into the screen, but my mind is screaming, "I like you, but I am not like you . . . I am not . . . *that way.*" Still, my thigh will not move, not listening to its own words. I wish he could read my thought, or perhaps I shouldn't. I wouldn't want him to have loved me this much. I scratch my face, making movements to disturb this stillness. Stillness scares me, so full of thoughts. My heart, cold and resolute, turns my leg away, and even as I wipe the sweat from my thigh, ridding the smell of our past, its palpitations consume the stillness of the dark room.

Jeannie

Mina Kumar

$\mathcal{B}$efore Neelam met Jeannie, it seemed such a strange, mysterious thing to like a woman. Neelam worried over what she was and why she was what she was and what women like her wanted and whether any woman *would* want her at all. She didn't think the latter was possible. There had been women who had liked her, liked the way she sucked their breasts, liked having her on their arm, liked dancing with her, but she wanted to be wanted. She wanted a woman to desire her body, as ludicrous and impossible as the idea seemed. She told herself all lesbians really wanted to be wanted by a woman or wanted to possess a woman more than they wanted to make love with a woman, and she had a lump in her throat of the cries it seemed she would never utter. It wasn't so much that she wanted a "butch" as that she wanted a woman who would desire the corporeal reality of her breasts, stomach, cunt, and this didn't seem altogether likely. Why would a woman want her pussy? She had never particularly been overcome with a desire to eat pussy. It didn't repulse her, and she was certainly willing to do it, but the idea didn't particularly excite her. She didn't know she just hadn't met the right pussy.

The night Neelam met Jeannie began with Neelam sitting alone in Sheridan Square after yet another failed date. The only other people left in the park were sleeping homeless men. Neelam stretched her arms out on the back of the bench and sighed. It had been a long damn day.

First she had gotten out of work late. She had rushed downtown to make her blind date with a pudgy, androgynous Chinese-American dyke who was not what Neelam had been expecting. After the movie, they walked down Seventh Avenue and Neelam had suggested they go to the Box for a drink. The Chinese-American dyke said she only went to Crazy Nanny's, the white bar, because she had heard that the women at Pandora's Box smoked crack in the bathroom. The date ended soon after.

Neelam continued sitting in the park after her date left. She didn't feel like moving. It seemed such a shame to be home on a ripe summer night. She took a sip of D&G's ginger beer and watched the women go by.

The furthest back Neelam could trace her sexual proclivities was to when she was eight years old and living in Kluang. Her mother passed the long, empty days sitting in a wicker chair in the garden, doing the crossword puzzle in every English-language magazine or newspaper she could possibly buy. When her mother went into the kitchen to get her lunch, Neelam would sneak up to her mother's chair and carefully pull out from the bottom of the pile the dew-moist Australian tabloids with the half-naked girls on page three. She would enter the house from the backyard and go into the room where she slept. There she sat hunched on the tile floor, poring over the pictures of bare-breasted girls, and listening for the sound of footsteps coming toward her, ready to shove the magazines under the mattress. "Why does that girl *sneak* the magazines away?" her mother once asked her stepfather. He had shrugged.

A cop came into the park to get the homeless men out and
Neelam rose along with them. She tossed the empty bottle into the
garbage bin and turned the corner.

The Box wasn't very busy. There were some women at the bar,
but the only people dancing were one couple and a vogueing
transsexual. Neelam stood at the edge of the dance floor. Jeannie
was standing against the speaker, her arms crossed.

She was tall and Junoesque, big-breasted and big legs, long
thin braids flowing over her shoulders. She was beautiful: her lips
lipstick-red, skin smooth and dry like cubes of dark chocolate.

Neelam walked back down the bar, and bought a screwdriver.
She was in no mood for rejection, and she thought Jeannie was too
femme to want her. She caught herself in the mirror behind the bar,
brooding over her drink like Amithab Bachchan, and laughed.

When she was a kid, nearly every weekend her mother, her
stepfather and Neelam went into the Indian section of Singapore to
eat at Komala Villas and watch a film, preferably an Amithab
movie. She spent her Saturday afternoons mesmerized. She would
sit in a narrow seat at the very top row, almost aswim in the
enormous screen. Neelam identified with Amithab completely.

He was tall and angry and misunderstood, usually abandoned
by his father, usually forced to rely on only himself. Amithab was
the "angry young man," a criminal, a man whom injustice forced
outside the law, illegitimate, fatherless, a drinker, a clubgoer, a
sophisticated lover of beautiful women, a wrecker of revenge, consumed by his past, lean and dark with a deep, rich voice, consum-
mately urbane, strong and unafraid, melancholy, a man who won in
the end or died. Neelam was all these things. But to her confusion,
she also identified with the women in the movies. She wanted to
wear makeup, lots of heavy gold jewelry, zari-bordered bright silk
clothes and be beautiful, with henna designs on her hands and
brow, and writhe and sing mujras like Rekha, Zeenat Aman,
Parveen Babi, Helen, and Bindu. She was torn between being
Amithab and being the heroine, knowing that she was both. And if

she was corrupted by being both, how would she have the only solace Amithab ever had—the love of a beautiful, sympathetic woman?

Amithab movies stirred her and consoled her and discomfited her. She watched Helen swivel her hips in the den of the dacoit Gabbar Singh and felt a strange wave of something between queasiness and joy. She watched the scene in *Muqaddar ka Sikandar* where the rich girl tiptoes out of her house in the dead of night. The poor boy who will grow up to be Amithab is sleeping on her front steps. He has nowhere to go and no one to help him. The girl leans forward, and without waking him, covers him with the blanket. Which one did she want to be? The girl or the boy? She thought about it until her head hurt. The blanket, she thought finally, but it was an answer both witty and inadequate.

Neelam took her half-finished drink to a table, and returned to the dance floor. One of the songs she had requested had come on. She stood facing the empty center of the floor and waited for the music to enter her. Neelam danced with a slowly disintegrating self-consciousness. This was exactly what she needed. The DJ played all her house anthems one by one. "Coming on Strong." "Ride the Rhythm." "Let No Man Put Asunder." "Love Dancing." Neelam's moves became deeper and showier. She slid and glided on the waxed floors. "But tonight is the night that I'm gonna make you mine."

The music slowed down. Neelam stood on the dance floor awkwardly for a minute, then went to sit down at her table. She dragged a chair in front of her so that she could stretch out her legs. She picked up a napkin and dabbed at her brow, looking around to see who else had come into the bar. The transsexual who had been vogueing up a storm was sitting at the table across the aisle, next to Jeannie. Jeannie leaned over to whisper to the transsexual, who turned around and looked at Neelam.

Neelam ignored it. The transsexual turned around again. What the hell was he . . . she . . . it looking at? What the fuck were they talking about? Neelam sucked her teeth. It was bad enough that she had to accept that a woman like Jeannie wouldn't want her, but did she have to also accept that Jeannie would make fun of her with some transsexual? Just as she was crushing the empty plastic cup, the transsexual loomed in front of her. "My friend is too shy to come over but she'd like to dance with you."

Neelam wondered if this was some kind of prank. She resigned herself to falling for it. Neelam looked down and nodded.

Jeannie strode to the dance floor and Neelam followed, her eyes lowered. They danced and Neelam felt too embarrassed to look up. She was suddenly hyperconscious of her body. A little liquor made Neelam feel dainty, but a little more made her acutely aware of her heaviness. Jeannie asked her name, where she lived, where she was from. "I'm Indian," Neelam said, stopping to catch her breath. "As soon as I tell a woman that, she offers to teach me to dance."

"That's ridiculous," Jeannie said. She pulled Neelam to her as the first beats of "Housecall" started. She leaned down and whispered in the shell of Neelam's ear, "You know you have rhythm." Neelam blushed. Suddenly, everything was going right, and her anxiousness was eased. She felt like she was floating in a dream. She rested her face lightly on Jeannie's chest, the soft cotton jersey against her cheek so she could smell Jeannie's musk on it. They were in a corner, near the speaker, and through her half-closed eyes, Neelam could see the lights fading down until the dance floor was dark.

When they became tired, Jeannie bought her a drink, and after Neelam downed it, Jeannie took her outside for some air.

The summer air was heavy and moist. Jeannie stood against the brick wall of the bar. "Do you want to see some pictures?" she asked. Neelam nodded. There wasn't anything else to do.

Jeannie fished her wallet out of her backpack and showed Neelam some faded snapshots of women in jaunty toques sitting around a table. "That's my grandmother when she was young." Jeannie flipped the page to a heavily airbrushed studio picture of a woman with a big white bow in her hair and gleaming white teeth. "And that's my mother."

"Where's your girlfriend?" Neelam asked flirtatiously.

"I don't have a picture of her," Jeannie replied, putting her wallet back.

"You have a girlfriend?"

"Yes," Jeannie said. "Don't you?"

"No. What the fuck are you doing plying me with alcohol?"

"Being friendly." Jeannie pulled the strap of her backpack over her shoulder. "I wasn't making a move on you." Neelam pouted. "Come on, let's sit down." Jeannie led her through a few deserted side streets to a church with wide, white steps. They sat down on the top stair.

Neelam was silent. She has a girlfriend, Neelam thought. There was always something wrong.

The first woman to make a move on her was a crazy Bahamian bank teller. Neelam had been a little over fourteen and had noticed Rosemarie right away when she went to deposit the forty dollars she had earned compiling listings at a real estate office. Rosemarie was tall and warm brown, with a big chest and expressive hands. The first time they spoke was weeks later, when they met by accident at the bus stop. Rosemarie said Neelam cheered her so much that she wanted to know Neelam always. On their first date, Neelam brought Rosemarie a teddy bear with a pink bow around its neck, since Rosemarie had said she liked stuffed animals, and Rosemarie had bought her a brooch and a purse.

They rode the subway to a tiny Palestinian restaurant on Bathhurst, and Neelam shouted to Rosemarie above the train rattle that she was beautiful.

"I'm not beautiful," Rosemarie protested, smiling. "I am not beautiful at all. You should see me without my clothes on." She paused. "If you come to my apartment, I'll take my clothes off and show you."

The train pulled into Lawrence station. They walked down the fluorescent-lit platform to the escalator to the street level, and, tentatively, Neelam took Rosemarie's hand in her own. Rosemarie squeezed, her gold rings pressing into Neelam's palm. At the end of dinner, as they said goodbye in the subway station because they were going home in separate directions, they stood close. Rosemarie leaned down, her thick lips an inch away from Neelam. Neelam reached up to kiss her lightly on the mouth. "You can't do that," said Rosemarie. "That's a devil thing."

Rosemarie, it turned out, was a Pentecostal. They talked a few more times, and she accused Neelam of trying to seduce her. Neelam wondered if she had misread the situation. How could one misread "let me take you home and show you my naked body"? Did women generally buy presents for other women they barely knew the first time they went out together? Did women generally make friends at the bus station? Neelam stopped calling Rosemarie. It was all too complicated.

The next woman she went out with was years later and in a different country, but the situation was just as ridiculous. This woman was a Texan, who told Neelam, "You are attracted to black women because you want a 'big, black buck,'" and Neelam wondered, if this was true, why she was with a woman who was decidedly wimpy in bed? Later, the Texan told her that they should be just friends and then told Neelam she wanted to fist her. And then she said they should be just friends, but she wanted to eat Neelam's pussy. After a few rounds, getting neither friendship nor sex, Neelam gave up. The Texan ran off with a Dominican girl who, it later turned out, was pregnant by her live-in boyfriend, who knew all about the Texan, so there was a modicum of karma. Then the Texan became the mistress of a rich butch chiropractor who took the Texan on all-expenses-paid holidays to Puerto Rico, so maybe there wasn't any justice after all.

And Jeannie had a girlfriend. Neelam sighed. Her butt hurt from the rough concrete stair. And the air was like a layer on her skin. She watched the flies buzz around the corner streetlight, screwing up her eyes until it was all a blur. She could hear crickets and cars and some people having a conversation around the corner. She took a bag of bagel chips out of her bag and ripped it open.

"Do you want one?" she asked, as chips tumbled from the packet. She held one out.

Jeannie shook her head.

Neelam ate it and held out her salty fingers.

Jeannie looked down at Neelam's outstretched arm, her fingers tipped with a paste of onion flecks and salt, and then back at Neelam's face. The streetlamp's yellowy light made Neelam's light skin and her white blouse glisten. And Jeannie said, "You know how bad I want to suck them."

Neelam felt her pussy clench. She barely perceptibly leaned toward Jeannie and then they kissed, Jeannie's tongue sliding into her mouth. Jeannie said, "Are you trying to make me unfaithful to my girlfriend?" and cupped Neelam's head, kissing her harder. Jeannie pulled Neelam toward her until Neelam sat, triumphantly ensconced between Jeannie's thighs, Jeannie's arms around her waist. Slowly, Neelam picked up Jeannie's right hand and examined it, the starkly pale palm, thick fingers, burn mark like a ring on the middle finger, neatly long unpainted nails. "Do you have a nail clipper in your house?" Jeannie whispered into Neelam's neck. Neelam nodded. "Let's go."

Once in the apartment, Neelam went into the bathroom and drew the bath. She unbuttoned her blouse and took off her pants. She was wearing a white lace teddy with satin cups. Nice underclothes gave her an extra bit of confidence on a date, but she wasn't thinking of her earlier date. It suited the moment; that was all.

Jeannie fingered Neelam's satin spaghetti straps. "I guess you were planning on bringing someone home with you," she said.

"I've never done this before," Neelam said truthfully, but the idea of being a deliberate, lingeried seductress was not displeasing. She reached over and turned the water off. She put a finger in the tub. The water was nice and hot. Jeannie pulled off her jersey and hooked it on the doorknob.

Neelam undid her ponytail. "You are beautiful," said Jeannie.

"I know," Neelam replied. And at that moment, she did.

"I know you know."

"But no one loves me."

Jeannie said, "You know if I didn't have a girlfriend, I would scoop you up." And then Jeannie scooped her up.

They sat in the bathtub with Neelam's back against Jeannie's chest. Neelam could feel Jeannie's stiff nipples poking against her. Neelam splashed the hot, soapy water over Jeannie's legs. There should have been music in the background, but Neelam knew it would spoil the mood to get up and turn some on. Without a great deal of gentleness, Jeannie entered her. "Didn't you ask about the nail clipper?" Neelam reminded her, wriggling away.

Jeannie rose, splashing water on the floor. She picked up the clipper from the countertop and clipped her nails, letting the cuttings fall on the floor. "There is a wastepaper basket right over there," Neelam remarked, getting out of the tub.

"Now you'll have to clean before you invite the next person up."

Neelam wrapped herself in a blue towel. "There doesn't have to be a next person, you know," she said tentatively, going into the other room.

But Jeannie had a girlfriend, she thought. She felt cold in the bed and got under the covers. She threw the damp towel on the floor. "Turn off the light," she said to Jeannie.

Then Jeannie crawled into her bed, shoving the blanket aside.

———

Neelam knew what the inside of her pussy felt like. She had felt it. And though it was fine, she couldn't imagine a woman wanting to be there. What for? It wasn't that she thought it was icky—just unexciting. And yet she wanted a woman to want it. Her fantasies abruptly veered into trying to imagine why a woman would want it. She knew that she wasn't overcome by the desire to be inside another woman, so why would another woman want to be inside her? Women probably did it out of politeness. Billy said he sucked dick because he liked his dick sucked. This was simply not good enough for Neelam, because fags have anal sex, which they can both feel. What a ridiculous thing a lesbian was. Two polite women doing boring things. She was forced to admit that she never looked at a woman and wanted to suck her pussy, or get inside her. The thought just never occurred to her. She never thought about the act of sleeping with a woman. Neelam somehow felt that it was impinging on another woman because the woman might not want to sleep with her. Neelam rarely appeared in the fantasies she used to get off. When she did succeed in suspending her disbelief, she felt like she had cheated. The only way she believed a woman could want another woman was out of pathology, like the Texan. The Texan wanted to be a man. In fact, the Texan liked to pretend her lovers were men. The Texan wanted to be a fag. This was too much for Neelam. She never had much luck when she tried to explain her quandary to other people. They would describe scenarios where two women could come at the same time, but that wasn't the point. She wanted a woman to be stimulated by what was stimulating her, not by the idea of stimulating her. "You think too much," said Marcia.

"What choice do I have? I never have any sex," Neelam replied.

As Jeannie got inside her, she wondered what was going on in Jeannie's mind, but knew better than to ask. Why were women so ridiculous, she wondered. Why couldn't she just believe?

"Do you have any lubricant?" Jeannie asked.

Neelam reached for her breast. "We have to do this the natural way," she said. "Besides, I'm so wet."

"You're so tight." Jeannie looked down between Neelam's legs. "And your clitoris is overgrown."

"Overgrown?" said Neelam. Not again. She pulled her thighs shut.

"It's enormous," Jeannie said. "It looks like a little dick."

"Shut up," Neelam drawled, half-laughing and half-insulted. It was no doubt the reason she was a lesbian, at least according to medieval Europeans. That and the porno magazines of her step-father's that she came across as a child, and her domineering mother, and some inner perversity that disposed her toward the impossible.

She leaned over to suck Jeannie's breasts. There was not a whole lot else she could do in the position they were in. Jeannie's pussy was beyond the reach of her hand. She wondered if Jeannie was bored with probing the guck of her pussy. Straight women had it so easy. All they had to do was lie there and a man would be satisfied. Besides, everyone always said that the only thing a straight man wanted was pussy. Straight women didn't have to ask themselves how and why and if this was true. Why did a woman want pussy, and did any women really ever want it at all?

Jeannie made her lie back, and plunged deeper inside her. Neelam arched up to accommodate Jeannie more easily. Jeannie tried to put all her fingers inside. Neelam clenched her teeth. She didn't want Jeannie to stop but it was beginning to hurt. Jeannie's powerful movements made Neelam's whole pussy shake. Finally she couldn't take anymore. "You're hurting my clit," she cried out, squirming, her body involuntarily lifting off the bed.

Jeannie said breathlessly, "Can't you move it?"

Neelam was dumbstruck. Jeannie was staring at her as if she expected a response. She doesn't want to stop, Neelam thought with astonishment. She wants to be inside my guck. If she is unwilling to stop, then it means she wants to. And suddenly she realized that it was possible and Jeannie wanted her and everything tumbled into place. She felt as if her lungs were full of cold, clean air, and she was almost crying. She moved Jeannie's hand out of her and pulled Jeannie on top of her. "You didn't even come yet," Jeannie said, reproachfully.

"It doesn't matter," Neelam replied, ridiculously happy. She wants it, she wants me. It's not just to make me happy.

They lay in silence for a while. Then Jeannie shifted to lie beside her. "I have to go soon," said Jeannie. "My girlfriend is expecting me." Neelam slipped on the ruby-colored nightshirt hanging from a hook by the bed.

She turned on the light and looked at Jeannie, her naked body. Jeannie was about to pull the covers over her, but Neelam stopped her. "Don't," she said. She parted Jeannie's legs. "I've never really seen a pussy." This was not strictly true, but close enough.

Jeannie unclenched her thighs. "I'll let you see mine," she said, ruffling Neelam's hair. And she did.

Right after Jeannie left, Neelam felt cold and sluttish and guilty, but not for long. She was full of Jeannie, and when a friend from high school whom she hadn't talked to in years called up, she helplessly started telling Kathy about what had happened.

Kathy was initially discomfited by the turn the conversation was taking, but then her curiosity overcame her other emotions. "So when did you know you were . . ." Kathy asked.

"What is there to know?" Neelam responded. "It has nothing to do with knowing. It has do with your pussy getting hot. Ask me when I knew a woman could feel the same way about me. That's what you have to realize. That's what you have to learn. Your pussy getting hot is an involuntary physical reaction. It's the other thing you have to figure out or find out or have shown to you, because the world does not want you to know." Kathy was silent. "All right, when I was in fifth grade, after reading Colette," said Neelam, to keep the conversation rolling.

Neelam didn't always believe she was right, but thinking of Jeannie always reassured her. Once, after eyeing a dark, hard dread all night, just as she was getting her coat from the coat check because it was obvious that this eye contact thing was not working and she was ready to go home, the dread touched her elbow. The woman made mildly flirtatious conversation and asked for her number, and just as Neelam was settling in to enjoy the moment, the woman said, "Let me ask you something. I see a lot of Indian girls with acne on their faces. Is that a really common thing?"

Neelam reeled from the shock and rushed out the door. It had been almost a year since that time with Jeannie, which was the last time she had been with a woman. She felt ugly and empty. She felt like it would never happen. The drinks she had downed and the year of celibacy made her feel weak and insecure. She would never find anyone, she thought, crying, but then she stopped. Maybe she was overdoing it, and besides, she *would* find her woman. At least, the women were getting better and better. One day, she would have a girlfriend.

She undressed and got into bed, remembering Jeannie's pussy. It had such pink petals. She had wanted to suck it, but it would have been her first time. She knew she would have been terribly depressed if her first time had been a one-night stand. She had contented herself with a swipe of her finger. Jeannie tasted slightly bitter, like appleseed or pink champagne. Jeannie's pussy was so pretty and rimmed with dark, tightly napped hair like a pink rose surrounded by baby's breath. She had leaned closer to the pink jewel at its heart, and she had seen, Neelam remembered with a smile—Possibility.

Roses

EVELYN LAU

The psychiatrist came into my life one month after my eighteenth birthday. He came into my life wearing a silk tie, his dark eyes half-obscured by lines and wrinkles. He brought with him a pronounced upper-class accent, a futile sense of humor, books to educate me. *Lolita. The Story of O.* His lips were thin, but when I took them between my own they plumped out and filled my mouth with sweet foreign tastes.

He worshiped me at first because he could not touch me. And then he worshiped me because he could only touch me if he paid to do so. I understood that without the autumn leaves, the browns of the hundreds and the fiery scarlets of the fifties, the marble pedestal beneath me would begin to erode.

The first two weeks were tender. He said he adored my child-like body, my unpainted face, my long straight hair. He promised to take care of me, love me unconditionally. He would be my father, friend, lover—and if one was ever absent, the other two were large enough on their own to fill up the space that was left behind.

He brought into my doorway the slippery clean smell of rain, and he possessed the necessary implements—samples of pills tiny as seeds, a gold shovel. My body yielded to the scrapings of his hands.

He gave me drugs because, he said, he loved me. He brought

the tablets from his office, rattling in plastic bottles stuffed to the brim with cotton. I placed them under my tongue and sucked up their saccharine sweetness, learning that only the strong ones tasted like candy, the rest were chalky or bitter. He loved me beyond morality.

The plants that he brought each time he came to visit—baby's breath, dieffenbachia, jade—began to die as soon as they crossed the threshold of my home. After twenty-four hours the leaves would crinkle into tight dark snarls stooping toward the soil. They could not be pried open, though I watered his plants, exposed them to sunlight, trimmed them. It was as if by contact with him or with my environment, they had been poisoned. Watching them die, I was reminded of how he told me that when he first came to Canada he worked for two years in one of our worst mental institutions. I walked by the building once at night, creeping as far as I dared up the grassy slopes and between the evergreens. It was a sturdy beige structure; it didn't look so bad from the outside. In my mind, though, I saw it as something else. In my mind it was a series of black-and-white film stills; a face staring out from behind a barred window. The face belonged to a woman with tangled hair, wearing a nightgown. I covered my ears from her screams. When he told me about this place I imagined him in the film, the woman clawing at him where the corridors were gray, and there was the clanking sound of tin and metal. I used to lie awake as a child on the nights my father visited my bed and imagine scenes in which he was terrorized, in pain, made helpless. This was the same. I could smell the bloodstains the janitors had not yet scrubbed from the floors. I could smell the human discharges and see the hands that groped at him as he walked past each cell, each room. The hands flapped disembodied in the air, white and supplicating and at the same time evil.

He told me that when he was married to his first wife, she had gone shopping one day and he had had to take their baby with him on his hospital rounds. "I didn't know where to put him when I arrived," he said. "So I put him in the wastepaper basket." When he returned the child had upended the basket and crawled out, crying, glaring at his father. "I had no other choice," he said, and he reached into his trenchcoat and gave me a bottle of pills. "I love you," he said, "that's why I'm doing this."

I believed that only someone with a limitless love would put his baby in a trash can, its face squinched and its mouth pursing open in a squawk of dismay. Only someone like that could leave it swaddled in crumpled scraps of paper so he could go and take care of his patients. I could not imagine the breadth of the love that lay behind his eyes, those eyes that became as clear as glass at the moment of orgasm.

He bought a mask yesterday from a Japanese import store. It had tangled human hair that he washed with an anti-dandruff shampoo, carefully brushing it afterward so the strands would not snap off. It had no pupils; the corneas were circles of bone. He took it home with him and stared at it for half an hour during a thunderstorm, paralyzed with fear. It stared back at him. It was supposed to scare off his rage, he said.

After two weeks his tenderness went the way of his plants— crisp, shriveled, closed. He stopped touching me in bed but grew as gluttonous as dry soil. I started to keep my eyes open when we kissed and to squeeze them shut all the other times, the many times he pulled my hand or my head down between his legs.

He continued to bring me magazines and books, but they were eclipsed by the part of him he expected me to touch. Some days, I found I could not. I thought it was enough that I listened to his stories. I fantasized about being his psychoanalyst and not letting him see my face, having that kind of control over him. I would lay him down on my couch and shine light into his eyes while I remained in shadow where he could not touch me.

His latest gift, a snake plant, looks like a cluster of green knives or spears. The soil is so parched that I keep watering it, but the water runs smartly through the pot without, it seems, having left anything of itself behind. The water runs all over the table and into my hands.

Tonight I did not think I could touch him. I asked him to hit me instead, thinking his slim white body would recoil from the thought. Instead he rubbed himself against my thigh, excited. I told him pain did not arouse me, but it was too late. I pulled the blankets around my naked body and tried to close up inside the way a flower wraps itself in the safety of its petals when night falls.

At first he stretched me across his knees and began to spank me. I wiggled obediently and raised my bottom high into the air, the way my father used to like to see me do. Then he moved up to rain blows upon my back. One of them was so painful that I saw colors even with my eyes open; it showered through my body like fireworks. It was like watching a sunset and feeling a pain in your chest at its wrenching beauty, the kind of pain that makes you gasp.

How loud the slaps grew in the small space of my apartment— like the sound of thunder. I wondered if my face looked, in that moment, like his Japanese mask.

The pain cleansed my mind until it breathed like the streets of a city after a good and bright rain. It washed away the dirt inside me. I could see the gutters open up to swallow the candy wrappers, newspaper pages, cigarette butts borne along on its massive tide. I saw as I had not seen before every bump and indentation on the wall beside my bed.

And then he wanted more and I fought him, dimly surprised that he wasn't stronger. I saw as though through the eye of a camera this tangle of white thighs and arms and the crook of a shoulder, the slope of a back. I scraped his skin with my fingernails. I felt no conscious fear because I was the girl behind the camera, zooming in for a close-up, a tight shot, an interesting angle. Limbs like marble on the tousled bed. His face contorted with strain. He was breathing heavily, but I, I was not breathing at all. I knew that if I touched his hair my hand would come away wet, not with the pleasant sweat of sexual exertion, but with something different. Something that would smell like a hospital, a hospital without disinfectant to mask the smells underneath.

And when he pushed my face against his thigh, it was oddly comforting, though it was the same thigh that belonged to the body that was reaching out to hit me. I breathed in the soft, soapy smell of his skin as his hand stung my back—the same hand that comforted crying patients, that wrote notes on their therapeutic progress, that had shaken with shyness when it first touched me. The sound of the slaps was amplified in the candlelit room. Nothing had ever sounded so loud, so singular in its purpose. I had never felt so far away from myself, not even with his pills.

I am far away and his thigh is sandy as a beach against my cheek. The sounds melt like gold, like slow Sunday afternoons. I think of cats and the baby grand piano in the foyer of my father's house. I think of the rain that gushes down the drainpipes outside my father's bathroom late at night when things begin to happen. I think of the queerly elegant black notes on sheets of piano music. The light is flooding generously through the windows and I am a little girl with a pink ribbon in my hair and a ruffled dress.

I seat myself on the piano bench and begin to play, my fingertips softening to the long ivory, the shorter ebony keys. I look down at my feet and see them bound in pink ballerina slippers, pressing intermittently on the pedals. Always Daddy's girl, I perform according to his instruction.

When it was over he stroked the fear that bathed my hands in cold sweat. He said that when we fought my face had filled with hatred and a dead coldness. He said that he had cured himself of his obsession with me during the beating, he had stripped me of my mystery. Slapped me human. He said my fear had turned him on. He was thirsty for the sweat that dampened my palms and willing to do anything to elicit more of that moisture so he could lick it and quench his tongue's thirst.

I understood that when I did not bleed at the first blow his love turned into hatred. I saw that if I was indeed precious and fragile I would have broken, I would have burst open like a thin shell and discharged the rich sweet stain of roses.

Before he left he pressed his lips to mine. His eyes were open when he said that if I told anyone, he would have no other choice but to kill me.

Now that he is gone, I look between my breasts and see another flower growing: a rash of raspberry dots, like seeds. I wonder if this is how fear discharges itself when we leave our bodies in moments of pain.

The psychiatrist, when he first came, promised me a rose garden and in the mirror tomorrow morning I will see the results for the first time on my own body. I will tend his bouquets before he comes again, his eyes misty with fear and lust. Then I will listen to the liquid notes that are pleasing in the sunlit foyer and smile because somewhere, off in the distance, my father is clapping.

Blood Links

II

The Word Love

Chitra Divakaruni

You practice them out loud for days in front of the bathroom mirror, the words with which you'll tell your mother you're living with a man. Sometimes they are words of confession and repentance. Sometimes they are angry, defiant. Sometimes they melt into a single, sighing sound. *Love.* You let the water run so he won't hear you and ask what those foreign phrases you keep saying mean. You don't want to have to explain, don't want another argument like last time.

"Why are you doing this to yourself?" he'd asked, throwing his books down on the table when he returned from class to find you curled into a corner of the sagging sofa you'd bought together at a Berkeley garage sale. You'd washed your face but he knew right away that you'd been crying. Around you, wads of paper crumpled tight as stones. (This was when you thought writing would be the best way.) "I hate seeing you like this." Then he added, his tone darkening, "You're acting like I was a criminal."

You'd watched the upside-down titles of his books splaying across the table. *Control Systems Engineering. Boiler Operations Guide. Handbook of Shock and Vibration.* Cryptic as tarot cards, they seemed to be telling you something. If only you could decipher it.

"It isn't you," you'd said, gathering up the books guiltily,

smoothing their covers. Holding them tight against you. "I'd have
the same problem no matter who it was."

You tried to tell him about your mother, how she'd seen her
husband's face for the first time at her wedding. How, when he
died (you were two years old then), she had taken off her jewelry
and put on widow's white and dedicated the rest of her life to the
business of bringing you up. *We only have each other,* she often told
you.

"So?"

"She lives in a different world. Can't you see that? She's never
traveled more than a hundred miles from the village where she was
born; she's never touched cigarettes or alcohol; even though she
lives in Calcutta, she's never watched a movie."

"Are you serious!"

"I love her, Rex." *I will not feel apologetic,* you told yourself. You
wanted him to know that when you conjured up her face, the stern
angles of it softening into a rare smile, the silver at her temples
catching the afternoon sun in the backyard under the pomegranate
tree, love made you breathless, as though someone had punched a
hole through your chest. But he interrupted.

"So don't tell her," he said, "that you're living in sin. With a
foreigner, no less. Someone whose favorite food is sacred cow steak
and Budweiser. Who pops a pill now and then when he gets depressed. The shock'll probably do her in."

You hate it when he talks like that, biting off the ends of words
and spitting them out. You try to tell yourself that he wants to hurt
you only because *he's* hurting, because he's jealous of how much she
means to you. You try to remember the special times. The morning
he showed up outside your Shakespeare class with violets the color
of his eyes. The evening when the two of you drove up to Grizzly
Peak and watched the sunset spreading red over the Bay while he
told you of his childhood, years of being shunted between his
divorced parents till he was old enough to move out. How you had

held him. The night in his apartment (has it only been three months?) when he took your hands in his warm strong ones, asking you to move in with him, please, because he really needed you. You try to shut out the whispery voice that lives behind the ache in your eyes, the one that started when you said yes and he kissed you, hard. *Mistake,* says the voice, whispering in your mother's tones.

Sometimes the voice sounds different, not hers. It is a rushed intake of air, as just before someone asks a question that might change your life. You don't want to hear the question, which might be *how did you get yourself into this mess,* or perhaps *why,* so you leap in with that magic word. *Love,* you tell yourself, *lovelovelove.* But you know, deep down, that words solve nothing.

And so you no longer try to explain to him why you *must* tell your mother. You just stand in the bathroom in front of the crooked mirror with tarnished edges and practice the words. You try not to notice that the eyes in the mirror are so like her eyes, that same vertical line between the brows. The line of your jaw slants up at the same angle as hers when she would lean forward to kiss you goodbye at the door. Outside a wino shouts something. Crash of broken glass and, later, police sirens. But you're hearing the street vendor call out *momphali, momphali, fresh and hot,* and she's smiling, handing you a coin, saying, *yes, baby, you can have some.* The salty crunch of roasted peanuts fills your mouth, the bathroom water runs and runs, endless as sorrow, the week blurs past, and suddenly it's Saturday morning, the time of her weekly call.

She tells you how Aunt Arati's arthritis isn't getting any better in spite of the turmeric poultices. It's so cold this year in Calcutta, the *shiuli* flowers have all died. You listen, holding on to the rounded *o*'s, the long liquid *e*'s, the *s*'s that brush against your face soft as night kisses. She's trying to arrange a marriage for Cousin Leela, who's going to graduate from college next year, remember? She misses you. Do you like your new apartment? How long before you finish the Ph.D. and come home for good? Her voice is small and far, tinny with static. "You're so quiet . . . are you okay, *shona?* Is something bothering you?" You want to tell her, but your heart flings itself around in your chest like a netted bird, and the words that you practiced so long are gone.

"I'm fine, Ma," you say. "Everything's all right."

The first thing you did when you moved into his apartment was to put up the batik hanging, deep red flowers winding around a black circle. The late summer sun shone through the open window. Smell of California honeysuckle in the air, a radio next door playing Mozart. He walked in, narrowing his eyes, pausing to watch. You waited, pin in hand, the nubs of the fabric pulsing under your palm, erratic as a heart. "Not bad," he nodded finally, and you let out your breath in a relieved shiver of a laugh.

"My mother gave it to me," you said. "A going-away-to-college gift, a talisman . . ." You started to tell him how she had bought it at the Maidan fair on a day as beautiful as this one, the buds just coming out on the mango trees, the red-breasted bulbuls returning north. But he held up his hand, *later.* Swung you off the rickety chair and carried you to the bed. Lay on top, pinning you down. His eyes were sapphire stones. His hair caught the light, glinting like warm sandstone. Surge of electric (love or fear?) up your spine, making you shiver, making you forget what you wanted to say.

At night after lovemaking, you lie listening to his sleeping breath. His arm falls across you, warm, *protective,* you say to yourself. Outside, wind rattles the panes. A dry wind. (There hasn't been rain for a long time.) *I am cherished.*

But then the memories come.

Once when you were in college you had gone to see a popular Hindi movie with your girlfriends. Secretly, because Mother said movies were frivolous, decadent. But there were no secrets in Calcutta. When you came home from classes the next day, a suitcase full of your clothes was on the doorstep. A note on it, in your mother's hand. *Better no daughter than a disobedient one, a shame to the family.* Even now you remember how you felt, the dizzy fear that shriveled the edges of the day, the desperate knocking on the door that left your knuckles raw. You'd sat on the doorstep all afternoon, and passersby had glanced at you curiously. By evening it was cold. The numbness crept up your feet and covered you. When she'd finally opened the door after midnight, for a moment you couldn't stand. She had pulled you up, and you had fallen into her arms, both of you crying. Later she had soaked your feet in hot water with boric soda. You still remember the softness of the towels with which she wiped them.

Why do you always focus on the sad things, you wonder. Is it some flaw in yourself, some cross-connection in the thin silver filaments of your mind? So many good things happened, too. Her sitting in the front row at your high school graduation, her face bright as a dahlia above the white of her sari. The two of you going for a bath in the Ganges, the brown tug of the water on your clothes, the warm sleepy sun as you sat on the bank later, eating curried potatoes wrapped in hot *puris.* And further back, her teaching you to write, the soft curve of her hand over yours, helping you hold the chalk, the smell of her newly washed hair curling about your face.

But these memories are wary, fugitive. You have to coax them out of their dark recesses. They dissipate, foglike, even as you are looking at them. And suddenly his arm feels terribly heavy. You are suffocating beneath its weight, its muscular, hairy maleness. You slip out and step into the shower. The wind snatches at the straggly nasturtiums you planted on the little strip of balcony. *What will you remember of him when it is all over?* whispers the papery voice inside your skull. Light from the bathroom slashes the floor while against the dark wall the hanging glows fire-red.

———

The first month you moved in with him, your head pounded with fear and guilt every time the phone rang. You'd rush across the room to pick it up while he watched you from his tilted-back chair, raising an eyebrow. (You'd made him promise never to pick up the phone.) At night you slept next to the bedside extension. You picked it up on the very first ring, struggling up out of layers of sleep heavy as water to whisper a breathless hello, the next word held in readiness, *Mother.* But it was never her. Sometimes it was a friend of yours from the graduate program. Mostly it was for him. Women. Ex-girlfriends, he would explain with a guileless smile, stressing the *ex.* Then he would turn toward the window, his voice dropping into a low murmur while you pretended sleep and hated yourself for being jealous.

She always called on Saturday morning, Saturday night back home. The last thing before she went to bed. You picture her sitting on the large mahogany bed where you, too, had slept when you were little. Or when you were sick or scared. Outside, crickets are chanting. The night watchman makes his rounds, calling out the hour. The old *ayah* (she has been there from before you were born) stands behind her, combing out her long hair. The hair lifts a little in the breeze from the fan, the silver in it glimmering like a smile. It is the most beautiful hair in the world.

And so you grew less careful. Sometimes you'd call out from the shower for him to answer the phone. And he would tease you (*you sure now?*) before picking it up. At night after the last kiss your body would slide off his damp, glistening one—and you didn't care which side of the bed it was as long as you had him to hold onto. *Or was it that you wanted her, somehow, to find out?* the voice asks. But you are learning to not pay attention to the voice, to fill your mind with sensations (how the nubs of his elbows fit exactly into your cupped palms, how his sleeping breath stirs the small hairs on your arm) until its echoes dissipate.

So when the phone rang very early that Tuesday morning you thought nothing of it. You pulled sleep like a furry blanket over your head, and even when you half-heard his voice, suddenly formal, saying *just one moment, please,* you didn't get it. Not until he was shaking your shoulder, handing you the phone, mouthing the words silently, *your mother.*

Later you try to remember what you said to her, but you can't quite get the words right. Something about a wonderful man, getting married soon (although the only time you'd discussed marriage was when he had told you it wasn't for him). She'd called to let you know that Cousin Leela's wedding was all arranged—a good Brahmin boy, a rising executive in an accounting firm. Next month in Delhi. The whole family would travel there. She'd bought your ticket already. *But now of course you need not come.* Her voice had been a spear of ice. Did you cry out, *don't be angry, Mother, please?* Did you beg forgiveness? Did you whisper (again that word) *love?* You do know this: You kept talking, even after the phone went dead. When you finally looked up, he was watching you. His eyes were opaque, like pebbles.

All through the next month you try to reach her. You call. The *ayah* answers. She sounds frightened when she hears your voice. *Memsaab* has told her not to speak to you, or else she'll lose her job.

"She had the lawyer over yesterday to change her will. What did you do, Missybaba, that was so bad?"

You hear your mother in the background. "Who are you talking to, Ayah? What? How can it be my daughter? I don't *have* a daughter. Hang up right now."

"Mother . . ." you cry. The word ricochets through the apartment so that the hanging shivers against the wall. Its black center ripples like a bottomless well. The phone goes dead. You call again. Your fingers are shaking. It's hard to see the digits through the tears. Your knees feel as though they have been broken. The phone

buzzes against your ear like a trapped insect. No one picks it up.
You keep calling all week. Finally a machine tells you the number
has been changed. There is no new number.

Here is a story your mother told you when you were growing up:

*There was a girl I used to play with sometimes, whose father was the
roof-thatcher in your grandfather's village. They lived near the women's
lake. She was an only child, pretty in a dark-skinned way, and motherless,
so her father spoiled her. He let her run wild, climbing trees, swimming in
the river. Let her go to school, even after she reached the age when girls from
good families stayed home, waiting to be married.* (You know already this
is a tale with an unhappy end, a cautionary moral.) *He would laugh
when the old women of the village warned him that an unmarried girl is
like a firebrand in a field of ripe grain. She's a good girl, he'd say. She
knows right and wrong. He found her a fine match, a master carpenter from
the next village. But a few days before the wedding, her body was discovered
in the women's lake. We all thought it was an accident until we heard
about the rocks she had tied in her sari.* (She stops, waits for the
question you do not want to ask but must.) *Who knows why? People
whispered that she was pregnant, said they'd seen her once or twice with a
man, a traveling actor who had come to the village some time back. Her
father was heartbroken, his good name ruined. He had to leave the village,
all those tongues and eyes. Leave behind the house of his forefathers that he
loved so much. No, no one knows what happened to him.*

For months afterward, you lie awake at night and think of the
abandoned house, mice claws skittering over the floors, the dry
papery slither of snakes, bats' wings. When you fall asleep, you
dream of a beautiful dark girl knotting stones into her *palloo* and
swimming out to the middle of the dark lake. The water is cool on
her heavying breasts, her growing belly. It ripples and parts for her.
Before she goes under, she turns toward you. Sometimes her face is
a blank oval, featureless. Sometimes it is your face.

Things are not going well for you. At school you cannot concentrate on your classes, they seem so disconnected from the rest of your life. Your adviser calls you into her office to speak to you. You stare at the neat rows of books behind her head. She is speaking of missed deadlines, research that lacks innovation. You notice her teeth, large and white and regular, like a horse's. She pauses, asks if you are feeling well.

"Oh, yes," you say, in the respectful tone you were always taught to use with teachers. "I feel just fine."

But the next day it is too difficult to get up and get dressed for class. What difference would it make if you miss a deconstructionist critique of the sonnets, you ask yourself. You stay in bed until the postal carrier comes.

You have written a letter to Aunt Arati explaining, asking her to please tell your mother that you're sorry. *I'll come home right now if she wants.* Every day you check the box for Aunt's reply, but there's nothing. Her arthritis is acting up, you tell yourself. It's the wedding preparations. The letter is lost.

Things are not going well between him and you either. Sometimes when he is talking, the words make no sense. You watch him move his mouth as though he were a character in a foreign film someone has forgotten to dub. He asks you a question. By the raised tone of his voice you know that's what it is, but you have no idea what he wants from you. He asks again, louder.

"What?" you say.

He walks out, slamming the door.

You have written a letter to your mother, too. A registered letter, so it can't get lost. You run outside every day when you hear the mail van. Nothing. You glance at the carrier, a large black woman, suspiciously. "Are you sure?" you ask her. You wonder if she put the letter into someone else's box by mistake. After she leaves, you peer into the narrow metal slots of the other mailboxes, trying to see.

At first he was sympathetic. He held you when you lay sleepless at night. "Cry," he said. "Get it out of your system." Then, "It was bound to happen sooner or later. You must have known that. Maybe it's all for the best." Later, "Try to look at the positive side. You had to cut the umbilical cord *sometime.*"

You pulled away when he said things like that. What did *he* know, you thought, about families, about (yes) love. He'd left home the day he turned eighteen. He only called his mother on Mother's Day and, if he remembered, her birthday. When he told her about you she'd said, "How *nice,* dear. We really must have you both over to the house for dinner sometime soon."

Lately he has been angry a lot. "You're blaming me for this mess between your mother and yourself," he shouted the other day at dinner although you hadn't said anything. He shook his head. "You're driving yourself crazy. You need a shrink." He shoved back his plate and slammed out of the apartment. The dry, scratchy voice pushing at your temples reminded you how he'd watched the red-haired waitress at the Mexican restaurant last week, how he was laughing, his hand on her shoulder, when you came out of the restroom. How, recently, there have been more late-night calls.

When he came back, very late, you were still sitting at the table. Staring at the hanging. He took you by the arms and brought his face close to yours.

"Sweetheart," he said, "I want to help you but I don't know how. You've become obsessed with this thing. You're so depressed all the time I hardly know you anymore. So your mother is behaving irrationally. *You* can't afford to do the same."

You looked past his head. He has a sweet voice, you thought absently. A voice that charms. An actor's voice.

"You're not even listening," he said.

You tried because you knew he was trying, too. But later in bed, even with his lips pressing hot into you, a part of you kept counting the days. How many since you mailed the letter? He pulled away with an angry exclamation and turned the other way. You put out your hand to touch the nubs of his backbone. *I'm sorry.* But you went on thinking, something *must* be wrong. Surely a reply should have reached you by now.

The letter came today. You walked out under a low, grey-bellied sky and there was the mail woman, holding it up, smiling. It was the registered letter to your mother, with a red ink stamp across the address. *Not accepted. Return to sender.*

Now you are kneeling in the bathroom rummaging in the cabinet behind the cleaning supplies. When you find the bottles, you line them up along the countertop. You open each one and look at the tablets: red, white, pink. You'd found them one day while cleaning. You remember how shocked you'd been, the argument the two of you'd had. He'd shrugged and spread his hands, palms up. You wish now you'd asked him which ones were the sleeping pills. No matter. You can take them all, if that's what you decide on.

You'd held the letter in your hand a long time, until it grew weightless, transparent. You could see through it another letter, one that wasn't written yet. His letter. You knew what it would say.

Before he left for class this morning he had looked at you still crumpled on the sofa, where you'd spent the night. He looked for a long time, as though he'd never really seen you before. Then he said, very softly, "It was never me, was it? Never love. It was always you and her, her and you." He hadn't waited for an answer.

Wind slams a door somewhere, making you jump. It's raining outside, the first time in years. Big swollen drops, then thick silver sheets of it. You walk out to the balcony. The rain runs down your cheeks, the tears you couldn't shed. The nasturtiums, washed clean, are glowing red. Smell of wet earth. You take a deep breath, decide to go for a long walk.

As you walk you try to figure out what to do. (And maybe the meaning of what you have done.) The pills are there, of course. You picture it: the empty bottles by the bed, your body fallen across it, a hand flung over the side. The note left behind. Will he press repentant kisses on your pale palm? Will she fly across the ocean to wash your stiff eyelids with her tears?

Or—what? *What?* Surely there's another choice. But you can't find the words to give it shape. When you look down the empty street, the bright leaves of the newly washed maples hurt your eyes.

So you continue to walk. Your shoes darken, grow heavy. Water swirls in the gutters, carrying away months of dust. Coming toward you is a young woman with an umbrella. Shoulders bunched, she tiptoes through puddles, trying hard to stay dry. A gust snaps the umbrella back and soaks her. She is shocked for a moment, angry. Then she begins to laugh. And you are laughing too, because you know just how it feels. Short, hysterical laugh bursts, then quieter, drawing the breath deep into yourself. You watch as she stops in the middle of the sidewalk and tosses her ruined umbrella into a garbage can. She spreads her arms and lets the rain take her: hair, paisley blouse, midnight-blue skirt. Thunder and lightning. It's going to be quite a storm. You remember the monsoons of your childhood. There are no people in this memory, only the sky, rippling with exhilarating light.

You know then that when you return to the apartment you will pack your belongings. A few clothes, some music, a favorite book, the hanging. No, not that. You will not need it in your new life, the one you're going to live for yourself.

And a word comes to you out of the opening sky. The word *love.* You see that you had never understood it before. It is like rain, and when you lift your face to it, like rain it washes away inessentials, leaving you hollow, clean, ready to begin.

Moths

G. S. SHARAT CHANDRA

I.

She said
while she looped her hair

helplessly high
over her tight breasts,

I sat spinning
snares in the bed,

so she hid to undress
in the closet

with the moths:
she came to know

the moth in me
bred also under shelves.

She moved out quickly,
I let her go,

tore her dress
to the outer world

then spun my body
with all my spit

to rise in my chest
the chant of moths,

my father waking
somewhere in a dream,

my brother turning
in the belly of the bulb.

II.

We sit in the closet
pretending

we're the one side
of darkness the walls

do not feel.
My brother tries

the red shirt of my father,
the one he hung

on the light bulbs
of strange harbors

to make his women glow
like lanterns of their true country.

Outside my wife drops
her robe humming

into the mirror
her naked dailiness.

She's our secret treasure,
our lookout for moths.

My brother aims
the golf club at her crotch,

the dark in the door ajar
is our wedge of bait,

our fingers drumming
on the flat breast

of the closet switch,
its back & forth nipple.

III.

I've been waiting in the closet
with the moths,

they stir when the lone bulb
flickers then gives up.

I remember my father
grown thin as a cat with cancer,

his quick leap into the birdless air,
the last surge of blood on his spit.

My wandering brother has found his passion
back this spring,

he explains to my wife
the trees that came in the way,

the thin wall of leaves
he mistook for moths.

She laughs softly as she makes tea,
if I touched her back she'd stiffen

to the moths in my sleeves drowsing,
at the cloud of wings if I wave.

IV.

Her daily gestures
naked at the window,

openings of her desire
she wants to cover,

are offerings to the world
in her small darts of eye.

Hair let loose,
head into the dishes

her buttocks seesaw
over the kitchen sink,

within her transparence
we know the silk

tracing the slopes of her vulva.
When she's finished,

she'll draw the blinds,
turn the lights off,

check the doorknobs
and come into the bedroom

to rub fragrance on her skin,
to climb into the mirror

next to the closet
where we practice the range

in our eyes for the dark,
the one perfect leap

we need to dare
in our blind flutter.

V.

Her moans we smother
with a necklace of lips,

father's thigh thrust
over her throbbing,

his right fingers
counting the heaves

of her left nipple,
in the powder smudge

on the mirror,
my brother's sniff:

then she's up & singing
of the blaze in the closet,

guides us there
for one last tango,

unplugs the darkness
to lock our thighs.

She'll catch that plane
to her mother's nest,

where the only dream
is the dream of dead moths.

She'll sleep the winter
hands tucked

under the gargantuan leaf
patched on her quilt.

The Cousins

Shirley Ancheta

Dear Jeanne,

Greetings from Honolulu. My grandmother is dead. The night she died, I was at home in San Francisco, and the sweet odor of tuberose filled the living room. The kids were scared that night because a small bird had rammed itself against one of the bay windows, creating a loud thud as its body hit the glass. Mark was attending a conference and wasn't expected home until later. I felt cold, really cold. I went to bed in my sweats and let the kids sleep with me. My mother called me the next morning to tell me about Lola's death.

The family here in the islands says she died on Wednesday, July 6, at 5:18 A.M. at St. Francis Hospital, but the old women at the marketplace say they saw her shopping Thursday morning around nine, holding her black umbrella to shield herself from the sun.

I'm here for the next eight days. Mark and the boys had to stay home, money being tight during the summer. I miss them.

Love,
S.

Dear Jeanne,

Sometimes you have to believe that something has been waiting for you all the time. This house on Ashford Street is far from my memory of my grandmother's house in Wahiawa. In her bedroom sits the same large bed with the mahogany headboard. Last night I lay on that bed and thought of her warm hands when she would take hold of mine and give me advice. "No fall down," she used to say.

I could hear voices down the hall and smell coffee being brewed by my aunties. I was homesick for something. It was hot, and a certain melody, a song by Edward Kaaina, kept going through my head. With every high pitch of his voice, I thought of the living room in my grandma's country house twenty-three years ago. Every image of memory possesses a sound, and inside that sound I remembered David.

David is my cousin. Our fathers are brothers. The summer I turned seventeen, my family came to Oahu to stay with my grandmother. My grandfather had just died, and my father wanted to make sure Grandma was okay. David, whose family stayed in Kauai, lived with Lola while he worked and attended college in Honolulu. He was nineteen and worried about getting drafted and going to Vietnam. He was good-looking with a square jaw and big dimples—everyone has dimples in my family. I loved listening to his deep, resonant voice when he played his guitar on the back porch. He didn't tune the strings the standard way. My uncles taught him a combination of Hawaiian and Filipino slack key.

He'd stare at my ripening body and say, "Too bad we're cousins, Cousin." I'd wait until he'd come in from his job at the gas station and serve up his lunch plate. No one noticed our growing relationship because they knew David had a girlfriend, Sharon, in Honolulu.

One night, David and I watched television in the living room after every one had gone to bed. I fell asleep, but woke up from my dreaming because I felt someone's hand cupping my breast. It was David. It seemed natural, and it felt good, except that I was aware that the same blood that pulsed in my father and David's father pulsed through us in unforgiving ways.

"Ever done it before, Cousin?" he asked.

"What's it to you?" I said. His mouth landed hard on mine then, and we rubbed our bodies together, urged on by something forbidden and desired.

For the next six nights, David and I would take drives and park along the dirt roads of plantations, making fast and thirsty love. It all ended one night in Kunia Village when the sheriff who shined his brights on the back seat of the car turned out to be our cousin James.

"Jesus Christ, you guys!" was all he said. Word got out to the family, and I was on my way back to California. My father didn't talk to David's father for almost two years, and my name was spoken only in hushed conversations.

Jeanne, that's what I mean about sound and memory. I haven't thought about my cousin in years. I had to tell this to someone. David is coming in from Seattle tonight.

Love,
S.

Dear Jeanne,

The funeral was yesterday morning. It was like a huge family reunion. Grandma and Grandpa had eleven kids and twenty-seven grandchildren, not to mention extended family. I watched as David and my uncles carried my grandmother's orchid-covered casket down the mortuary steps. I noticed David's broad shoulders and imagined his lean back muscles beneath his dark suit. Our relatives watched as he greeted me at the cemetery. We gave each other a quick hug and our cheeks touched. He said, "Let's talk later."

After the funeral and luncheon, I stopped by Tamashiro's Market to pick up some tako and ahi for the big family dinner. Without turning, I felt David standing at the doorway watching me. I was pulled by his stare, and I looked up and waved to him. He looked handsome in his black tank top and shorts. I opened the door to the refrigerated goods and took in the cool air slowly. I tried to breathe evenly. When I looked up again, he was gone.

Stepping out into the bright heat, I saw David leaning against the shaded side of the store building. He took the grocery box from me and set it on the ground next to him.

"Cousin, howzit? We need to talk this time," he said.

I tried to look at him. His sunglasses were covering his eyes, and I couldn't read him. I studied his mouth and noticed his arms relaxed at his side.

"Are you free tonight?" he asked.

"We're all having dinner at Auntie's, remember?"

"You're right, but . . ." he said, his sentence slipping into local style. "After dinner, leave with my sister Josie. I'll clear it with her. Let's see, the Waikiki clubs will be swarming with our partying cousins. I'll think of something."

I ate dinner nervously that night amid all the relatives. David introduced me to his wife, Janet, and their two sons. Then I made my way through the crowd of aunties, who told me, "Eat more, get plenny food," until Josie came up and said, "How about that film tonight?"

I was grateful for Josie's coolness. She hugged me in the car and said, "Now you're free of family judgment calls. You two need the time, yeah?"

We drove to her place in Waipahu. I paced around while she told me to make myself at home. David met us there a few minutes later.

"Okay, kiddo, you're on your own," Josie told me. I felt like a kid, all right. I wanted her to stay. David must have seen the expression on my face because he nodded for her to leave.

"You're making it hard for her," he said.

We stood in silence for a while. He found the liquor in the cabinet to the right of the kitchen sink. "Drink Scotch?" he asked. I nodded, and he poured a couple of single malts.

We sat at Josie's kitchen table, and he asked me about Mark and the boys. We talked about sweet, polite things. I found out he taught middle school in Seattle, was a musician on weekend nights and that he'd been married about as long as I. David was still attractive, probably more attractive than I remembered.

"What are you doing tomorrow?" he asked. "Let's just drive around. You know. I can't cram twenty years into three hours. I think Janet talked about going shopping . . ." And then he stopped. He studied my face, then glanced quickly at my breasts before turning away. I put my hand on his and then withdrew it. He stood up and walked outside.

I sat there a long time, watching the red cat clock on the wall. The eyes and tail moved rhythmically. I sat still. Why was I in Waipahu? This was not my home. I was older now. I was supposed to know better. I thought about Mark and the kids, David's wife and kids, us. Us.

I stepped outside and saw David standing near his car. I was shaking, although it was an easy eighty-five degrees.

"Come here, Cousin," he told me, motioning for a hug. It was the kind of hug you save for old friends. "We were pretty silly," he said, and I guessed he was referring to earlier times.

"We were young and horny," I replied.

"I was so attracted to you," he said.

"And now?"

He held me close and whispered, "There is still so much night inside you."

That night, I felt the seventeen-year-old woman entering me from across the dark fields, and leaned back into a kiss. I thought I tried to walk away once, or maybe it was David who hesitated, but then I heard myself say, "I've come a long way to be with you."

Love,

S.

Dear David,

There is nothing to be done. I can taste you now, the dark flame of your mouth and the kiss that goes on without us. The smell of your love remains in my hair and the blouse I wore when I saw you last.

In another life, I might have called you husband, but in this life you are my cousin and lover. When we were young in a house deep in Wahiawa, our grandmother saw us barefoot and half-dressed, kissing in the dark, your hands touching my inner thighs. She threw her slipper across the room with enough force to shatter the small, stupid ceramic cat on the coffee table. She took me to church the next day and told me, "No do dat wit' your cah-sin! You no feel shame or what? Get plenny other boys heah. No good fo' cah-sins fo' make li' dat!"

Lola visits me in dream and tells me, "Decide now, anako. No fall down." But I have seen a mirror in you and have seen myself with burning lips unable to walk away. Time is the size of an i'iwi bird, and all the small wishes it contains is expelled in one breath. The wind blows and lifts the leaves. I listen with mixed feelings. I love, knowing we are tied in blood.

S.

Reunions with a Ghost

AI

For Jim

The first night God created was too weak;
it fell down on its back,
a woman in a cobalt blue dress.
I was that woman and I didn't die.
I lived for you,
but you don't care. You're drunk again,
turned inward as always.
Nobody has trouble like I do, you tell me,
unzipping your pants
to show me the scar on your thigh,
where the train sliced into you
when you were ten.
You talk about it with wonder and self-contempt,
because you didn't die
and you think you deserved to.
When I kneel to touch it,
you just stand there
with your eyes closed,
your pants and underwear bunched at your ankles.
I slide my hand up your thigh
to the scar and you shiver

and grab me by the hair.
We kiss, we sink to the floor,
but we never touch it,
we just go on and on tumbling through space
like two bits of stardust that shed no light,
until it's finished,
our descent, our falling in place.
We sit up. Nothing's different, nothing.
Is it love, is it friendship
that pins us down,
until we give in,
then rise defeated once more
to reenter the sanctuary of our separate lives?
Sober now, you dress,
then sit watching me
go through the motions of reconstruction—
reddening cheeks, eyeshadowing eyelids,
sticking bobby pins here and there.
We kiss outside
and you walk off, arm in arm with your demon.
So I've come through the ordeal of loving once again,
sane, whole, wise, I think as I watch you,
and when you turn back, I see in your eyes
acceptance, resignation,
certainty that we must collide from time to time.
Yes. Yes, I meant goodbye when I said it.

Memento Mori

Ai

For Turner Davis and Jim Davis, Artists

Twenty years ago, you were the man
who tended my roses, Jim,
but that ended in the garden of friendship,
where nothing grows
so much as serves its time,
frozen in the poses of love.
Those scissors you wielded like a surgeon
cut away that version of me
and now you don't know who I am
beneath my clothes.
My body's changed.
It's grown older
and rearranged itself to suit
some other truth, or lie.
I said goodbye. I meant it,
until I met you
stumbling through the rye again.
I could have let you pass,
but I caught a reflection of you
in a shot glass
and when I raised my eyes,

your son was standing there to my surprise.
Now he's the one whose touch
I dream sends me reeling
from desk and chair to bed
to rest my face on the pillow
where he lays his head,
where I take him on my tongue
like a sacrament,
where I am the paint he strokes on the canvas,
until the image he creates is my face
transfigured by desire,
my body surrounded by flames
and pierced by a single arrow.
I'll die for art, but not for love
and I sense he'll give me what I want,
still I choose to rendezvous
with him only in sleep,
until he crosses over the boundary
of the unconscious
when one day, I run into him
at the Lucian Freud show (how fitting, no?)
Afterward, we go out for drinks.
He thinks he's so daring
when he says, "Damnit, let's go to bed,"
or something more romantic (I forget)
and we do,
though I mostly find lust a bore now.
I'd just as soon mop the floor as make love.
He understands. He knows I go
from one passion to the next
without a fixed destination.
He knows my inclination is to do
my loving with my mind, not my body.
I don't use men. I lose them

in the rough seas of my imagination,
where aroused and afraid,
they give in to my domination,
before they disappear.
Cleverly, he plays the role of slave so skillfully,
I decide to free him,
but he says, "Beat me, use your fists."
I use a whip instead.
When I draw blood, I stop,
because the world is red enough,
but he begs me to go on
and I do, until my strength is gone
and we lie gasping in the long shadow
of night among the starving,
where you find us, Jim.
At first, you stare at us
as if we were merely objects,
then take up the brush
and paint us just
as if we'd died this side of Paradise.

Kala: Sitting on Our Bikes

by the Catholic Church

LOIS ANN YAMANAKA

You get yours yet?
Your rags, dummy.
You dunno what rags is?
Stupid, eh? Where you from?
Your madda neva tell you?
You neva see *Time of Your Life* fourth grade?
Faaack. I bet you wen' close your eyes, ass why.
When you get yours, you cannot ride bike, you know.
'Cause going be so-wa, stupid.
Of course I get mines.
I seventh grade already.
What grade you?
Sixth?
You going ge-et yours,
you going ge-et yours,
and going be all bloooooo-dy.

My madda told me they call um rags
'cause before time neva have Modess
so they use the rice bags

and after they bafe,
they wash the rags in hot water.
No believe then, dummy.
I going tell all the old man wait for you
'cause you neva have yours yet
and you almost ripe.
Hoooo, tita, you better lock your doors
and pray to the Lord above
that you *neva* get yours
'cause I going tell
the old man that dinner
is almost ready to be served.

Sacrament

Tanith Tyrr

I'm cruising over the Bridge doing an easy sixty-five, the sunroof of my car open, the wind lashing at my long, dark hair. He lives just past Japantown, where the bright and bustling streets are filled with faces that remind me poignantly of the relatives I have not seen for years. His own face does that, sometimes, when I'm not careful; and it frightens me.

I grew up swearing I would never marry the nice Japanese boy Okaasan wanted. I was almost thirty years old before I dated another Japanese. He has been familiar to me since the day I met him, yet the anticipation of seeing him is still keen and almost painful. My palms are sweaty, and I wipe them on the red upholstery.

Past Geary Street, where the gaily colored lanterns from the Obon festival are still wired to the streetlamps, and paper carp swim against the breeze. Down Folsom, where the Japanese cultural line is drawn like a barrier, and the Gay, Spanish and Chinese neighborhoods take over in noisy profusion.

There are no guards and no jailers to keep them in, but I seldom see a Japanese face crossing the line. I myself visit Japantown only rarely. I revert too quickly to the submissive, self-effacing habits and accents of my childhood, and I have worked too hard to win free of them and to fit more easily into a Western world. My jailers live inside.

His door opens. I give him a quick hug and an unexpected invitation. The trunk of my car is filled with cool drinks, thick steaks brushed with olive oil for grilling, blankets, camping gear, a new tent. The weather is oppressively hot, sultry and lazy in the city. My suggestion of escape is irresistible. He grins from ear to ear as he gets into my car, scratching his head, half astonished and half pleased at my boldness. We have been dating for nearly a year; we touch one another in restaurants casually, like lovers. We have never spent a night together.

I was brought up in a strict Japanese family, expected to conform to my role as a good little Japanese girl, quiet and virginal, until I was married. Then I would have been expected to be a good geisha-wife to my husband, servant and nonentity. Studying history, it comes as no surprise to me that the Japanese never bound their women's feet. They never had to; we bound our own.

I spent years violently excising those taboos, teaching myself to speak up aggressively instead of waiting patiently for the last bowl of rice. I learned how to drive a truck and shoot a gun. I shouted at marches and at rallies. I had sexual adventures. I broke taboos until my imagination was exhausted and there were no more to break. Beyond all of that, I learned finally that my body belonged only to myself, and that all of it was worthy of respect.

My years of taboo-breaking had their consequences. After a while, nothing really shocked me anymore, and few things excited me. Until I met him. His familiarity is my new forbidden.

His dark eyes and quirky, slanted grin, his taut, lean-muscled body and his defiantly long, utterly black hair are mine. The graceful arch of his back, the poetic textures of him, the liquid play of muscles beneath tawny skin are beloved to me. My hands love this man as much as I do; they have a consciousness of him that is entirely their own. With daring fingers, they brush his dark mane aside. I touch his neck, his arms, his casually bared chest.

His feet were as bound as mine, and like prisoners who have shared a common jailer, we both know where the cell walls are. We laugh together about mothers who still talk in Japanese, who only know the shameful Japanese words for the places "down there." But those shameful words are at the core of us now, and the laughter is only skin-deep.

I don't yet know where we're going. We steal kisses at stop lights and clear stretches of highway; we hold hands and touch when we can do nothing else. His hand strokes my thigh, and the contact is electric even through thick, worn denim. Vallejo, Fairfield, Napa and other cities pass before us in a swift and marvelous daze as he continues his merciless attentions. His touch arouses me almost beyond bearing, but somehow I manage to keep driving.

Since I first started seeing him, we have touched, kissed, necked frantically like teenagers until my white cotton panties were soaked through and his erection pressed painfully tight against the thin, rough fabric of his belted jeans. We have never made love.

We have been so careful with one another, never pushing past the boundaries we have somehow agreed upon without ever speaking. I have walked through life unseeing, in a kind of sexual delirium, for days after our short and stolen interludes together. I ache for more. My thighs are damp.

When we reach the perfect place, we leave the car under the spread of a shady tree and hike away from the road until we reach a hidden grove. We can see the green branches reaching overhead, and the piercingly blue sky between them. The smell of freshly crushed leaves and the dark, moist earth nearly overwhelms our senses. We kiss, and laugh, and talk, and set up our tent.

By the time dark falls, a fire is blazing merrily and we have started dinner. The steak and foil-wrapped potatoes, slightly burned at the edges and still hot from the fire, taste incredibly good. I start a tape playing softly, and we sit for a while, looking at the fire, listening to music. Kissing, touching until the tension is unbearable.

I break away from his embrace for a moment, breathless. The fire has died down to coals, delicate formations of pink ash that flicker and dissolve in an incautious breath. We crawl awkwardly into the tent, taking our shoes off and staring at each other self-consciously. Neither of us is quite sure of what we want, neither of us as confident as we would like to appear.

Hands reach tentatively under clothes to pat and stroke and squeeze, withdrawing at the first sign of uncertainty. They grow more bold with practice, and later, they do not withdraw. Clothes become an encumbrance rather than a necessary protection.

Finally, skin to skin, we each shed pieces of clothing like water after rain. I am hardly conscious of the act of disrobing. The feel of his hands on my body and mine on his have merged into a single, diffuse sensation. His touch arouses me almost beyond bearing. He smiles, knowing what he can do to me. Liking it. It is still new to him, the realization that women can become aroused, and that he could be the cause of it.

I am afraid. I am frightened of causing pain, of making him need what I may not be able to give. And I am afraid of needing too much.

He is afraid. He is scared that he is inadequate to the task, that he cannot perform well enough to satisfy. He is old enough to vote, to drink, to enter bars without challenge. Yet he is still a virgin. While I violently shattered myself out of the mold my parents had cast for me, he shrunk up within it and refused to emerge whole. From the same cell, we escaped in opposite directions. It is possible that parts of us never escaped at all.

My fears and his fears talk to one another, sometimes; and they seem to leave us out of the conversation. And we both have one strike against us from the beginning: our parents would finally approve.

And now we are naked. Naked not only in the sense of being without clothes, but without defenses. There is a basic honesty about nakedness that appeals to me. Clothes come with pretensions, and here there are none.

His skin is an electric shock on mine, hot and impossibly silken. My hands wander delightedly over him, more freely than they ever have before. His body is lithe and pantherlike, his haunches curving gracefully into the taut bow of his back. His long, black mane flows like liquid darkness over his tawny shoulders, tickling my face. He covers me like a blanket.

I ask him in whispers whether my flesh feels cool to him, since his feels so warm to me, and he replies in the same hushed tone, telling me that I feel warm to him, too.

I giggle, wondering what it is about being naked in the wilderness that makes us want to whisper. We are in the presence of the Great Mystery, and it awes us. The enormity of the act that we contemplate leaves us both with diminished voices.

My ancestors from East and West understood sex and sacredness; they did not separate them as rigidly as we do now. In ancient Europe, there was the initiator. A sultry, dark-haired priestess with a body as ripe and brown as an ear of wheat for the boy on the verge of manhood. A bearded and gentle priest with skilled hands for the woman newly past menarche. No hint of laughter, unless it was a free and honest mirth, would ever mar the ritual. This rite was sacred, and the priest and priestess and celebrant were always honored.

It was a heavy responsibility as well as an honor; but all strove to be chosen. The altars of the temple bowed under the weight of their gifts: purple-black grapes half bursting out of their skins with sweetness, rich roasted meats, the silver-skinned bounty of the sea. Jewels, fine necklaces of emerald and alexandrite and tourmaline strung on beaten copper. Cups of yellow gold and slender daggers of bright forged steel, casks of good wine, cattle tethered for slaughter in the temple yard.

In Japanese legend, the ripeness and bounty of the earth comes from the Goddess of the sun, who can appear in many forms. She is an inhumanly beautiful woman, a bird on the wing, a golden shaft of light. Yet today, our correct model for a woman has been a drab-winged sparrow, efficient and self-effacing, not a bright and shining goddess with sunlight in her hair. Western culture is not alone in its contradictions.

No one gifts the old gods anymore; and the initiators go without honor. Women who should have been priestesses are reviled in the streets for their sex, and the worst words we know are the most sacred parts of a woman. Our world is upside down.

Western women are taught to deny their sex and their sacredness, and to fear the desires of a man. Eastern women are taught to submit to a man's desire, and to utterly submerge their own. The men of both worlds learn to despise women for their denials and to become automatons in the search for sexual fulfillment. Is it any wonder that we know shame and fear? Is it any wonder that we live with jailers?

I will teach him pride, I vow silently. I bend to press my lips against his phallus, manifestation of the God rampant. I will show him no shame. I shall be his priestess.

He is past caring for consequence, aroused beyond denial. His cock is a jutting tower of need, a ripened fruit sweet and nearly bursting in my hands. I cup him in my hands and feel the silky smoothness of his rigid shaft, the soft, heavy down of his tightly rounded balls.

I close my eyes, and I can see bunches of grapes laid on a temple altar, heavy with the promise of ripeness and fertility. His hips move slowly and involuntarily in a jerky, breathless rhythm as I stroke. I lower my head to sip the sweet nectar that overflows from him, and he groans. The taste of him is intoxicating, better than any wine; and it heightens my senses like a rare drug. I want him more than I had ever imagined wanting, and I tell him so without shame.

This time, his answer is final. Lying on his back, his arms spread wide, his naked vulnerability is heartbreaking.

I touch him, and my voice is solemn. Thank you for trusting me, I tell him quietly. I have wanted to be your lover. Gently, I smooth a lock of hair from his face, tracing the familiar and beloved lines of him. I bend to my task, to the sacred trust that I have been honored with.

I am aroused enough to take my pleasure with ease. I could come from taking his cock in my mouth. I could have a dozen orgasms if I wanted to, pressing myself against him, kissing him, delighting in his warm, sensual body. But I have held back, balancing on the knife's edge of explosive release. My prolonged ecstasy becomes unmeasured and transcendent.

This is sacred, this most ancient of rituals. My body is a holy sacrament which he worships with growing delight, his tongue flicking as rapidly as a serpent's on the altar of my breasts, my belly, my thighs. Hesitant, then hot and demanding, he buries his face in my holy cunt, my sacred womanhood, and worships me to orgasm after orgasm. I am Goddess, I shout, as waves of pleasure come crashing over me like the moon-called sea.

I clasp him to me and we press together, moving inexorably with the rhythm of tides. We surge forward violently and then draw back, readying for the final embrace. Thou art God, I cry out softly.

Stallion, goatfoot god, golden phallus of the sun, his cock fills me as if I have never been empty, as if I will never again be empty. I clutch his lean, tautly muscled body to mine.

We plunge together, bucking and twisting, sacred bull and rider locked in the ancient dance. He rises like the sun, limned in glory. My body is the full moon, moving to cover him in the sky, and our joining eclipses the Earth. Again and again, until our backs arch and our mouths open wide in a rictus of uncontrolled pleasure.

As I ride the cresting waves of orgasm, I hear him cry out, high and wild. In my mind I see two birds flying freely, beyond the prison walls and for home.

from

Tokyo Bound

Written and Performed by Amy Hill

The show opens in black with music and slides of Japan and Amy's own photos.

VOICEOVER: When I was seven, I would tell people I lived in a mansion on Broadmoor, with servants and chandeliers. Instead, we lived off a gravel dead-end street in the Rainier Valley. My father, a Finnish-American transplant, had moved us all from Deadwood, South Dakota, to make it big as a heavy-equipment operator. But it rains so much in Seattle that construction is shut down a good part of the year. My mother, a Japanese war bride, helped ease the financial burden by first cooking part-time in a Japanese restaurant, then full-time in the Group Health hospital kitchen. Growing up, I sensed our family situation was unique, though not necessarily to be envied—so I made it my job to reinvent who I was.

Lights up on AMY sitting on a large geta (Japanese wooden shoe) on its side, center stage. The words "Tokyo Bound" are written on the bottom of the shoe in Japanese characters. There is a large noren (Japanese hanging curtain) upstage, against the back wall.

By the time I got to high school, I had plans to move to Paris and become a bohemian: sit around in cafés, smoke nonfilter Gauloises and converse about politics, poetry, art and change my name to "Josephine." Dad said he'd pay if I went to Finland. Mom said she'd pay if I went to Japan. "You make me so happy if you go!" . . .

That's how it began. I was eighteen, first time away from home. Alone. And, everybody's Japanese: small, dark, neat . . . and they all looked the same. I mean, it's not like I've never seen them before. My mom's Japanese. But, we're talking nothing but Japanese faces everywhere. *(Beat)* The first six months, I cried everyday, called home a lot and wondered if I could handle it all: new school, new language, new lifestyle . . . nude body. *(She glances down at her body and cringes slightly)* No one had ever seen me naked before. Not even my doctor. My first apartment in Tokyo didn't have a bath or shower, which is very common. I would have to use the public bath house. A room full of naked people. All women. But . . . naked. I must have waited at least a week before going.

AMY WALKS PAST IMAGINARY STORES, ETC., TAKING HER TIME.

I walked that long, lonely two blocks. Until I found myself in front of it. A large wooden building with a giant smokestack coming out of the center of the roof . . . with sliding frosted glass doors. *(Opens door and enters cautiously)* To my right I saw shelving with several pairs of very sad-looking shoes. People who had their own bathrooms probably had nice shoes. I looked down at my own sorry-looking Dr. Scholls and thought, "Nobody'd steal these either." *(Takes off shoes and enters)* To my right, a handful of women in various stages of undress. To my left, a wooden wall, about six feet high, separating the men's side of the bath house from the women's. I could hear their voices . . . and wondered if they were listening, too. *(Cowers slightly)* I found an empty locker and undressed. What was I supposed to do? Leave? No. I had to get used to this. No one else seemed to care.

LOOKING AROUND HER. SHE COVERS HERSELF WITH HER ARMS AND SCURRIES TO THE FINAL IMAGINARY DOOR, PAUSES AND OPENS IT SLOWLY. SHE IS AWESTRUCK.

A bunch of naked women cleaning themselves very thoroughly. I mean, scrubbing real hard and getting really clean. They were all kind of moist and pink. And, for the first time, I realize that the Japanese woman comes in all shapes and sizes. I mean, they were right there, in full view, sitting on little stools. I grab a stool and wait to see if it belongs to anyone. No one protests.

SITTING ON HER IMAGINARY STOOL. SHE CAREFULLY WATCHES AND THEN MIMICS THE WOMEN AROUND HER. SHE FILLS A BUCKET WITH WATER. POURS IT OVER HER HEAD. LATHERS HERSELF AND THEN RINSES OFF. SHE THEN NOTICES A LARGE COMMUNAL TUB. SHE STANDS AND STARTS TO GET IN. AS HER TOE REACHES THE WATER, SHE IMMEDIATELY PULLS IT OUT AGAIN. IT IS VERY HOT, BUT SHE GRITS HER TEETH AND FORGES AHEAD. AS SHE MANEUVERS HERSELF INTO THE WATER, SHE GRIMACES AND GROANS IN PAIN. FINALLY SETTLED, SOMEWHAT UNCOMFORTABLE YET VICTORIOUS, SHE NOTICES THAT A SMALL GROUP OF WOMEN HAVE TAKEN NOTICE OF HER. SHE WAVES MEEKLY AND INDICATES THE WATER IS . . .

Atsui.

DECIDING THAT SHE HAS BEEN IN A SUFFICIENT AMOUNT OF TIME, SHE EMERGES FROM THE TUB, WAVING GOODBYE, AND RETURNS TO HER STOOL. SHE THEN NOTICES SOMETHING ODD NEXT TO HER.

There's a leg next to me. Kind of hairy. An arm. Hairy.

SHE JUMPS TO HER FEET AFTER A QUICK DOUBLE-TAKE. SHE COVERS HERSELF WITH A WASHCLOTH.

A man! He's not naked. He's wearing a loincloth. But no one

blinks an eye. He gathers some used razors and empty shampoo bottles and moves on, cleaning and shuffling stools and buckets as he makes his way through the bodies . . . *(beat)* . . . Of course, if I'd gone to Finland, I'd have been buck naked in a sauna, slapping myself with birch branches and jumping into a snow bank. How'd I end up with a mom and dad from two cultures that think of bathing as some kind of ritual?

DROPPING THE TOWEL, SHE MOVES TO ANOTHER AREA OF THE STAGE.

My first day at Sophia International University, I noticed a group of kids sitting on the steps outside the student lounge. They were laughing and talking. One of them, Kimiko Gelman, became a friend of mine.

I wanted to be just like Kimiko. Be Japanese when I wanted to, or American or . . . both. I enjoyed being around her because, growing up, I never had any friends with a family like mine. *(Beat)* I cut my hair, got a perm and went . . . shopping . . . When you entered a department store, there was always someone to greet you at the entrance. As you moved through the store, the clerks would welcome you as you passed their counters. And, at the foot of the escalator, there was always a young woman, wearing white gloves, holding a handkerchief, continuously wiping the handrail of the escalator as she bowed and purred, "Welcome, welcome."

ESCALATOR GIRL.

(Bowing to passing customers) "Irasshaimase." The rooftop beer garden is now open as well as the children's insect zoo. In the first-floor basement, American beef is now on sale at the same price as Australian and New Zealand beef, sliced thin for sukiyaki and shabu shabu. Dresses are on floors three, four and five. All clothing is marked size M, but shoes range from size 21.5 to 24.5.

BECOMES AMY.

I was at least an L and wore a size 25 shoe, so everything was a bit tight. I was soon walking like a Japanese girl, naturally . . . (*As if in pain, she starts to walk slightly pigeon-toed*) And, lacking any basic knowledge in the finer points of Japanese womanhood, I studied tea ceremony, calligraphy and flower arrangement. My ikebana teacher was perfect—so soft, gracious, feminine. I liked her a lot . . . Koike sensei. (*Becomes very feminine Japanese woman arranging flowers*) This is "shin," representing the heavens, "hikae," the earth and "soe" is the sun. (*Dropping pose*) She had a way about her that was utterly compelling. So . . . cool. So I assumed her persona outside of class as well. I'd try it on new acquaintances. Japanese acquaintances—okay, men.

AMY APPROACHES AN IMAGINARY MAN, SHY AND COVERING HER FACE AS SHE GIGGLES.

How are you? I'm fine thank you. Would you like a piece of fruit? An apple? Let me peel it for you. (*Laughing*) Oh, you are so funny! Hot? Oh, no, I'm not hot. I'm fine. (*Suddenly concerned*) Are you hot? Let me fan you! Feel better? (*to audience*) Sometimes I got carried away. (*Returns her attention to the man*) You are so smart. You are so strong. Thirsty? Oh, no. Don't move. Let me get it for you. Tired? Let me massage your shoulders. Stop! You are so funny, you make me laugh too much! My name? Amy. Yes, it does mean "laughing beauty" in Japanese.

TO AUDIENCE, AS SHE KNEELS AND BOWS.

I was every Japanese man's dream.

RETURNING TO HER FEET. WE HEAR A JAPANESE RADIO TALK SHOW "KONNICHI WA, AMY DESU."

I did all sorts of things in Japan—well, what I was allowed to do. As a foreigner, I could teach English, translate, do language tapes . . . host a radio show. But as I learned to speak Japanese fluently, I would often be treated differently—not so special. Or rather—like a Japanese woman. There's a lot of baggage attached to either identity and I knew I had to start making some choices. Something my Japanese-American friends had little trouble making . . . or so I thought.

Candy Takanaka and I were in the same class in high school. I ran into her in Tokyo.

SHE DISAPPEARS BEHIND NOREN. SHOUTS FROM BEHIND SCREEN.

I'm not Japanese!

BURSTS FORTH AS CANDY WITH RAY• BAN SUNGLASSES ON.

I got really burned! I mean, I came here to get in touch with my roots, you know. Get down with the "people." And all they can do is get on my case! Like, I let them know right from the get that I am American. Like they can't just tell by looking at me? *(Points at herself)* "I am an American." I use my hands a lot. *(Grimacing and carefully pronouncing)* "America-jin desu." I mean, isn't it obvious?! *(Almost shouting and pronouncing with American accent)* "Nikkei desu! Wakarimasu ka?!" *(Giving up)* Wakarimasu nothin'! They got pissed off! They thought I was trying to bullshit them . . . like I could speak Japanese but I was pretending I couldn't! *(Beat)* Okay, I guess I coulda studied harder in Japanese school. I mean, my parents forced me to go every Saturday of my life! But, be serious. Nobody learned Japanese there. We only went to play basketball. I mean, I didn't want to have nothin' to do with all that bowin' and scrapin' and shit. You act like some foreigner in my neighborhood, honey, you get your butt kicked. We were tough. We had to be. But, you wanna know the truth? This is tough. I feel like . . . like my own people have turned on me . . . shit!

CANDY TURNS AND TAKES OFF HER GLASSES, THEN REFACES AUDIENCE AS AMY.

All this time, I thought "J-As" had it made. They had assimilated into America . . . with teriyaki hot dogs, baseball leagues, cheerleading squads, Buddhist church dances. They had their own thread, but I found out they felt "different," too. They'd come to Japan hoping to fit right in, but they didn't.

SHE WATCHES THE TRAIN PULL IN, SLOWLY MOVING TO A HALT.

I lived by the train and subway schedule. All Tokyoites do. The train has a very tight schedule. If you calculate the time you leave, the time it takes to get to the station—trains depart every 1.5 minutes, then, you figure 2.5 minutes for every stop it makes between the time you get on and your destination, and—you're never late . . . When I got on at Nakano Station, there weren't any seats left. I manage to find the only hand-grip available and settle in for the duration. As we pull into Shinjuku Station, I can see we're in trouble. The Japanese call it "rashu." Rush hour. The doors opened and in they came. Five million, bazillion people. Being packed in by these guys in white gloves. Some had to use their whole body to force people in. I ended up with my breasts in the face of the man sitting in front of me. I didn't think he could breathe. *(Suddenly startled)* Then, I felt something odd behind me. A hand? *(Realization strikes)* A chikan?! One of those guys who feel you up on the train?!

SHE VAINLY ATTEMPTS TO GET OUT OF HIS REACH, BUT UNABLE TO MOVE, SILENTLY SURRENDERS. AT FIRST SHE IS ANGRY AND SUSPICIOUS OF THOSE AROUND HER, THEN PERHAPS A BIT EMBARRASSED BY A STRANGER'S INVASION, THEN——BY TURNS——SLIGHTLY CURIOUS AND HESITATINGLY AROUSED.

Then, I remember my father: stern, hard-nosed Finnish-American, devout Lutheran.

THE TRAIN STOPS AND AMY DISEMBARKS.

We arrive at Tokyo Station. I manage to catch a glimpse of my chikan. He's cute. Young *(Long pause)*. I wonder if he'll be on this train tomorrow? *(Continues to walk through station)* You can find everything you want in a train station: magazines, gift shops, department stores and . . . restaurants. *(Enters noisy restaurant)* "Saaa. Heee. Hooo." Japanese love to make noises. *(Sits at counter)* Especially when they ate. Take noodles for instance. They could suck up a bowl of noodles in one breath, right into their stomachs, without spilling a drop. *(Reaches out to accept a large bowl)* You have your spoon in one hand, your chopsticks in the other, and . . .

SHE DIVES IN, SUCKING AND SLURPING NOODLES, UNTIL SHE STARTS TO COUGH AND CHOKE. SHE STOPS AND SLOWLY LIFTS HER HEAD. SHE FINDS A STRAY NOODLE ON THE TIP OF HER NOSE, THEN IN HER HAIR AND ON HER CHIN, CLOTHING ETC. UNTIL SHE TAKES HER HANDS AND JUST WIPES HER WHOLE FACE CLEAN. SOMEONE SITS DOWN NEXT TO HER AND SHE SHRINKS IN EMBARRASSMENT AND DEFEAT.

In the midst of my humiliation, a guy sits down next to me. He asks if I'd like some tea. *(Doing him)* "Ocha o nomimasenka?"

How sweet. But I already had some, so I passed on it. But he insisted. Said he loved tea. *(Doing him, with a little more energy)* "Ocha o dai suki da!"

Said he'd love to have some with me. *(Doing him, gradually building)* "Ocha o nomimashoo!"

He really had a hankering for tea. *(Doing him, just a touch crazed)* "Ocha o nomitai!"

What he meant was . . . at his place. Or, if that wasn't convenient, we could pop into a local love motel for a quick sip or two. He wanted some *(imitating his desperation)* tea! I may have been young, but I whacked him with my chopsticks and left. I could still hear him screaming *(Doing him, wailing and grabbing his crotch)* "Ocha! Ocha!" as I walked out the door.

SHE STANDS OUTSIDE THE RESTAURANT.

Soon after the noodle incident, I took a long walk around the Imperial Palace, past the National Theater and through the gardens, when I ran into a couple of young Japanese students who started a conversation with me in very good English. Exchange students to the University of Michigan? Show me around the city? *(She appears to be taking a tour, until she stops, pokes her head through a door and looks around)* "Nice apartment, Kenji." Several of his friends were there and we all sat around and talked. Slowly, I noticed that the size of the gathering had dwindled to just . . . us two. He pulled out some pictures of his days at U.M. His girlfriend. His host family. His other girlfriend . . . naked on the bed. His trips around the U.S. *(Hesitates)* Naked? Well . . . it probably wasn't meant for others to see. Then he got up and went to his bedroom. When he emerged again . . . *(stunned)* he was . . . *(She can't believe what she sees)* buck naked with a hard-on. *(Beat)* Up to this point in my life, I'd never had the opportunity to see an erect penis. And, I must say, it was quite a sight. And, it seemed so . . . large. I remembered a girl in high school health class had insisted she'd seen one at least a foot long. Well, we might have laughed then but . . . I believed her now.

He asked me to dance.

SHE LOOKS UP AT HIM AGAIN, AS IF SHE CAN'T BELIEVE WHAT SHE'S JUST HEARD.

SHE PAUSES A MOMENT TO THINK IT OVER, BRACES HERSELF AND THEN STANDS. SHE CAUTIOUSLY MOVES TOWARD HIM, STEALING QUICK GLANCES DOWN TO HIS GROIN. SHE RAISES HER ARMS TO HIS SHOULDERS, CAREFUL TO KEEP HER BODY WELL AWAY FROM HIS AND ATTEMPTS TO SLOW DANCE. AFTER SEVERAL AWKWARD MOMENTS, SHE BREAKS AWAY INTO A DISCO DANCE OF SORTS.

I knew this was not the reaction he was hoping for, but not having had any sexual encounters up to this point, I wasn't sure how to react. *(Turning to him)* "Maybe I should leave?" He put on his clothes and took me home. We never danced again.

RECALLING A WARM MEMORY, SHE SITS BACK ONTO THE GETA.

One summer, I went to a tiny island called Yoron, located halfway between the Japanese island of Kyushu and Okinawa. It was very small and very untouched. You had to get there by dinghy. It was like one of those places you see in *National Geographic,* where the water is warm and clear and the sky is as blue as the starfish in the ocean and the beaches are covered with "star sand," shaped that way because it was formed from white coral. *(Beat)* I loved it, so I decided to stay behind for a few days to just relax. I loved telling people I was from Tokyo. I had married into a Japanese family and my Japanese was pretty good by then, too. And I made friends with the guy who rented out the boats. He and I could talk about all kinds of stuff for hours. I admired how he'd left everything behind to just kind of live off the land, enjoy life, escape. *(Beat)* One night we were sitting on the beach, talking. I was filling him in on my background: being born in Deadwood, South Dakota, raised in Seattle. My dad's Finnish-American. My mom's Japanese. He stopped me there. He wanted to know how my parents met. *(Stumped)* Well . . . I'm not too sure. I know that my mom had told me that while my dad was in Japan during the Occupation, he had pursued her very heartily and finally won her over, but I didn't know the details, so I said, "I don't know."

VO: "Why don't you know?"

AMY RESPONDS, A BIT PUZZLED: "Well, I just never asked. I had more important things to think about like . . . if I was ever gonna have a boyfriend."

VO: "Was there something your mom wanted to hide?"

NOT QUITE COMPREHENDING THE LINE OF QUESTIONING, AMY ASKS: "Hide? That's one thing my mom never did. She was always totally honest and blunt and 'in your face'! Sometimes I wished she'd disappear when my friends were around."

VO: "Maybe she didn't tell you because she didn't want you to know . . ."

AMY BEGINS TO UNDERSTAND: "What? I started to feel my heart race. He's saying my mother was . . . *(Quietly defiant)* what?"

VO: Maybe she couldn't do any better because no Japanese man would have her. Maybe she sold herself to the first American who would take her. What'd he do? Offer her nylons and candy?"

HARDLY CONTAINING HER RAGE: I wanted to kill him. Just grab him and make him stop thinking what he was thinking. I flashed to my childhood. "Your mother is so cute! Does she speak English? Can she eat American food?"

SHE JUMPS UP FROM GETA AND TURNS TO AUDIENCE.

She was a freak to me. My father told me once that even my own relatives didn't talk to her for six months after she arrived in Deadwood. We got hate letters and rocks in our mailbox in Seattle. We, her own children, would make fun of her accent. "Mom, say 'Phyllis Diller,' come on!" *(As mother)* "Firis Diris" . . . *(As Amy)* She spoke English so poorly we questioned her intelligence. I thought it was her fault that I didn't fit in—"What are you? Indian?" They called me "half" and asked me which half was which. I'd say *(Tracing a line down her face)* "This half is Japanese. This half is American." Sometimes I'd switch. *(Beat)* My mother tried to deal with it once by showing me an article in *Life* magazine about "Ainoko"—"love children" . . . like me . . . living in Japan. It painted a pretty bleak picture. I guess she wanted me to feel lucky. But I didn't. *(Long pause)* Yet, here I was, years later, defending this woman—realizing how much I loved her and how much she had influenced me. She made a very difficult choice in life: turned her back on everything she knew, faced extreme racism, held a marriage together through sheer force of will and, through it all, maintained her dignity.

AMY PULLS A LETTER FROM HER POCKET AND LEANS BACK ON THE EDGE OF THE GETA.

One day, I received a letter from my mother. For the first time, she had written to me in her own language. Watakushi no aisuru Amy . . . My beloved Amy . . . All during my childhood, she had never held me or kissed me. Not that I can recall. Yet here she was, professing her love—Amy no akarusa ga mo arimasen no de, kono ie wa naka naka samishii desu ne. Hayaku, Amerika ni kaette hoshii desu. Without your brightness, this house seems so empty. Hurry home . . . She went on, in a very literary, poetic way to describe the weather, her thoughts on life . . . her loneliness in my absence.

SHE FOLDS THE LETTER AND PUTS IT AWAY.

My mother was transformed—from this goofball illiterate who could barely read or write English—to this formidable, intelligent woman. I think this was finally an opportunity for her, in her own language, to communicate to me like she was unable to with anyone else in her new life in America, particularly those closest to her —her own family. My mother had begun to perceive me as the one who is "Japanese" in the family, that I should understand. I did. And . . . I do.

AMY STANDS UPRIGHT.

All these years, my mother held on fiercely to who she was, hoping that one day her children would find their strength in the strength they had seen in her. She knew who she was and was proud of it. I always wanted to be someone else from somewhere else. I thought I needed to create an acceptable "Amy." Instead, I learned that I need to find and accept "Amy" just the way she is. I knew then that I could go home. And I'm glad I went to Tokyo.

Tongue

JULIET S. KONO

Dust flew into my eye.
My mother took my face
into her hands like a melon,
came at me with her tongue
and placed her lips around my eye.
It looked as if she were sucking
out my eyeball,
the way she sucks out fish eyes to eat.
She swirled her tongue
and cleansed my eye of its irritant.

Honeycomb of lungs,
sticky with infection
held me to the sick bed for days.
She placed her mouth over my nose
and sucked the green muck
as if she were slurping noodles.
Her tongue helped clear

my blocked nasal passages,
and heaved my wheezing out like bathwater.

After a walk in the canefields,
a bee in the ear
had me spinning like a top.
I banged into the wash buckets, gate, clothesline,
zigzagged like a drunk,
or someone blind.
Mother grasped my hands
and secured me between her legs
and came down on my ear with her tongue.
She slid the tip in and left it there.
Without a flinch,
she retracted her tongue,
the bee curled on its tip.

My lips on your lips,
my lips holding your tongue
a learned truth:
the old ways of love and survival.

Embracing the Female Body

III

preceding page:

Photograph by Jana Monji

Lipstick

WANG PING

*I*n some deep corner of the dinner table, I found an old lipstick.

The cover was gone, its green plastic body coated with dark greasy dirt. I wiped it with a tablecloth and held it under my nose. I smelled the fragrance of wild roses. Slowly I turned the tube as far as it could go. About an inch of scarlet red appeared between my fingers. The print of someone's lips on the top, its angle so tender that I dare not touch it. Whose lipstick could it be? Who still had the guts to keep a lipstick in 1971, the prime time of the Cultural Revolution? Anything which was related to beauty, whether Western or Oriental, had been banned. Gray *zhongshanzhuang*—Mao's suit—became the uniform for the middle-aged and old people, and the green and navy blue uniforms became young people's most desirable objects. All the women had short hair cut just below their ears. Some girls tied their hair with rubber bands into two brushlike pigtails. They were called revolutionary brushes, because they resembled the brushes people used to write critical big-character posters.

Whose lipstick could it be? My sister Sea Cloud's or my mother's? Sea Cloud's power seemed limitless. Although she was only twelve, and was two years younger than me, she was three inches taller—five foot, five inches—and looked like my older sister. In fact she had me completely under her thumb. She made me do her share of the housework, which was only one third of the work I had to do. Her excuse was that I had no friends to see and no places to go to anyway. She made me tell her a story every evening. If I refused, she pinched and cursed me as my mother did: *dead ghost, wooden-head, abacus.* Sometimes when the pinch was too painful and I grabbed her wrists, she would holler for my mother. My mother always punished me with the bamboo stick behind the door. She said that since I was the oldest daughter, I should love and take care of my younger sisters and brother. I had two sisters and one brother. Fortunately, my youngest sister stayed with my grandma in Shanghai, and my brother was not as wily as Sea Cloud. Everyone said Sea Cloud looked exactly like my mother: big double-lidded eyes, long clean eyebrows, straight delicate nose, and clear white skin. She looked like a foreigner, people also said, with admiration in their voices.

I couldn't understand why Western books and ideas were poisonous but to look foreign was desirable. Whenever I couldn't bring any food from the food market or broke a bowl or burned rice, my mother would sigh: If only you were half as smart as Sea Cloud. I talked back in my heart: If only she could do her own homework.

Every Chinese New Year, my mother killed one of the chickens I raised and made chicken broth. She asked me to bring a bowl of chicken soup to Sea Cloud, who was always sick in bed with a stomachache or a bad sore throat just when every hand was needed for the holiday preparations. I hated Chinese New Year. It meant endless washing of dishes and vegetables in cold water and listening with an empty stomach to guests feasting and laughing. I slowly dried my swollen frost-bitten hands on my apron, staring at the hot chicken soup with hatred. I'd been washing dishes piled up to my chest from nine to three o'clock. My mother said, "Don't pull a long face. You should love your sister and take care of her. She's sick." As soon as my mother turned her back, I spat into the soup and stirred it with my greasy finger. Then I brought it to Sea Cloud with a big smile.

The lipstick. My sister wouldn't have hidden it inside the table. She had her own steel box with a lock on it. If it had been hers, she would have shown it off long ago.

Then it must be one of Mother's old belongings. Somehow it had escaped the Red Guards' confiscations in the fall of 1967 and had been lying in the table since then. The dinner table was the only piece of furniture that survived the confiscation. All other pieces were taken away or burned, together with books. It was an eight-fairy table made of *nanmu* wood, square, with heavily decorated legs and edges, and a drawer on each side. The drawers were no longer there. The vacated space was perfect for hiding my books. As long as I kept them in the center, no one could reach them. Only my thin arm could get through the six-inch-wide and two-and-a-half-inch-high drawer space.

Today was my lucky day. At fourteen and a half, I had my first lipstick.

There was some dust on top of the lipstick. I wiped it on the ball of my left thumb, the only spot on my hands not covered with frostbite scars. The bright red mark startled me and the slightly sticky lipstick on my skin sent an unspeakable sensation along my arm to my scalp. I trembled as I rubbed the lipstick mark on my hand. I was remembering a scene in my childhood.

I was five years old, a senior in the Navy Boarding Kindergarten. That night we were going to give a performance in the Navy Auditorium. My parents would come to the show. I hadn't seen them for two weeks. The weekend before, my father's ship was on duty in the East China Sea, and my mother was too sick to take me home. I was too excited to nap, so I stole into the playroom. The teacher had forgotten to lock the closet where the costumes for the performance were stored. I picked up the general's hat with its shiny beads and two long striped whips sticking out on each side. Since I'd be singing behind the curtain with the chorus, the teacher had said I didn't need to wear any costume. I tried on the hat. As I was looking for a mirror, I found a basket with some lovely round boxes and tubes in it. I opened one of them. Rouge. How beautiful the pink color was! The teacher had said she'd put the makeup on for us after dinner. This must be it. I lifted the pad and rubbed it on my cheeks. I wished my parents could see me. I wished I had a mirror. Someone grabbed my pigtail and pulled me out of the closet. It was the teacher. She yelled and shook me like a mad-woman. "You smelly beauty, you little bourgeoisie! Just like your mother." Her screaming was so loud and piercing that soon I couldn't hear anything, although her mouth was still opening and closing like a stranded fish on the beach. She dragged me into the room where twenty other children were napping and walked me around. I must have looked strange with that general's hat on and rouge all over my face. The children laughed and called in chorus: *smelly beauty, smelly beauty.*

I was taken out of the performance and delivered to my parents that night.

I rubbed some lipstick from the ball of my thumb onto the back of my hand, its scarlet red thinned and faded into pink, like the color that always glowed so splendidly on my sister's cheeks. Whenever I saw her, I'd pray with an aching heart: Oh, God, please give me beauty like Sea Cloud! But I remained the ugliest in the family. My eyes were small and my eyelids were single-layered; my eyebrows short and thick; my nose bony and too big on my small face.

Whenever we had a fight, my sister would call me "small-eyed devil." I was pathetically thin and pale. My mother sometimes ground her teeth in anger and told me that I deliberately made myself skinny so that I could make the neighbors pity me and accuse her of maltreatment.

I looked at my rosy hand, hoping for a miracle.

It was nine o'clock. I had three hours to perform this experiment, find my book, and cook before Mother came back for lunch. Little by little I lifted the table from the floor. I was actually looking for a book that I'd hidden in the table the night before. I'd pushed it inside in a hurry and pretended to study English when I heard Mother's footsteps. Its title was *Deep Is the Night,* written in semi-ancient Chinese about a woman warrior disguised as a man who somehow remained pure among the lustful and corrupt men. After the five-year ban, books were very hard to get. The bookstores had only Mao's books on their shelves. I'd secretly been trading books at school through a well-organized underground book network. Everyone obeyed its strict rules: Never betray the person you got the book from; never delay returning books; never re-lend without the owner's permission; pay back with three books if you lose a book. I owned some very good books: *Grimm's Fairy Tales, The Blossom of Bitter Herb,* and some Russian spy novels. I had torn off the covers and wrapped them with the red plastic covers for Mao's works. I traded for books about herbs, medicine, stars and constellations, and of course, I cherished novels. Once I got a porno book about monks and nuns digging tunnels between their temples to meet at night. Something called *Burning the Red Lotus Temple.* My sister caught me reading it in the public bathroom and threatened to tell on me unless I let her read it. I had no other choice but to give it to her. She wasn't as skillful as me in terms of keeping books away from my parents. Maybe she just thought they wouldn't punish her. My father caught her and hit her for the first time. He hit her so hard that he broke the handle of the broom. The book was thrown into the stove; my sister had to write three self-criticism papers and read them in the family training class my father organized. To my surprise, my sister, who had told on me and gotten me in trouble with my mother so many times in the past, took the punishment alone with heroic silence. I really admired her for being such a good sport, and I willingly gave up three of my best books to my friend as a compensation for the lousy porno book.

I straightened the table, locked the door, and stood in front of the mirror on the wardrobe door in my parents' room. I looked at myself in despair. My features were still as bad as they were a month ago—white patches of fungus and strips of peeling skin on my dark face, the result of the strong liniment my father had applied to my face to cure the fungus. He had believed that my face was infected with athlete's foot. My jacket—passed down from my grandma to my mother, then from my mother to me—was splotched with dirt on its shredded sleeves, patched elbows, and front. I looked pathetic. I was pathetic. I'd graduated from high school two months ago, the youngest graduate, with straight A's in every subject. Still I couldn't go to college. Universities were open only to peasants, workers, soldiers, and the students who had received reeducation for more than two years in the countryside, factories, or army. Nor could I get a job in town. Factories and other businesses had stopped hiring people since the Cultural Revolution started; they could hardly give the salaries to their old employees. No one worked, no one was allowed to work. Making revolution was more important than production. My only choice was to go to the countryside to receive reeducation from the poor and middle-class peasants. I was willing to go. After two or three years, I might have a chance to be recommended to college. But

Mother said I was too young. She wanted me to stay home to grow fat and learn some English. The truth was she wanted a free maid. Since graduating in February, I had taken over all the housework, cleaning, washing, shopping for daily food, and cooking. My mother didn't have to do anything except sit down for meals and take naps at noon. It was my mother who grew fat. I got thinner and paler.

The lipstick was the only bright color in the room. Everything else was gray or brown—my face, the walls, the furniture, the sheets. I held it up to my mouth. It brightened my face.

I applied it to my lips. The first touch was frightening. I practically jumped as the lipstick left the first red mark on my lips. It was like being kissed. I laughed at the idea. How much did I know about kissing? I'd never been kissed on the lips or anywhere else. My mother never touched me except when she knocked on my head with her knuckles. Not that I wanted her to touch me anyway. I put some lipstick on the ball of my thumb and rubbed it on my cheekbones. Then I turned to the mirror.

The figure in the mirror was grotesque, with her scarlet lips and uneven red rouge over white patches of fungus on dirty cheeks, the tube of lipstick between her chapped, stained fingers. The effect was like a rose in cow dung. I pushed the mirror away. There was no miracle. Was I destined to be a housemaid all my life?

I poured some hot water into my mother's basin and washed my face. No one must see any trace of lipstick on me. As I rubbed my cheeks, rolls of dirt came off. I hadn't been to the public bathhouse the whole winter. I took off my clothes and soaked my mother's washcloth in the water, breathing in the warm comforting steam. Little by little I cleaned myself, from my face to my legs, until the water in the basin turned black. Then I picked the coal out of my nails and the folds of my knuckles with my mother's toothbrush. Yesterday I had made coal balls from coal powder for the stove. It was cheaper than coal. Mother said we must be more economical since we had an idler at home, meaning me, of course. I opened Mother's bottle of Vaseline on the dresser and applied some to my face and hands.

Finally I took hold of my braids. They were the only thing on which the neighbors ever complimented me, thick and glowing with bluish darkness. They hung loosely down to my waist and swayed as I walked. It was almost a miracle that I still had them. Long braids, together with curly hair and colorful clothing, were considered the tails of capitalism at the beginning of the Cultural Revolution. I still remembered how the Red Guards patroled the streets with scissors in hand and jumped at passersby who were wearing tight pants or had long hair. After they cut open the legs of the pants or cut off the braids, the victims had to recite Mao's words and express their sincere gratitude to the Red Guards for saving them from the horrors of capitalism. Although things had quieted down a lot, my long hair could still bring me trouble. My parents also hated my hair. My father thought it was dirty. Whenever he picked out a long hair from the food I cooked, he'd stare at me and roar, "Cut it off tonight!" My mother kept telling me my hair sucked all the nutrition out of my body. "You look like a ghost with long untidy hair," she screamed with her beautiful voice. Slowly I unbraided my hair and brushed it with my mother's hairbrush. It worked much better than my little plastic comb. My hair was so thick even my mother's brush couldn't get through it.

When I turned back to the mirror, I saw a different person. She was clean, had shapely lips, a slender neck, long legs, and breasts that were firm like pigeons' bellies. I turned to see my back. Once my mother measured my hips to make me a pair of shorts. After the measuring, she pinched my behind and said, "You have a big ass." My big ass looked fine in the mirror. It traced a smooth curve below my waist. I raised my arms, holding two handfuls of hair. It looked like the wings of some powerful black bird in the sunshine. Tears filled my eyes. I wasn't going to be ugly all my life.

I wrapped the lipstick in a piece of white paper and put it back into the dinner table. No one else except me could reach into that two-and-a-half-inch-high, six-inch-wide drawer. I had an hour to clean my mother's towel, hairbrush, and toothbrush, and to cook lunch. Today's menu was fish, pickles with sliced pork, sprouts, and seaweed soup.

The Handbook of Sex

of the Plain Girl

MARIAN YEE

She calls herself the plain girl, but I
am plainer. Nothing is homelier
than the floor of my breasts; this house
of bones. Everything I know of sex
is large-breasted, blue-eyed, and blonde.

I am woman learned in these ways—
lie still, I will teach you.
I have pulled back the quilts,
swept clean the pillows, softened
the lamp. I will unfasten my robe,
set my hair free. Quietly
let me smooth your skin into peace.
This is how you please a man.

I ran away from the first boy who said I
was beautiful. What do I know
of pleasing a man? Mother will not answer
my questions, and these pictures she gives me—
do men and women really do this?

Come into my red—let white
iron burn, reshape and find its form
in heat. My Master,
my Emperor. I am yours tonight.

On the page, she crouches to receive him
as a glove enfolds the hand.
But this man beside me—who is he?
He calls my plainness beauty, and I,
who have little enough to give, will find
this reason enough to give
everything.

Men know nothing of sex—ask a man
what sex is and he will show you
his penis—we have much to teach:
my Master, my child, let me teach you
about your lips, your thighs,
your cheeks, the bones
of your hip.

But what can you teach about the pain
of his entrance and, later, the ache
of his departure? You, who taught
the Emperor to live forever,
teach me what to do with love.

Volcanology:

Curtain of Fire

Garrett Hongo

One night, under a midsummer half-moon, I took a long hike across the broad black caldera of Kilauea from Volcano House on the crater rim to Halema'uma'u, the old fire pit of the volcano where a lava lake had boiled for over a hundred years, from 1823 to 1924. I wanted to see earth-shimmer on the black lavas, to see moonlight pooling in the crevices of fumaroles spouting their vaporous ghosts. I wanted to feel whatever there was from starlight glistening over new skin on the earth.

At dusk, I made a quick descent through stumpy *'ōhi'a* and the fern forest against the north rim of the crater. Kāhili gingers bloomed by the trailside. Their thick yellow scepters radiated out of the deep greenery I passed through. When the evening wind came up the trail, I saw fingers of mist stirring through every friable green thing. After a while, I could see that a soft rain was splashing on the upturned face of the dark, volcanic sea ahead of me. Clouds breezed through the cool arms of the ginger flowers, *origami* cranes alighting like bundles of white flames on the fleshly leaves of the forest.

In less than an hour, it was past nightfall and I stood on a fissure line ripped open from the caldera floor, the spatter rampart of an eruption that had sent a curtain of the fire fountaining along its entire length for nearly a full day in 1982. There had been a long red wall of volcanic blossoming, sheets and spinnakers of incandescence. The lavas had thrown themselves up from a boil of old rock, sending new gouts and slashes up through a slit in the earth nearly two hundred yards long. On one side of the split were low hummocks and hogbacks slumping inward toward the long crack in the earth. But, on the other, there were huge, cowling crests like ocean waves just about to crash onto the black shore of the caldera. Standing next to them, I felt those lifting shapes were as immense and powerful as any set of waves I'd surfed, only thicker and completely substantial.

I scrambled up beside a huge lip of purple and gray seven feet high. There were ocherish reds streaked with white under its concave side. In moonlight, the gray-buff and reddened lava looked like the nippled line of skin upraised on the mound of a woman. I imagined the way the earth had opened itself—the flap of molten matter, partly congealed, the covering tufts of spatter shaped into a single part thrown upward with the surge of sudden fountaining, coolish rock curling against the heightening spume, the long ridge along the fissure gradually shaping itself into a chain of lips boiling with earth's passion. It seemed to me that I stood on the body of a woman, and the glistening lavas were her hills and thighs.

I wanted to kiss and lie down. I wanted to taste weariness and feel an infinite ache. I curled myself inside one gigantic lip and gave in to the smell of its sulphurous climate.

A blue night dropped upon Kīlauea. Around me was the whirling, nocturnal depth. I felt burning and cold all at once, encircled by a curtain of fire that coiled away in shrouds of sleepy mist. I surrendered to the earth, body of a woman.

Skin Diving in Bombay

GINU KAMANI

*T*he taxi screeched to a halt in front of her. The driver stuck his astonished face out of the window, jumped out of the car and hurriedly opened the back door for Neena. She hesitated, not knowing why he was excited. The taxi driver mopped his sweating brow and flashed an ingratiating smile. Neena took a deep breath and entered the car. The driver closed the door respectfully and turned down his meter. As he slid into his seat and put the car in gear, she directed him.

"Andheri station."

He nodded vigorously and turned onto the main road. Neena looked about the cab, then noticed that her door had no handle. She looked to the other passenger door. It was the same. In place of the curved handle there was only the metal fitting from which the grip had been removed. The driver looked at her through the rearview mirror every few seconds. She idly wondered whether he was Palestinian or Latino, then remembered that she was hurtling through a suburb of Bombay, not the streets of New York.

"Srimati Chawla," the driver intoned shyly in Hindi. "May I call you Juhi? You are like my own flesh and blood; you see, I have seen every one of your movies at least ten times! You are top-A-one dancer." *Top-A-one dancer* was enunciated proudly in English.

The taxi driver's short speech was so melodious in its ingratiation that at first Neena thought he was singing a song. But he stared at her expectantly through the rearview mirror, waiting for her response.

"What?!" she spluttered.

"Madam, please!" The driver put his hands together in supplication. "I love you like myself. I have been waiting for this day. Ask any of my friends. I keep your picture right next to Lord Shiva and every day I do puja that one day you will need a taxi—and it will be mine! With god's blessings"—again his hands joined in supplication—"that day has finally come. You are my goddess, Juhi-ji!"

Neena racked her brains. Juhi . . . Juhi Chawla.* She had to be one of the younger stars of the Hindi screen. Neena had adored film actresses as a child and lovingly collected their pictures in scrapbooks. Each of the actresses had exuded her own special charm and sophistication. Neena had sat and admired their beautiful wide-eyed faces for hours. But over the years, the newer stars had transformed into interchangeable sirens who all simulated uninhibited sexuality. In reality, these bombshells never ventured far without a chaperone: they were prize catches. Their reputations had to be maintained until they finally contracted that highly desired marriage with a VIP, after which time they generally retired from public view.

Juhi-ji must be an actress. Nothing else could explain the daft behavior of this cabbie. Neena had been told to keep her eye on the meter to make sure the taxi driver wasn't cheating her, but looking at the meter brought her gaze right in line with his. He stared at her reflection in the mirror, unblinking. She was repelled by the entreaty in his moist eyes. At the stop light, she noticed that the driver was slowly massaging his crotch. Her face flushed with anger. She felt like stopping the car and getting out, but the driver read her mind.

"Madam, station is close by. Do not worry, I will let you out.

* One of the popular young heroines of Hindi films.

But, madam, please, it is my lifetime dream. I am sure you will understand. No harm will come to you. But how much I love you!" He massaged his crotch faster. They halted at another stop light. The driver gasped and panted, panted and gasped, and then moaned in submission to climax. The light changed and the cars lined up behind started a terrific honking. The driver struggled to his senses. Cars overtook him left and right. His foot seemed to have trouble pressing down on the accelerator.

"Madam, when the time comes, don't marry one of those big filmwallahs. Marry a taxi driver like me. I have lots of juice. I can make you very happy." He began massaging his crotch once again.

Wear a sari while you're in India, her aunt had advised her that morning. *It's the best protection.* But Neena could never recognize herself in a sari, and the vision was almost frightening. Most probably her well-padded aunt hadn't encountered masturbating taxi drivers in her silk-and-organza protected world. Right as Neena was leaving the house, Mrs. Charan the neighbor had dropped in. She took one look at Neena and said, *Shall I give you the address of my tailor? He's very good. He'll make that dress much more presentable. How can you walk out of your aunt's house looking like* that!

Neena banged her fist on the roof.

"Open the door!" she snapped. "I have to catch a train."

The driver slowly stepped out of the car and swung open the back door. Neena rushed past him, cursing him for reminding her that she was on display. *This dress isn't for you!* she wanted to scream. *It's for Jeet, and only Jeet.*

As she dashed up the steps of the station, she automatically checked the front buttons on her dress. Her aunt had warned her about eve-teasers who snipped off hooks and buttons from women's clothing as they journeyed through public spaces. A south-bound commuter train was preparing to pull out, and she broke into a run.

"Does this train go to Churchgate?" she asked the thin man

overtaking her on the platform. He looked her up and down as she raced alongside him.

"Hurry, hurry, train is leaving!" he beckoned her.

He jumped up the three metal steps and swung himself into a compartment. The wheels squeaked into motion as she swung herself up right behind him. Satisfied that she was on board, the man dove into the thicket of bodies that crowded the compartment and disappeared from view. The train pulled out of the station at a steady pace. It was a fast train to Churchgate, an express with no stops. Neena stood at the open doorway for a moment, savoring the breeze.

The open carriages were a godsend in the humid heat. They had no doors to obstruct the healing, cooling breeze. These were the surface trains of Bombay's commuter railway, transporting upward of two million people a day in and out of town. Facing Neena at the carriage entrance were a threesome of young men, all nattily attired in crisp white shirts and pleated office trousers. They were rubbing against each other like cats. Neena blinked her eyes to clear her vision. The tall man's hand was definitely on the short one's crotch, while the middle one whispered intimately into both the other men's ears. From the corner of her eye she saw that the other passengers were giving this trio a wide berth, no doubt repelled by their erotic play.

Turning away to give the threesome their privacy, Neena realized with a shock that she was completely surrounded by men. There wasn't a woman in sight. A sudden thrust from the side pushed her into their midst and she clung to the wall of the compartment. She had forgotten about the segregated women's compartments! That very morning her aunt had coached her about looking for the word LADIES in English or MAHILA in Hindi, painted on the sides of the carriages reserved exclusively for women. The male bodies pressed closer in, and an elbow glanced her breast.

The men surrounding her were of slight build, and dressed in the same cheap, heavily starched office shirts with gray pleated office trousers. They worked in South Bombay as errand boys, assistant secretaries, typists, clerks. Five or six days a week they packed themselves into trains and commuted as human jam, jumping off at their stations soaked right down to the skin. Usually it was only against each other that they dissolved their pent-up desires. But standing in their midst that day was the eternally longed-for goddess, right out of the Hindi movies. "Madhuri Dixit!"* a man whispered in her ear, and the name rippled through the throng in hushed tones, drawing them in nearer. A tentative hand reached for the strap of Neena's sleeveless dress, and she cried out in alarm. Her arms were pinned to her sides by the encroaching bodies and she could not move.

Neena shrank back against the wall of the compartment. The men moved in closer. She looked at the faces swaying in unison from side to side. There was something very familiar about their movements; then it struck her: they moved like a school of fish underwater. It was just like skin diving, surrounded by look-alike creatures who stuck together in order to navigate the dangerous depths.

Neena had forgotten about this contact, the indifferent public caress that could enfold one's body without notice—in buses, trains, ticket lines, shops, temples, weddings, festivals, schools. As a child, she had crushed into the mob at movie theaters for snacks and drinks. And then there was the mad rush of girls tripping over each other to get through the school gates at the end of each day. But most intoxicating of all had been the eager crowds that jammed the court to watch Jeet in action playing championship squash. She had known without a doubt that Jeet would never touch her; after all, their families knew each other, so she dove in with his fans, who clung to each other like sand on the seashore, cheering him on to victory.

Neena recalled the intense face of Jeet, his laughing eyes crinkling with pleasure as he listened to her talk, the sweat falling from his brow after his daily rounds of squash. She remembered the time his sweat landed on her arm as he left their customary table by the pool. She licked up the drops one by one, tasting carefully. There was stinging salt, faint talc and a pungent peppery vanilla that filled her mouth like a cloud of steam.

The men of the compartment were exhaling excitedly in her face, stepping right up onto her toes. Dark skins, big eyes, mustaches hiding fleshy upper lips. They communicated their burning desire in short, nervous breaths, flapping their arms repeatedly so their elbows could brush her breasts. Still they said nothing, faces blank, bodies tensed with anticipation. Her skin felt numb. The mingled odor of sweat, hair oil and cheap aftershave was unbearable.

Puppy love, her aunt had smirked when Neena mentioned Jeet's name. *Puppies in heat,* Neena reflected in amusement. Sitting across from him at the Club day after day had been enough to flood her underpants. When she got home she would find the opaque droplets of her desire stuck to the cotton crotch like old glue. On her return to Bombay, Neena had decided to track him down. He was a businessman now, but his main place of work was still the Club, still drinking beer after his contests, except now the competition was for money and not titles. The train would get her to Churchgate, from where she could walk across to the Club, then take a taxi to the New Year's party where she was sure to find him. She dressed for the evening. As she walked out the door, it occurred to her that she had dressed for New York. Basic, form-fitting black. Did anyone in Bombay wear black?

The train jerked to a halt in the middle of the tracks, dislodging Neena from her protected spot against the wall. Figures quickly closed in behind her. Like eyes adjusting from a dark tunnel to the light, it took a minute for her skin to detail the various bulges of flesh pressed up against her body. Then something twitched against her leg. And then again, on the other leg. Frogs? she wondered. Grasshoppers, perhaps. She couldn't look. The twitching multiplied until her body was beset with leaping creatures on all sides. It felt exactly like those Mexican jumping beans enclosed in boxes that had fascinated her in childhood. A man behind her groaned passionately and the hair stood up on Neena's neck. *Oh god!* She shivered in horror. *They're rubbing their things against me.* She couldn't twist her arms around to push away the man whose erect member pressed keenly into her buttocks. She felt panic rising as she counted the number of erections pressed up against the back and front of her thighs and hips. When she managed to turn away from one man, another positioned himself in place and thrust against her. All around her eyes flashed with questions about who she was, where she was from, when she would succumb to the pleasure of being penetrated by adorants from all sides.

When they finally pulled in to Churchgate, most of the men jumped onto the platform while the train was still moving. Neena waited to make sure that everyone had disembarked before she unglued herself from the wall. The last man out of the compartment was the thin clerk whom Neena had first followed into the carriage. She glared at him as he dashed past her and down the steps. He nervously offered her a helping hand from below but she steered clear of him.

"Madam!" he called urgently, matching stride with her down the length of the platform. "Madam, please, you are from good family, why you are not marrying only? All men are wanting to know why Madhuri Dixit is not marrying." His sweeping gesture took in the entire train station, and he puffed up in pride at being a spokesman for the masses. Without waiting for an answer, he scurried away.

Neena walked cautiously, on guard against all pedestrians. She held her arms like a boxer, fists close to her chin and elbows protecting her chest. But whatever had been the allure on the crowded train seemed to have diminished in the open street. The lush green lawns signaled that she was entering exclusive territory. She sighed with relief and smoothed her dress down before entering the fan-cooled Club.

At the front desk, Neena signed herself in with her family's life membership number. The registration clerk peered at the ledger entry, then looked at Neena with delight.

"Madam, you are Mr. Sunil's daughter?" She nodded. "Welcome back!" he bowed to her, then wiped his face. "Madam," he continued apologetically, "please, you are not married? Only unmarried daughters can use family membership." Neena nodded again. "Oh," the clerk looked relieved, but a moment later he shook his head sadly. "Madam, no husband? But do not despair. Now that you are in Bombay, you will find very easily. Your bad luck with husband is American only. I swear you will be getting one-two offers today only!" As the clerk chattered animatedly about her plight, Neena perused the signatures, hoping to see Jeet's name.

Neena settled into a wicker armchair and put her feet up, even though the portly waiter sternly shook his head at her. She remembered this man as one of Jeet's adoring retinue. He looked right past her with years of well-rehearsed snubbing. It was clear even to the waiter that she was single, and single women above a certain age were not encouraged at the Club. Casually, with a quick pinch and pull, the man adjusted his genitals through his white trousers. Neena was shocked at his gesture, because she realized exactly what he had just done—he had readjusted his erection to keep from tenting in his pants and drawing embarrassing attention to his crotch. She couldn't believe his insolence. It was something Jeet himself used to do, unconsciously, every time he stood up to take his leave. On one occasion, purely by accident, his eyes met hers as he performed the quick adjustment, and seeing her curiosity, he blushed deeply to his ears. *Is your underwear too tight?* she'd asked jokingly. *Not tight enough,* he had mumbled. *I can't help it, it has a mind of its own.* Later on she got accustomed to noticing men adjusting themselves at bus stops, ticket lines, parking lots, parties. It seemed to her that most men in Bombay were trying to subdue their uncontrollable erections while moving around in public.

Neena sat in the stifling formality of the British-built Club. The balcony gradually filled with the lunch crowd, tinkling the bells that summoned blank-faced waiters. These were the adults she had hated as a child, their voices hammering out disparaging remarks about friends, family and strangers; their faces sneering and contorted with bigoted disdain. Right under their noses she and Jeet had exchanged the books they called their "bedtime stories": books reveling in explicit, torrid affairs, mad heights of passion between skillful lovers, tireless, conscienceless prostitutes, gigolos, nymphos, harems, lesbians, slaves, exotics, virgins, sadomasochists, whackos, jailbirds, animals.

Neena started to dose as the small type of paperback novels flew through her head. She used to have hundreds of those passages memorized by heart, but now only bits and pieces stood out in her memory as she struggled to recapture the phrases. She had loved whispering the words aloud, savoring the weight and texture of them on her lips and tongue.

"Excuse me, madam, was that one more beer, you said?" Without realizing it, Neena had been mouthing erotic phrases at the pompous waiter. Neena angrily waved him away. It was evening. From where she sat she could see anxious office workers rushing to Churchgate station. Across the street, long lines of impatient commuters mopped their brows and tidied their clothes as they waited for their buses to appear. Darkness descended with swiftness, a final orange glow burning the rims of clouds journeying by.

Neena gathered her purse and slipped into her shoes. All around her businessmen joked in loud groups and gulped down liquor. A few curious faces turned her way. She scanned them intently. Jeet might have walked past her a dozen times and she would never have known. As Neena stood up, she felt the old dampness between her legs. Soon she would be able to rub together the streaks of mucous till they stuck to her fingers like cotton candy.

"Believe me, madam, it is too far to walk. How would it look—one of our lady members in the open road? All the hooligans are knowing right away you are not married, madam. Five minutes only, madam! I am fetching a taxi for you."

"But how do they know I'm not married?" Neena demanded angrily.

The Club doorman dropped the whistle he was about to blow, and wiped his mouth nervously. "Uh . . . uh . . . I am knowing very little, madam, please, I am not wanting trouble, madam . . . We men are just knowing some things, madam, from working at the Club only, madam," he finished in a rush.

"What?" Neena demanded. "Tell me, for god's sake. What is it that you know?"

The doorman looked Neena up and down, then looked around to make sure no one was listening. He spoke rapidly, authoritatively, inducting Neena into the mysteries of the male perspective.

"Madam, after marriage, no lady is coming to the Club sleeveless, no lady is showing her legs without trousers, no lady is coming without husband or children, no lady is coming without car and driver." The doorman took a deep breath, and made sure that he had Neena's undivided attention before exhaling generously. "No married lady is sitting like this"—he splayed his palms to mimic a woman sitting with her crotch open to the world—"and no lady is standing like this"—the doorman spread his legs apart in a wide stance. While Neena had dozed in her solitary reverie, all the attendants had apparently been watching her.

"But biggest problem, madam, is you are looking like Anu Aggarwal."* With a smirk on his face and a quick twitch to his crotch, the doorman turned away. As he blew shrilly on his whistle time and again, Neena couldn't help but shrink back into the shadows.

Taxi after taxi filled with passengers raced by. The doorman blew his whistle diligently and waved at the drivers to stop. Finally, a taxi crawled to a halt. Neena climbed into the back seat and the driver searched frantically through his audiotapes for a film soundtrack. He kissed the desired tape and slid it into the player. The blaring music was so distorted that Neena could not understand the lyrics. But by the high-pitched keening of the female voice—coy, contrite and giggling by turns—Neena understood the taxi driver was sending her a message lusting for unempowered, unpenetrated, virginal love.

"Slow down! Slow down!" she shouted. "We're here."

The actual address was two streets over but Neena wanted to get out of the car. The driver turned back, beaming.

"Would you mind," the driver gushed in Hindi, "if I told my friends that Raveena Tandon* herself sat in my car? They would be so impressed!"

She stepped out of the cab and was about to cross the street when she thought better of it and climbed the front steps of the nearest building.

"Madam." The cabbie waved at her as she entered the foyer. "These days you have stopped wearing sari? My friends and I like very much seeing you in tight sari!"

Hidden in the dark interior, she waited for the taxi to leave— the driver would have continued to harass her if he realized that she had gotten out too soon.

Thank god it had been books and not music that she and Jeet had in common. Neena had heard he loved hamming it up at Karaoke clubs. She was minutes away from the party where they were supposed to meet. She had hardly thought about what Jeet had become: a wealthy businessman who owned prime real estate, imported cars, a penthouse in London and a wife acquired through arrangement. His business cards were rumored to list his current worth. What were the two of them going to talk about after all these years?

The party was being held in the same illegally constructed rooftop duplex wing where Jeet lived and worked. It was enormous, fantastically domed, with a black ceiling studded with flashing lights to emulate the night sky outside. In the dim light the shapes of what appeared to be hundreds of people slowly emerged.

"Coffee?" a deadpan waiter paused to offer a trayful of beverages to the parched guests. Neena snatched a glass of cold coffee to steady her nerves. The waiter looked her up and down, adjusted his crotch and moved on. A man pushing through jostled the coffee out of her glass. She felt a hand on her back—sticky fingers pressing on her sweated skin. Neena turned around, certain it was Jeet. The impatiently pushing man took his hand off her back as she turned her questioning eyes on him. Another hand landed on her back, burning holes in her sweating skin. She focused her impatient gaze on the bodies around her and suddenly realized that for the second time that day she was surrounded entirely by men. Where were the women? She rose up on her toes and looked around. Could they all be cooking in the kitchen?! She laughed grimly to herself. These party-goers had instinctively separated themselves: males on one side, females on the other. Hot, wet skins pressed against her, plastering her dress to her person. The pressure on her back was insistent, guiding her farther into the crush of silk jackets and safari suits.

She pushed, and a man turned around. "Hello, hello!" He laughed and grabbed her hand. For a minute she was confused. Jeet? He looked at her expectantly. Wrong man. She slid sideways, tucked her head in and gently butted a shoulder. "Having a good time? Where's your drink . . ." She pressed her fingers lightly against a suited back. "So sorry, my fault." She raised herself on tiptoe and set the coffee tumbler onto a waiter's tray. "Scotch, madam . . . ?" She felt a man step back onto her toes and she cried out in pain. "Oh! So sorry, darling, didn't quite see you there."

Neena extricated herself and shouted in a sing-song, "Excuse me, excuse me please, oh so sorry, my fault, hello, hello, yes, yes, of course we've met, at the Club perhaps? Excuse me, oh *pardon* me, I'm *so* clumsy. Here, I have a hanky in my bag, why don't you just keep it . . . yes, lovely gathering, isn't it. *This* dress? Yes, it is a nice color, nice meeting you, sorry again."

"Scotch . . . madam!" The insistent waiter came around again. She snatched the glass and gulped down the liquid. The Scotch brought more sweat onto her brow and thickened her tongue. She wished that it would thicken her skin, which felt raw from being brushed against every body in the room.

She whirled through the elastic crowd and was propelled onto the balcony like a stone from a slingshot. She kicked her heels into a corner, leaning gratefully against the cool, concrete balustrade, gulping in air. The breeze from the Arabian Sea made her shiver. The waves shuddering along the sea wall were low and sluggish, heavy with silt and strings of marigolds. The neon sign boards atop the buildings blinked on and off, buzzing noisily like flies at a windowpane.

The chant of the coconut men rose over the splash of idling waves. The dark, lithely muscled men stood along the sea wall, enticing their last customers with gleaming knives and big green coconuts. Neena used to love drinking the sweet liquid slowly, sucking for long moments on the creamy coconut pulp, then coaxing the velvety meat along her tongue till it slid irretrievably down her throat. She wanted one right then. But the barricade of sweating socialites blocked her escape to the thirst-quenching fruit below. Her skin felt numb again as it had that morning, scorched by the hot flint of commuter lust. Her body prickled with an old familiar alertness—as though she had an eye in every pore.

She felt a presence behind her, still and silent and male.

Oh, Neena, it's you. So! Are you in Bombay to find yourself a man? I hear those American gandus don't know how to handle our Indian girls. Never mind those jokers, it's high time you got yourself a husband. Ha ha! Did you ever meet my cousin the doctor? Thirty-five years old and still a frustrated bachelor . . .

The man cleared his throat and Neena swiftly turned around. Jeet? He wore a pale silk shirt and white trousers. He cocked his head at Neena.

"My friends over there"—he pointed at a group of men standing back to one side—"have made a bet with me. Are you Manisha Koirala?" He leaned in closer and added in a whisper, "Even if you aren't, just say that you are. They've bet a thousand. I'll take you out to dinner."

The group of friends were no more than twenty years old. They fidgeted nervously as she looked them over. Clean-cut, good-looking, eager as puppy dogs. She strode up to the group and offered her hand. "Hi, I'm Manisha, but my friends call me Neena." The boys hesitated for a respectful moment before shaking her outstretched hand, then tripped over each other trying to introduce themselves: Amit, Sudhir, Mansoor, Nakul and the man who'd just won a thousand rupees, Rohit. They stood back at a deferential distance to avoid any undue contact. They peeked at her shyly, waiting for her to make the next move.

"Let's go," Neena directed Rohit, and the boys rapidly cleared a path for her through the crowd down the length of the room.

"Where's Jeet?" Neena asked Rohit.

"Jeet? You mean, Jeet Chandani, the bigshot?" Neena nodded. Rohit rose onto his tiptoes and surveyed the room. "There!" he pointed, guiding Neena into position to get a good look. She found herself looking at the bald spot on the back of a head, and the loose skin on the back of a neck. Jeet had his arms around the waists of two glittering sari-clad women. Facing him were three more shimmering and bejeweled women. There was something familiar about the way they tossed their hair back, adjusted their low bodices and interrupted each other to get Jeet's attention. Behind them stood several eagle-eyed older women, flashing hard smiles at each other to mask their obvious rivalry. Shrewd, conniving chaperones to the dizzy lacquered stars.

At that moment Jeet turned and looked Neena right in the face. She stared back at him but his gaze drifted off without recognizing her. It was his face all right, but puffier, duller. He looked spent.

"Do you want me to introduce you?" Rohit offered blandly, then added with a grin, "He's a real ladies' man, you know, he can rape at fifty feet—"

"—sixty if you're a virgin," interrupted Mansoor.

"—but forty if you're an actress!" Amit ended with a shout.

The boys snickered and snorted, and looked bashfully at Neena for approval. She turned away, repelled by the entreaty in their eyes no different from that of the masturbating cabbie. They waited for her to smile, to giggle coyly, to denounce their boldness with mock outrage. But she pushed the boys out of her way, marched down the steps and out of the building to where a taxi stood vacant. She slid into the front seat right next to the driver, who moved away with a start, unaccustomed to having a woman in the seat next to him. Pressed up against his door as far from her as he was able, he took off at full speed, training his gaze directly on the road ahead. Neena settled back against the seat and closed her eyes, relishing the cool night air. It would be a quick ride back to where her impatient aunt was waiting to unburden herself of the latest juiciest movie-star gossip, as spicy as any pickle that piqued her evenly seasoned meals.

from

Body

WOON PING CHIN

Blue spotlight on the Woman standing in front of mirror, placed at an angle so the audience sees both the Woman and her reflection. She wears the underpants she put on over her leotards in Part I. With one arm raised above her head, she is giving herself a breast examination using the other free arm and hand. She rotates her fingers over each breast in a slow, methodical, attentive fashion.

The mood is solemn and meditative. This part is played in adagio. You might hear snatches of shakahachi music. Or, the Chorus makes the solemn sounds of Noh voices—Eeyo-oh! etc.

Woman

(Dreamily, seriously)

Over and over I return to Body. It is a precious jar, vessel of life, receiver of goodness. Whole, it bursts into fullness. Over and over man writes on it his imagination, his bewilderment, his inadequacy, his potency. Over and over, he writes on it his punishment, his wrath, his magnanimity, his fickleness. In darkness and health, he clutches at me and wreaks his jealousy and his longing.

(Draping a long, silky veil over her shoulders, pulling it over and around her and luxuriating in its soft folds. Breathlessly, intimately, with growing excitement, as if narrating a special secret)

I know a place where the water convolvulus grows in dense clutches and jackfruit heavier than worry sit low on the branch. The banana leaf is smooth to touch, dollops of dew roll down its downy parts until you touch innermost recesses of flowering center. There the spirit of banana tree lives, curled in crimson, pert as a virgin's nipple, a promise of golden form, great clump of sweetnesses. The spirit is snowy, silent. He sidles into bed, he is sleek upon first caress, oh lighter than silk, muscularly made.

When he enters, you sigh several times with bliss, he hisses his wants into your ear, he loves to lick. The touch grows heavier as he strokes, he has many ways of lavishing attentions, now cool, now fiery, lapping at your sorest points, he is too cruel, too tender, oh keep the rough handlings right there!

When ghost birds call and the flying fox swoops, he is still cool, still pointed. Aroused to a pitch, you are turned into his purple blossom flaring at edges. He knows the tenderest places and will find them, no moaning will keep him at bay, he is not full, he's working at the mouth.

(With growing sadness, as the Chorus makes correspondingly sad sounds)

The breeze will not die down, he swells larger, all color is draining from you, oh he will snort your life away! When dawn clicks on, a slant of light behind the bamboo blind, he is too soon, too sadly gone.

(Removes the veil. Shoulders drooping, moves to another part of the stage. Finds a patch of cloth and sticks it {with Velcro} on her right breast. The patch is an irregular red piece that looks like a puddle or a big ugly scar. She clutches it as if it hurts, or she's been badly hurt)

But what if your body is no longer beautiful, will not be beautiful, never was beautiful? What if it is not desirable, not gorgeous, not a piece of cheesecake? What if it is not a piece, not a whole, not a one, NOT, NOT, NOT? How do you live with flatness? How do you live with plainness? How do you live with ugliness? How do you live with emptiness?

(In different voices of ordinary women)

"Every time I looked in the mirror and saw this chicken-breasted figure or walking down the street thinking about it, I felt deformed."

"I'm five-foot-nine, I wear a size twelve and I wore a size A bra. You know, it means so much for a woman because God didn't make her enormous."

(She finds and puts on a bra. It is more a falsie, decorated with lace, ribbons and bows. Taking a bicycle pump, she inserts its nozzle into an opening in the bra. She pumps vigorously, so the bra inflates her chest. The Chorus chants solemnly)

SILICONE IS SEXY, SILICONE IS SEXY, SILICONE IS SEXY . . .

(She puts the pump away, pleased. Now she straightens herself and puts on a doctor's white gown. She picks up a pointer and points to the mirror as if it is a blackboard.)

Lesson Number Five: Hand. A hand is for holding and for plucking and for massaging. Hand over what you have when asked. Never handle more than you can keep. Keep your hand soft, shapely and attractive. I recommend Nail Polish Number 42, Watermelon Excess, or Nail Polish Number 4, Brazilian Brassiness, or Handcream Number 99, Mushy Magic.

(Reading the following translation from Sutardji Calzoum Bachri as if from an imaginary blackboard, with deadpan seriousness)

it must be that a hand is not only a hand but a hand that is a hand not merely a hand but a hand that's a hand positively a hand absolutely a hand that can beckon that can wave hello

it must be that a hand is not a clump of fingers writing in vain just a mere thorn writing wounds rubbing eyes yet still the drizzle has not stopped

even a complete hand feels maimed although nearly a hand it feels amputated although one hand it is lopped off although half a hand it's amputated the dismembered hand feels cut off the chopped hand is amputated hand amputated

(She mimes with hands stretched out as if they are amputated)

all amputated all not hands
only clocks are complete their hands pointing
who knows where

(Removes the white gown. Runs to the other side of the stage, puts on a diaphanous kimono)

Lesson Number Four. Do you like your mouth? For a mere princely sum you can have your mouth enlarged, thickened, lengthened, voluptuized, desensitized, defamiliarized. Would you like to look like Kim Basinger, or Jean Paul Belmondo, or a Bez Denage? Come to Fanciful Flesh Farms. Leave your mouth to us. Never leave home without your instant, chewable Mouth.

(Finds a huge, Raggedy-Ann doll upon which she inflicts various acts of anger and violence as she chants the following, with the Chorus making accompanying sounds)

When he cuts into me when he slices into me when he
     stabs me
When he stalks me when he hits me when he slaps me
When he throttles me when he poisons me when he
     maims me
When he chains me when he traps me when he sells me
When he brands me when he ropes me when he tattoos me
When he cripples me when he dumps me when he
     burns me
When he hangs me when he shoots me when he snuffs me

(Now she cradles the doll like a child, showering upon it gestures of affection and tenderness)

Is he saying he has forgotten
How to comfort me how to look at me how to tame me
How to work with me how to walk with me
How to lighten me how to learn from me
How to live with me how to cherish me

How to comfort self how to tame self
How to lighten self how to learn from self
How to look at self how to love self
How to heal self how to cherish self

(*Removing the kimono, removing the bra and the underpants, standing straight and facing the audience, in an even voice, repeating the chant as many times as she likes, with growing conviction*)

I am not my breasts I am not my chin I am not my arms I am
not my neck I am not my womb I am not my lips I am not
my breasts

(*Moving to another part of the stage. Puts on a pretty gown and a gardenia in her hair. Sings, in Billie Holiday fashion*)

I'm not much to look at, nothin to see
Just glad I'm livin and lucky it's me
I've got a man crazy for me
He's funny that way

Mangoes

Hsu Tzi Wong

Silk, her touch was like silk. When she first put her hand against my cheek, I thought of a red silk jacket I had as a child. She brushed my skin, first one cheek then the other, in slow rhythmic strokes. My breathing became deeper. As I melted into her hand, I thought of being a child. I thought of a red silk jacket I was given as a child by my great-grandma. The jacket was padded, with a high stiff collar and sleeves that dangled below my fingertips. My mother said the jacket was much too good to give a child, but Great-grandma had no use for it anymore. Too sick to go out, Great-grandma hadn't worn it in years. The jacket lay in the bottom of a drawer, discoloring from mildew and age. "Come," Great-grandma said, "I won't use this again." She put it on my shoulders, and my mother said, "All right. But I don't know why you want to spoil her."

The jacket became my most prized possession. I loved the soft thick feel of the padded silk, and even wore it to bed. I found great pleasure in cupping the long hanging sleeves over my upheld fingers and rubbing the extra fold of silk across my face, over my eyes and down my cheeks. I did this without thinking. It became a habit, this and burying my face in the soft folds which smelled vaguely of cedar and camphor. Her touch brought this back to me. In one searing flash, I remem-

bered the touch of padded silk, and out of gratitude for this
gift, I kissed the center of her palm.

Lie down, she said, and I'll cool you off.

She took a hand towel and soaked it in a bowl of icy water.
Starting from my toes, she washed the summer sweat off my body.
It was hot, but even in that sweltering heat, the rough edges of her
towel made my skin rise up in goose bumps. I was so excited my
body reacted. A sound escaped my lips and, hearing me, she
stopped. She leaned over and kissed me. "You are so beautiful," she
whispered. Her words wrenched something deep inside of me. The
feelings welled to the surface, ready to stream forth tears. Suddenly
I wanted to cry. Stopping myself, I pulled her face to face. She
wrapped her ivory arms around my waist and I knew I had to tell
her. She was the one who was beautiful. Not I.

"I'm not beautiful," I stuttered. "I'm fat."

She laughed and turned my gaze toward hers. "Where?" She
asked, then grabbed the jelly roll around my waist. "This?" she
asked. "Is this what you're ashamed of?"

My back and legs stiffened automatically. I couldn't say anything because I knew how it would end. I had heard all the things
men say to fat women after they've gotten what they wanted, and I
didn't want to be disappointed again. She shook my jelly roll and
leaned closer. I pulled back nervously, but she drew my body into
her arms, then leaned her face so close I could feel her breathe on
my lips. Her eyes probed, then her lips forced my mouth open. Her
tongue slipped in as she shoved her top leg between mine. My heart
started beating faster. I felt my reserve break apart. She withdrew
her tongue, then asked, with her lips still pressed to mine, "Have
you always been fat?"

I jerked back, but she pressed her leg deeper and rubbed the
small of my back the way a mother does to calm a child. I shook my
head—no. I stiffly waited for the next attack, when suddenly the

answer to her question popped into my head. No—I hadn't always
been fat! It had only been the last five years, since David and I
started living together, that I started to have a weight problem. Yet
the shame of the folds around my waist made it seem like forever.
The pounds had become a colonizing force, taking over what had
been before. The rolls of jelly flesh impregnated my mind with the
belief that what was had always been. And that was not true. It was
a lie.

The lie started when David had insisted I have a beer every
time he had one. He never got fat, and after a year, when I put on
ten pounds, David said, *If you get fat, don't expect me to get it up.* I
looked at him like he was crazy but he scorned me. He said he
would leave if I got fat. We were together for four years, and
throughout that time, David always had to be in control. Even in
bed, he had to have his way. What I put into my mouth wasn't
simply pleasure. I tried to stuff back a question David should have
never made me ask. *If you get fat . . . if you get fat . . .* If what,
David? . . . If I get sick or old, will you still love me?

"I want to make love to you," she said.

Her hand moved up my back, slithering up and over my face,
exploring every inch as if her fingers were sensory transmitters. I
was shy. I had never made love with a woman before. I closed my
eyes and with a sudden sense of relief realized that her mouth on my
thigh felt no different than the lips of a man. The fingers are the
same, they have no gender. It is only the mind and soul that are
different.

Use me, she said. Teach me how to love you. Do you like the
way this feels?

Yes, I said. Your hands feel so right. It has never been like this
before.

Never? She asked.

Never, I replied.

At the point of orgasm, it is not just the two of us. She brings me into myself, and in doing so, I fall into a current of life so full and throbbing I become one with a great expanse of light. I slip into feelings and remembrances of something far greater than I. Instead of feeling jealous, like David did, she is glad that I lose myself in pleasure. *Yes,* she says, *I want you to come. I want you to sing in all your glory.* And saying these words, she strums my body, pushing me beyond until finally I enter layers of myself I had forgotten. I remember the comfort of my red jacket and the loss I suffered when Mother tossed it into the garbage. I see a thick full tree spreading its arms, and the image of the sheltering branches melds into the feeling of warmth suffusing my body. Then floating in a shimmering net of branches, I drift from my body. I feel lighter than air. Before my eyes sparks of light shoot off like beams of light shattering into crystals. I see these fleeting vignettes without feeling the need to share or offer my thoughts, and instead of feeling angry, like David did, she is glad. She does not need explanations. She treasures my ecstasy as if it were her own.

The fingers are the same. It is these details which create the differences. David and almost all my boyfriends before him thought my flights of ecstasy left them alone. Once, as I started to have an orgasm, a boyfriend slapped my face and said, *Stop it, stop it.* I jerked upright in bed. *You were leaving me,* he said. *You were going someplace I couldn't follow.* I couldn't comprehend what he was saying. I was so shocked by the slap, I jumped out of bed and grabbed my clothes. He begged me to stop, to listen to him. To forgive him. I ran out in the rain, but he came after me. I returned to his apartment, but not for long. I could never trust him again. After him came Ying, who returned to China, then David. I asked him once, why do you resent my orgasms, and he said, *It's unfair. You can have one after the other, but all I get is one.*

David, I said, you can hold back until the explosion is a volcano. You know that's possible. But David would get angry at what he called my "wavy gravy" metaphysical ideas. He wanted me to put on black lace and red lipstick, then, kneeling between his legs, look up at him with the adoring lust of porno starlets. Lips wet. Mouth open. David . . . I don't know if it was a gender thing or if it was David, but David had no idea of the sublime pleasure achieved through surrendering. And through that surrender, merging with a beam of light breaking into rainbows. He knew I could have an orgasm without his touching me, but refused to think this possible for him. Ying understood. Ying understood and delighted in giving pleasure. He would hold himself back, not coming for hours. He could have an orgasm without ejaculating. So it was not a male thing. Ying had a wonderful curving cock. David's was penetrating, a blade which had to cut and slice. To push and conquer. As I said, David was a control freak.

She wants to know only this—did you come?

Every man has asked this question, but the difference is she does not ask out of a rhetorical need for reassurance. She asks this knowing her touch reminds me of silk, and instead of feeling afraid of my memories or the rolls of flesh around my body, she embraces them, knowing that the layers can slip away and all that will remain are our hands in one another. Did you come means something different. It means I love you. I want you to drink in pleasure. I want your body to take the moisturizing oils of my saliva and to rain out joy. I want you to cry out, your flesh streaming out joy, your thighs juicing out saliva, come and joy.

It means I lay between your legs and bring you pleasure because the pleasure you feel is my pleasure. I love every inch of you.

Show me, I ask.

"It is like eating a mango. Place your hand around the fruit. Hold it. Slip your hands up my legs, down my belly. Touch the skin. Let your fingers savor the texture of the soft baby skin nestled between my thigh and groin. Press the fruit and feel the flesh at the nipple. Slowly then, slowly unpeel the fruit.

"Use your hands and mouth to explore the regions. Don't be afraid. If you are afraid of a woman's smell or juice, you cannot understand her pleasure. You will never savor the taste of a mango. A mango is delicate. It is rich. It is the taste of a tropical woman in heat. Aroused, her skin ripens and exudes a sweet flavor. Inside is tender, candylike flesh waiting to surrender. If you are squeamish or afraid, you will take the coward's way out and stand at arm's distance, prodding the mango open with a knife. That's easy, but with a knife, you will never understand the full pleasure of a mango slipping down your throat. You will never learn how to milk the mango of its juices. You will stand, at arm's distance, from the true pleasure of pleasing a woman.

"To the connoisseur, to those who love women, each woman is unique. Each woman is unto herself. The Tomkins are larger mangoes. They are best eaten when the ripened flesh is soft to the touch. The flesh can be stringy, with fibrous strands and a large hairy pit. Kents can be eaten hard and green. Their flesh is always yellow, but sweet. Kents are the only ones whose green skin belies their sweet inner flesh. Haden are smaller than Tomkins. They are the best. Their skin is yellowish-red. They fit in the palm of your hand and have a small pit, very little hair. They have the smoothest flesh, with sweet, nonfibrous, silky meat. They can be eaten firm.

"If you reach for the obvious, all you will find is what is obvious. Not the sublime. If your hands know only how to find the obvious—man-sized—you won't know how to use your fingers to hold her lips, or how to cup her mound and rub, bringing the ripe scent from inside the fruit to the surface. Or rousing her body. But you are a woman. You know this by instinct. Do to me what pleases you."

————

I am aware of the smaller lips and vales of her body, of her inner thighs and outer hips. Each breath I take meshes with the rise of her thighs so perfectly synchronized to my tongue licking between her crevices. My mouth surrounds her lips, nibbling and sucking. Every part of my body is made alive by this act of eating. By the perfect rise and fall of my lips against hers. She moans, and her sounds are utterances of my own delight. My tongue strokes her as I use first one finger, then two and three. She moans, *Yes, yes, yes.*

I tell her, "Yes, my darling, come."

Using my mouth, lips and hands, I bring her to a bursting sunrise. Her rays spray out over the terrain, her body subsides. Her body pours out pleasure. "All of this," I murmur, "is my harvest of joy."

Curling my tongue, I partake of her feast, whispering, "Mangoes. You taste of mangoes."

Krista Rising

Julie Shigekuni

The morning I am to leave I awaken at the same moment as my lover Richard. He and I are face to face when we lift our heads from my pillow. As if we'd been dreaming the same dream, we share the same canny frown; thick dewy lines transect our cheeks and the pungency of garlic and red wine lingers in our mouths. We may well be thinking fire, emergency, disaster, if we are thinking at all. For an instant our posture remains frozen, symmetrical as a mirror image that is shattered by my move to turn off the alarm clock.

He doesn't say good morning, or I'll help you pack, or I'll miss you, because to him it isn't a good morning. A blankness settles around his features, shrouding whatever he may feel about my departure. I want to say it's not the same, I'll be back. We'll be honest, faithful, adoring this time, but moments pass and the words do not come. I manage to pack well enough on my own, and as soon as I have finished, he takes my bags downstairs to the front of our building, where we will wait for Isabelle.

It's full-steam summer on the street, but even the heat doesn't slow the pace of traffic. A delivery van is ticketed while its driver escapes the heat in a corner deli; too enervated to negotiate the wire planter, a dog lifts his leg on the sidewalk. A jet passes overhead and I recall a missed flight and how I once spent a morning with the roar of jet engines in my ears watching tearful departures. I waited alone that day, defiant witness to my own leave-taking. Goodbye is something I dread saying. I prefer to say I'm sorry, I love you, I'll miss you, words full of promise, and then to disappear when no one is looking.

Richard has never gotten along with Isabelle. He says he finds her money distasteful, but that's not it—not really. The fact is that she and I became friends at a difficult time in my relationship with Richard, and it's easy to blame her. Even though he and I discussed being separated over the summer and agreed that we needed a break from each other, he acts as if she has come between us. Without a glance her way, he loads my suitcases into the trunk of her car. He is a poet and his final words to me are a quote from Pablo Neruda. "Your duty," he says, "is to leave and return."

He is both dead serious and half-joking. He says, "Think about that."

Goodbye, I wave. "I'll call you soon."

Isabelle and I are headed for her family's summer home in the Berkshires, where she will work on a novel and I on developing my eye. I took up photography last year, after graduating from college and finding myself edgy. I've been told I have talent, but I'm still an amateur. Isabelle is farther along in her career and it's not hard to tell why when you figure that she spends most of the year at vacation homes and spas. I don't think of myself as a greedy person, but certain advantages are not unappealing to me. Isabelle's house is less palatial than I had expected, but staffed in a way I could never have imagined. A uniformed man takes our bags from the trunk and leads the way first to Isabelle's room, which is elegant and spacious, then to mine, which is less elegant and small. It has its own darkroom attached, though, and a bed, a worktable, and a view. I can look out at a plush green valley through one window and a graveyard through the other, or enjoy pale blue walls surrounding me.

Accustomed to a house run by my mother, I find that I have more affinity for the servants and grounds crew than Isabelle's family members, who don't seem to have much to say to me either. At the dinner table, Isabelle's mother asks me polite questions about myself, and then continues on another subject without listening to my answers. Then one night she tells me that her maid is Japanese.

"Really?" I am not quite sure how to respond to this comment.

"I think so. I believe her last name is Kitano. Is that Japanese?"

During my first week, I enjoy the garden, where I spend my time planting herbs, mulching, and chopping firewood while Isabelle writes.

"You're working too hard," Isabelle likes to say. "You look exhausted."

"Not really." I am tired, but I don't mind the work. My day is filled with the scent of lilacs and pine. I don't think about Richard; often I don't think about anything.

Late in the afternoon of my second week, I go to the kitchen for my routine lemonade only to find the cook gone (her six-year-old son was hit by a car), and dinner an hour behind schedule. And there, alone, is Krista. I identify her vaguely as the woman Isabelle's mother had mentioned at dinner, but there is something else I respond to—something about her presence that resonates like a familiar song humming in my head. Her dark hair falls across her face and her skin is pale and flawless. Even bent over the counter she stands tall and beautiful as a statue. Her deep voice is both serious and playful when she tells me that she is just out of school. I ask which one, what she studied, and if she went straight through.

Vassar, she says. Sculpture. And yes. Together we pore over recipe books, dog-earing pages until we decide on pizza.

My third crust is a major success—perfectly round, slightly wedged at the edges. For a moment I am so happy I imagine I can go on this way forever, performing simple tasks with Krista, without a care in the world. We work steadily until she is rolling out the last crust. Her palms leave fissures in the soft yeasty dough and she catches me eyeing them.

"Do you read palms?" she asks.

"Sort of," I tell her.

Eyes gleaming, face alight, she holds hers out. "What do you see?"

They are large, fleshy, and white as a Noh mask. I take the right and then the left to examine them. What shocks me is how similar our lines are—I am reading her like I'd read myself. I am about to say hasty, honest, gentle, but I realize the ingenuousness of these observations.

"What?" she demands. "You're not telling me what you know."

I am grinning, teasing her for wanting me to tell her about her life. It's funny how people act when they think you might know something about them that they don't understand about themselves. That's why a good palmist assesses the entire person—bags under the eyes, strain in the voice, the shape and color of the skin, its texture, touch.

"It's obvious," I tell her.

"Obvious to you," she says.

"I'd prefer it if you'd tell me," I say.

Her studio, just down the path from the main house, is filled with sensuous shapes. Clay and wax sculpture line her worktable and an unfinished plaster work hangs from a hook in the ceiling. It's huge, so unabashedly there, in the middle of her room. I wonder if she tried to hide it in a closet, or cover it with a sheet before I arrived. If I were she, that is what I would have done. But we are so different, she and I. She seems not to care what people think, and I admire her for this.

On three sides of her studio are windows. I make a circle, glancing out into the night and then stopping at the far wall to admire a row of pastel drawings. The colors are vibrant, and the detail intricate, revealing something about her that her sculpture did not. My imagination is triggered by bold lines straining to solidify, and then running off scared.

"It's difficult for me to fall in love," she says.

"Really?" I say. "It's difficult for me to stay in love."

She looks at me as if I've caused her to have an epiphany, as if it were I and not she who out of the blue said, It's difficult for me to fall in love.

"My lover, Louise," she begins. "She called me on New Year's Eve to tell me she was seeing someone else. She wouldn't tell me who. She didn't want to talk about it. I tried calling her back for the next four days, got her machine. Then finally she called me and said, 'Now we can talk about Katie' . . . Or Patsy, whomever."

She is telling me a story in which New Year's Eve, another woman, four days, all have meaning. But her face says that she doesn't understand, that she doesn't want to know. What intrigues me is the emotion attached to her words. Her expression, her body, her movement all betray her. If I can't figure out why she is telling me this story, or where exactly her words are coming from, it's because I am distracted by what I see. She is so open, so gentle. I wonder how much it matters to her that I am in her room, watching her.

"Do you know what I mean?" she asks.

"Yes," I say, although I am no longer listening to her words. "Sometimes you just don't know."

"There's something I want to show you," I tell her.

I run down the stairs that lead out of her studio. I run blindly into the night not knowing what I want her to see but needing to escape the pressure that has been building in my head. Back in my room, my desktop is piled with portraits. They are nudes, women, some of my best work yet. The collection is entitled "Passion." I am not in the habit of showing my work, but I select samples to show Krista, gathering them like the curtain I want to lift from her eyelids.

I drop the stack of photographs into her lap. While she shuffles through them I rethink what she has told me. "It's not always possible to know what's right," I tell her. "You act on what you believe until what you believe changes. Sometimes overnight."

Not more than an hour ago, she had said, "You just don't know." Now she says, "You know what is right. You know what feels right."

I rock back and forth, watching her take in my work until she looks up, and for a moment her eyes hold mine.

"I like this one," she says, holding up a self-portrait of me. I am flopped over the back of a chair, my dark eyes intense from restless sleep. Early morning light softens my black hair, enveloping my head with a bluish hue. I knew I had to take that photograph when I awoke. I looked into the mirror before rinsing my face and what I saw astonished me. "You look like someone I know," she says, looking from the photograph to me and back to the photograph. And when she looks at me again I wonder if she can see the sweat beaded on my forehead, or feel the quickening of my heartbeat.

Needing to fill the space between us with words, I tell her

something Isabelle once told me, something I don't really believe. "Isabelle says, 'At least once in our lives we appear to ourselves who we are.' "

"I know," she says excitedly, not listening, "you look like me. Don't you think? A little?" She turns her face to the side, shining a half-grin my way, and holds her hair back, exposing a delicate ear.

"Not at all," I say giddily, thinking *you are so beautiful.* And I am so flattered I can barely sit still.

"Uh-huh," she insists, not taking her eyes from me.

She produces a sketchbook that looks like one I have kept. Inside is a drawing that reminds me of a room I once lived in. "This looks like my room," I say.

"That's my room." She laughs.

"How long have you lived here?" I ask.

"I moved from Poughkeepsie a month ago."

I am piecing together a puzzle—her life in the room with the lover who broke her heart, her move from Poughkeepsie a month ago. She was in love. No, she is still in love with the woman who broke her heart. She is telling me how one person can be your whole life, and her heart is so present that I can hear it beating, irregularly, straining to rectify itself. I can see the muscles in her cheeks flex in and out. I am consumed by a passion that is not my own when a face I haven't seen in two years appears like an apparition before my eyes. It is an image lost, like the face it belonged to, long after the love affair had ended—a snapshot of Kenji, and of my room where I patiently awaited his visits. Long after the relationship ended, I made sure that his face was the last image I saw before closing my eyes at night. For a whole year, I tucked a photograph of him beneath my pillow, waiting for my lover to return. Now, if only for a moment, I reclaim the lost image. Reaching across the table, I place Krista's palm face up in my lap.

"Tell me. What do you see?"

"A love affair."

"You look like someone I know," I tell her.

"Really?" She blushes.

"No, really," I tell her. "I once dated a man named Kenji Miyata and you have eyes like his."

"Kenji Miyata?" She crosses her legs and looks away.

"Um-hmmm," I tell her. "I loved his eyes."

"Oh?" And her gaze returns to me.

"I would have married him, I loved him so much. But it didn't work out." In my head I can still hear Richard narrating his dream to me over the phone while Kenji waits for me in my bed.

"Why?"

"Long story," I tell her, though this is a lie. I couldn't let go of Richard; end of story. *"Love is so short, forgetting is so long."*

"Isn't that Neruda?"

"Yes."

Didn't Kenji say *I'll call you?* And I waited, knowing he never would. I thought to call him, but I never did. I went back to Richard instead. Krista's presence confronts me with what I no longer believe because Kenji's leaving me that night was not the end of the world, and I am back with Richard. I've heard that in order for love to last both partners must love the same way. To me, love is a fantasy tucked beneath the eyelids.

Krista sits rosy-cheeked in front of me, her hand balanced on my lap, and I steer the conversation away from love because she is scaring me. It is as if her eyes are seeing me for the first time. I am wondering what it would be like to love her.

"Do you want to go to sleep?" I ask. "Shall I leave?

"No," she says. "Actually, I don't. I had a horrible nightmare last night and now I'm scared to go to sleep."

"What was it about?"

"I dreamèd I'd been shot.

"Right here," she says, covering her abdomen with both hands. "When I woke up I was in so much pain I couldn't even move my head out from under the blankets. I was sure someone was going to break into my studio and kill me."

"You don't have to worry about that," I say.

"I know," she says. "But have you ever had a dream that seemed so real that even when you wake up you're still having it?"

"Sometimes," I tell her.

"I felt so vulnerable," she says, "like a long needle was piercing my stomach."

I nod only because I cannot speak. I have a fierce desire to protect her, or maybe I want to wrap my arms around her and cry. Instead, I reach for the camera lying in front of me on her table. Looping the shoulder strap around my neck, I examine the body. Krista says nothing, but when I point the viewfinder at her she turns away. I wait, and the instant she turns toward me I shoot. She is lovely, modest, unpretentious.

When I ask Krista to tell me about her work she says, "I clear my mind, and I create, and I do the best I can. I work from the unconscious." The next time someone asks what I do I will say to them what she has said to me. But for now I will take her words with me as I leave to practice them. "Good night," I say.

"Already?" She looks hurt, dejected.

"Yes." I'm afraid if I stay another minute, I might not want to leave.

"Good night."

On the stairs that lead down from the studio I lose my balance. I am hanging from the banister by one arm when I hear Krista call, "Don't go!"

"What?"

"Please stay."

She tells me again, "I had the worst nightmare last night. When I woke up I ached for someone to hold. I just wanted to hold someone, to feel someone next to me." She yawns and stretches out her arms, the same strong arms that carried a bowl of pizza dough across the kitchen floor.

The air is tense with her words, but I do not respond. Where do we begin, now that we have begun? I tell her that if she has nightmares she can come knock on my door.

She tells me not to fall down the stairs.

When I left Richard he told me my duty was to leave and return. He said, "Think about that."

I waved goodbye. I told him I'd call soon, and back in my room I pick up the telephone. I am dialing home when I hear footsteps outside the door, and I hang up.

Although I see her every morning at breakfast, Isabelle looks surprised to see me the next day. "I came by your room last night and you weren't there," she says.

"I know," I tell her. "I was visiting with Krista."

"What's she like?"

"I like her."

"I do too."

"What?" I tell myself, You are tired, you are not thinking clearly.

Krista doesn't talk to me that day, or the next. It seems that every time she is near, I am crouched over a bag of fertilizer or pulling weeds. I imagine myself picking up a hoe and shaking it at her. What am I to do?

And then I awaken early one morning from a nightmare. The sun is just rising, but I am wide awake. I approach Krista's room from the backwoods, clearing a path as I go. I am thinking of a line from Antonio Machado, one of Richard's favorite poets, and I am laughing. There is no road, I tell myself. The road is made by walking. I make a half-circle around Krista's studio, snapping shots of the door, the stairway, a mass of footprints leading every which way in the dirt, but there is something more I want, another reason I am here this early. With the camera strapped around my neck, I find myself doing something I haven't done since I was a child. An old fruit tree stands not far off the path, and I straddle its rough bark and hoist myself up until I am seated in its dense branches, a bit scraped up, but comfortable. From high up in the tree I see Krista. She is naked, limbs wrapped in a fetal position, the way I imagined she'd sleep. I take a few shots and wait, prepared with my zoom lens for the first signs of movement.

I develop the film in my darkroom, watching as colors bend under ripples of wash water. Rows of prints hang on the line to dry, and I assess each one in the dim red light. Leaves blur the edges, beyond them her windowpane. And in the center of each frame is Krista rising, magnificent, and her work, unsteady but bold, the way it has always appeared to me. I am transfixed, unable to believe what I see. I collect a few photographs and run to Isabelle's room, wet images flapping in my arms.

Isabelle takes the bundle from my outstretched arms, her blue eyes sparkling. Her hands tremble as she spreads the prints across her worktable. She examines them with reverence, letting me know that she sees what I see. It does not occur to her to ask why I've done this.

"Am I on to something?" I ask.

"Yes," she says. "These are really beautiful."

"I want to include them in my collection," I tell her.

Isabelle lights a cigarette. I watch her eyes wander from the prints to her computer screen. "The first task of an artist," she says, "is knowing what to leave in your life, and what to put into your work."

I don't know why she says this or what her words imply where I am concerned, but I figure that's because I am so confused. I have shown Isabelle my work because I need her to approve of me and Krista. I could use some help to steady my desire, but help does not come. That night I place the photographs in an envelope which I slide beneath Krista's door; in the morning I am awakened by a muffled knocking and a whisper calling my name. "Illysa, Ill-y-sssssa."

"Yes," I say, half-asleep. "What?"

For a moment there is no answer. And then, "Phone call for you."

"How the hell are you?" Richard greets me.

"Fine," I tell him dreamily. "It's good to hear your voice."

"Why haven't you called?"

"I've tried to call," I lie. "You're never home."

He lets this one pass, or maybe he hasn't been home. "It's good to hear your voice too."

"I'm covered from head to toe with bug bites," I tell him.

"Are you sure that's all it is?" he asks.

"No," I tell him, my eyes still closed. "I just woke up."

On the other end of the wire a siren is sounding, jarring me back to the city when all I have heard for weeks is the breeze, the birds, the intense quiet of country nights.

"Are you there, Illysa?"

"I'm here."

"Something's wrong."

I tell him I'm sorry, nothing's wrong. I press my eyelids shut until I see stars, white with yellow casings, and a streak of blue that flashes like lightning through a pitch-black sky. "I miss you," I say, clutching the receiver to my ear.

"I miss you too," he whispers, and I believe with a trembling hand that I can feel the power time has to bind two lives, and the force of our history tugs at me.

"Do you remember the night we drove out to the Sound and watched for shooting stars?"

"Uh-huh," he says. "It was a great night."

"It was," I say. "I made a wish for us to last that night."

"I hope your wish comes true," he tells me.

I open my eyes to the brightness of the morning and all around the room shadows are dancing in the breeze. "Goodbye," I whisper. "I'll be home soon."

Having no idea how to proceed on my own, I have become superstitious, convinced that the true meaning behind Isabelle's comments about art and Richard's phone call is that I should forget about Krista: they are the clearest signs I have. And so I believe that in the passing of the longest day of the year, in the withering of the lilacs and the appearance of deep red, wild roses, and in the air hanging thick with anticipation of fall, I can see the movement of time, and I pray it will bloom in my head with a wild forgetfulness.

Practically every afternoon a thunderstorm passes, ridding the air of bugs and heat in its wake. Then, with my routine over and a shower between me and the day, I take my camera from its shelf and head back to the garden to photograph my vegetables. Isabelle says she will use her connections to get my work into a local gallery. She says the photographs tell a story of New England in the summer, but that is not my intention. I take the photos because I am proud of my hard work. My tomatoes are ripe and red and firm, I

have never seen squash the size and shapes and textures of the ones
I've grown, and maybe when I am finished I will write a cookbook
because I have discovered more recipes for summer vegetables than
I ever thought possible. I tell myself it is enough to stir sauces with
Krista, to shred the lettuce she has washed and I have grown, to
smell traces of paint and bits of plaster that stick to her clothing
and make me dizzy when I stand next to her. It is the paint, the
plaster, the hard work, I tell myself. I have Richard and she has
someone else: not me.

The city can inure a person to noise, but in the country I am aware
of every sound. One night, cicadas warming up like streetlights, I
hear footfalls up and down the hall outside my room. There is a
knock at my door and I open it to find her there. Her eyes dart past
me, into my room, and her hair is wet and tangled. "Are you busy?"
she wants to know.

"No," I tell her. "Come in."

She surveys my worktable, where I have been arranging a col-
lage of magazines clippings and cut photographs; then she seats
herself on my unmade bed with her arms stretched out behind her.
"I'm sorry it's so late," she says. "If you were working I could
leave." She says *I can leave,* but the way she sits back on my bed-
sheets informs me of her desire to stay for a while.

"I saw Louise," she says, and I know at once that it could not be
good.

"Here?" I ask, imagining Krista's studio with its big windows,
full of her artwork.

"Yes," she says. "She came to tell me that she wants me
back."

I sit with this information for a minute, not knowing what to
say. "And you?"

"I thought that's what I wanted. I was so lost when I came
here, and now I don't know."

I look through her web of black hair into her eyes and it is as if I am hearing myself speak. I hear only one voice and I think it must be Krista's, except the words are ones I have spoken before. What is her? What is me? I ask, but I do not need to ask what I want.

"Come here." She arches back her neck, and I go to her. I sit beside her on my bed, close enough that our thighs are almost touching, and at first when her lips brush against mine I cannot be sure that it is really her I am feeling. I reach for her face because I want to feel her, but she takes my hand in hers and holds it still in her lap so that only our mouths are moving, until I cannot be sure where she begins and I end.

"I know that you have someone else, and maybe I do too, but I want to make love to you," she whispers, inches from my face. *Isn't that what we have been doing?* I want to ask, but I say nothing because kissing her has left me unsteady and scared. In my bed, she spoons my body, covering my back with her breasts, her stomach against my buttocks, our legs entwined. I fall asleep to the sound of her breath in my ear; I fall asleep, believing I cannot fall asleep at all.

Gloriously

KITTY TSUI

first night of the new year.
we are guests for the night.
bedding together,
down bags on tatami
in a meditation room
warmed by a blazing woodstove.

moonlight through
rice paper shutters
falls on our bodies
as we talk and touch
and taste each other
for the first time.

mouth on mouth, thigh
on thigh, hand on breast,
my fingers circling
your nipple, a long moan.
i take you in my mouth,
a sharp intake of breath.

shoulder to thigh
i push my tongue
inside your depths,
hands on your ass,
fingers down your crack
and feel your passion rise.

i sink my teeth
into bicep muscle,
feel your wetness,
stroke your lips,
tongue soft folds, then
part and penetrate you.

tongue inside mouth,
hand on breast,
fingers circling clitoris.
how do you like to come? i ask.
you reply simply:
gloriously.

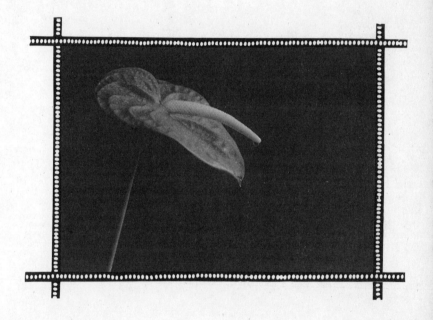

The Size of It

IV

The Size of It

TIMOTHY LIU

I knew the length of an average penis
    was five to seven inches, a fact
I learned upstairs in the stacks marked 610
    or HQ, not down in the basement
where I knelt behind a toilet stall, waiting
    for eight and a half inches or more
to fill my mouth with a deeper truth. The heart
    grows smaller, like a cut rose drying
in the sun. Back then I was only fourteen,
    with four and three-quarters inches
at full erection. I began equating
    Asian with inadequate, unable
to compete with others in the locker room
    after an icy swim (a shriveled
bud between my fingers as I tried to shake
    some semblance of life back into it).
Three times a day, I jacked off faithfully, yet
    nothing would enlarge my future, not
ads for vacuum pumps, nor ancient herbs. Other
    men had to compensate, one billion

Chinese measured against what? Some said my cock
    had a classical shape, and I longed
for the ruins of Greece. Others took it up
    the ass, reassuring in their way,
yet nothing helped me much on my knees at night
    praying one more inch would make me whole.

Asian Penis:

The Long and Short of It

L. T. Goto

*P*oor, poor Asian males. We sure are taking a beating these days, aren't we? If it's not our height, it's our lack of might. We aren't handsome enough, loud enough, considerate enough, paternal enough, aggressive enough, masculine enough, horny enough—maybe not that last one. And, according to popular myth, Asian men have smaller penises!

Smaller penises! Doesn't the world know that we have enough to worry about other than the size of our "wee-wees"? It's bad enough that people think we're overcompensating for our inadequacies by setting outrageous goals in education and profession without having to worry about being smaller. Smaller than what? Or who? Well, that all depends on what standard of measurement you use.

"The Dirty 230"

Back in college, I took a class called Sexual Psychology 230, otherwise known as "Dirty 230." My professor said the average penis size is five and a half inches, when erect. When flaccid or limp, the average size is about two and a half inches.

Dr. Sooth, *Gentlemen's Quarterly*'s "Dear Abby" of the sexually sublime, wrote, ". . . the average erect penis measures somewhere between five and seven inches." Let's pick an arbitrary average then. How about six inches? If the average guy is six inches, then, by the law of averages, most of the world's men lie, er, uh, stand around that number.

That also means that a few men are below six inches long. They are the small fry, shrimp chip, pinky—the tiny tots of this world. Understand that to be labeled as such, you really have to be "tiny tot" size. That means in the neighborhood of about three and a half inches long, give or take about an inch.

Then you have the men who are above the average. They are the Long Dong Silvers, the Wun Hung Los, the Ball Park Franks of this world. They are the X-rated movie actors whose prerequisite for a lead role is a tree trunk size, flesh monster that measures bigger than eight inches. They are the ones that make the *Playgirl* centerfolds and the *Hustler* pictorials. They are the ones who strut around the locker room without a towel wrapped around their waist after they've showered.

So what about this Asian penis thing anyway? Is it average, is it a tiny tot or is it Wun Hung Lo?

Male Anatomy 101

Perhaps the course we really should be addressing is Philosophy 101, to find out why men lie or exaggerate about their male anatomy.

One answer is because they can.

Women have a much harder time lying or exaggerating about their breast size, save for surgical implants or the use of a push-up bra. Women wear their "God-given glory" for all the world to see.

Men keep theirs bunched up in an old pair of Jockey underwear for safekeeping. The old saying "Don't judge a book by its cover" wears true in this area. Despite a man's height or build, women just don't know what they're getting into until the heat of passion compels them into finding out.

While researching this subject, a woman asked why men feel it so important to worry about the size of their penis. The average male chauvinist pig probably would have written her question off as rhetorical and moved on. I mean, come on! Isn't everyone concerned about the penis? Doesn't the world revolve around the male's sexual anatomy?

Well, probably not. But I can remember the time a young boy who lived near the city of Seattle, Washington, was kidnaped, molested and sexually mutilated by this crazy pedophile. A man in his late twenties took this young boy, mutilated his penis and left it in a rather unusable condition. Understandably, there was a tremendous outcry of anger and attention surrounding this little boy's mutilated penis by the public and media in Seattle. Then, when the national media became involved, further outcry and support arose from all over the world. Several trust funds were established for this boy, thinking: "Well, he has a screwed-up penis. So, will a few hundred thousand dollars make it better?"

All that attention over a little boy's mutilated penis—I thought, "Wow, I've seen it all."

Then came John and Lorena Bobbitt.

Instantly, a story with very little worldly importance caused reverberations far and wide. Almost every country in the world covered the story.

All this attention over a man's severed penis. A severed penis that was later resewn on and, through some weird kind of physical therapy, made to work again.

Yes, for the second time in my life, the world revolved around the penis. So—to the woman who asked in vain, "Why are men so concerned about the size of their penis?" I answer, "Why aren't you?"

Frankly, I could give a damn too. But manhood is manhood, and when the penis is in question, so too is the manhood.

The Men's Institute

In 1993, a Beverly Hills urologist by the name of Dr. Melvyn Rosenstein combined his expertise in urology with a marketing expert named Ed Tilden. They developed the Men's Institute and made penile enlargement and lengthening surgery as accessible as, well, getting your hair trimmed.

The Institute reportedly takes more than two thousand calls a day at their twenty-six sales offices, resulting in more than 150 operations a month. They spend $200,000 per month on newspaper advertising and are starting to take calls from all over the world.

Reportedly, the operation is only partially effective. Penile enlargements are the most effective since body fat is transferred to the shaft of the penis. (The glans or head cannot be thickened.) This process can add as much as an inch to the girth or circumference of the penis. However, the results can be temporary, since the body fat can be reabsorbed.

As far as the lengthening process is concerned, that's a little trickier and, at this point in time, a little experimental.

Apparently, about one third of the penis is in the body. The surgery involves cutting an incision at the base of the penis, exposing its root. The ligaments that suspend the penis at an upright angle are snipped, and the root of the penis is literally pushed out from inside the pelvis. The pubic area is then restitched to prevent retraction.

The actual gain in length is nominal (about an inch) during an erection, but most noticeable (by up to three inches) during the flaccid state. This increase during the flaccid state is obviously of no use during sexual intercourse. But depending on how much a man's penis retracts, the operation reportedly can give a man a great "psychological boost," especially in public situations such as the locker room.

Since 1991, Dr. Rosenstein has performed about fifteen hundred operations on over nine hundred men at a package price of almost $6000. Yes, penile surgery is big business.

Whether or not Asians tend to invest in this type of surgery more often than others is a well-kept secret that the Men's Institute's marketing department wouldn't divulge.

Not to worry, though. The shortest distance between two points is a straight line, and the best way to get data is to ask men and women directly.

"Going to the Source"

A Japanese-American female, early twenties, said, "Okay, let me think about this. I have to think how long six inches is. Well, I guess the Asian men I've been with were average. Yeah, they were about average."

A Vietnamese-American in his early twenties admitted he was "below" the average of six inches. Asked if he was ever concerned about the length of his penis, he simply answered, "No."

A Chinese-American woman named Marilyn said, "I guess I've been pretty lucky. Every single guy has been at least six inches. One was eight inches, another was seven inches. They were mostly Chinese men."

"Asian penises are not big," said Donna, a Columbian-American who has had several Asian boyfriends. "I guess that's always why I liked Asian men. I strongly believe that that's because of their bodies. Their bodies are not big."

I told her the average size for all males is about six inches. She replied, "Yeah. They are average."

Her friend, a Chinese-American, said she dated one Asian male whose penis was "about six and a half inches, but it was big in circumference." She added, "Not all Asian men are going to have smaller penises in the same way that not all Black men have huge penises."

I even found one Asian male, a Japanese-American, early thirties, who said he has a seven-inch penis. He even offered to show it to me, to which I immediately declined. He boasted that "girls would point at me," and admitted, "It was a pretty big ego boost!"

I assumed that the women's accounts of penis size to be more reliable than the men's. However, while conducting my research, a gay Caucasian who prefers Asian men volunteered, "I would say that from a purely statistical point of view, [the myth of the Asian penis being smaller] is basically true . . . However, the smallest I've experienced was on a Caucasian." He added, "What I've found among Asian men is the absence of really 'big ones.' But if you were to put White men and Asian men on two separate bell curves, there would be a lot of overlap."

A Korean-American man recalled a conversation with his Caucasian girlfriend. They had just finished making love when she brought up the subject. "She said she had heard about the size myth, and she was initially concerned," he said. "It was something that was in the back of her mind, before we ever made love. But after making love, she found out it wasn't a problem, that [the myth] wasn't true."

He said he was always a little uncomfortable with the subject of penis size because all of his Caucasian friends joked about "how little Asian men's penises must be . . . After a while, it plays on your psyche."

One of the last women I asked said the Japanese man she dated was "average," then added, "I can't believe you're asking these questions!"

To be honest, I can't believe I'm asking people these questions either. Women probably think it's some sort of pickup line. Men? Well, I'm sure they understand that this is strictly research. Remember, the world revolves around the penis, and men understand this.

Does Size Matter?

Back at the college where I took the "Dirty 230," I was one of about two hundred Asians on campus. I will never forget the experience of being asked daily, "Do you eat rice? Do you use chopsticks?" But these questions were nothing compared to the graphically sexual ones I heard about Asian women.

"I heard that Asian women are 'tighter,'" several acquaintances would say in reference to the vagina. Another reference never ceased to amaze me: "I heard that Asian women's 'slits' are horizontal instead of vertical so that it would get tighter as they spread their legs."

You would be seriously amazed by all the questions I have heard about Asian women's genitalia. But let's get back to this Asian penis thing.

The woman who asked why men are so concerned about size also said, "Even though women say 'size doesn't matter,' it really does . . . Women are just too kind to shatter men's egos with a simple statement about something so sensitive to men."

So what size is the right size?

Donna said she dated a Columbian man whose penis was so big that it hurt. "He was someone I could've married but I wouldn't. One reason was because [his penis] was too big. My friends said, 'Oh, you'll get used to it.' But I never did. I couldn't stand it!"

The woman I refer to as Marilyn admitted she doesn't particularly like sex with a man much bigger than six inches. "With someone that huge, it really hurts," she said. "I don't ever want something that big inside me again."

The Unbearable Lightness of Being Average

One of the females I interviewed was curious as to what the consensus was on Asian penis size. I told her that the results were about average. Some bigger, some smaller, mostly average though.

She was surprised to hear "some bigger." I was talking to her on the phone, but I could just imagine her eyes growing wider with amazement. Having heard the myth of the small Asian penis, she was surprised to hear that Asian men were about average.

Being an Asian male myself, I never expected to find results that were smaller than average, nor did I expect to find results that were bigger than average. I just found what I found: Asian penises are about average in length when erect.

There is a trick to being objective: don't look for certain results. If a non-Asian male or female had attempted this story, the results may have been different. People, in general, tend to "find" the results that they expect. It's the self-fulfilling prophecy at work. Perhaps if I had searched long and hard, I may have come up with more men who were smaller than average.

My favorite interviewee, Marilyn, made an interesting point about penis size, on an individual basis. She said, "There is an erection—and then, when he's really turned on, there is an *erection!*"

Well put, Marilyn.

from

Re-Placing Angels

ALLAN DESOUZA

Luke's father was afraid of dirt.

Dirt. Contamination corruption decay defilement excrement filth impurity ordure pollution putrefaction putrescence soilure sordidness squalor suppuration tainture uncleanness.

Dirt. Shit spit piss cum blood.
Shit spit piss cum bleed.

Dirt was his consuming obsession and lifelong torment.

A misplaced torment, a displaced obsession. Dislocated fears: his desires, his brown body, his capacity to love. He was afraid of who and what he was. Fears barely hidden behind veneers of discipline, propriety, routine.

Luke had once hated him, but with time, he also learned an all-forgiving compassion. His father did not know how to live in this new world which treated him as less than human and not nearly as well as an animal. He was fond of saying, and they laughed each time they heard it, that the English cared more for their dogs than for their children. "And they care even less for the coloreds." Luke grew up on tales of untrustworthy whites, of how they would smile to his face and plunge the dagger in his back the moment he turned. And yet he was also taught to seek their approval and their company.

A primer for Luke had been the time his father invited his boss for dinner. For three days beforehand his mother was in the kitchen trying to surpass her previous culinary wonders. On the evening of the man's arrival, Luke had to put on his Sunday outfit—white nylon shirt, charcoal Stayprest trousers and black Tuf shoes. He was spared a tie. The family kowtowed to the man's every whim, laughed at his inane attempts at humor, kept his glass filled, nodded sagely at his solutions to world problems, kept his plate filled, ignored his stupidity and overwhelming ignorance. They made him feel like a great emperor who honors the home of a lowly servant, an illustrious traveler sampling the delights of an exotic, gracious eastern hospitality.

Until he left. Then Luke's mother put on the kettle for a pot of tea, provided Luke with a glass of milk and sat with the rest of the family around the dining table making jokes about the fat white slug who'd come to dinner. As much as Luke's parents attempted to teach him the values of assimilation, of working hard, of obeying the masters' law and the masters themselves in whatever manifestation they appeared, by their own behavior they instilled in Luke a mocking defiance: to hold in disdain this new world and its pale people.

Luke watched his parents being stripped of the humanity they once proudly wore. Leaving naked, frightened creatures, their vulnerability a torment for Luke to behold. At the time, it was an anguish he never understood, but accepted as a routine of life.

———

On weekends Luke's father took a nap for an hour after lunch because, as he unfailingly insisted to ears which had long since ceased to listen, "that is what babies do, and they must know since they do what is natural." If the weather was warm, he read the papers in the garden for a further hour, otherwise he sat in the front room trying to listen to classical music. It was a torture for him, but he believed that to be cultured one had to appreciate such things. Luke admired him for trying.

On Sunday afternoons, after his two hours of digestion time, he would traipse upstairs to the bathroom for his weekly bath. Turning the lime-encrusted hot tap full on, he would return downstairs while the water tank disgorged a spluttering trickle.

All this Luke observed, or rather listened to, sitting on the floor of his room, his ear pressed against the door. He knew every sound in the house, recognized every footstep. He could distinguish the rattle of the hot tap from the rumble of the cold, the squeak of the third step from the bottom from the squeal of the fifth step from the top. He could tell who was where and what they were doing, all from listening at the door or lying on the bare floor of his room, casting his senses like a radar scan across the house.

When his father reached downstairs, that was Luke's cue to crawl into the clothes-airing cupboard on the upstairs landing, shut the door behind him and climb up into the narrow space above the top shelf where a metal grille overlooked the bathroom.

Judging by the deepening sound of the splashing water when the bath was nearly filled, his father would return. Lock the door behind him, test the handle to make doubly sure: disrobe. From his vantage point far above his father's head, Luke could watch the whole sordid scene, his vision marred only by the rising steam.

His father hung his toweling robe on the hook behind the door and meticulously folded his shirt, trousers, underpants and socks. He never hurried, as if the completed ritual were timed to the last second. Standing naked in front of the mirror, he slowly turned around and bent forward, presenting his fleshy buttocks to the mirror. Firmly gripping each haunch, he pulled the cheeks apart, at the same time craning his head round to see in the mirror the reflection of what lay between.

Luke never had the unfettered pleasure of sharing baths with his father, of his expansive body as a visual and tactile part of his developing childhood. Finally, when he did see his father's nakedness, not through a casual familiarity with flesh but through guilty voyeurism, it was too frightening an event. His substance—corporeal and symbolic—was too big, too alien from Luke's own.

The once lithe body now mellowed into heavy flab, every ounce of flesh weighted down, dragged toward the earth. The thick forests of black hair spread from his chest onto his shoulders, arms and back, and down to join the knot of darkness at his groin. His penis, to Luke's ten-year-old eyes, a monstrous brown chorizo ending in a tumescent purple-red bulb; his balls, a swollen sac, puffed out from beneath the black thatch.

He spread a towel on the floor and knelt onto it, his knees spread wide. Opening a bottle of baby oil, he poured a glistening pool into the cupped palm of his right hand. Leaning forward onto his elbows and raising his haunches, he dipped the first two fingers of his left hand into the liquid and rubbed them into his anus. Inserted the fingers, first one, then the other, as far as they could go, teasing them round, creating a slippery entrance into his body. With his right hand he massaged the excess oil onto his steadily rising shaft. It was an animal, with its own momentum, its own tropism. The neckskin rolling back to reveal the helmeted head.

What was going through his mind as he oiled a brush handle and inserted it, inch by inch, into his waiting hole? What did he fantasize about as he knelt there, gripping the brush with his heels and rocking back and forth onto it. His sphincter emitting a whispered, sucking sound each time he reached his apex and relaxed to push back down onto the brush. By this time, his member was a grossly swollen limb compared with the finger length of Luke's own penis.

Luke watched dry-mouthed, barely able to contain his feelings of shock, fear, disgust . . . and arousal. He is able to name them now, but at the time, his head was aswirl with unknown emotions, his body riven by fearsome passions.

The brush handle was fully inserted into his father, the brush hairs protruding like a foxtail: an electrocuted fox, its tail rigidly on end. A vision appeared in Luke's head of the cartoon roadrunner-chasing coyote, frazzled by one of its own acme gadgets. It wasn't such an incongruent idea: the scene below Luke was equally bizarre, infinitely more bestial.

His father's breathing quickened. Beads of moisture erupted from his skin, a combination of steam from the still-running bath and the sweat from his own exertions. Half-strangled grunts, birthed deep in his belly, escaped through his lips. He began to swivel his hips, grinding the brush handle deep within him. One hand cupped his balls, the other was jerking the foreskin backward and forward over his purple glans. Faster and faster moved his hand in a painful blur. His whole body began to shudder. Luke wanted to rush out, call his mother, call an ambulance—Father's gone into a fit!—but he remained rooted. He watched as his father's penis jerked, and spat out globs of thick white . . . Thick white what? Thoughts and visions were fighting in Luke's head: questions, snippets of information and misinformation garnered in the school playground, glimpses of television before he was sent out of the room, returning to find the channel changed.

It became as much a habit for Luke as it was for his father, but after a few weeks of spying the blood-tingling excitement began to lose its heat. Each time, his father shrank a little more; each time, Luke grew in stature, unaware that he also increased his burden of shame. Watched from above, his father shriveled in Luke's estimation, an increasingly pathetic man. It was a forced independence; Luke wasn't yet ready to abandon him, to outgrow him. His father's diminishment, and Luke's expansion, were too sudden, too early in his climb toward maturity. Luke had nowhere to go, no other models to follow. No means of absolving the sin of transgression. His father molded him in his own image, or rather, by intruding on him, Luke transposed into himself his father's shame, his guilty desires.

In the early mornings Luke waited in the toilet, ready for his father to perform his ablutions. His father entered, untied the pajama cord around his waist and let the pants drop to his ankles. Luke knelt behind him, arms encircling the naked thighs, pressing his nose into the furry darkness between his father's sweat-glistening buttocks, delirious in the sanctification of his intestinal perfume. As his father bent forward, Luke clamped his mouth onto the ring of puckered muscle, teasing open the cavernous hole with his tongue. Squatting down, his father released a torrent of thick manna onto Luke's face and with his heaving, rotating haunches rubbed its heat into the pubescent skin. After his benediction Luke licked him clean. His father then went about the rest of his morning activities, got dressed in his usual immaculate manner and went to work as if nothing unusual had taken place. The Immaculate Deception.

Luke awoke from these nights of passionate debasement appalled by the wickedness into which he had drawn his father. That they were only dreams further inflamed the shame and terror he felt in his father's presence. Had these events actually taken place, Luke was sure that the intimacy in them would have created at least a symbiotic bond between his father and himself. A shared degradation.

———

Luke had learned to mimic every action and nuance of his father's solitary pleasure. As he watched his father's face, the pupils moving behind the closed lids, the teeth biting into the lower lip, the slight wince as the brush handle entered, Luke already knew from his own body each sensation that enflamed his father's flesh. He had learned to stroke the shaft to and beyond the aching stiffness, to tease the bulb toward a thunderous climax and, at the last moment, halt it by circling his fingers tightly behind the head. Then beginning again, seducing himself toward ecstasy.

After the initial thrills of his voyeurism had subsided into familiarity, Luke began to tire of his father's limited and unvarying routine. Its monotonous precision felt alien and incomprehensible and, despite the pleasure he had learned to give and receive from his own body, it began to profoundly depress him.

He was unable to fuse the double-edged image of his father; two existences, two forces precariously separated by the one-inch thickness of the bathroom door. The two-faced masquerades of the man, public and private, paragon and nemesis, inseminator and penetrated, father and lover, pounded Luke's thoughts with their seeming irreconcilability. He had wanted to scream at the man, I know who you are, I know what you are, I know what you do. But the only part of the accusation that held any truth then was that Luke knew only the actions of his father, not who or what the man was.

By the time of his eleventh birthday, the diminishing excitements of danger and transgression had failed to overcome his growing, condescending distaste. Luke forged an escape from his anger and confusion by feigning disinterest; when his father went upstairs for his weekly bath, Luke remained in his room with the door firmly closed.

Once, a few months into his eleventh year, he tried to squeeze back into the airing cupboard, more out of boredom than any revived arousal. He could no longer fit into that narrow space. The blocking of his entry, his inability to pass through, was to him a rite of passage, a sign, if one were needed, that he had outgrown his father's sexual hold over him.

Who was this man? Luke has spent his whole life trying to understand that question. Looked at in another way, his whole life has been distorted because his father never answered that question for himself. He was afraid of even posing such a question, and instead locked himself behind a multitude of doors. Now that Luke is his father, with his own doors to unlock and open, he is still asking the same, or at least a similar, question: Who is this man?

So many years later, at the age his father was then, Luke realizes that no one—man or woman—ever escapes their father's sexual shadow.

He continues to measure himself, literally and symbolically, physically and emotionally, against his father. He had thought earlier that he hated him and perhaps, then, he did. Perhaps, then, he hated him with a singular clarity that only a child can have.

A few years ago, Luke wanted to write his father a letter, explaining this hatred which had over the years given way to an infinite sadness. A sadness born of isolation during those long years they lived under the same roof, years in which they witnessed and mutely shared each other's deepest intimacies without once breaking their mutual silence. Luke wishes that he could say to his father, I forgive you.

I forgive you.

Not for his father's actions, but for his weaknesses: his inactions and silences. I know you. I know who you are, and what you are. I know what you do. I know.

His father was afraid of dirt.

————

*H*e forgives his father for his fear. Father, if only you could have embraced your fear, transformed it to sanctify your desires, your actions.

But Luke knows that the way of sanctity is the hardest to bear; salvation, with its promises of penance and absolution, was too great a temptation and his father, in his weakness, could not be blamed for taking the most trodden path.

My Body, Singing in Silence

NORA OKJA COBB

I lay straining against my skin, feeling its heaviness covering me like a blanket thick as sleep. I wait, paralyzed, for the popping of my blood that signals Induk is near, also waiting, wanting me.

When she was alive, she did not seem so impatient. But then, I knew her only at the comfort stations, when she had to hide between layers of silence and secret movements. I want to say that I knew she would be the one that would join me after death. That there was something special about her even then, perhaps in the way she carried herself—walking more erect, with impudence even —or in the way she gave the other women courage through the looks and smiles she gave us.

But I am trying not to lie.

There was nothing special about her life at the recreation camps, only her death. In front of the men, we all tried to walk the same, tie our hair the same, keep the same blank look on our faces. To be special there meant only that we would be used more, that we would die faster.

Though we were not afraid of death, only of dying under them, like dogs.

One of the women there—I do not know her real name and will not use the one assigned to her—I think she came from *yangban,* high class. She spoke of a dagger her mother used to wear about her waist. Smaller than the length of her palm, the hilt encrusted with gems, it was to be hers when she married. The knife would have shown her pride in her virtue; if she had failed in guarding it, she would have turned the weapon on herself.

The rest of us were envious, not of the rich things she indicated having, not of her aristocracy, but of her right to kill herself. We all had the obligation, of course, given what had happened to us, but it didn't have the status of privilege and choice.

That is what, in the end, made Induk so special: she chose her own death. Using the Japanese as her dagger, she taunted them with the language and truths they perceived as insults. She sharpened their anger to the point where it equaled and fused with their black hungers. She used them to end her life, to find release.

I cannot believe she chooses to come to me, a coward. But I am grateful.

My body grows heavy, but inside I am crackling like hot oil. She is going to peel back my skin, then cover me, like steam: gentle, insistent, invasive.

I do not see her, but I know Induk is with me. She licks at my toes and fingertips, sucking at them until my blood rushes to greet her touch. I feel her fingers wind through my hair, rubbing my scalp, soothing me, while her mouth caresses my chin and neck. My body prickles.

With infinite care, Induk slides her arms around my back, cradling me into her heat. Her lips press the base of my throat, into the hollow underneath my jaw, then travel lower to brush against my nipples. I feel them pulling, drawing my milk, feel the excess liquid trickle against my sides and down my belly. Induk laps it up, her tongue following the meandering trails.

Her hands knead my ass, shaping them to her hands, spreading them apart. Her fingers dip into and flirt with the cleft, from anus to the tip of my vagina where my blood gathers and pulses until it aches. She combs my pubic hair with her long nails, pulling at the crinkling hairs as if to straighten them. I stifle a groan, try to keep my hips still.

I cannot.

I open myself to her and move in rhythm to the tug of her lips and fingers and the heat of her between my thighs. The steady buzzing that began at my fingertips shoots through my body, concentrates at the pulse point between my legs, then, without warning, explodes through the top of my head. I see only the blackness of my pleasure.

My body sings in silence until emptied, and there is only her left, Induk.

Once I was not quiet when Induk came to me. I must have cried out, for I attracted the attention of my husband. He knelt by my bed, watching me until I became aware of the sound of his harsh breathing. When I looked at him, he moved the covers off me and crowded into my bed.

He pushed his forehead against mine and, firmly, unknowingly, replaced Induk's hands on my body. His fingers, rough and harsh, lifted my nightgown and pressed into the skin of my breasts and hips. When he felt the fabric of my underwear, he pulled it aside and fit himself between my legs.

I felt his arousal probing the entrance to my vagina and tensed. He found it slick, made ready by Induk's endless caresses, and thrust into me.

Jesus, he said. He pulled out slowly, then entered me again, stretching me. As he thrust and thrust again in long, slow strokes, he lifted my hips against his, forcing me into a counterpoint rhythm.

And, suddenly, it was as if Induk was still there, between us, inside of him and inside of me. The buzzing that I felt with her unfurled within me, gaining strength until I could not contain it. As it burst over me, I cried out against my husband's shoulder and was answered by his own shout of pleasure.

Afterward, when my husband had returned to his bed, I dreamed of Induk and of him and of his shouts that sounded too much like the shouts the men at the camps gave as they collapsed over the women in release and triumph.

The next morning, my husband told me. Masturbation is a sin. I blinked.

Hanyok un chae ok ida, he repeated in Korean.

Realizing he was referring to what he had witnessed between Induk and myself, I laughed. How could he compare what went on between men and women's bodies with what happened spiritually?

I was not alone, I said. Did you not see her touching me where your hands touched me? Suckling me where your mouth suckled?

When he asked, "Who?" I laughed harder.

He licked his lips and looked at my laughing mouth. Succubus, he whispered.

I saw in his eyes the lust, dark and heavy and animal, that I'd seen in the eyes of men at the camps. And I also saw the fear.

I knew then that he would not come into me again like that. I knew then that he could not.

Skin Flowers

ANN SHIN

when Marla dances
she dances without accompaniment.

lifting her small table like a basket
above her head, she goes
where she's wanted.

the smile on her lips

she takes steps so small
it seems she will never get there
slipping in and around tables—
there are so many tables,
she keeps an eye out for potentials.

a guy
with a NY
Giants cap
is staring.
there's a $20 bill

looking everywhere
looking anywhere
as she sets down the table

held between
two fingers.
she sees the man.

testing with her feet, then stepping up.
she knows the borders of her round table
          and moves within.
     she never looks down.   *closer*
                                            you're not
                                         shy now are you.

               and so,

Debbie's finishing   Marla's legs
up on stage.
                     feel for the grin—

               look at his lips

                    ho . . .

               and bending down
      her shoulder wavers, as if she's slipped
         as if her whole cover's shot—   there's
                                                  laughter
                                                  over at
                                             Sheila's table.

          her hand reaches up
               (quick reflex)

     but her arm bends behind her head now,
               to untie the straps.

three heads   she watches
turn her way.
                    his desire laid naked.

               she prolongs
               her smile,
          like butterfly's dust—

          or the grainy smoke of evening
     in a bar that's about to close,
     lit cigarettes and cash
     having all changed hands.

     the stage
     has changed

and lights come on at random:
tables of squinting faces,
coats hastily pulled on.

Debbie's done the last act
now it's just table girls and regulars.

   Marla picks up her stuff
   slips her feet through the G-string,
   awkward elbows as she reties the strap
        at her back.

she takes her money as he finishes his drink.

it's temporary.

from

Aomori

JULIET S. KONO

After their golf
games, Aomori and his friends ate, drank, and sat with the bar girls
in the Pearl Lounge to talk story. The men told each other sick
jokes. The cruder the better—women, race, deformity. When
Aomori first went to one of these Korean bars, he felt shy and
uncomfortable, out of place. Drinking gradually took the edge off
most of his inhibitions, and now he felt like a regular Joe Blow.

It was here, at this club, that he first met Susu. One night, he
had been so drunk she had been kind enough to take him home
with her after the bar's mandatory 2 A.M. closing. Too drunk to
drive home, she had sobered him up with coffee and splashes of
water on his face over a bathroom basin, and had later sent him on
his way. While this became a regular thing with them, Aomori
never thought to thank her, or to do anything for her; it never
occurred to him.

At the bar, Susu took it upon herself to take care of
Aomori, extending him small favors while the men drank. She
served him his drinks, gave him extra *pupus,* sat next to him.
Once in a while she massaged his head and neck. Sometimes she
would tease him by putting her hands between his legs and
crotch, and massaging him in the area. He would push her

hands away and she would laugh. "What? Cannot, huh, Aomori-san? You drink too much, no?"

The young Korean bar girls liked the doctors and their friends. The girls fed the men a lot of food: meat and fish *jhun,* barley rice, pig intestines, *kim chee,* lobsters, steaks, shrimps. *Ono* food. Delicacies. The doctors spent their money freely and bought rounds of drink. At someone's whim, maybe for a handjob under the table or a feel up one of the girl's skirts, the champagne flowed. Hundred dollars a bottle. Dom Pérignon.

The women began to tease Aomori with the nickname "Tako," or octopus, because they said he had eight hands. He gained a reputation among the girls, enticing them to sit at his side, then grabbing their asses. The women in turn played into his hands. It was safe for all of them—the men getting their jollies without getting involved; the girls not having to put out much. The girls squealed and badgered the men. Like children.

But Aomori liked Susu the best. She didn't "expect" as much as some of the other women did. Some of them wanted expensive gifts or for him to buy good champagne. Susu never asked for anything and she was always full of fun.

Aomori's involvement with Susu began naturally and slowly. She always brought him to her house to sober up if he was too drunk, and often, on her days off, he would appear at her small high-rise apartment on Kanunu Street before going home. Because there wasn't much they had in common or they could talk about, their relationship slipped easily into sex.

For the first time in his life, Aomori learned that sex could be fun. He could make love with abandon. He laughed as they teased each other across the sheets. He didn't need to talk to her about anything of consequence; there was not the resentments, tiredness, and sameness of marital sex. He never knew what Susu felt or what was on her mind, but he didn't care. Anything and everything was light, a joke. Susu laughed at whatever he said, even when she didn't understand what he meant. He could be silly. He could try things with her. He could never have had fun like this with his wife Carolyn; he couldn't recall if he ever did. What he couldn't play out with Carolyn, he played out with Susu. She was his best audience.

One evening, during one of the first times he made love with Susu, Aomori demanded in a voice that sounded new to himself, "Come here. I want you." He pulled her toward him, ready to glide his hands and arms all over her body. It didn't occur to him that he should maybe ask her if she wanted him too. If there was some hesitation on Susu's part, it was fleeting. The tiny woman was easily overcome by his presence. She slowly slid to his side of the bed. "Come here, I said."

Aomori grabbed Susu around the waist, and whatever made her hesitate slipped away as quickly as her clothing. She responded fully. He pulled her roughly onto him and made her lie the length of his body. They rolled off the bed and fell to the floor, where they thrashed about like fish. He had never made love like this—ever. Urgent. Demanding. "I want to fuck you badly," he said. "I want to fuck you hard!" Overcome by the harsh reality of the words that passed his lips, he could no longer hold himself back. He sought Susu's lips eagerly. There was something about saying the base words that made him dig his hands into the small of her back, raising and dropping her body onto himself.

"Fuck!" he cried out. It felt terribly good to say the word, to have it hurtle out of his mouth and tumble over his lips. In all his life, he had never used the word before. When he was a young boy, he was not allowed to swear; later, he never allowed himself. The repressed barriers that had been held back in his loins for years burst warmly inside of him, and were released, with the word's strong utterance.

It might have been a significant moment, something to reflect on, but once satisfied, he hiked up his pants, went home, and never gave Susu or what happened that night another thought.

from

The Hemisphere: Kuchuk Hanem

Kimiko Hahn

"Flaubert's encounter with an Egyptian courtesan produced a widely influential model of the Oriental woman; she never spoke of herself, she never represented her emotions, presence, or history. *He* spoke for and represented her." (Said, *Orientalism*, p. 6)

I am four. It is a summer midafternoon, my nap finished. I cannot find her. I hear the water in the bathroom. Not from the faucet but occasional splashes. I hear something like the bar of soap fall in. I cannot find her.

Flaubert's encounter, Flaubert's encounter, Flaubert's encounter—

I stand outside the white door. Reflected in the brass doorknob I see my face framed by a black pixie-cut. More splashes.

I hear humming. It is Mother's voice in the bathroom through the closed door and it is midafternoon. No light from beneath the door. I twist the knob and hang my weight to pull the door open. In the half-light I see Mother sitting in the bath: the white porcelain, gray, the yellow tiles, gray. Her hair is coiled and pinned up.

I see her breasts over the edge of the tub. I have never seen my mother without clothes. Her nipples.

"[S]he never spoke of herself, she never represented her emotions, presence, or history. [Flaubert] spoke for and represented her." [Said, 6]

Her nipples appear dark and round. They are funny and beautiful. I leave, perhaps to lie down on my pillow or find my bear. What did she say to me? Did she scold? Laugh? Just smile or ignore me? My breasts have never looked like those breasts.

"He was foreign, comparatively wealthy, male, and these were historical facts of domination that allowed him not only to possess Kuchuk Hanem physically but to speak for her and tell his readers in what way she was 'typically Oriental.' " [Said, 6]

In 1850 a woman with skin the color of the sand in the shade of the Sphinx, midday, meant little and of course mine was seen more than veiled and I could earn a living "dancing." What I liked best were gifts of chocolate. Usually from French thinking I'd consider the evening amorous and reduce the rate. Paris must be lovely but for the French.

Maybe I want a penis. Maybe that's why I love sitting on an outstretched man and seeing his prick between my legs, rubbing it as if it were mine. Maybe that's why I love to put a cock in my mouth, feel it increase in size with each stroke, each lick, each pulse. Taste the Red Sea. Look over or up and see the man barely able to contain himself, pulling on my nipples or burying a tongue into my Persian Gulf. Also barely able to contain my own sluice. Maybe it's my way to possess a cock. For a moment feel hegemonic and Western.

I have an addiction to silk and chocolate—gold a little. But coins are a necessity. Now chocolates—if there's a plate of chocolate, I cannot stop my hand. I tell the Nubian to take it to the kitchen and store in a cool place. I will sniff it out. Find her fingerprints on the sweaty sweets.

It is midafternoon.

We both use our mouths, professionally.

"My heart begins to pound every time I see [a prostitute] in low-cut dresses walking under the lamplight in the rain, just as monks in their corded robes have always excited some deep, ascetic corner of my soul . . ."

Maybe it's my way to possess a cock. For a moment feel hegemonic and Western.

". . . The idea of prostitution is a meeting place of so many elements—lust, bitterness, complete absence of human contact, muscular frenzy, the clink of gold—that to peer into it deeply makes one reel. One learns so many things in a brothel, and feels such sadness, and dreams so longingly of love!" [Steegmuller, 10]

I watch white couples. See how they touch the clitoris. A cat lapping, a cat pawing. Think about betrayal and loss.

I stand outside the white door.

The two girls invited her cousin Conrad in the little pool, to see his small penis wobbling about like a party favor.

Playing with the costume jewelry in her mother's drawers, then hiding under her vanity, the bathroom door opened, steam poured out and she saw her father naked from the waist down. Swollen balls. Penis dangling. A raw red.

For a moment feel hegemonic and Western.

It's true, when all is said and done, I am less a dancer than a whore. Men pay me money, stick their cocks in me, laugh, weep, curse or silently ride my body. And leave. That's what I am, a whore and alone. To be despised by the men because who else would let them come as they come but someone with vagrant morals? Despised by wives, mistresses, fiancées for my abilities, independence, the peculiar attention I receive. I am scorned by the religious. By the courts and by my parents. But I do not fear a man's departure. Know that.

And I have made a name for myself that will, Flaubert boasts on his own behalf, not mine, that will cover the globe. Know that. That the image is not my own. My image does not entirely belong to me. And neither does yours, master or slave.

I cannot find her.

Kim

JANA MONJI

Can you keep from hating a roommate who gets all the looks? You know, the one that makes a man's pulse jump by just walking across the floor. Of course, sometimes it helped that the skirt was so short bare cheeks flashed brazenly from the black thong worn underneath. And Kim took time. Each painful step of the patent leather stilettos radiated forbidden pleasures and broadcast the smothering scent of Opium, Kim's trademark perfume for these nights.

"Those silly white bitches think you need breasts. You just need attitude. Look like yes, but say no. Men like what they can't have," Kim would say.

I learned a lot about life from Kim. It was like Aesop's city mouse and country cousin fable. When I first came to Los Angeles, I was prepared for hitting the books—living in a library. But I didn't belong in LA and certainly not in Hollywood.

I found Kim through an ad in the *LA Weekly*. The rents in Hollywood were cheaper than Westwood. It wasn't the best way to find future roommates, but I didn't know that then. There was so much I didn't know.

Kim was willing to teach me. After a month, Kim squinted, looking at me like a piece of blank canvas, and said, "You know, you could be real good-looker. Hot stuff. You just need little change." Kim smiled, tossing the long waves of auburn hair, permed out of its natural straightness.

I don't know what I liked about Kim. Our bond was perhaps dependent on bridges built on false assumptions of sameness—the Asian factor. But I had never known war. Kim had.

Kim warned me about white men. "They only want one thing, girl," Kim would say, winking. "Madonna even knows that. You make good life here, you learn that fast."

"What about Asian men?" I asked one day when Kim had finally convinced me to forgo the usual sweatpants and ponytail and was deciding how to achieve an attractive but tasteful hairstyle for me.

"Asian boys, they nothing but paper dragons. They too afraid to spit fire, but they make good bonfire," Kim said with a throaty laugh steeped in bitterness.

Our bedrooms were separated by rattan screens and curtains. But these were walls, just the same. "Privacy is only a state of mind," my mother once said. I saw that in Kim, too. With curtains pulled, Kim was alone and I was too. Kim's futon folded up into a chair for company and, without the throw pillows, my bed was the couch.

Kim had been a student, but was now caught up in the Holly-wood movie rush. "My life, like this shit," Kim once said, turning on the garbage disposal to whirl away the remains of our stir-fry dinner. When Kim was working, doing makeup or hair on a shoot, I had no roommate. Otherwise, Kim would sleep late and watch grainy videos borrowed from Vietnamese friends.

When Kim's money thinned down to pennies in a jar, Kim worked at a local Vietnamese-Chinese restaurant owned by a nice woman Kim called "Mother-lady." Kim's real mother belonged to another world that Kim had left behind. This Mother-lady had a big heart. Her real children were *bits of dust*—ashes in a man's war. At least, she thought they were dead.

We were her city orphans, sent to give her good karma and

comfort. She liked feeding us. Kim and I were both so thin—like baby birds who have to be brought food and too stupid to get it by yourself, she would say.

But we ate a lot. Kim took me to the best cheap eats. "Don't worry. Floor dirty, but kitchen clean. I never get sick here, not like American hamburger shit." Kim would sniff with disgust.

Other times Kim fretted about my safety. "If you out too late, call. No funny look, call. Call. Don't wait for RTD," Kim would say then, picking me up in a very dented white Datsun B210. "Good brakes, so-so tires. No one want steal. That best car for Hollywood."

Despite little changes, some of which I admit I liked, I never let Kim take over my appearance. Still, Kim never gave up. "You could be hot stuff, real hot number, girl." I just nodded and went back to my books.

Listening to Madonna on a shiny yellow Walkman, Kim would sometimes dance half-naked to empty air as I studied. With paper thin walls, our neighbor, a sickly thin old woman who rarely left her apartment, would complain loudly. If Kim's antiquated stereo broke the old woman's serenity, *bang! bang! bang!* went the old woman's cane against the wall.

On hot days, Kim would leave the door open, dancing madly and sometimes catching our neighbor watching. She didn't approve of the life Kim led, but she still worried. We returned the favor, shopping for her.

Kim would yell from the kitchen, "I go market. You need something?" The old lady would poke her head out ten minutes later. Holding a worn purse in hand, she counted out the dollars and pennies.

After knocking three times on her door, Kim would leave the old lady's small items on the hallway floor. Then, with our door open, Kim would dance passionately while putting everything away in our kitchen. Unless I was studying, Kim would try to get me dancing. "You need to relax, baby-girl," Kim would say. But as with all of Kim's wildness, I resisted until the summer sun melted my reserve.

With the quarter over, I was locked in a mind-numbing dead-end summer job.

"Let's celebrate summer, baby-girl," Kim said. "I give you my fuck-me-look special." I gave in. "Trust me, baby-girl. You look nice yuppie tomorrow. I make sure," Kim said, and fiendishly began the transformation. Opening a great tool box, Kim washed my hair, cut and sprayed. "My mother taught me how. You know, best bucks go to best-looking girl." Kim laughed. "Now, we go shopping."

Kim favored black miniskirts and stiletto heels. "Show some flesh, not too much. Don't want to be mistaken for Miss Saigon," Kim said sarcastically. Kim wore tastefully tight black pants with rather understated silk shirts.

We went to small clubs at first. But as Kim saw my confidence grow, we tried better places. Sometimes, the bouncers were only letting in certain girls and very few couples. One night, we couldn't get in at all. Kim didn't mind if white guys with Rolexes got in while we waited. Kim winked and said, "Kiss ass. I get even. You see, next time we have good laugh."

The next weekend, Kim came out dressed in high black platforms, a skin-tight leather miniskirt studded with silver and a low-cut black blouse. "You not shocked, baby-girl," Kim said with wide-eyed coyness. "Beauty, it's just dust and imagination," Kim said, blowing face powder off a brush. It held the lamplight briefly, sparkling as we began our enchanted evening.

This time, the bouncer took one look at Kim's long smooth legs and smiled as if his brain had evaporated. Kim stooped over sideways to give him a good view, pretending to pull up the stockings—not quickly, but slowly. "Give man his money's worth, baby-girl. Gotta sell merchandise," Kim hissed with a false smile.

After that, we always got in. The club managers, those white men with slick ponytails and overly bright smiles, liked having

Kim there. Asian girls were exotic, but humble enough to not cause trouble. We never went to Asian hangouts dressed like this. Kim advised, "We live two worlds. One, real. Two, white-boy fantasy."

It was a game. Meat on the market before slobbering dogs that couldn't afford the entry fee. Kim's standard lose-them line was, "You nice fella, but my family don't like no white boys. But white boys so nice-looking and fun to dance with. I can't bring you home. No, I can't go your place. I get killed if I don't make breakfast for old man. My cousin, here, she same. We neighbors." Kim would smile and feign shyness.

Kim got to know all the bouncers by name so if some Romeo got too hot, we would call for help from our bouncer friends. "You know, we good girls. We don't want no trouble," Kim would say coyly.

Summer nights became our realm of magic. After selecting our costumes and taping for cleavage ("I learn this from pageant," Kim confided), we would meet in the bathroom. Our mirror ritual would begin with careful plucking of facial hair. "I no like Brooke Shields. Look like man or horse," Kim would say.

We would sponge on foundation and then lightly brush our faces, necks and shoulders with Kim's "fairy dust" mixture of translucent powder, rice polishings and pearlescent eye shadow for an otherworldly glow.

Next, we would brush two different tones of brown to form expressive eyebrows. "Think young Liz Taylor," Kim would chant softly. Then Kim would whisper, "Delicately—no Connie Chung eye," while applying eyeliner for both of us. We would then curl, mascara, powder and re-mascara our eyelashes, sweeping eye shadow up from our eyes to our eyebrows, blending from wine purple to a soft pink at the crest of our brows. After a slight whisper of rouge, we applied lipstick—first outlining our lips with pencil. Kim favored china red or blood reds while I used rose colors. Kim would mousse and lightly spray our hair.

We applied perfume. Opium for Kim ("It like history, you know. China and white man," Kim once explained) and Shalimar for me. Kim had bought me a bottle as a surprise one day. "I think it you," Kim explained nonchalantly. Pulling on our black stockings and slipping into high heels, we walked incognito, night-time creatures feeding off the fantasies of strangers.

But it couldn't last like that, could it? I had seen those two watching us. Sometimes they would just stare at us, panting like dogs hoping for a phantom meal. I mentioned them to Kim, but Kim laughed them off. "They frightened we too hot for them. We are."

One full moon, we slipped into an abyss, falling before we even knew we were in danger.

We were sitting down, drinking Perrier, when the two watchers sat down on the stools next to us. The shorter man was muscular, sweaty and tanned with stubble glistening on his chin. He sat next to Kim. He leaned over and said something to Kim. Kim shot me a look of disgust, but still got up to dance. Kim was a good dancer. I liked watching Kim dance.

The taller man also favored that Don Johnson "Miami Vice" sleaze look. He came and sat next to me, touching my leg and taking hold of my thigh. "Don't," I said as I tried to squirm out of his reach. He relaxed his hold and asked me if I wanted a drink. I could feel his fingers stroking my inner thigh as he ordered two margaritas. His fingers stole under my skirt. I tried to push him away, but he tightened his grip until it hurt. Then he kissed me like a slobbering bulldog, tasting of stale alcohol, stinking of Old Spice.

Kim saw, then began looking for a bouncer. Turning Kim's face, the short man pulled Kim toward him. I couldn't catch the eye of the nearest bouncer boy; he was socializing with a new girl at the club—a bleached blonde.

The margaritas came. I gave mine to the man's pants and

jumped up. Kim joined me as I stormed out the door. Kim shot a kiss at that same bouncer who had just scored the blonde's phone number. Kim shouted, pointing with a black sequined bag toward the two men. "We too hot for those boys. You cool them off?"

We escaped into the night, our heels beating an erratic retreat cadence. While unlocking the passenger door, Kim offered me comfort by kissing my forehead, nose and lips. Kim looked solemnly into my eyes for a moment before I got in. I felt unclean, but now curiously excited by the feel of soft hairless skin slipping tenderly against my own. But Kim couldn't erase my fear; I was shaking in the car. Kim cursed and chanted, coaxing the Datsun into action. Finally, we jumped into traffic. Kim held my hand, turning to smile and say comforting words until we got home.

Kim kissed me like a lover while opening the building's front door, and then hurried me inside. "I sorry, baby-girl, I never want you get hurt. You don't know men. You be okay. I make you some tea." Kim stroked my hair and murmured gently.

That night we slept together. Kim stroked me like I was a lost kitten. "You baby-girl, not ready for city. You gotta be tough, baby-girl. Okay, I be tough enough for both."

The next morning, Saturday, Kim went out early to work at the restaurant. "Tonight we have quiet dinner, okay, baby-girl? We have good talk. You rest. I be back maybe eight."

At seven-thirty, the doorbell rang. I thought Kim was laden down with goodies from Mother-lady and couldn't open the door, so I opened it. There they both stood—those two men.

"You damn cock-teasing dykes," the taller one began. I screamed and tried to shut the door. "Where's your friend?" the shorter one asked. They checked our rooms, ripping open the curtains and pushing aside the rattan screens, destroying the barriers like cobwebs of Asian dreams. "Get out," I cried, trying to grab the phone. But the tall one ripped it off the wall. I tried to escape.

"I'll show you what a real man feels like," the tall one said, grabbing me. Slobbering like a rabid dog, he gave me a deep-tongued kiss before throwing me onto the sofa. The throw pillows that gave my bed a different daytime reality scattered. Tightly pinned down, I couldn't breathe. He tried to get me out of my pants. With his massive bulldog mouth, he swallowed my face. I bit his lip, and he slapped me hard. The shock made me momentarily stop kicking. I kept thinking "breathe," and "no." That, and "no more."

"You dykes are afraid of real men, but you'll like it," he grunted in my ear. "You just need a good one." He grated my face with sandpaper stubble, stinking of Old Spice. My pants were off and now he forced my hand down to touch his slimy dull weapon. I turned my face away to breathe. I prayed for life and death, unable to choose.

"Hey, white boy. You no real man. You don't know real man when you see one." Greasy from the heat of the Mother-lady's kitchen, Kim stood defiant at the doorway, holding plastic grocery bags.

"Who the hell are you?" said the tall man. His grip relaxed enough for me to squirm from under him. The short man couldn't speak.

"You don't know me, white boy? I tell you, you don't know nothing." Kim laughed sarcastically. Kim put down the bags and sauntered up to the short man, walking his Saigon slut strut and running his fingers up the man's chest. "You remember me, white boy? Last night, you say you win toss-up. I yours. You say you give me good time."

Stepping back, Kim leaned against the kitchen counter and slowly unwound the bun. Letting out a tide of wavy auburn hair, Kim smiled slyly. The scent of Opium and rancid sesame oil engulfed us.

The tall man looked back at me, "You, you," he shuddered.

The short man only stuttered. Kim said nothing, but then

coyly stood straight, presenting himself with a great flourish of his hands. He began to laugh wildly, recklessly. And then he just posed, smiling with his hand on his hip.

I laughed hysterically. "I'm the only woman here, you stupid assholes."

"No." The short man shook nervously. Looking at me, he muttered, "She said you were always jealous."

"White boys like me best. That why. Who want me first?" Kim smiled coyly. "White boys like rice queens with tight asses." The short man shook his head. "Maybe you hit wrong club, white boy. Go look for white love. Maybe you get three-way boy love."

"No," the short man, said. "I like women."

"White boy don't even know woman when he see." Kim laughed.

"I know women," the taller man stuttered, staring uneasily at Kim.

"But you've never seen him naked. I have," I screamed.

Our neighbor popped her head in. "I called the police. You better go. We don't want no trouble here."

They left puzzled and angry. Afraid to touch Kim or look at me. Before they reached the front door, Kim called out and exposed himself. With a defiant laugh, Kim slammed our door.

Kim embraced me in his sinewy arms and fed me from cartons of food, scolding me like a mother bird feeding her chick. "Baby-girl, I told you about white men. You believe now? Don't worry, baby-girl, I no paper dragon. I keep you safe."

Afterimages of Leung Kar Fai

WAGNER WAI JIM AU

Anne's fantasy of the last few nights goes something like this: she is dressed in muted silks, in a glass penthouse above the neon pandemonium of some Pacific Rim city. The place is humid with incense; it seems to drift along the floor, misting over the black-lacquered furniture, the vases of moonlit porcelain, the futon with sandalwood frame.

He grips her from behind, by the wrists. She lets herself sink into his torso, imprinting its lean frame against her. He speaks to her in the lilting dialect of Mandarin. He twitches off her gown with his long, ascetic fingers.

He makes Anne kneel down on the futon, ass high. He makes her reach back to grip her own ankles, so her face ends up planted into a thick pillow that smells like jasmine. Sitting beside her, he lights an opium pipe. He takes a long drag on it, watching her all the while, idly stroking her face; the pipe's glow flickers across his beautiful slanted eyes. He holds the inhalation in his mouth as he strains himself up and crouches behind her. He places one hand on her back, anchoring it there. She can't see him. She feels his other hand running up her thigh, then along her cunt. Then careful fingertips, warm and dry, teasing her lips open. Gingerly easing them wider. Pushing down on her back with the other, firmly.

He puts his mouth on her cunt, opened slightly. And Anne feels the opium begin to curl into her cunt. A downy, drowsy heat billows inside her, then dissipates to smoke wisps that trail their way up her womb.

Somewhere in there, she bolts upright in bed. Her image flashes at her from the mirror in the opposite wall: neck flushed scarlet, auburn hair a flurry across her face, teeth bared, hand working furiously between her legs. The Asian Man of her mind's eye seems to dissolve over her reflection like a cinematic cross-fade, and as it does, she watches herself to the end, watches her eyes blaze over, watches her fingertips blurring over her clit, watches the shudders burst and spread from her cunt in five directions.

She smiles as she remembers this, walking up Columbus, along the edge of Chinatown. Now a little embarrassed by all the arch, ethnic accoutrements of the fantasy. But it is a new discovery for her, an erotic avenue she'd never considered before, never would have imagined herself considering, until only weeks ago. And now, here she is, making herself walk toward a party to which she's coaxed an invitation—from a woman at the gallery, a Japanese girl who wears black, paints with slow, dreamy motions . . . and talks with the gulping, amphetamine accent of a San Fernando mall rat. When she gets there, she expects to find the men she'd not noticed all this time, and be ready for them.

It began with a film, where so many exotic yearnings begin, where they are put up before you in looming chiaroscuros that make the Excluded Other seem, suddenly, infinitely desirable. A friend dragged Anne to it, to a small theater, through the thick wafts of cappuccino in the lobby, and into the cramped seats.

It was about the self-imposed concubinage of a luscious, awkward French girl to a young Chinese gentleman of inherited wealth. Played, the flier in the foyer informed her, by a Hong Kong actor named Tony Leung. *(His western name; from Leung Kar Fai, his original, Chinese name,* notes the copy, which intrigues her even more.) In the film, she meets him by day, off a teeming Saigon market street bleached by the sun, in a small bachelor's apartment. Now, Anne imagines what it must feel like for the girl; thighs pasting together as she walks, filmy with sweat, and then to open that narrow door, and feel that dark cool rush out at her.

Tony Leung is all smooth, austere limbs. She waits in the doorway. He sweeps toward her in long strides. His hair is slicked back, along the elegant angles of his face; when he bends to her, into the threshold and out of the light, they resolve to hollowed triangles; his bare skin is resilient, surfaceless; when she opens his robe, it seems to shimmer on his frame like golden chocolate. His dark eyes disappear into narrow crescent shadows when they near hers.

Then he is fucking her on the dusty floor, without preamble. He falls between her thin legs, and she wraps them around the lazy V of his waist. She has a firm, spacious butt, a Gallic horse's ass; it makes her back arc off the ground as he thrusts into her. Slowlike, to begin with, meditatively, inside her.

His own ass is beautiful. It's a slender ass, the ass of an earnest choirboy. And as she watches them fuck from straight on, she can see it just over his straining shoulders; she can see it, hovering and kneading above the girl's cunt. Her gawky legs begin to grip him to her. Feet locked together, toes curled, pushing down into the small of his back.

Then he is thumping into her quick and hard, impact absorbed by the spread width of her ass, then pushing her across the floor. She yelping, arms out, damp hair on her cheeks. Slithering together down the shallow flight of stairs, sprawling. He hovering above her, making boyish tenor gasps. Now at the foot of the bed, fucking her madly.

———

*E*xquisite, Anne decides. Lovely. And in the back of her mind, in that erotic salon of her imagination, where she keeps the furniture of male features she desires most, a remodeling begins. Exotic objets d'art uncrated, polished, gingerly arranged with the older favorites. In among the looping forelock of blond hair, and the sidelong glance of hazel-green, go new items to luxuriate over: the melancholy shape of dark, almond eyes . . . an expanse of smooth, hairless flesh the color of dark honey.

She thinks of these things, climbing the steps at the top of Chestnut. She wonders why she had never thought of them before. There they were at UC, in her core classes, Asian boys with furtive glances and mousy mannerisms. She recalls one, at her MFA show, approaching her with two glasses of white wine. His hair was cut in a high crest poky with bleach-red tips; they spoke for several minutes. He was saying something enthusiastic about her art; he was holding a glass out to her. But all she can really remember now was his accent. He was from Sydney. Anne smiles now; she didn't hear a single word, dazed with the surrealism of that bleach-blond Aussie drawl coming out this guy's mouth. She can't quite remember what he looked like, and this bothers her. Seems like he was after her, come to think of it now; he was trying to be charming, seductive; he was trying to take her to bed.

It never would have struck her then, that's for damn sure; that possibility simply would not have occurred to her. Now here she is, at the foot of the stairs of a Nob Hill Victorian painted bird's-egg blue, from which colored light and a muffled synth throbbing emanates.

Here I am, finally. I won't overlook you. I promise.

*I*nside, she makes slow figure 8s through jostling elbows and shoulders in leather, linen, and padded lycra. She herself is dressed in airborne boots and wool greatcoat, in lace stockings and a pearly choker around her neck, a sort of capricious combination of Back Off You Goddamn Yuppie Poseur and Bend Me Over a Chair and Fuck My Guts to Steaming Lasagna.

She says banal things she forgets a moment after spoken. She drinks in a saliva froth of alcohol and steaming sensimilla. She smiles tightly at the collarbones of the people who gush foolish things about her paintings, trying to confine the textured darkness of her work into cubicles of trite phrase.

But eventually, through it all, she picks out two top contenders.

His name is Robert Akiyama; he has long hair, dark but for a single brushstroke of ivory down the middle, and a beard trimmed in exact angles around his lips, which are full; he is wiry tall. He is an industrial designer, or something. She meets him in a group, and before she has the chance to detach him from the others, he is dragged away by a shrieking woman. He grins at Anne, helplessly, as he goes. His smile is sharp, sardonic, and beautiful.

The other one, she does not meet; he's someone, rather—as he appears in various parts of the room, in various angles—that she spots and itemizes: eyes rounded to a mournful, downward slant; Chinese, then. Not very tall, but muscular. Broad chest and shoulders above an impossibly slender waist. Armani jacket, nice touch. And he does an odd thing, from time to time. His eyes will glance up to hers, shy but expectant, with half a dimpled smile. But by the time they do meet hers, for a retreating instance, the smile is gone, and the gaze is cold; and then he appears vaguely annoyed or bored. This frustrates her; it also beguiles her.

Then Robert Akiyama smiles at her again, but this time, he's standing off in a corner. A trim blond man is beside him, resting on his shoulder; eyes closed, lips parted, like he's sound asleep. The blond man's left hand is idly stroking Robert's denim crotch. Robert's cock is hard beneath it, an obtuse angle parallel to the caress-

ing fingers. Then just before he bends and nuzzles into the crook of
the man's chin, hair draping across his face, here comes the shit-
eating grin. *Sorry, I thought you knew.*

Anne straightens. All right. The Armani man, then.

She turns to find him standing in the doorway, leaving alone.
Glancing back at her one last instant, with that same shifting
expression. And at that moment, she intuits its meaning. All this
time, he has been imagining what it would be like to meet her. In
his mind, he has been envisioning an awkward approach, an introduction, a faltering conversation, a politely stinging indifference.
This scenario has been playing across his face as he looks at her. And
she realizes that he has played it out before, with other women like
her—other *white* women, why not say it?—and has no intention of
repeating it again. Much as he may want to.

The realization shames and infuriates her at the same time. But
before she can reach him through the crowd, to remedy all this, he's
gone.

So. An hour later, she's making morose on the divan, slouched and
spilling her fifth rum and Coke, arguing loudly about art and the
corrosion of modern et cetera with someone she doesn't know.

Another hour later, fishing about for her greatcoat among the
dwindling pile on the rack, an impish headache threatening to
pounce on her temples, someone steps up behind her.

He has thick chestnut hair, and a cheeky, cherubic grin. He is
holding out her coat in one hand; he twirls her around with the
other. He slips it on, gliding up her arms and over her shoulders.
He smooths it out for her. His hands feel nice, but she glowers at
him for a moment anyway, just to keep him on his toes.

They end up walking down Mason together, several arm's lengths
apart. His name is Loren; a writer. He has seen her work, and

liked it, and he spends most of the way downhill listening, *really* listening, as she tells him about it, a grave look fixed to his face.

Anne tries to keep her sentences coherent and linear, but she's really burning more brain cells trying to guess his ethnic background. Something Southern Europe, maybe; he has the strong-nosed profile of the men she studied with in Florence. Or say a Latin mix: his skin is the color of richly creamed coffee. Even Arabic, going on the sad sensuality of his eyes. But then there's the kicker: a British accent, and not the working-class drawl of Pakistani immigrants, either: no, fully mellifluous, in spot-on BBC intonations. *So, will you be having a go at another series of paintings, whilst your current show is running?* Jesus Christ, where did he come from?

She begins to take the mystery as a challenge, and this excites her. So by the time they intersect Columbus, she's wholly forgotten about her headache. And when he invites her upstairs to his North Beach apartment, she follows.

They enter embracing, moving together into the darkened apartment with flicking tongues down each other's throats, clawing their way across the room. Hands locked on her waist, he thrusts Anne into the shadows. She feels languid, and dangerously safe in his grip; she feels herself falling into a couch, sinking into a softness that doesn't seem to stop. Loren straddles her, unpeeling the greatcoat from her shoulders. His cock bobs against her as he labors, furtively jabbing at her belly, her tits. Now he's grunting, teeth bared, trying to strain her skirt over her ass. It would almost be comical, all his furious machinations, but for the trilling buzz coming from her cunt. So she helps; she squirms up, to let him shimmy it past her open thighs.

He falls between her, grinding his cock against the thin lace over her cunt lips. They feel unbearably heavy, and yearning, and when his cockhead thumps against them, it comes away with a strand of saltwater taffy that stretches through the sheer fabric.

Loren is already in a fugue of thrusting, eyes rheumed over, and whimpering, as if he's unable to do anything past this maddened humping on her crotch.

Oh, for Christ's sake. Her whole womb is quaking. Anne spreads her legs wide, starts scrabbling down there with both hands, ripping at them with her fingernails. They unseam in a wet tearing sound, and her cunt is in the clear. She feels a warm breeze ripple along the surface, and then his cock plummets in.

Now she's gripping her ankles, draped way over her head. He's fucking his full weight into her, into that single point of sloppy joy. Anne shrieks, grabs at the clenching muscles of his ass, tries to hop herself off the couch, to reach up and swallow the full length, forever.

"Oh, fuck . . ." Loren says it gasping, but with that accent, he sounds like an RAF officer about to expire. Then he begins to babble, a throaty, singsong guttural. At the top of his voice, as his hips pound into a desperate flurry between her legs.

And . . . oh, sweet baby . . . Anne suddenly realizes what he's saying. Just as her own orgasm goes whirling away from her outraged clit, just as she feels it pinwheeling through her body, and her screams begin to drown his entirely.

Loren is coming . . . *in Cantonese.*

A few hours afterward, he explains to her. *My father is British. He met my mother in Hong Kong.* Now he's holding her legs wide, his head bobbing over her cunt. *No one can tell what race I am. Not even other Chinese people.* He is flicking his tongue over her clit, and when it becomes too intense for her to bear, he slinks it inside her. *I don't tell women that, no. Why should I? It would only complicate matters.* And back to her clit in glorious velvet flashes, until the fluttering begins in her again, and she can do nothing but ram his head to her, and howl, and let the pleasure overwhelm her, and contemplate the karmic balance through the mantra of her thrashing body.

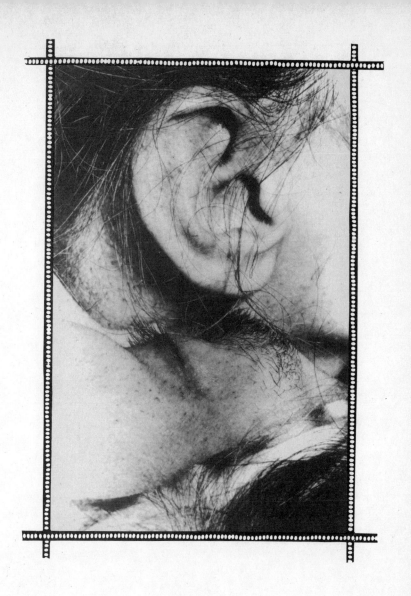

Mating

V

from

Obasan

Joy Kogawa

The town of
Cecil, Alberta, is one hundred and fifty odd miles northeast of
Granton, and I have been teaching in the same room now for the
last seven years. Every month or so, I try to drop in to see my uncle
and my aunt, Obasan, who are both now in their eighties. But at
the beginning of the school year, I'm quite busy.

It usually takes me at least two weeks to feel at home with a
new class. This year there are two Native girls, sisters, twelve and
thirteen years old, both adopted. There's also a beautiful half-Japa-
nese, half-European child named Tami. Then there's Sigmund, the
freckle-faced redhead. Right from the beginning, I can see that he
is trouble. I'm trying to keep an eye on him by putting him at the
front of the class.

Sigmund's hand is up, as it usually is.

"Yes, Sigmund."

"Miss Nah Canny," he says.

"Not Nah Canny," I tell him, printing my name on the blackboard. N A K A N E. "The *a*'s are short as in 'among'—Na Ka Neh—
and not as in 'apron' or 'hat.'"

Some of the children say "Nah Cane."

"Naomi Nah Cane is a pain," I heard one of the girls say once.

"Have you ever been in love, Miss Nakane?" Sigmund asks.

"In love? Why do you suppose we use the preposition 'in' when we talk about love?" I ask evasively. "What does it mean to be 'in' something?"

Sigmund never puts his hand up calmly but shakes it frantically like a leaf in the wind.

I am thinking of the time when I was a child and asked Uncle if he and Obasan were "in love." My question was out of place. "In ruv? What that?" Uncle asked. I've never once seen them caressing.

"Are you going to get married?" Sigmund asks.

The impertinence of children. As soon as they learn I'm no disciplinarian, I lose control over classroom discussions.

"Why do you ask?" I answer irritably and without dignity.

"My mother says you don't look old enough to be a teacher."

That's odd. It must be my size—five feet one, 105 pounds. When I first started teaching sixteen years ago there were such surprised looks when parents came to the classroom door. Was it my youthfulness or my Oriental face? I never learned which.

"My friend wants to ask you for a date," Sigmund adds. He's aware of the stir he's creating in the class. A few of the girls gasp and put their hands up to their mouths. An appropriate response, I think wryly. Typically Cecil. Miss Nakane dating a friend of Sigmund's? What a laugh!

I turn my back to the class and stare out the window. Every year the question is asked at least once.

"Are you going to get married, Miss Nakane?"

With everyone in town watching everything that happens, what chance for romance is there here? Once a widower father of one of the boys in my class came to see me after school and took me to dinner at the local hotel. I felt nervous walking into the Cecil Inn with him.

"Where do you come from?" he asked, as we sat down at a small table in a corner. That's the one sure-fire question I always get from strangers. People assume when they meet me that I'm a foreigner.

"How do you mean?"

"How long have you been in this country?"

"I was born here."

"Oh," he said, and grinned. "And your parents?"

"My mother's a Nisei."

"A what?"

"N-I-S-E-I," I spelled, printing the word on the napkin. "Pronounced 'knee-say.' It means 'second generation.' " Sometimes I think I've been teaching school too long. I explained that my grandparents, born in Japan, were Issei, or first generation, while the children of the Nisei were called Sansei, or third generation.

The widower was so full of questions that I half-expected him to ask for an identity card. The only thing I carry in my wallet is my driver's license. I should have something with my picture on it and a statement below that tells who I am. Megumi Naomi Nakane. Born June 18, 1936, Vancouver, British Columbia. Marital status: Old maid. Health: Fine, I suppose. Occupation: School teacher. I'm bored to death with teaching and ready to retire. What else would anyone want to know? Personality: Tense. Is that past or present tense? It's perpetual tense. I have the social graces of a common housefly. That's self-denigrating, isn't it?

The widower never asked me out again. I wonder how I was unsatisfactory. I could hardly think of anything at all to ask him. Did he assume I wasn't interested? Can people not tell the difference between nervousness and lack of interest?

"Well," I say, turning around and facing the general tittering, "there are many questions I don't have answers for."

Sigmund's hand is waving still. "But you're a spinster," he says, darting a grin at the class. More gasps from the girls.

"Spinster?" I grimace and have an urge to throttle him. "What does the word mean?"

"Old maid," Sigmund says impudently.

Spinster? Old maid? Bachelor lady? The terms certainly apply. At thirty-six, I'm no bargain in the marriage market. But Aunt

Emily in Toronto, still single at fifty-six, is even more old-maidish than I am, and yet she refuses the label. She says if we laundered the term properly she'd put it on, but it's too covered with cultural accretions for comfort.

"I suppose I am an old maid," I say glumly. "So is my aunt in Toronto."

"Your aunt is an old maid too? How come?"

I throw up my hands in futility. Let the questions come. Why indeed are there two of us unmarried in our small family? Must be something in the blood. A crone-prone syndrome. We should hire ourselves out for a research study, Aunt Emily and I. But she would be too busy, rushing around Toronto, rushing off to conferences. She never stays still long enough to hear the sound of her own voice.

"What's her name, Teacher?"

"Emily Kato," I say, spelling it. "That's 'Cut-oh,' not 'Cat-oh,' or 'Kay-toe.' Miss E. Kato." Is there some way I can turn this ridiculous discussion into a phonics lesson?

Someone is sure to ask about her love life. Has Aunt Emily ever, I wonder, been in love? Love no doubt is in her. Love, like the coulee wind, rushing through her mind, whirring along the tips of her imagination. Love like a coyote, howling into a "love 'em and leave 'em" wind.

The Tenant

BHARATI MUKHERJEE

$\mathcal{M}$aya San-yal
has been in Cedar Falls, Iowa, less than two weeks. She's come, books and clothes and one armchair rattling in the smallest truck that U-Haul would rent her, from New Jersey. Before that she was in North Carolina. Before that, Calcutta, India. Every place has something to give. She is sitting at the kitchen table with Fran drinking bourbon for the first time in her life. Fran Johnson found her the furnished apartment and helped her settle in. Now she's brought a bottle of bourbon, which gives her the right to stay and talk for a bit. She's breaking up with someone named Vern, a pharmacist. Vern's father is also a pharmacist and owns a drugstore. Maya has seen Vern's father on TV twice already. The first time was on the local news when he spoke out against the selling of painkillers like Advil and Nuprin in supermarkets and gas stations. In the matter of painkillers, Maya is a universalist. The other time he was in a barbershop quartet. Vern gets along all right with his father. He likes the pharmacy business, as business goes, but he wants to go back to graduate school and learn to make films. Maya is drinking her first bourbon tonight because Vern left today for San Francisco State.

"I understand totally," Fran says. She teaches Utopian Fiction and a course in Women's Studies and worked hard to get Maya

hired. Maya has a Ph.D. in Comparative Literature and will introduce writers like R. K. Narayan and Chinua Achebe to three sections of sophomores at the University of Northern Iowa. "A person
has to leave home. Try out his wings."

Fran has to use the bathroom. "I don't feel abandoned." She
pushes her chair away from the table. "Anyway, it was a sex thing
totally. We were good together. It'd be different if I'd loved
him."

Maya tries to remember what's in the refrigerator. They need
food. She hasn't been to the supermarket in over a week. She doesn't
have a car yet and so she relies on a corner store—a longish walk—
for milk, cereal, and frozen dinners. Someday these exigencies will
show up as bad skin and collapsed muscle tone. No folly is ever lost.
Maya pictures history as a net, the kind of safety net traveling
trapeze artists of her childhood fell into when they were inattentive,
or clumsy. Going to circuses in Calcutta with her father is what she
remembers vividly. It is a banal memory, for her father, the owner
of a steel company, is a complicated man.

Fran is out in the kitchen long enough for Maya to worry. They
need food. Her mother believed in food. What is love, anger, inner
peace, etc., her mother used to say, but the brain's biochemistry.
Maya doesn't want to get into that, but she is glad she has enough
stuff in the refrigerator to make an omelette. She realizes Indian
women are supposed to be inventive with food, whip up exotic
delights to tickle an American's palate, and she knows she should
be meeting Fran's generosity and candor with some sort of bizarre
and effortless countermove. If there's an exotic spice store in Cedar
Falls or in neighboring Waterloo, she hasn't found it. She's looked
in the phonebook for common Indian names, especially Bengali,
but hasn't yet struck up culinary intimacies. That will come—it
always does. There's a six-pack in the fridge that her landlord, Ted
Suminski, had put in because she'd be thirsty after unpacking. She
was thirsty, but she doesn't drink beer. She probably should have
asked him to come up and drink the beer. Except for Fran she hasn't

had anyone over. Fran is more friendly and helpful than anyone Maya has known in the States since she came to North Carolina ten years ago, at nineteen. Fran is a Swede, and she is tall, with blue eyes. Her hair, however, is a dull, darkish brown.

"I don't think I can handle anything that heavy-duty," Fran says when she comes back to the room. She means the omelette. "I have to go home in any case." She lives with her mother and her aunt, two women in their mid-seventies, in a drafty farmhouse. The farmhouse now has a computer store catty-corner from it. Maya's been to the farm. She's been shown photographs of the way the corner used to be. If land values ever rebound, Fran will be worth millions.

Before Fran leaves she says, "Has Rab Chatterji called you yet?"

"No." She remembers the name, a good, reliable Bengali name, from the first night's study of the phone book. Dr. Rabindra Chatterji teaches Physics.

"He called the English office just before I left." Fran takes car keys out of her pocketbook. She reknots her scarf. "I bet Indian men are more sensitive than Americans. Rab's a Brahmin, that's what people say."

A Chatterji has to be a Bengali Brahmin—last names give ancestral secrets away—but Brahminness seems to mean more to Fran than it does to Maya. She was born in 1954, six full years after India became independent. Her India was Nehru's India: a charged, progressive place.

"All Indian men are wife beaters," Maya says. She means it and doesn't mean it. "That's why I married an American." Fran knows about the divorce, but nothing else. Fran is on the Hiring, Tenure, and Reappointment Committee.

Maya sees Fran down the stairs and to the car, which is parked in the back in the spot reserved for Maya's car, if she owned one. It will take her several months to save enough to buy one. She always pays cash, never borrows. She tells herself she's still recovering from the U-Haul drive halfway across the country. Ted Suminski is in his kitchen watching the women. Maya waves to him because waving to him, acknowledging him in that way, makes him seem less creepy. He seems to live alone though a sign, THE SUMINSKIS, hangs from a metal horse's head in the front yard. Maya hasn't seen Mrs. Suminski. She hasn't seen any children either. Ted always looks lonely. When she comes back from campus, he's nearly always in the back, throwing darts or shooting baskets.

"What's he like?" Fran gestures with her head as she starts up her car. "You hear these stories."

Maya doesn't want to know the stories. She has signed a year's lease. She doesn't want complications. "He's all right. I keep out of his way."

"You know what I'm thinking? Of all the people in Cedar Falls, you're the one who could understand Vern best. His wanting to try out his wings, run away, stuff like that."

"Not really." Maya is not being modest. Fran is being impulsively democratic, lumping her wayward lover and Indian friend together as headstrong adventurers. For Fran, a utopian and feminist, borders don't count. Maya's taken some big risks, made a break with her parents' ways. She's done things a woman from Ballygunge Park Road doesn't do, even in fantasies. She's not yet shared stories with Fran, apart from the divorce. She's told her nothing of men she picks up, the reputation she'd gained, before Cedar Falls, for "indiscretions." She has a job, equity, three friends she can count on for emergencies. She is an American citizen. But.

Fran's Brahmin calls her two nights later. On the phone he presents himself as Dr. Chatterji, not Rabindra or Rab. An old-fashioned Indian, she assumes. Her father still calls his closest friend "Colonel." Dr. Chatterji asks her to tea on Sunday. She means to say no but hears herself saying, "Sunday? Five-ish? I'm not doing anything special this Sunday."

Outside, Ted Suminski is throwing darts into his garage door. The door has painted-on rings: orange, purple, pink. The bull's-eye is gray. He has to be fifty at least. He is a big, thick, lonely man about whom people tell stories. Maya pulls the phone cord as far as it'll go so she can look down more directly on her landlord's large, bald head. He has his back to her as he lines up a dart. He's in black running shoes, red shorts, he's naked to the waist. He hunches his right shoulder, he pulls the arm back; a big, lonely man shouldn't have so much grace. The dart is ready to cut through the September evening. But Ted Suminski doesn't let go. He swings on worn rubber soles, catches her eye in the window (she has to have imagined this), takes aim at her shadow. Could she have imagined the noise of the dart's metal tip on her windowpane?

Dr. Chatterji is still on the phone. "You are not having any mode of transportation, is that right?"

Ted Suminski has lost interest in her. Perhaps it isn't interest, at all; perhaps it's aggression. "I don't drive," she lies, knowing it sounds less shameful than not owning a car. She has said this so often she can get in the right degree of apology and Asian upper-class helplessness. "It's an awful nuisance."

"Not to worry, please." Then, "It is a great honor to be meeting Dr. Sanyal's daughter. In Calcutta business circles he is a legend."

On Sunday she is ready by four-thirty. She doesn't know what the afternoon holds; there are surely no places for "high tea"—a colonial tradition—in Cedar Falls, Iowa. If he takes her back to his place, it will mean he has invited other guests. From his voice she can tell Dr. Chatterji likes to do things correctly. She has dressed herself in a peach-colored nylon georgette sari, jade drop-earrings and a necklace. The color is good on dark skin. She is not pretty, but she does her best. Working at it is a part of self-respect. In the mid-seventies, when American women felt rather strongly about such things, Maya had been in trouble with her women's group at Duke. She was too feminine. She had tried to explain the world she came out of. Her grandmother had been married off at the age of five in a village now in Bangladesh. Her great-aunt had been burned to death over a dowry problem. She herself had been trained to speak softly, arrange flowers, sing, be pliant. If she were to seduce Ted Suminski, she thinks as she waits in the front yard for Dr. Chatterji, it would be minor heroism. She has broken with the past. But.

Dr. Chatterji drives up for her at about five-ten. He is a hesitant driver. The car stalls, jumps ahead, finally slams to a stop. Maya has to tell him to back off a foot or so; it's hard to leap over two sacks of pruned branches in a sari. Ted Suminski is an obsessive pruner and gardener.

"My sincerest apologies, Mrs. Sanyal," Dr. Chatterji says. He leans across the wide front seat of his noisy, very old, very used car and unlocks the door for her. "I am late. But then, I am sure you're remembering that Indian Standard Time is not at all the same as time in the States." He laughs. He could be nervous—she often had that effect on Indian men. Or he could just be chatty. "These Americans are all the time rushing and rushing but where it gets them?" He moves his head laterally once, twice. It's the gesture made famous by Peter Sellers. When Peter Sellers did it, it had seemed hilarious. Now it suggests that Maya and Dr. Chatterji have three thousand years plus civilization, sophistication, moral virtue, over people born on this continent. Like her, Dr. Chatterji is a naturalized American.

"Call me Maya," she says. She fusses with the seat belt. She does it because she needs time to look him over. He seems quite harmless. She takes in the prominent teeth, the eyebrows that run together. He's in a blue shirt and a beige cardigan with the

Kmart logo that buttons tightly over the waist. It's hard to guess his age because he has dyed his hair and his mustache. Late thirties, early forties. Older than she had expected. "Not Mrs. Sanyal."

This isn't the time to tell about ex-husbands. She doesn't know where John is these days. He should have kept up at least. John had come into her life as a graduate student at Duke, and she, mistaking the brief breathlessness of sex for love, had married him. They had stayed together two years, maybe a little less. The pain that John had inflicted all those years ago by leaving her had subsided into a cozy feeling of loss. This isn't the time, but then she doesn't want to be a legend's daughter all evening. She's not necessarily on Dr. Chatterji's side is what she wants to get across early; she's not against America and Americans. She makes the story—of marriage outside the Brahminic pale, the divorce—quick, dull. Her unsentimentality seems to shock him. His stomach sags inside the cardigan.

"We've each had our several griefs," the physicist says. "We're each required to pay our karmic debts."

"Where are we headed?"

"Mrs. Chatterji has made some Indian snacks. She is waiting to meet you because she is knowing your cousin-sister who studied in Scottish Church College. My home is okay, no?"

Fran would get a kick out of this. Maya has slept with married men, with nameless men, with men little more than boys, but never with an Indian man. Never.

The Chatterjis live in a small blue house on a gravelly street. There are at least five or six other houses on the street; the same size but in different colors and with different front yard treatments. More houses are going up. This is the cutting edge of suburbia.

Mrs. Chatterji stands in the driveway. She is throwing a large plastic ball to a child. The child looks about four, and is Korean or

Cambodian. The child is not hers because she tells it, "Chung-Hee, ta-ta, bye-bye. Now I play with guest," as Maya gets out of the car.

Maya hasn't seen this part of town. The early September light softens the construction pits. In that light the houses too close together, the stout woman in a striped cotton sari, the child hugging a pink ball, the two plastic lawn chairs by a tender young tree, the sheets and saris on the clothesline in the back, all seem miraculously incandescent.

"Go home now, Chung-Hee. I am busy." Mrs. Chatterji points the child homeward, then turns to Maya, who has folded her hands in traditional Bengali greeting. "It is an honor. We feel very privileged." She leads Maya indoors to a front room that smells of moisture and paint.

In her new, deliquescent mood, Maya allows herself to be backed into the best armchair—a low-backed, boxy Goodwill item draped over with a Rajasthani bedspread—and asks after the cousin Mrs. Chatterji knows. She doesn't want to let go of Mrs. Chatterji. She doesn't want husband and wife to get into whispered conferences about their guest's misadventures in America as they make tea in the kitchen.

The coffee table is already laid with platters of mutton croquettes, fish chops, onion pakoras, ghugni with puris, samosas, chutneys. Mrs. Chatterji has gone to too much trouble. Maya counts four kinds of sweetmeats in Corning casseroles on an end table. She looks into a see-through lid; spongy, white dumplings float in rosewater syrup. Planets contained, mysteries made visible.

"What are you waiting for, Santana?" Dr. Chatterji becomes imperious, though not unaffectionate. He pulls a dining chair up close to the coffee table. "Make some tea." He speaks in Bengali to his wife, in English to Maya. To Maya he says, grandly, "We are having real Indian Green Label Lipton. A nephew is bringing it just one month back."

His wife ignores him. "The kettle's already on," she says. She wants to know about the Sanyal family. Is it true her great-grandfather was a member of the Star Chamber in England?

Nothing in Calcutta is ever lost. Just as her story is known to Bengalis all over America, so are the scandals of her family, the grandfather hauled up for tax evasion, the aunt who left her husband to act in films. This woman brings up the Star Chamber, the glories of the Sanyal family, her father's philanthropies, but it's a way of saying *I know the dirt.*

The bedrooms are upstairs. In one of those bedrooms an unseen, tormented presence—Maya pictures it as a clumsy ghost that strains to shake off the body's shell—drops things on the floor. The things are heavy and they make the front room's chandelier shake. Light bulbs, shaped like tiny candle flames, flicker. The Chatterjis have said nothing about children. There are no tricycles in the hallway, no small sandals behind the doors. Maya is too polite to ask about the noise, and the Chatterjis don't explain. They talk just a little louder. They flip the embroidered cover off the stereo. What would Maya like to hear? Hemanta Kumar? Manna Dey? Oh, that young chap, Manna Dey! What sincerity, what tenderness he can convey!

Upstairs the ghost doesn't hear the music of nostalgia. The ghost throws and thumps. The ghost makes its own vehement music. Maya hears in its voice madness, self-hate.

Finally the water in the kettle comes to a boil. The whistle cuts through all fantasy and pretense. Dr. Chatterji says, "I'll see to it," and rushes out of the room. But he doesn't go to the kitchen. He shouts up the stairwell. "Poltoo, kindly stop this nonsense straightaway! We're having a brilliant and cultured lady-guest and you're creating earthquakes?" The kettle is hysterical.

Mrs. Chatterji wipes her face. The face that had seemed plump and cheery at the start of the evening now is flabby. "My sister's boy," the woman says.

So this is the nephew who has brought with him the cartons of Green Label tea, one of which will be given to Maya.

Mrs. Chatterji speaks to Maya in English as though only the alien language can keep emotions in check. "Such an intelligent boy! His father is government servant. Very highly placed."

Maya is meant to visualize a smart, clean-cut young man from south Calcutta, but all she can see is a crazy, thwarted, lost graduate student. Intelligence, proper family guarantee nothing. Even Brahmins can do self-destructive things, feel unsavory urges. Maya herself had been an excellent student.

"He was First Class First in B. Sc. from Presidency College," the woman says. "Now he's getting Master's in Ag. Science at Iowa State."

The kitchen is silent. Dr. Chatterji comes back into the room with a tray. The teapot is under a tea cozy, a Kashmiri one embroidered with the usual chinar leaves, loops, and chains. *"Her* nephew," he says. The dyed hair and dyed mustache are no longer signs of a man wishing to fight the odds. He is a vain man, anxious to cut losses. "Very unfortunate business."

The nephew's story comes out slowly, over fish chops and mutton croquettes. He is in love with a student from Ghana.

"Everything was A-okay until the Christmas break. Grades, assistantship for next semester, everything."

"I blame the college. The office for foreign students arranged a Christmas party. And now, *baapre baap!* Our poor Poltoo wants to marry a Negro Muslim."

Maya is known for her nasty, ironic one-liners. It has taken her friends weeks to overlook her malicious, un-American pleasure in others' misfortunes. Maya would like to finish Dr. Chatterji off quickly. He is pompous; he is reactionary; he wants to live and work in America but give back nothing except taxes. The confused world of the immigrant—the lostness that Maya and Poltoo feel— that's what Dr. Chatterji wants to avoid. She hates him. But.

Dr. Chatterji's horror is real. A good Brahmin boy in Iowa is in love with an African Muslim. It shouldn't be a big deal. But the more she watches the physicist, the more she realizes that "Brah-

min" isn't a caste; it's a metaphor. You break one small rule, and
the constellation collapses. She thinks suddenly that John Cheever
—she is teaching him as a "world writer" in her classes, cheek by
jowl with Africans and West Indians—would have understood Dr.
Chatterji's dread. Cheever had been on her mind, ever since the late
afternoon light slanted over Mrs. Chatterji's drying saris. She remembers now how full of a soft, Cheeverian light Durham had been
the summer she had slept with John Hadwen; and how after that,
her tidy graduate-student world became monstrous, lawless. All
men became John Hadwen; John became all men. Outwardly, she
retained her poise, her Brahminical breeding. She treated her crisis
as a literary event; she lost her moral sense, her judgment, her
power to distinguish. Her parents had behaved magnanimously.
They had cabled from Calcutta: WHAT'S DONE IS DONE. WE ARE CONFI-
DENT YOU WILL HANDLE NEW SITUATIONS WELL. ALL LOVE. But she knows
more than do her parents. Love is anarchy.

Poltoo is Mrs. Chatterji's favorite nephew. She looks as though
it is her fault that the Sunday has turned unpleasant. She stacks the
empty platters methodically. To Maya she says, "It is the goddess
who pulls the strings. We are puppets. I know the goddess will fix
it. Poltoo will not marry that African woman." Then she goes to
the coat closet in the hall and staggers back with a harmonium, the
kind sold in music stores in Calcutta, and sets it down on the
carpeted floor. "We're nothing but puppets," she says again.
She sits at Maya's feet, her pudgy hands on the harmonium's
shiny, black bellows. She sings, beautifully, in a virgin's high
voice, "Come, goddess, come, muse, come to us hapless peoples'
rescue."

Maya is astonished. She has taken singing lessons at Dakshini
Academy in Calcutta. She plays the sitar and the tanpur, well
enough to please Bengalis, to astonish Americans. But stout Mrs.
Chatterji is a devotee, talking to God.

————

A little after eight, Dr. Chatterji drops her off. It's been an odd evening, and they are both subdued.

"I want to say one thing," he says. He stops her from undoing her seat belt. The plastic sacks of pruned branches are still at the corner.

"You don't have to get out," she says.

"Please. Give me one more minute of your time."

"Sure."

"Maya is my favorite name."

She says nothing. She turns away from him without making her embarrassment obvious.

"Truly speaking, it is my favorite. You are sometimes lonely, no? But you are lucky. Divorced women can date, they can go to bars and discos. They can see mens, many mens. But inside marriage there is so much loneliness." A groan, low, horrible, comes out of him.

She turns back toward him, to unlatch the seat belt and run out of the car. She sees that Dr. Chatterji's pants are unzipped. One hand works hard under his Jockey shorts; the other rests, limp, penitential, on the steering wheel.

"Dr. Chatterji—*really!*" she cries.

The next day, Monday, instead of getting a ride home with Fran— Fran says she *likes* to give rides, she needs the chance to talk, and she won't share gas expenses, absolutely not—Maya goes to the periodicals room of the library. There are newspapers from everywhere, even from Madagascar and New Caledonia. She thinks of the periodicals room as an asylum for homesick aliens. There are two aliens already in the room, both Orientals, both absorbed in the politics and gossip of their far-off homes.

She goes straight to the newspapers from India. She bunches her raincoat like a bolster to make herself more comfortable. There's so much to catch up on. A village headman, a known Congress-

Indira party worker, has been shot at by scooter-riding snipers. An Indian pugilist has won an international medal—in Nepal. A child drawing well water—the reporter calls the child "a neo-Buddhist, a convert from the now-outlawed untouchable caste"—has been stoned. An editorial explains that the story about stoning is not a story about caste but about failed idealism; a story about promises of green fields and clean, potable water broken, a story about bribes paid and wells not dug, But no, thinks Maya, it's about caste.

Out here, in the heartland of the new world, the India of serious newspapers unsettles. Maya longs again to feel what she had felt in the Chatterjis' living room: virtues made physical. It is a familiar feeling, a longing. Had a suitable man presented himself in the reading room at that instant, she would have seduced him. She goes on to the stack of *India Abroad*s, reads through matrimonial columns, and steals an issue to take home.

Indian men want Indian brides. Married Indian men want Indian mistresses. All over America, "handsome, tall, fair" engineers, doctors, data processors—the new pioneers—cry their eerie love calls.

Maya runs a finger down the first column; her fingertip, dark with newsprint, stops at random.

Hello! Hi! Yes, you *are* the one I'm looking for. You are the new emancipated Indo-American woman. You have a zest for life. You are at ease in USA and yet your ethics are rooted in Indian tradition. The man of your dreams has come. Yours truly is handsome, ear-nose-throat specialist, well-settled in Connecticut. Age is 41 but never married, physically fit, sportsmanly, and strong. I adore idealism, poetry, beauty. I abhor smugness, passivity, caste system. Write with recent photo. Better still, call!!!

Maya calls. Hullo, hullo, hullo! She hears immigrant lovers cry in crowded shopping malls. Yes, you who are at ease in both worlds, you are the one. She feels she has a fair chance.

A man answers. "Ashoke Mehta speaking."

She speaks quickly into the bright-red mouthpiece of her telephone. He will be in Chicago, in transit, passing through O'Hare. United counter, Saturday, two P.M. As easy as that.

"Good," Ashoke Mehta says. "For these encounters I, too, prefer a neutral zone."

On Saturday at exactly two o'clock the man of Maya's dreams floats toward her as lovers used to in shampoo commercials. The United counter is a loud, harassed place, but passengers and piled-up luggage fall away from him. Full-cheeked and fleshy-lipped, he is handsome. He hasn't lied. He is serene, assured, a Hindu god touching down in Illinois.

She can't move. She feels ugly and unworthy. Her adult life no longer seems miraculously rebellious; it is grim, it is perverse. She has accomplished nothing. She has changed her citizenship but she hasn't broken through into the light, the vigor, the *bustle* of the New World. She is stuck in dead space.

"Hullo, hullo!" Their fingers touch.

Oh, the excitement! Ashoke Mehta's palm feels so right in the small of her back. Hullo, hullo, hullo. He pushes her out of the reach of anti-Khomeini Iranians, Hare Krishnas, American Fascists, men with fierce wants, and guides her to an empty gate. They have less than an hour.

"What would you like, Maya?"

She knows he can read her mind, she knows her thoughts are open to him. *You;* she's almost giddy with the thought, with simple desire. "From the snack bar," he says, as though to clarify. "I'm afraid I'm starved."

Below them, where the light is strong and hurtful, a Boeing is being serviced. "Nothing," she says.

He leans forward. She can feel the nap of his scarf—she recognizes the Cambridge colors—she can smell the wool of his Icelandic sweater. She runs her hand along the scarf, then against the flesh of his neck. "Only the impulsive ones call," he says.

The immigrant courtship proceeds. It's easy; he's good with facts. He knows how to come across to a stranger who may end up a lover, a spouse. He makes over a hundred thousand. He owns a house in Hartford, and two income properties in Newark. He plays the market but he's cautious. He's good at badminton but plays handball to keep in shape. He watches all the sports on television. Last August he visited Copenhagen, Helsinki and Leningrad. Once upon a time he collected stamps but now he doesn't have hobbies, except for reading. He counts himself an intellectual, he spends too much on books. Ludlum, Forsyth, MacInnes; other names she doesn't catch. She suppresses a smile; she's told him only she's a graduate student. He's not without his vices. He's a spender, not a saver. He's a sensualist: good food—all foods, but easy on the Indian—good wine. Some temptations he doesn't try to resist.

And I, she wants to ask, do I tempt?

"Now tell me about yourself, Maya." He makes it easy for her. "Have you ever been in love?"

"No."

"But many have loved you, I can see that." He says it not unkindly. It is the fate of women like her, and men like him. Their karmic duty, to be loved. It is expected, not judged. She feels he can see them all, the sad parade of need and demand. This isn't the time to reveal all.

And so the courtship enters a second phase.

When she gets back to Cedar Falls, Ted Suminski is standing on the front porch. It's late at night, chilly. He is wearing a down vest.

She's never seen him on the porch. In fact there's no chair to sit on. He looks chilled through. He's waited around a while.

"Hi." She has her keys ready. This isn't the night to offer the six-pack in the fridge. He looks expectant, ready to pounce.

"Hi." He looks like a man who might have aimed the dart at her. What has he done to his wife, his kids? Why isn't there at least a dog? "Say, I left a note upstairs."

The note is written in Magic Marker and thumbtacked to her apartment door. DUE TO PERSONAL REASONS, NAMELY REMARRIAGE, I REQUEST THAT YOU VACATE MY PLACE AT THE END OF THE SEMESTER.

Maya takes the note down and retacks it to the kitchen wall. The whole wall is like a bulletin board, made of some new, crumbly building material. Her kitchen, Ted Suminski had told her, was once a child's bedroom. Suminski in love: the idea stuns her. She has misread her landlord. The dart at her window speaks of no twisted fantasy. The landlord wants the tenant out.

She gets a glass out of the kitchen cabinet, gets out a tray of ice, pours herself a shot of Fran's bourbon. She is happy for Ted Suminski. She is. She wants to tell someone how moved she'd been by Mrs. Chatterji's singing. How she'd felt in O'Hare, even about Dr. Rab Chatterji in the car. But Fran is not the person. No one she's ever met is the person. She can't talk about the dead space she lives in. She wishes Ashoke Mehta would call. Right now.

Weeks pass. Then two months. She finds a new room, signs another lease. Her new landlord calls himself Fred. He has no arms, but he helps her move her things. He drives between Ted Suminski's place and his twice in his station wagon. He uses his toes the way Maya uses her fingers. He likes to do things. He pushes garbage sacks full of Maya's clothes up the stairs.

It's all right to stare," Fred says. "Hell, I would."

That first afternoon in Fred's rooming house, they share a Chianti. Fred wants to cook her pork chops, but he's a little shy about

Indians and meat. Is it beef, or pork? Or any meat? She says it's okay, any meat, but not tonight. He has an ex-wife in Des Moines, two kids in Portland, Oregon. The kids are both normal; he's the only freak in the family. But he's self-reliant. He shops in the supermarket like anyone else, he carries out the garbage, shovels the snow off the sidewalk. He needs Maya's help with one thing. Just one thing. The box of Tide is a bit too heavy to manage. Could she get him the giant size every so often and leave it in the basement?

The dead space need not suffocate. Over the months, Fred and she will settle into companionship. She has never slept with a man without arms. Two wounded people, he will joke during their nightly contortions. It will shock her, this assumed equivalence with a man so strikingly deficient. She knows she is strange and lonely, but being Indian is not the same, she would have thought, as being a freak.

One night in spring, Fred's phone rings. "Ashoke Mehta speaking." None of this "do you remember me?" nonsense. The god has tracked her down. He hasn't forgotten. "Hullo," he says, in their special way. And, because she doesn't answer back, "Hullo, hullo, hullo." She is aware of Fred in the back of the room. He is lighting a cigarette with his toes.

"Yes," she says, "I remember."

"I had to take care of a problem," Ashoke Mehta says. "You know that I have my vices. That time at O'Hare I was honest with you."

She is breathless.

"Who is it, May?" asks Fred.

"You also have a problem," says the voice. His laugh echoes. "You will come to Hartford, I know."

When she moves out, she tells herself, it will not be the end of Fred's world.

In Between and Around

JOHN YAU

And all the while we were kissing,
the two of us, and the many we are,
were standing, kneeling, or spinning
upside down in the long wet arms
of prayer, waiting to be kissed.
Pimply slumps of postmarked muscles.
Closet behind schoolyard
back alley train station
midnight morning
lifts through blue light
locked inside eyes and breath
held in wet palms.
Hands and mouth gripping.
Tepid, slippery teeth and tongue
first joyful snake stabs.
All the while we were kissing
on a dusty summer afternoon,
someone was standing outside us,
watching our shadows perpetrate a body
on soft asphalt beneath cloudless sky.
Walking, as if there is somewhere to go.

Petulant scowl, lips that flower,
scorched red petals swelling
neither to be caressed nor plucked.
One of them thinks, always afraid
to fill the thought with words, breathe
outside the boundaries of the third person,
though eyes in hazy half-light
watch the lips parting with each breath,
and the body beside the one
who is sleeping sweats.
The sweat rolling down the face
mingles with tears, and the tears
moisten the lips. The lips of the one
who wished and waited and finally spoke
or the lips of the one who didn't and didn't.
Rows of mouths, closed, open and twisted
open or shut in dunes and curtains
flowering under the monument's hammer.
Of these tears and the tears beside them,
the ones about which you cannot speak
and are afraid to see, of these and others
the *Book of Trembling* is written.
And the body one sees beneath
and within the fabric rustling
and shifting with every breath
drawn across the taut sweep of skin,
eyes fixated, air held in lungs,
smoldering there, the sounds
swelling louder and louder
than the thoughts releasing them.
All the while the voices are rising
toward one's mouth, borrowed, broken,
or temporarily possessed, two tremulous
ropes are kissing behind and beyond

the ones who are crawling, shifting
away from and toward,
near and under and beside
this around and near.
Sometimes a pleasant shrieking,
gurgles and wriggling gasps.
A sigh like that of one in pain.
And all the while the ones
we imagine ourselves to be
go on kissing and kissing,
hands prying apart,
fingers squeezing
twisting hard buttons,
plucking at metal and cloth,
and the rippling overlap of two
consecutive, stretching, pushing forms
located on the physical plane
between liquid and solid disintegrates
the dorsal trajectories,
as they go on,
as if that is all they can do,
the only place of sustenance
being where mouths mesh,
all they want being the mouth
opening and closing around, over and between.
And the kissing goes on
even when the body grows lax,
soft and malleable as a spoon of lead or wax,
something to thud against the wind.
And the wind moves aside,
as the kissing continues,
and the mouths move aside,
as the bodies become plants

on the ocean floor, spinning within
the motions of air's sweet tremors.
And the kissing begins to take hold,
while inside the ones who are kissing,
the ones whose mouths have merged
into a single speaker of divided thoughts,
are other mouths, hands and feet.
And their voices begin rising, expanding,
and there is no end to the clamoring, whispers,
whistles, mumbles and screams,
while the ones who are kissing go on
because there is nothing and nowhere else,
no other hospital but here
where lips are meeting.
Shoulders, arms, fingers, eyelids,
and elbows join with feet, ribcage, and legs,
Mouths open, words or sounds
resembling words emerge
and melt among the sounds of cars honking,
curses of the hurt and shunned,
tremors of the astronauts dreaming,
sunlight drifting across shutters.
And the sounds of the kissing
reach the ones lined up inside
waiting to be kissed.
Some feel a mouth or mouths,
and others don't,
while the two people
in the hallway their bodies form,
keep kissing, lips
pressing and pushing against lips,
teeth and tongue.
They become silhouettes of the ones

waiting, wanting, refusing, afraid.
The kissing that goes on and on,
and the kissing that brings
something more, something else,
is just a sign of what will happen,
a taste or touch. Murmurs leading to more.
And this taste or touch
that some mouths never know
and about which they cannot speak,
having never tasted or been tasted.
The one tied to the chair obtained by the family.
The one strapped in the chair provided by the state.
And all that they have to say about kissing
that has never been heard by those who have kissed.

The Movers

DAVID WONG LOUIE

$\mathcal{A}$ week earlier we had left our old jobs, friends, and habits, and had driven across the state so we could start over fresh. Now we were in the place we had just rented, waiting for the Salvation Army to deliver our furniture. I was sitting on the edge of the kitchen sink fidgeting with the twin spigots, both running cold, when Suzy came right out and said we were out of love. She had this way of talking when she was mad: her lips scarcely moved, and she would point her hip at you and pat it as if it were a dog about to pounce. "We've made a mistake," she said. "We don't love each other anymore."

What could I do in that situation? Tell her she's wrong? That she's loved? I told her her news was no news to me, that her very thoughts had been incubating in my head, but I managed to keep them to myself. I wanted to believe that as long as we kept our mouths shut and let the negative thoughts that popped into our brains die there, there was hope for us. I told her this. She slapped her hip black and blue. Then, in menacing detail, she catalogued all that was wrong with me. She surveyed our common history, touching on incidents I thought were at worst benign, some even happy, that she now cited as reasons for her discontent.

Minutes into her testimony—by then I had already heard enough—someone knocked at the front door, and I gladly left the kitchen, thinking it was the furniture, anxious to catch my breath. A small kid was standing there. "Collect," he said.

"What?"

"Collect."

"They moved," I said, finally catching on.

"Collect," repeated the boy. We went on this way for a few more rounds. The kid was a tangle of woollies. Snot was frozen on his face. "Can't you see," I said, "you've never seen me before?" I heard Suzy coming to the door. "Send it back. We won't be needing the furniture anymore," she was saying before she saw I was talking to a kid. "Collect," he said the moment he laid eyes on her. "You're making a mistake," I told him.

"Ha!" Suzy said, brushing the boy aside as if he were a swinging gate. *"You're* the mistake." She ran out to the car. When she slipped on a patch of ice and almost fell, my heart stopped. But she quickly regained her balance, and so did I, and while the kid held back the storm door, I peppered her with insults, mostly names of barnyard animals, each leaving my lips with the ease of habit. All my screaming did little to mitigate my rage, so I cocked my middle finger and waved goodbye as she drove off in our car.

The kid stuck his mittened hand in my gut. "Collect," he said one last time. I reached into my pocket and brought out a crumpled dollar bill. I promised him more if he'd go. Then I apologized for the scene he had witnessed. "She's not always so difficult," I said as he left me.

I waited alone for the furniture. The manager at the store had promised delivery at three. By my watch it was already past four.

In the empty living room I sat on the floor near a window that faced the street. Cool air whistled through the cracked panes. Snow clouds darkened the sky. Beneath me the cold of the linoleum seeped through my pants; I felt as if I were sitting on a block of ice.

I got up and took down a set of bamboo blinds left by the

previous tenants. As I unrolled the blinds, each slat clicked against the polished floor like beetles underfoot. I stretched out on this mat, hands dug deep in my pea jacket, and pretended I was dead, lying in a morgue in China. This succeeded where obscene gesture had failed. I felt transported, dead in a foreign land where the language of Suzy wasn't spoken. Who would understand our petty complaints there? Who could translate our squabbles and make them palatable to another tongue? No, I was a dead man, and all I had to do was shut my eyes and listen for the Salvation Army to come.

In time, I fell asleep and when I woke my legs were filled with sand. They were open in a V to the corner of the room reserved for Suzy's loom—there, she said, the northern exposure was perfect for selecting colors of thread. I scanned the adjacent wall where the fireplace stood. Above the mantelpiece there was a large opening of exposed lath, perhaps the work of a shotgun blast, over which Suzy's tapestry was to hang, hiding the blemishes of our domesticity.

Then I returned to the morgue. A heat vent nearby started to hiss, blowing damp, refrigerated air against my cheek. I needed to have the gas turned on, but I couldn't call because I didn't have a phone yet and I couldn't go because Suzy took the car. No phone, no heat, no car. No electricity at least for another day. I was out of love. And, even worse, I had no modern conveniences.

I had almost dozed off again when someone knocked at the front door. I got to my knees and peeked out the window but saw no truck on the street.

I heard the storm door pulled back, the lock turned in a single, sensuous click. Although a wall separated the vestibule from the living room, still I crawled quickly into Suzy's corner, where my hands came to rest on mounds of dirt that someone had swept up and left there.

"You're crazy, George," a girl whispered.

"Nobody's here," said her companion. "You heard me knock."

The door was shut and the lock secured.

She said, "I still think this is crazy."

My visitors ran upstairs, their footsteps echoing throughout the empty house. I remained frozen in place, afraid I might be discovered. Even though my pulse thumped loudly in my ears, I was still able to hear every word that passed between them.

"But where's the bed?" she asked.

"My parents just took everything out," said the boy. "Just be glad nobody's moved in yet."

She said, "We're trespassing, you know."

"Phyllis," he said, "I opened the door with my own key. How's that trespassing? Can't you be more spontaneous?"

I crept to the foot of the staircase.

"Here, smoke this gizmo," the boy said. "Who's going to hassle us? This is my house."

"But you don't live here anymore."

"Don't be so picky. Nobody lives here. This is open territory, like outer space. Now hold your breath."

The heavy scent of marijuana rolled down the stairs.

"Slow down, George. You're strangling me," she said. "Shut the door, at least."

I guessed by their voices they were in their teens. My watch said it was four-thirty, and according to the wall, where trees earlier had been shadowed, the sun had set. The furniture probably wasn't going to show.

Someone shut the door upstairs. I could no longer hear them. And so, I reasoned, they couldn't hear me. I climbed the stairs.

I peered through the old-fashioned keyhole in the door of the room Suzy and I had designated as our bedroom. Inside, the light was as gray as a low-contrast photo. Still I saw plenty through my sharpshooter's squint: with his jeans knotted at his knees, his jacket half off, his arms free of his sweater, which was still looped around his neck, the boy thrashed about between the girl's skinny, naked legs. Her arms were extended out to her sides, each hand clutching a piece of clothing. At once, my intruders looked like a spirited heap of laundry and an exotic form of torture. But when their taut young bodies touched who could mistake the sounds of the wondrous suction of love, like water slapping up the sides of a tub? My intruders improvised with a bamboo blind. I wondered, if she were here—I didn't think of Suzy by name; names are for parents to give and strangers to learn—would we also make a mattress of bamboo, or would we dutifully wait for our bed's arrival? And even then, would we spontaneously fall onto our new used mattress where countless others had slept and loved, or would we wait longer still for our sheets due COD from UPS?

"What's that noise?" The girl pushed up on her elbows.

I heard the noise too. Another set of knocks at the front door. Sharp and urgent, a bare fist, I thought. The boy sat back on his heels and threaded his arms through the sleeves of his sweater. He scanned the room and then finally said, "Relax. It's the dumb paperboy. He collects on Fridays." The boy pushed the girl down onto her back. Her white hands disappeared inside his sweater. She lifted her knees. He rooted for her lips. She shook her head.

My name is Grey," said the silhouette at the front door. His voice was full, confident, mature. He said, "I believe you know my daughter Phyllis. Our children are schoolmates."

With his back to the streetlight—or was it the moonlight?— my visitor didn't have a face. I couldn't see the scar that might've slashed his cheek in two or the desolate hole that once was home to a missing eye. All I was certain of was the silhouette's general shape —rounder and squatter than my own—and his voice, not just its sound, but the way it looked as it billowed in the chilled night air in fat, legible puffs like the speech of comic-strip characters.

"I didn't mean to barge in," he said, "but I tried calling, and the girl said your line had been temporarily disconnected." His presence sent the temperature of the house plunging. "Have you seen my daughter?" he asked.

I thought of my intruders up in the bedroom. Pictured the tiny figure of this man's daughter, her white knees, bare and strangely luminous, two moons in the gray light of the room, reaching for the ceiling—or, more ambitiously, straining for the heavens—as they cradled the boy.

"I can assure you," I began, "your daughter's safe with my boy." Those last two words, "my boy," thudded in my ears. I was astonished by my daring, and certain, despite my thirty years, that my voice lacked the easy authority of a parent. Without question, my "my boy" had just made its maiden voyage from my lips. So I took a precautionary step back into the dark house, where age could best be discerned by a careful touch of my skin.

"Phyllis has to come home right away," the silhouette said. "My wife and I—it's our anniversary, and she has it in her head the kids should come to the restaurant with us." He sounded like a man who fretted over what his children dreamed at night. He said, "I asked her, 'Where were those kids when we got married?' But what's the use? When she gets something locked in her skull, you might as well be talking to a snail. You know how things go a little sour when kids come on the scene."

"Sure I do," I said. But what did I know? I took another step back from the door. I imagined having a man-to-man talk with the silhouette one night. And after a few beers he would say, "I'll get this eye fixed. Put in a fake one like that Sammy Davis, Jr. The ladies like that sort of thing. Makes a man mysterious, and gets the woman feeling sorry for you. I tell you, my wife can keep the kids. She can take them for burgers the rest of her days. You and me, we'll go out, we'll make a great team."

"That's right," I'd say. "Fathers have to stick together." And we'd shake hands like men.

He said, "Would you call Phyllis for me?"

"If she shows up," I said, "I'll send her straight home."

The silhouette's shoulders rose and fell. "She's not here? Look, I'm sorry I've troubled you. Please ask her to call home. But your phone, it's out of order."

I reassured him I'd send her right home.

"Thanks," he said, "thanks." The silhouette extended his hand toward the storm door, but when I didn't make a move to offer him mine he clumsily stuffed his back into his pocket. Then he switched subjects and advised me to work things out with the phone company. "Drive a person mad being cut off from the outside like that," he said.

"I'll have it fixed first thing in the morning."

"Good. Now how about your lights? No juice, is there?" He cleared his throat. "Through our children, you can say we're friends. Phyllis has told me about your money troubles. Let me know how I can help."

"That's kind of you," I said, "but I'm okay. I'm just trying to conserve energy." I started to laugh, but he didn't follow my lead. "Forget about me and Phyllis. Go have a nice dinner, and wish Mrs. Grey a happy anniversary for me."

I watched the silhouette step into the night. I was almost rid of him when his body was suddenly cut in half by a set of oncoming headlights.

It was the Salvation Army truck. The driver honked at the silhouette, who stopped to talk to a man hanging out the open passenger window of the truck's cab. The silhouette then turned and came halfway up the front walk toward the house. He stopped and called, "Are you expecting some used furniture?"

"Me?" I said indignantly. "What does a man like me need from the Salvation Army?"

"That's what I thought," said the silhouette. "But something's odd. They have the correct address on their invoice but the name's all wrong. I'll just send them on their way."

"Wait. Let me." I almost stepped out of the house, but thought better of it. "You've done enough already. Mrs. Grey's probably wondering where you are."

He stood there as still as a tree stump and stared in my direction.

"Mrs. Grey," I said, and finally he left, shrugging his shoulders at the truck as he passed.

You got a Suzy Tree here?" the guy in the passenger window asked. Half a fat, unlighted cigar tugged at the corner of his mouth. He had on an old felt baseball cap, its bill tipped so low on his brow that his face seemed to start at his nose.

"That's us," I said.

The cap leaped from the cab. "Who's your boyfriend?" he asked as he pumped past me on his stumpy legs. "He almost chased us away."

"I should've let him," I said, watching the cap unlock and then disappear into the truck's dark trailer. "You're over two hours late."

"The snow," the cap said. "It's the damn snow."

"What snow? It's not snowing."

"Of course no snow," he said. "I'm talking about the idea of snow. People do things different when they're living with the idea of snow."

I didn't try to answer him. All I knew was if Suzy were here, this guy would be apologizing for their tardiness; he'd be almost too polite. I said, "Let's say I don't want this stuff anymore."

"Can't do," said a deep voice behind me. I turned and saw the driver, a man a head taller than the cap. He was wearing gloves with the tips cut away, exposing sausage-thick fingers that scissored what must've been the other half of his partner's cigar. "We only unload," he said. "If you don't want the merchandise, call the office and they'll send the pickup crew over."

I didn't care for these two men, but they certainly could work.

At first, I thought it was an illusion of their cigars and stubble and utilitarian jumpsuits that gave me this impression. But in no time they had the vestibule filled with a gigantic tangle of wood, steel, Formica, and foam.

"It's a wrap," the driver announced as he carried in an armchair and lowered it on top of the heap.

"What do you mean?" I said. "Where's the bed?"

"What does that mean, where's the bed?"

Now that we were in the house, I could no longer see their faces. My guests had turned into shadows in the vestibule where there were no clean edges, no distinct boundaries.

"You say you got a bed coming?"

"No, I just said that so you'd stay a little longer."

"Hey, he's a pretty funny fellow," said the cap. "I better get me a chair so I don't fall over from laughing."

"Drop it," the driver said. "Let's get moving before I starve to death. You see anything left in the truck?"

"Nothing I'd put my back on," said the cap.

His partner chuckled.

"There was something rolled up and standing in a corner."

"Sounds like one of our mattresses all right." The driver clapped his big hands. "Let's get it and get going." They moved for the door.

"Hold it," I said. "I'll carry it in." This was one of Suzy's ideas. She wanted us to bring the bed into our new home, a variant of the bride-over-the-threshold ritual. I had opposed such a scheme from the start. And this she interpreted as proof that I didn't want to live with her. So she pointed her hip at me. Then the paperboy came.

"Can't do. Totally against regulations," the driver said.

"This is no time for amateurs," said the cap.

I clenched my fists. I could feel the muscles in my neck coiling into snakes. A sudden rush of heat thawed the tip of my nose. My breath turned quick and shallow.

But who was I mad at—the movers? Suzy?

I said in the voice of reasonable men, "Let me do the mattress. I'll make it worth your while."

The mattress was damp and musty. In all likelihood it had labored in a dank basement for years under piles of *National Geographic*s and cracked clay flowerpots. I dragged it out into the night air. It seemed to sigh as it folded in half across my shoulder.

By the time I reached the house, I was in a sweat from the struggle the mattress had put up. I propped it against the wall but it slowly slithered to the floor as if it were filled with heavy syrup. "This isn't the one we bought," I said.

"We only unload," the driver said. "You don't want, call the office."

"Look, feel this. This is Jell-O. Would you want to sleep on this?"

"Sorry, bub," said the driver, chomping moistly on his cigar, "you're not my type."

The cap danced in carrying the box springs. He was whistling an inane tune. "You have to admire the work of a professional," he said as he let the load slide off his back. "Hey, what's the matter here?"

"He doesn't want the mattress."

"What's the matter? It's too firm for you?"

They chuckled.

"Forget it," I said. "Just leave me alone."

"Love to. But first we need Miss Tree to sign this invoice." The driver's heavy fingers tapped a clipboard he had magically produced out of the night air.

"I'll sign," I said, reaching for his pen.

"Can't do. We need the lady's signature. Company policy, see: 'Accept only the signature of the party named on the invoice.'"

The cap struck a match against a table leg and held the flame over the clipboard so I could see their silly rule. On the same match they lighted the cigars. With each puff I saw their faces, like gruesome orange masks. I could tell the driver from the cap by the relative height of the burning nib at the tip of his cigar.

"If I sign, you can go."

"I see we're dealing with a devious individual," the taller nib said. "You want us to break Army policy. Joey, should we give him an opportunity to deceive us?"

The shorter nib bobbed up and down.

"Okay then, what's your relationship to Miss Tree? You Mr. Tree?"

I told them no.

"Her brother?"

"No."

"I know you're not her father."

"How can you be so sure I'm not?"

"You don't sound like anyone's father," said the shorter nib, and instantly I touched my throat and thought back to the silhouette.

"Face it," the taller nib said, "no self-respecting father would let his kid near this kind of crap."

"For your information," I said, "I have a sixteen-year-old son."

"Sure you do. And my father's Smokey the Bear."

"That's not so hard to believe."

The shorter nib came at me, puffing wildly, but then suddenly stopped.

"Leave him," said his partner. "Tell me," he continued, "are you Miss Tree's sweetheart?"

I had to chew that one over. "You could've asked her yourself if you showed up when you were supposed to."

"S-s-shit," the taller nib hissed. "We're wasting our time. Let's move this stuff out of here."

"I thought you only unloaded," I said.

"We load, bub, when it's our mistake."

"So you admit you're wrong."

"Sure we're wrong. We'll take the rap for everything wrong in this town, in this state, on this planet. So what?"

The orange nibs floated through the vestibule burning smoky orange loops onto the black canvas while the hands and boots of the movers untangled the furniture pile.

"I paid for this junk," I said. "It's legally mine."

"Not till Miss Tree signs."

"Gentlemen," I said, wondering where that word had come from, "if you don't stop I'll be forced to call the police."

The shorter nib said, "Hey, you suppose we get overtime for this?"

I backed away to make good on my threat. I heard the tear and creak of furniture in distress. I heard the movers' steamy breaths, the *clomp clomp clomp* of their boots. Then I turned my back to the vestibule, and immediately, involuntarily, I threw my arms out in front of me. I saw nothing. My eyes were useless. In the dark the hands are what count. My fingers combed the air for the phone's smooth shell, solid and sleek, but I soon realized my movements lacked purpose. I was, of course, phoneless. But I continued on, simultaneously hoping for and dreading collisions.

There are no directions in the dark. All one has is memory and I had no memories of that house. I took recklessly long strides away from the vestibule, as if I were trying to outstep the darkness, as one steps over puddles. I waved my arms like a drowning man, groping for anything solid. I heard the nibs curse and grunt. They could've been singing "Whistle While You Work" and I wouldn't have been surprised. But what spooked me was the peculiar way their voices seemed to come at me from every angle, even though I hadn't veered from my original course.

A brief eternity later, finally, a collision. Two walls, one on either side of me—a narrow hallway. Here I moved with confidence. Each hand pressed flush against the walls, my fingertips tracing the cracks they found there as a palm reader follows a lifeline to its end. I stepped easily now, content inside that enclosed space, when without warning the walls gave way to air, and my arms spread open like the bellows of an accordion. My hands once again swatted at nothing. My legs turned wooden, my body froze, but my mind traveled on, back to Suzy and dark rooms where we once lay, where I extended my arms and at the ends of my fingertips I'd find her. It took a few moments, but soon I realized my flailing hands were moving in a distinct pattern. She was within reach. My hands had molded her from air.

Then I heard fresh footsteps. Not the dull thuds of the movers' boots, not my own because I still hadn't budged, but bright steps —a child's, perhaps, tentative in their approach.

"I'll sign," said a female voice.

I turned in time to see a match struck. Through the sulfurous smoke I saw illuminated by the fragile flame a most implausible trio—the bovine faces of the movers sandwiching Suzy's likeness.

"Where you been hiding?" asked the cap.

She answered by blowing out the flame. "Where do I sign?"

"Smart. She blows out the light and then wants to know where to sign. Sign in the dark, lady." The cap struck another match. The trio reappeared. The lambent flame washed over her close-set eyes, her fringed forehead, her brown lips, giving substance to the voice that said, "Where?"

"Right there, Miss Tree," the driver said. She signed and then blew out the flame.

The nibs bobbed toward the door. "Enjoy the bed," the shorter nib said, and they were gone.

"Thank you," I said to the darkened room. "You've been a great help." I moved in the direction where I believed I saw her last.

Those tentative footsteps suddenly took life. Quick, whispery steps, louder and then fading, the way an echo loses energy. They were somewhere behind me, and when I turned, they were behind me again. I spun around once more and saw the door opening.

"Go home," I said. "Your father wants you."

She was momentarily silhouetted in the doorway. She briefly looked in my general direction.

"Tell him I sent you home," I said as she left me, with a slam of the door.

I realized my hands were clutching the front of my shirt. Beneath it my ribs felt loose; my heart needed massage; in my stomach a little man was trying to punch his way out.

Before I knew which foot to move first, I heard a voice from above: "Hey, mister, I want you to have this key."

"Who's that?"

"You don't need my name. I used to live here."

"It's you," I said. "You're the one." I could tell he was on the stairs. "Please, strike a match." All I wanted was to see his face, to see myself there as I had seen Suzy in the girl's face.

"I don't have a match," he said. "I don't smoke. But, mister, here's the key."

I heard the metal clatter on the floor. Did he expect me to catch it? "Why didn't you leave with the girl?" I said.

"We meant no harm," he said. "Just taking a look around the old place." The stairs creaked under his weight as he started his descent. "You get the key?"

"Why did she leave you?"

"I'm coming down now," he said. "I don't want any trouble."

"You should go after her. Tell her you're sorry you did what you did. Tell her you love her, if that's what it takes."

"She's at dinner with her folks. You met her dad."

"He's not a very happy man," I said. "You give him so much to worry about."

"*Me?* You lied to him. Man, that was great. I swear, you really messed with his head." The boy stepped onto the floor.

"That was my mistake. I shouldn't have done such a thing. And don't get carried away. I didn't do it to impress you."

"Okay, mister, don't get hot." He pushed aside some furniture, clearing a path to the door. "Stay back now," he warned. "I'm leaving now."

"Wait. Give me a hand upstairs with the bed." I felt his body close to mine. I could reach out and turn his hand away from the door. But how long could I keep him? What did I have to say to a boy his age? I'd tell him about Suzy, then what? We could count snowflakes, if it snowed, and in the first light of the new day, I might see all we had in common. Surely there would be something —the slant of our eyes, the breadth of our noses, the cut of our hair, and, should Suzy appear, our mutual love for the same woman.

"Pick up the key," I said. "I want you to have it. Come back with the girl anytime."

"I'm gone, mister."

"No, not yet."

"I'm late." He turned the doorknob. I cupped my hand over his. How warm it felt.

"Where are you going? Maybe I'll come along."

He opened the door. An icy wind struck our faces. "I have to go eat dinner. That's all." He stepped outside. I didn't try to stop him. I asked if he had gloves, a hat, a scarf. I told him zip up tight. "Don't run if it starts to snow," I said.

"I'm okay, mister." With his back to me he looked up at the low sky. He took a step and made a half-turn toward the house. "Thanks for the visit," he said. "I think you'll like it here."

from

Native Speaker

CHANG-RAE LEE

I didn't notice her come in. She curled in beside me. She said all over the house things were in piles. The amount of the work was beginning to overwhelm us. Neither of us was ever much of an organizer. Picture albums, address books, receipt-keeping, these were the happy tasks of people completely staked to one another, so that they could produce a chit on demand, order and reorder their memories for a future day. We used to enjoy those legions of collectables, and we were glad for them, their happy messes. Bulging photo albums, corks of wines we'd drunk at restaurants in overcoat pockets. Boxes of mostly useless paper. Those tapes of Mitt, terrifying audio. Trails of frayed odd ribbons and precious bits of gift wrap and other junks of the past.

And if I remember everything now in the form of lists it is that these notions come to me along a floating string of memory, a long and lyric processional that leads me out from the city in which I live, to return me here, back to this place of our ghosts, to my wife who lay beside me with her eyes shuttered wide.

If I go back now, it's a game we've invented just tonight, the point being how to breach each other the right way—it's got to be sudden like that—and the contact of our spooned bodies lets me see again the sheer turn of her burnished cheek diving to the corner of the eye, that bare sexual angle you glimpse in the half-dark, with your half-mind.

I began stroking her. Shoulder down her arm to the rise of her hip, with one hand. I was being slow. I wanted to be slow with her. She was being slow with me, because of what I was doing I wasn't sure, and she wasn't responding to the graze of my fingers but she wasn't ignoring it, either, and just as I was about to cease my movement and fall back I heard her breathe, once, heavily, through her mouth. She whispered, *Easy.* It didn't matter what she was referring to. She was referring to it all. And tucking my face into her hair, I kept going, stroking, holding down my rhythm to the slowest ache I could bear. Holding up the line. She broke the seam of her legs and scissored one back and hooked my ankle with her instep, pulling my knee between hers to the other side. Rub of old jeans. I smelled her washsoap on the back of her neck. Not flowers, lilacs, more like sweetened milk. I kissed there, the lightest way I knew. So she wouldn't jump or freeze. I kissed her again, this time my lips half on her skin, on the pale soft hairs of her neck, and she craned so that the white skin inched up past the cover of her shirt fabric. Bone white, purple white. I felt a heat anyway. Her mouth was open. She was trying to stay herself and I understood. I was doing the same. I was watching my hand stroking and watching my face closing in against her. I pushed myself up on the bed and tugged her to roll and face me and she did. I kissed her neck and the bone between her breasts and I pressed my face maybe too hard against her belly. She pulled me by a beltloop of my trousers and then I slipped my thumbs into two of hers and the bed suddenly seemed too small and fragile and I started to take her with my head up against the angled ceiling painted dead flat white by my father in a long fit of mourning and she said, *No, sweetie, not here,* and she swung her legs to the floor and led us out of the room and then down the back stairs to the kitchen.

She asked if it was locked up out there.

I shook my head. We'd never locked the garage. Even my father, who safeguarded his possessions with a military order and zeal, never bothered with it, considering it a colony of junk that was mine. I looked around for something to put on my feet but I didn't see anything. I started for the front door where I'd left my shoes.

"Just take off your socks," Lelia said, already undoing her feet in kind.

I did what she said. She slid open the glass door and we walked out gingerly onto the slick redwood deck and down steps to the slatestone path leading to the garage. It was raining hard enough that we were already wet to the skin by the time we reached the side door to the apartment. I was shivering. When we got upstairs Lelia stripped me of my clothes and then she stripped herself. She walked naked to the far wall and knelt and turned the dial on the baseboard heater. She stood up. I watched the straightness of her as she moved, her long belly, the dark collapse below that. I felt a melancholy before her nakedness. She gripped at my breast and collarbone and tore me down to the carpet.

I had forgotten how to make love to my wife.

Five months, since I had seen her body, maybe eight or nine since I'd really touched her. My low and narrow hips wanted to be lost in her width, the chute of her sternum my sole guide to the one place where we came in the same basic size and shape and flavor: that good piece, the mouth.

We were always oral. We were forever biting, we bit hard, we spit and shined each other, we licked each other, we slobbered, we gorged, we made elaborate meals of ourselves, we made holiday feasts Scotch and Korean, the cold strange meal of tongue, of ankle, of toe, we made a mess. She was given to anything vampiric, went wild for Blackula, Christopher Lee, Lugosi, bats, Venus fly traps, we kept buying those plastic fangs, and she said it was the best way, to use your mouth, that this was it, this was the thing that made us human, not the thumb but the mouth.

Maybe the paralyzed know. It's the tendering of lips, the tongue as parchment, that writing of teeth along the ridge of backbone, snare down the crack. These are the tools for our living. We don't need a language to learn. We have every weapon.

"Hey," she said, gripping me, breathing like there wasn't enough air. "Hold me now."

"Okay."

She fell back on the floor and winged her arms wide. I asked her if she wanted to get on the couch. She shook her head.

I rolled on top of her and grabbed her at the wrists. The old carpet was threadbare against her back, my knees scraping the rope webbing. I kissed her, and she nibbled at my lips as I pulled away. I pushed her hands together above her head and held them there tightly with one hand, my free one searching the scallops of her ribs, her taut neck, now unfolding inside her needy working mouth. She was tasting herself on my fingers and wet nose and my chin. The room was still freezing. She kept eating. I kept eating, too, wanting every last fold of her, the taste brand new to me, or at least, a reconfection of what I knew.

She wanted me to push down on her harder. I couldn't, so then she turned us around and pushed down on me, the slightest grimace stealing across her face. her body yawing above me, buoyed and restless. I held on by her flat hips, angling her and helping her to let me in, her movements agitated. Mixed up memory, hunger. At that moment we're revisiting pleasure or fear. Or not. We don't know what we're doing. We want to make love. Or fuck. Like lonesome dogs, all wags and tongues and worn eyes. I can't hold myself back. This is the woman I promised to love. This is my wife.

Song for Lovers

LONNY KANEKO

Whenever he rolls her onto the bed
the people upstairs move. He knows
because the chandelier rattles.
He wonders if they hear them love
and decide to join, being too old,
too old to do.

Whenever he opens the front door
down the hall another clicks closed.
Sometimes he races to the door
expecting to see a fragile
figure bent eye high to the knob.
He never does.

In the laundry room someone
is always adding clothes to the wash
or taking sheets from the dryer.
He lies awake dreaming that it's
the husband's private detective.
How would he know?

The hall has ears. The ceiling eyes.
The light outside the door burns off
and on whenever they arrive.
The lovers burn; their sheets are moist.
And above them, the building whispers,
"We know. We know."

Winston and Samantha

CHARLIE CHIN

The doctor slowly shook his head. He stared out the window as if trying to find the best words to use.

"Mr. Chu, I'm sorry. There is no medical explanation. We've taking all the standard tests and they're all negative. If you want, we can pursue some other options." I shrugged; it was pretty much what I expected. Before getting dressed I stopped to check the creases in my trousers and the material on the back of my jacket before putting them on. I detest it when my suit becomes wrinkled. It makes one look boorish and thick.

"Thank you, Doctor, that won't be necessary. I check every couple of months on the remote chance something has changed. This has been going on, or should I say, not going on for quite a while. I've seen specialists, herbalists, acupuncturists, and therapists of every description. I've grown quite accustomed to the situation. Thank you again."

"When did you first become aware of the problem, Mr. Chu?"

"Oh, about ten years ago. I was just beginning in the commodities market then, you know, keeping late hours, making too many meetings, that sort of thing. At first I thought it might be because I was not getting enough rest, but the situation continued even after I became established. My ex-wife did what she could, but nothing seemed to help. I suppose if we'd already had children she might have, well, she was young and didn't take it very well."

The doctor shook my hand and showed me the way out. Physicians don't like it when they don't have an answer. As I walked out the door he called out as an afterthought, "There's nothing physically wrong perhaps?"

I knew what he was alluding to and I didn't want to hear it. There was nothing wrong with me mentally. Another quack, like the rest of them, he was grabbing at straws. I checked my wrist watch as I stepped out of the building. In ten minutes I was to meet Samantha at the Plaza Hotel. Checking my wallet to make sure I had my credit cards and enough cash, I stepped into the street and hailed a cab going north.

It was obvious to me why she had called for a lunch date after a silence of three months. She must have broken up with that Neanderthal she was dating. This last one had been typical of the kind of brute she favored: a broad-shouldered, blond, blue-eyed, athletic clod with a constant erection. A Philistine whose idea of culture was going to films that had Roman numerals in the title. None of her bovine boyfriends ever lasted very long. The thugs would become infatuated with Samantha, her beauty and natural sense of style, like gorillas entranced by a bright bauble. It pleased them to have a little "Oriental doll" on their arm as they swilled beer at ballparks.

Sam would play the submissive role in order to seduce them into bed. She was very good at that. Wearing dresses that made her look common, pretending to be empty-headed, laughing at their locker-room jokes. She would go through the charade for a while, but for all their crude attempts at making love, she always ended up in a state of profound dissatisfaction.

The problem was simple: they couldn't give her what she really needed. They only wanted to dominate her, control her. That might work well with the uneducated cows they normally rutted with, but not with precious Samantha. Her proper milieu was a society that appreciated music, art, theater, and good taste. She needed delicate handling and space to indulge her whims. I did that for her, without demanding anything in return. That's why after her silly schoolgirl flings, she always returned to me.

Samantha had arrived at the Plaza before me. She was sitting at a "good" table in the Palm Court restaurant and looked very smart. Every adult male in the room was staring at her. Her dress was an off-the-shoulder affair with a plunging neckline. Even from halfway across the room her legs looked stunning. She must have shaved only an hour ago. She had chosen a pair of black open-toed high heels with thin heel straps. They had a tiny ruffled leather bow on each of the uppers.

She pretended not to see me coming. There was a half-empty cocktail glass on the table in front of her. I hoped it was her first. She could become disagreeable when in her cups. A distinguished-looking white man with gray hair at the next table was shamelessly exchanging flirting glances with Sam, much to the annoyance of the middle-aged woman sitting with him. When I stopped at the velvet rope the maitre d' politely looked up from his reservation book. I commented, "I'm meeting Miss Chang," and motioned at Sam's table.

It appeared as if Samantha's glass was almost empty. To save time I ordered a couple of sweet Manhattans directly from him. He nodded and turned to snap his fingers at a passing waiter. I walked over to the table and smoothly slid next to her on the banquette. Glancing down, I noticed that her high heel shoes were quite new. Worn enough times to imprint her scent but not enough to mar the finish on the thin leather. The gold buckles were microscopic and the black string straps glistened against the smooth porcelain of her ankles. It pleased me that her legs were naked. I dislike stockings; they obscured the cleavage of her toes. A powder-blue vein was beginning to show across the pale white skin of her left instep. It forked gently and disappeared into the warm pink hue of her deliciously high arch. The vermilion red of her toenail polish was drops of fresh blood on warm rice. I was momentarily dismayed to see a slight build-up of callus on her left heel. It wasn't much, but I made a mental note to soak and pumice it before it became unsightly. That is, if she would let me. When she was being especially contrary, she would purposely neglect her foot care purely out of spite.

Without turning around, she reached into her miniature handbag and pulled out a thin cigarette. She held it up to her lips and whispered, "You're late, Winston. Light me."

She only called me Winston when she was annoyed or nervous. She hadn't taken her eyes off the man at the other table.

"Samantha, this is a no-smoking section and that fellow is old enough to be your father."

"Must you be so clumsy, Winston? The gentleman is *tres gallant* and I'm just being pleasant." The "gentleman" was lingering and trading significant looks with Sam while paying for his check. His stocky wife was huffing her way to the exit on a pair of hideous orthopedics.

"Yes, and the woman with him is quite angry. Do turn around and face me, Sam. We are at the same table, are we not?" She made a point of turning her head slowly and staring deeply into my eyes. She knew the effect it would have on me.

"At times you can be so"—she hesitated for a second to let the patronizing tone sink in—"very middle class, Winston." It was clear that she had had more than one cocktail. I became mildly annoyed with her.

"Oh really, Samantha? I was not aware that working for a living had become a social stigma. And I notice that you were not above accepting my very middle-class offer to pay for your classes at the New School, several weekends on Martha's Vineyard, and not a few little trinkets that you developed an affection for, all with the sordid profits of my middle-class income."

She knew I was miffed and used her old ploy. She silently leaned forward in her chair, resting her elbows on the white linen tablecloth, the front of her dress falling open to reveal her breasts. The soft brown of her nipples could be seen peeking out from their flimsy covering.

I suppose she imagined that a cheap trick like that was enough to make me defenseless. I wrenched my gaze away from her cleavage and back up to her eyes. She looked at me with practiced indifference.

I cleared my throat. "Sam, I don't like it when you do that on purpose." Her eyes opened wide in mock surprise.

"Whatever do you mean, Winnie?"

"When you display yourself rather than answer the question. You know how it distracts me."

"But you enjoy it. Don't you, Winnie?" She reached under the table and playfully squeezed my knee and let her hand rest on my thigh. She walked her fingers up my leg to my groin and fondled my private parts. I was soft. She knew I would be. That was her idea of humor. She gave me a little "nice puppy" pat on the crotch, and drew her hand away so that she could pick up the menu with both hands.

"I would adore some escargots. What are you having, Winnie?"

"I'll try the pâté. You do that just to be cruel, don't you, Sam?"

"Now, Winnie, don't be cross." Her eyes softened a bit. With a tone that almost sounded compassionate she teased, "If you're a good boy I'll let you have a sniff later."

I couldn't tell if she was joking or not. It would be just like her to promise something and then forget all about it. We ordered two more Manhattans and went through the rest of the meal avoiding serious subjects. It was agreed that we would visit the Boone Gallery in SoHo after lunch and see Mary's latest discovery. I motioned for the check and paid while Samantha went to freshen up. We took our time strolling through the hotel lobby. I waited patiently while Samantha stopped to look at some mediocre cultured pearls in a shop display case. The Plaza doorman hailed us a cab with that silly little whistle they use and an old-fashioned Checker cab pulled up to the curb.

In the back of the taxi Sam leaned against the leather seat and crossed her legs. The hem of her dress rode up and the smooth whiteness of her thighs came into view. She wiggled her foot so that her left heel shoe strap slipped off and then used her bare toes to playfully balance the shoe loosely on the front end of her foot. The indentation lines on the sides of her upper foot and the back of her heel caused by the thin straps first showed pink, then slowly faded to match the bone-white of her skin. When I realized that I was unconsciously leaning forward to get a better view, I straightened up abruptly and made a point of staring out my window. The cab became trapped in midtown traffic.

The Jamaican driver turned up his radio and tapped his hand in time with the music on the steering wheel while he waited for a break in the crush of cars. As the loud reggae patois drowned out the traffic sounds, Sam fanned herself with her hand for a moment and commented it was very warm in the cab. Without thinking I started to crank my window down to let in more air but she stopped me by putting her hand on my wrist. I stopped and turned to see what she wanted. She was gesturing with her left hand and pointing at her lap.

"No, Winnie, I need more air here." She opened her thighs slowly, lifted the edge of her skirt with her other hand and gently led my fingers under her dress. Sinking down a little on the seat to offer a better access, she rubbed my palm in the tuft of hair on her mound. I was about to draw my hand away when she drew up her knee, reached down and slipped off her left shoe and then coyly held it up to my face. The fragrance of her pump drifted into my nostrils and immediately my heart pumped gallons of adrenaline into my blood. My face became flushed. I tried to maintain some semblance of self-control, but as I deeply inhaled the mixed scent of her sweat, perfume, and the new leather, the old and constant craving caused me to surrender. I used my free hand to press the leather to my cheek and rubbed my face across the top. I tenderly kissed the leather uppers several times. As I nibbled the tiny leather bows I glanced at Samantha's face to see if I was to be permitted to go further. Sam didn't pull it away, so I became bolder and reached inside the toe opening with my tongue to taste the salty pad that the ball of her foot rested on.

I was dimly aware that her hand was insistently squeezing mine. She wanted me to fondle her. When I didn't respond at once, she took her shoe away from my face and pretended as if she were going to put it back on. I moaned in the negative and pulled the shoe back to my lips. To keep her happy I groped under her dress, found her moistness, and began to explore it with my fingers. It was, I thought, similar to putting your fingers in a bowl of warm oyster stew. I really don't know what all the fuss is about when it comes to a women's private parts. It is hairy, slimy, and looks like a surgical operation that hasn't healed properly. On the other hand, a pair of shapely woman's feet, well taken care of and properly shod, are capable of elegance, grace, beauty, and texture. She interrupted my thoughts with a hoarse whisper.

"Not so hard. Softer, Winnie, softer." I did as she asked. I tried my best to block out the unpleasant sensation of rubbing her internal mucus membranes and concentrated on the magnificent scent of her shoe.

In a few minutes she moaned, "Faster, it's good, faster." I had no doubt that she was fantasizing about one of her simian boyfriends. Her body twitched several times. Her mouth formed a silent O, her pupils dilated widely, and then her legs straightened out uncontrollably as the full orgasm hit her.

When the last of the twitching subsided, Sam allowed her body to go limp. The light of recognition returned to her eyes and she smiled weakly at me. I slowly lifted my hand from beneath her skirt and carefully wiped my damp fingers on my pocket handkerchief. Impregnated with her vaginal scent, it would only make me gag if I used it again. I thought about tossing it out the window but instead I stuffed it into the door-arm ashtray.

She reached up and took back her shoe, inspected the inside by cocking her head to one side, and made a little "tsk-tsk" face. She took out a clean tissue from her handbag and dabbed out the moisture left by my tongue. As she put the pump back on her bare foot she whispered, "That's enough for now. If you're nice, I'll let you have the other one later."

Sam smiled broadly, hugged my arm, and entwined her fingers with mine before reclining back in her seat. I wasn't quite sure what to do next. My state of arousal was not resolved, but then, with my little affliction, it never can be.

There was a loud exclamation from the driver and the cab suddenly lurched forward. Whatever had been holding up traffic was now over and the driver was trying to make up for lost time. It occurred to me that he must have watched us in his rearview mirror but I didn't care.

I reached across the top of the headrest to cradle Sam's head in the crook of my left arm and admired her profile. She was quietly staring at the ceiling of the cab, lost in her own thoughts. My own pulse rate was slowing down and I became aware of the tenderness I felt toward her. We might not verbalize it often, but we had feelings for each other. If nothing else, I was certain of that. I leaned my head closer to hers to kiss her upturned lips, but she turned away her face, pretending to look out the other window. She remarked in a clinical voice, "Please, not on the mouth, Winston. It's not sanitary."

Sea of Grace

Geraldine Kudaka

I

Sleep weighs down my eyes as I wind up the cameras and let rivers
of images float past my hands. I made my mother's country dish for
you. Eat, I said, you're too thin. You sliced off a small piece of tofu
and gingerly tasted it. In that distant past, that time when we were
too new to fear the pain of loving, you pulled back shyly. Arm's
distance. The instep of your palms walked across my face, leaving a
warm impression of valleys crossed, of terrains waiting to be explored. When we made love, you asked me if you were too scrawny.
No, I whispered, reaching out for your thin warm body. Drowning
myself in the ocean of your skin, I let myself go. I floated, carried by
the eddying tow of your currents.

The ceiling cannot hold back stars floating on a horizon drawn
across my mouth. Two separate continents, male and female, tun-
neling over thighs, bellies, testicles and viscous fluids of self-con-
tained ecosystems rose in a hurricane of desire. Swelling with need,
my waters began to drip. Your hand moved over my breast, squeezing small twin mounds into sharp peaks which lift up and down in

the vale of my breath. Surely this must be heaven, I whispered, as you rubbed your erect cock head against my sweet moist labia. Surely, there must be a god to bring you back so quickly, so hard and erect. Surely, you plunged; surely you pierced, surely you probed. Surely—you went deeper and deeper. You broke the barriers of my reef, flooding me with your essence, driving words from my lips, leaving me spent.

After you came, you said, "Thank you." Your hands reached out, wrapping my fingers in an intricate sailor's knot. My lips murmured a pattern across your skin.

II

The land which held us together was our bodies. Your desire was my desire. Your cock rose, hard as sinewy otters traversing wet shores. Proud, relentless, you punctured my soft white body. Look, you said, how dark I am compared to you. Your fingers traveled through my hair, curling straight strands into fine braid as you explored the mounds between my legs. Look, you said, this is where Africa begins. This is how the Boers raped the land and made it theirs. And like a fierce Zulu, you rose, mounting me until I screamed over and over, calling out god's name, begging you to travel the vast distance between our continents.

Kissing the small of your back, I closed my eyes, ears and mouth. "This is what we do best," I said. You laughed, your tongue traveling down the neck, along the clavicle, between the breasts. Reaching the tip of my clitoris, you rocked the buried dragon. Grains of sand rolled in a luminous chamber between my legs. Tips of your fingers stirred up storms. A pounding surf chased away songs. Waves upon waves washed over us. Looking for music, I floundered upstream. Your constant hardness silenced questions, but I was frightened of the void. Please, I whispered, don't leave me carved like smiling pumpkins outside our door. Kissing the softest spot of my palm, you answered, "I'm not a doctor. I don't know how to make you well." You slept, dreaming of your wives chewing on your bones, and holding you close, our song began to fade.

Like grains of sand enveloped in an oyster, we adjusted to the sound of silence.

III

It is hard to be a mapmaker. There are so many ways of erosion that details listing each would be a pointless waste of paper. Precipitation, storms, age, everything in nature points to a shifting mass of evolving continents. Without taking the time to get to know one another, we fell into an easy feast of our bodies, and our bodies knew things about ourselves that our minds could only glimmer.

"I am afraid," you said. Sucking your weapon erect, I tried to stem the parting seas. Love will come, you said, tonguing me into submission. Moving your hands over my face, exploring my eyes, ears and mouth, your cock spelled out the terms of surrender. "Love may come, but fear will keep us alive. It is fear which has the power to move." No, I cried, but your thin wiry arms pushed me beneath the sea. I opened my mouth and water filled my throat, my pores, drowning me in what we know best. My legs spread of their own accord, my nails dug into your back, until crazed with desire you laid me flat on the table and spread my legs into a V-formed universe where we once found god.

"God has left us," I whispered. "In his absence there is only silence." Nonsense, you replied. Fear will never cause my cock to rise. Erect, you pressed against the small of my back. This ferocious beast I saw as stallion you called squirrel. (Size, why is size so important? Size, is that all men think about?) You pressed, harder and harder, and the waters that moved between us drained into the ocean.

My body spoke its own language, you were master of my body. You said I am afraid, but the hard erect beast between your legs knew no fear.

IV

A thorny bramble grows around your heart. Unable to pull its branches free, you sink into my body and gasp out a meager, perfunctory thank you. I hold on to you, grasping for gossamer strands to tie fear into little bundles of firewood. Though strong and fierce, I cannot pull you through calcified layers of fossilized hopes, dreams and pains. You sink beneath the waters, drowning in the brambles of your past. "Swim," I shout. "Damn you. Lift up your arms and swim." Anchored down by fear, you sink, your black hair a mass of floating seaweed. I search the shores for stones to build you an altar. A virgin throws you a line. You sail up her skirt. Pride writes its name across your face and fear makes you bleed between her legs.

Wandering amidst stars, I find remembrances of things past. On my right are all the possibilities of what could have been; on my left, things which should never have been. Behind me is everything we shared. On the road ahead, the relentless weight of fear. A tremor breaks open the universe. A chorus of voices rise, reminding me of the existence of god. Riddled with faults, the earth shakes. Continents drift apart. Your songs drown in a river of tears. This is the devastation we do, rending apart that which we love. We forget the language of the body, and trapped beneath pride, lose the grace of god.

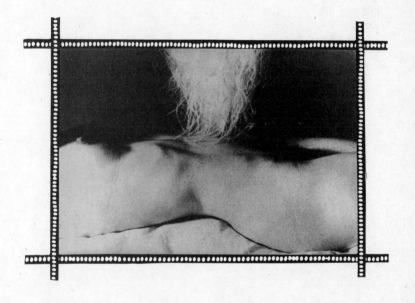

Colors of Love

VI

preceding page:

Photograph by Gaye Chan, from *Angel on Folding Chair*

Fear of Flying

from *American Knees*

SHAWN WONG

Brenda Umeki says she's disgusted every time she sees an Asian man with an ugly white woman. She's not saying all white women are ugly when they're with Asian men. She's not a racist. When she sees it, she just sees some pathetic Asian man so desperate to smack up skin to skin with a white girl, he'll pick anyone who'll have him. In the cases where the Asian man is actually pretty nice-looking, he looks kind of guilty when she's staring at him.

Aurora says, "Maybe because it's the way your mouth gets all twisted up in that sneer."

"He's got this look like he's been caught in the headlights, and he doesn't know which way to run."

"That's fright, not guilt."

"For Asian boys there's no difference."

Brenda says for the handsome Asian men with the truly gorgeous white girl, you know, some awesome Barbie babe with the blond curly mane and legs and the tits, great beach material, those boys just stare her down or ignore her like "go ahead and hit me with your headlights, I'm indestructible." He's with the woman all men lust after. Brenda says she's the kind of girl she wanted to be when she was thumbing through the pages of *Seventeen,* harboring some self-contempt while Mom's telling her the advantages of straight black hair.

"What about the ugly nerd Asian boy and beautiful white girl?" Aurora asks.

"I don't mind. I'm not threatened. No love or lust there," Brenda says. "It's a charity case or more likely it's study hall time. She needs a passing grade in calculus in order to stay on the cheerleading squad. Henry's there to help. He has his day in the sun. Then he melts, unless he's too rich to melt."

"Why do you care, Brenda?" Aurora asks. "You don't go out with Asian men."

Brenda says she's tried to but doesn't know how. She's Sansei and never knew any Asian boys growing up in the suburbs, never went to school with them, never been around them except in college. She was in a sorority, and there weren't any Asian guys in the frats. She got invited to some Chinese Student Association dances but felt out of place. A lot of the Chinese girls froze her out because she was a sorority girl, she was Japanese, she was from the suburbs, Japan invaded China, hell, pick one of the above. Brenda went on a date with a Korean guy, but both sets of parents nearly went on full tilt just thinking about the Japanese-Korean thing. The stereotypical monumental and monolithic rudeness of Koreans and the invasion and occupation of Korea by the Japanese was too much to overcome. Brenda went out with a couple of black guys, but she couldn't handle the vicious backbiting and the looks among the black women she met. Some of the women would talk loud enough for both her and her date to hear, "Got hisself a yearning for high yellowness so high he got a chink." The chorus behind her voiced its uh-huhs. If you can't fight back, you can't survive in that environment. One time Brenda got so mad she said something about this black woman wanting to be Asian so bad she ironed and processed her black hair straight until it was a toxic waste dump of chemicals. Brenda's date had to step between them.

Over his shoulder Brenda said something about the woman's mother and her pubic hair. Brenda's date got a black eye.

The Korean and the black experience even made Dad much easier to handle when she started dating white boys again. Brenda asks Aurora which was the lesser of the evils. Koreans and Japanese head the hate list dating back to Japan's invasion of Korea followed by their rudeness and abrupt manner. Japanese practice *enyro* and *gaman*. You know, nobody takes the last piece of chicken no matter what; let it go uneaten back to the kitchen, defer and be patient. Fight over the bill until you tear it in half. Send a thank-you card as soon as you get home. Next time make an excuse to go to the bathroom, and pay the bill secretly in the back. Chinese scrimp on things at home, clip out coupons, never buy retail; warehouse stores are made for Chinese shoppers, but they too will fight to the death over paying the restaurant bill. Gives them "big face." Chinese Americans and Japanese Americans have patched things up between them over the invasion of China. Chinese buy Japanese cars until they can afford a Mercedes. Ever see a Mercedes with clear plastic seat covers protecting the leather? Chinese and Japanese have been out of the Chinatowns and Japantowns a long time now, been neighbors in the suburbs together.

Korea invaded the black neighborhoods and took ownership of the corner grocery store, and an urban war started. Filipino boys in their leather jackets, tank tops, gold chains, and Monte Carlos with the tinted windows go hot and heavy for the tinted blondes. It's the American dream they've been reading about in their American textbooks and watching in the American movies and television back in the Philippines. Every Filipino boy wants to rescue Ginger from Gilligan's Island. But they marry Filipino girls in the end out of filial duty and Christian and familial guilt. Sometimes people can't figure out what they are and simply refer to them as "that Spanish kid."

Brenda says the Thai boys at the Thai Take-Out are polite and have beautifully smooth skin. The mother of the family that runs the take-out looks young enough to be the boys' sister. She wonders if they can dance.

Streetwise Vietnamese and other recent immigrant boys are always staring at the Asian-American women who shop in their grocery stores, coming up to them and saying, "Hi, how are you?" with an accent that begins with forming their mouths as if each word begins with an "O." Sometimes they walk up to Brenda dragging the heels of their shoes on the floor, which drives Brenda crazy. She wants to yell, "Pick up your feet!" They want to know what you are to see if it's okay to go out with you. "Are you Chinese? I'm Vietnamese Chinese." Sometimes she tries to be friendly and joke with them, but they don't allow themselves to laugh properly, you know, the way Brenda's Japanese grandmother says she shouldn't. At the grocery store their family runs, they try too hard to make strained casual conversation out of what you buy, what you eat, what you drink, what magazines you read. Brenda buys aspirin and they want to know if she's "making a headache?" Brenda never buys tampons from them.

Brenda says Asian men have great bodies. She doesn't want to date them, or have sex with them, or marry them. Brenda says, "Let someone else marry them. We've been married to them for four thousand years." She actually just likes the way they look: that hairless look, that Bruce Lee muscle tone. Brenda likes going to the kung-fu movies and the samurai movies, likes her Asian men to be virile and heroic and strong. Her support of them in this way has something to do with history and loyalty to the race. Privately to Aurora, Brenda will put Asian men down as mates, but in public she'll defend them when she hears a non-Asian say something racist about them. Too bad white guys can't have Asian bodies. Brenda hates chest hair and hairy backs. She's sometimes afraid she'll end up married to some white guy that'll wear his jeans too low and the crack of his hairy white ass will show when he bends down. Too bad Bruce Lee had that accent.

Aurora tells Brenda the men aren't the problem and that 75

percent of Japanese-American women are marrying out of the race compared to 20 percent for the men. Aurora herself is the product of a statistic, the offspring of the rule rather than the exception. According to the statistic, the odds favor Brenda becoming one of those hyphenated women keeping their identity correct in their names—a Umeki-Miller, or a Umeki-Polanski, or a Umeki-Washington. Aurora tells Brenda about the time Raymond and his buddy, Jimmy Chan, were walking down the street and saw this Vietnamese guy, obviously fresh off the boat, walking hand in hand with a white girl. Raymond nudges Jimmy and says, "Look at that guy." Jimmy says, "Shit man, FOB's be stealin' our women."

"Umeki-Washington, now there's a thought, Ro." Aurora wonders if black men who have a thing for Asian women are less likely to be racists than the white men who have a thing for Asian women. Do they have to have that black hair down to the waist fantasy? Subservient, submissive, docile geisha?

Brenda says she likes black coffee, black silk, little black dresses, black tights, black shoes, black leather pants, oversized black T-shirts, black bras, black cars, black linguini.

Brenda's aunt married a white man during the war when she was sprung from Minidolka Relocation Center to go back to school in Chicago. She says it's better for the kids so that the next time the country wants to round up the Japanese and haul them off to camp, they won't be able to recognize them, like the Germans and the Italians who got off easy during the war. Brenda's aunt says the sooner the Japanese all marry out, the better. The whole country is going to be Hispanic in a few years; maybe we can pass for Hispanic in a generation or two, then pass for white after that, even change our names like the Jews and the Mexicans. "Buy American" means a whole bunch of things.

Brenda's aunt says the kids got it all wrong in the sixties with all that search for identity and self-determination crap. "What is it you kids don't know? Why do you want to draw attention to yourself? You kids didn't even know we were in camp until you read about it in your high school textbooks. Then you come home wearing black armbands wanting to know why we never told you about the camps. You never asked."

Brenda's aunt and uncle took their family to Disney World after they got their $20,000 redress money and an apology from the President for the internment and bought a new fishing boat and named it *Camp Harmony* after the first camp they were sent to during the war, or, as the War Relocation Authority called it, "Assembly Center." Meanwhile the letters-to-the-editor pages of every newspaper in America are filled with readers who can't tell the difference between Japanese Americans and Japanese. They want to know if redress will be paid to the "Americans" who died at Pearl Harbor.

Brenda says when she was growing up, she didn't want to be Japanese; she wanted to be like all the other kids. In the sixties "Orientals" suddenly became "Asian Americans" looking to establish ethnic studies classes, going into Chinatown clothing stores and buying *mee nahps,* taking judo and karate lessons, and spelling out ten non-negotiable demands on a bullhorn.

Brenda has a very un-Asian body. Brenda says it's all natural. She's tall, long-legged, short-waisted, and has breasts. Her breasts she got from her mother, but otherwise her mother and father are short, bow-legged, and long-waisted. Vitamins and stretching her limbs, says Brenda's mother, are what did it. Brenda's mother says she pinched Brenda's nose when she was a little girl to make it thin. At birth Brenda's mother was relieved when she saw her daughter had all her limbs, and toes, and fingers, *and* double eyelids. She's an all-American girl.

"They shouldn't give Asian women large breasts because we have enough problems as it is," Brenda says to Aurora. "In American culture, the boobs become your identity. You know, 'Hey, she's got big tits,' instead of having an identity first. Even Asian women mention it. Men come up to me and actually point at my breasts and say, 'Oriental girls don't usually have those.' "

Brenda says the best of both worlds would be to marry a white guy and have 100 percent Asian babies "because they're so cute." Brenda is a mass of contradictions. Aurora says that white girls who marry Asian men want 100 percent Asian babies too. White couples want little blond boys and want to adopt Korean girls. American society is a mass of contradictions.

Brenda went out with Glenn Tompkins once. Everybody in the Asian community calls Glenn Tompkins "Red." It's a real cliché because of his red hair, but then none of the kids growing up in Chinatown ever got to call anyone Red. Glenn floats between Chinatown and Japantown, dabbling in things Chinese and Japanese because he likes Asian women. Red joins the Japanese Buddhist Church, volunteers to drive the church van and takes the old-timers out for their excursions, cooks for the bazaar potluck, buddies up to the Nisei aunts who might introduce him to their daughters, tutors English down at the Chinatown community service center, and takes Chinese and Japanese language classes. Red is not some midwest sailor who, on R&R in Hong Kong first time away from the family farm, gets a taste of some Oriental poontang and a massage and signs himself on the waiting list back home. Red knows the difference between the stereotypical Hollywood image of an Asian woman and the real Asian-American woman. He's more comfortable being a white guy immersed in a culture he can study and understand, instead of being what he is—part Scottish, Irish, French, and, as always, a sixteenth Cherokee. A lot of Asian women have gone out with him once, but he doesn't know that he falls into the same category as the other boys their aunts set them up with—a boring wimp, and, in this case, a boring wimp who wants to talk about Asian culture.

Red is trying to be like the guys, hang with them, be polite so maybe someday one of the women will like him back and think of him as a brother because he's been hanging around so long. For a while some thought Glenn was gay and was cruising through the community in order to get hooked with some rice queen, as they call them. Asian men stayed away from Glenn and wouldn't even walk on the same side of the street. It's odd that when they found out he was after the women, they didn't mind his presence.

One time three gay guys, one white, one black, and one Asian, came to a community fundraising dance put on by the younger members of several of the Asian organizations to "celebrate diversity" among the new Asian populations. After asking several Asian men to dance and being refused, they wondered out loud about the theme of "diversity" and how discrimination and homophobia seemed to be well protected by a double standard. Three of the women asked them to dance, saying that would be "celebrating diversity" for them.

In the movies Chinese men very rarely play real men: Hop Sing, Charlie Chan, Cain, Fu Manchu. They rule by proverb, not brawn. Most times in movies Chinese men can't even play themselves and have white actors in yellow face with latex slanted eyes stepping in for them. On "Bonanza" a white woman can be shy about showing her ankle to Hoss or Little Joe, but she can walk around Hop Sing's kitchen with her corset on without fear. Everyone knows nothing will happen to her. Hop Sing talks a line of excited jibberish, but he's no real man. Chinese men have been defined by these role models for decades. Raymond's friend Jimmy Chan, a writer for the *Oakland Tribune,* says that apes have made greater strides in self-determination in the movies than Chinese-American men. Apes went from King Kong pounding on the gates of Skull Island to speaking and taking over the world in *Planet of the Apes.* Meanwhile Chinese men have gone from Charlie Chan to Cain in the television series "Kung-fu," both proverb-spouting effeminate men played by whites in yellow face. Cain does fight, but it's artistic, not lethal. Asian men in the movies never have names like Bo or Max or Leroy or Scarface.

Jimmy Chan says, "Why is it every time I go to the bank to withdraw cash and I get an Asian woman teller, she's got to go in the back and check my signature and my bank balance? I've been banking at the same bank for years, and they've got two Asian women tellers. They know me. I give them a break and think maybe I've got an attitude. So I go up to the window of this one woman all friendly-like and look at her name plate and call her by her name, 'Hey, Angela, how are you doing today?' She says, 'Fine,' like a robot, and before I can begin speaking again, she spins around and heads for the back again. She's fuckin' with me."

"You're being paranoid," Raymond says, even though he knows it's true. "Maybe she's got a crush on you. Likes to have you linger around. Wants to see if you got enough money to keep her happy!"

"I know what it is; they're prejudiced."

"Why is it," Raymond joins in, "every time I get on an airplane and walk down the jetway to the plane I see ten, twelve people walk by the flight attendant and she stops me and wants to see my boarding pass? Is it because I'm cute and she wants to make small talk? Is it because she thinks I'm sitting in first class and she wants to greet me? No! She thinks I can't read or speak English and I might be getting on the wrong damn plane, that I'm too stupid to match flight numbers! These days I make it a point of walking right up to them and getting all chatty, holding up the line, just so they won't ask, and I say, 'Howdy! (I never say howdy.) Howzit goin' today? Hope we'll have a humdinger (I never say humdinger) of a flight!' Do I look like I'm from Japan?"

Jimmy Chan says one time this white Moonie holding a flower out at the airport tries to stop him by speaking Japanese to him, and Jimmy stops and launches into a tirade on this poor sucker about how his family has been living in California for five generations, he's a writer for the *Oakland Tribune,* he's Chinese, and every Asian ain't a Japanese tourist and he better get his sorry Moonie pin cushion haircut back to the temple before he really gets mad.

"What's the worst thing about flying?" Jimmy asks.

Raymond says the worst is when he's given a seat next to another Asian. The flight attendant automatically thinks the two "Orientals" are together. If he or she is from Asia somewhere, neither Raymond nor they really care. Maybe he can even help them out with the English. It's a relief to them because Raymond can tell they would rather be sitting next to another Asian than not. Like the time Raymond and Jimmy were flying to New York and Jimmy tried to use his bad Cantonese on this woman about the choice in meals on the plane, one was beef, *nowyuk,* Jimmy pronounced it, and the other was shrimp, but Jimmy said the word for lobster instead. The woman chose lobster, but smiled when she got her shrimp because Jimmy meant well. It's why foreign-born Chinese call American-born Chinese *jook sing,* hollow bamboo; we look Chinese, but we're hollow inside, no substance. But if the other passenger is an Asian-American woman, and it's the bank teller from Jimmy's bank, we're in big trouble. The flight attendant is going to come by and ask, "What would you two like to drink?" Everybody gets irritated by the assumption. It becomes a contest of body language that says, *I'm not with him, I don't know him, I speak English, I don't date Asian men because they're domineering wimps.* "No, I don't want tea. I'll have coffee—black."

"Then there's the Asian woman with the white husband who have been assigned the seats next to you," Jimmy adds. "They go through this dance thing where they're trying to figure out who is going to sit next to whom. What makes the best sense. We're all trying to be polite standing in the aisle while trying to suppress the fear in our eyes, trying to suppress the apologies for even considering what might look better, trying not to be racists about it all. Finally the woman sits by the window, I sit on the aisle and there's this oversized hairy white guy sitting between us like a human demilitarized zone. I'm looking to see if there's an empty seat nearby next to someone with a more reasonable color combination. It'll help settle the question as to whose wife she is in the flight attendant's mind. I want to tell her that I've got no problem with her marrying a white guy. I'm a nice guy. I want to make small talk with her husband about sports and regular guy stuff."

"It's like a black guy walking down the block at night behind a white woman carrying a bag of groceries. She turns from time to time and looks over her shoulder. The black guy sees she's kind of nervous about him being there, so he crosses the street and slows down a bit so she doesn't think he's a mugger even though he has to cross back across the street later to get home."

"Exactly." Jimmy sighs. "I look for another seat on the plane so no one feels ashamed, or guilty, or defensive."

Raymond talks about traveling with his old girlfriend, Gretchen, the one after ex-wife Darleen. She was an attorney he had met when he went back to work at the Orange County Department of Human Rights as a temporary replacement for a woman on maternity leave. Gretchen was blond and has these looks people have seen somewhere before but can't place it—a magazine ad, a television commercial. Jimmy remembers her very well.

Men at airports and in hotels would come right up to Gretchen as if Raymond weren't there and start talking with her or offer to help her with her bags. They assumed Raymond was (a) not with her, (b) a business partner, (c) an employee of the hotel, (d) a driver delivering her to the airport, and/or (e) someone named Hop Sing. Get back to the kitchen. Those who didn't approach her would stare at her, openly flirt with her, or say something crude, and Raymond would either have to pretend he didn't hear them or have Gretchen restrain him. Gretchen would try to mollify Raymond's irritation by saying men do that to her all the time. She doesn't go to war over their ignorance; why should Raymond?

"I'm no threat to them," Raymond once said to her. "This thing between you and me couldn't be anything real. They've seen houseboys like me on television. By not standing up to them, I prove them right—Asian men are wimps."

"You don't have to prove anything to me. I know who you are.

Believe me, Raymond, men's IQs go way down when they see blond hair. It's not you."

"Yeah, like when they open the door for you and follow you through while I'm left on the outside."

"That's happened only six or seven times. You know I'm always holding your hand or being affectionate in public. It's not like I pretend I'm not with you. Plus don't you even notice that when I'm with you these white women think they can come up to you and start talking to you? They're racists too. They think I'm going to share my 'houseboy' with them. I've had friends as well as strangers ask me what it's like having a Chinese lover. You don't think I know something about racism because I'm white and Norwegian. I'm not one of those white girls you see in Chinatown walking around in those black kung-fu shoes, eating vegetables their Midwest mothers never heard of, wearing silk Chinese jackets, and speaking Cantonese phrases to the store clerks. You Chinese boys should be ashamed of yourselves for chasing after and seducing those ninnies like your friend who memorized some phrases out of the *I Ching* and recited them over dinner at the Lotus Pod restaurant."

Gretchen says that Raymond is too sensitive. What she leaves unsaid is that part of his discourse on identity and Asian male masculinity is very much part of his conceit—that trying to prove something about how men react to her is also trying to prove something about dating a white woman in the first place. Gretchen knows Raymond takes real pride in being *able* to date her. He thinks other Asian men might be in awe of him or at least green with envy. She's used to it and doesn't really mind. She's not interested in going out with some white guy with a red Camaro wearing Blublockers and deck shoes.

Raymond remembers that Gretchen was right about her display of public affection and that he very rarely returned her affection in public, at least in the same enthusiastic way. He couldn't be affectionate toward her and vulnerable while at the same time steeling himself for the next racist affront. One time Raymond and Gretchen were holding hands while walking down the street, and he saw an Asian woman walking toward them about a block away. Pretending he had an itch, Raymond dropped Gretchen's hand, not out of guilt but to again steel himself against a racist affront, even a racist thought never spoken. Racists come in all forms. No one white guy has ever come up to Raymond and said, "Keep your slimy yellow paws off our women." And no one dressed in a white sheet has ever come up to Gretchen and called her a "Chink lover." In the end most of it was blown out of proportion in Raymond's mind, because Asians are generally accepted anywhere, and no one ever said an unkind word when he was with Gretchen. Only the Asian woman walking down the street who had seen Raymond drop his girlfriend's hand had said to herself as she passed them, *Look up the word "double-standard" in the dictionary and there would be a picture of that jive dude.*

Guilty.

Happiness: *A* Manifesto

MARILYN CHIN

So, the sun shines through the jacaranda trees; the purple flowers opening, opening imperceptibly. And it is only Charles and me, Charles and the feeling of him inside me. And that strong angle of descent, the visage of his pink fleshy torso; starting from his sinewy neck down past his swollen yet hard chest/clavicle down to his groin. His beauty, his male beauty is a feeling that *I know*. It is not anything that I could sum up, pontificate on, illuminate via a terse and explosive gender discussion with my radical women friends. On our "mindful" level, in the great dialectic of things, he shall always be the hegemonist/oppressor/invader. The imperialist other—who keeps us oppressed, dissatisfied, yearning. As politically correct as I am, in that verbal bliss of the university, despite my own personal contentment, I continue the usual, feminist dyed-in-the-wool diatribe against male domination: jeer at that Hemingway specialist down the hall with his love of spare, laconic, fishing lore—or Moby-Dick reduced to some male patriarchal writer's swollen cock —too large to be conquered in one sitting.

Yet, this woman of the world secretly goes home and lives for a simpler love—somebody to look over the Beaujolais and say, "Darling, the pasta is superb . . ." that wonderful combination of garlic and extra-extra virgin olive oil, that pungent tang of fresh Roma tomatoes and of course, the secret three fingers of green chiles, preserved in vinaigrette à la Charles . . . Naked under his rococco apron, he would hum Debussy and meander in our small connubial kitchen, strutting all that love he harbors in his beautiful heart. He is the softer part of my "double consciousness." When I cross his threshold, I could kick off my sensible shoes, slither into my silky, sequined skin, lie back like some self-appointed goddess. And all weekend long, the birds are chirruping and the sea is savagely beautiful . . . And we would feast and fuck, feast and fuck, breaking all the ideological barriers until Monday morning . . .

When the cold slap of "conviction" jars me awake and I put on that postcolonial/scruffy tweed jacket and on to the local southern California State University to teach Introduction to American Ethnic Literature, and I, the infernal goddess—with hanks of black unruly hair, thick wire-rimmed spectacles, brown sensible shoes—I shall represent all the oppressed female intellectuals of the Third World. I shall begin each day by reminding these spoiled blond surfing children that their forefathers were slaveowners, their grandfathers were Chinamen-killers, their fathers were patriarchal pigs . . . their boyfriends were possible rapists . . . their Presidents were institutional criminals, their police force—a testosterone parade with nightsticks and battering rams.

And this month, in my office I call "the tenth orifice," I shall secretly preside over meetings with five powerful women litigators to initiate Project Alpha. We shall try to find a loophole in the university law code to get rid of fraternities forever—those hellholes that suck up decent, malleable young men and turn them into opportunistic, money-grubbing, women-raping, racist, warmongering, hegemonic Republicans! We have dubbed our secret society "the nutcracker suite." At least two of us are black belts in some exotic martial art. I, naturally, fancy Wing Chun, a close-range form invented by a very small Chinese woman, four feet tall, eighty-five pounds. The idea is to move closer into the opponent, that is, two inches from his chest; in a deceptive embrace gesture— and then, powwww—a short fist up the nose. He would see stars and a burst of technicolored rainbows before a panoramic blackness grips him.

Meanwhile, the five o'clock bell chimes. My shoulders shrink back to normal size, and a smile spreads across my face, a pinkness blossoms, and I am hungry and wet and thinking about my love— and how wonderful it would be to have his beautiful penis within me. I want him, this instant as I am writing my last memo of the day, an endearing note via e-mail to my chairman:

"Dear Chairman George Washington Franklin Hancock—Your memo of yesterday, regarding reinstituting the 'canon' as a main-stay of our literature department, disturbs us greatly; it rings of fascism, reactionary racism and sexism—and we, the 'feminist nut-cracker suite' demand that you illuminate us as to your true inten-tions . . ." (Secretly, I still adore some of the dead male writers like a rich opium I snort privately behind closed doors. Inhaling goopy lines of Keats is an onerous addiction I acquired during graduate school. I get turned on to his poetic death rattle: the sputum coagulating in his frail lungs, his coughing, hacking blood while he woos in that great European epistolary tradition . . . and oohh how a lugubrious love sonnet to Fanny makes me sticky.)

Now back to my paltry memo and to that great tradition of memo invective . . . and right on the word "intentions"—which I guess the impingement is upon the absent modifiers of "good" or "bad"—and the word "bad" conjures many a wonderful fucking vignette involving Charles and myself . . .

One particularly succulent episode was executed in "my tenth orifice" during a sudden California earthquake delivered by the

gods. Charles and I had the most glorious October morning for-
nicating on my desk. I remember the elaborate maneuvering.
First we had to remove my computer and laser printer and place
them gracefully on the floor, unstack and restack my present research on a Cantonese women's colony—silkworm breeders who
all collectively swore to be celibate and never marry. Although
it had not been thoroughly documented, the entire colony of
eight thousand-plus silkworm breeders and mulberry tree attendants were known to be militant lesbians. I went to this village
in 1988, and taped oral histories of these women's daily lives,
and to my dismay, the research turned out to be long, personal,
boring narratives on horticulture—and on fish emulsion/
peatmoss/nitrates—human fertilizer/humus and the mandibles of
caterpillars . . . that in its lack of metaphorical interest—there
were no fructifying double-entendres to be found—I couldn't
pry them open to talk about their sex lives. . . . The project
bored me and I had long abandoned it—twenty audiotapes/his-
torical books/copious notes and all—to collect dust on the
nethercorner of my giant, power desk.

Now, when Charles and I finally removed this dinosaur off—oh,
the dusty spines and femurs—paper clips, notecards galore—for a
morning of naughty, insolent, remarkable romping, and I had worn
that invaluable red thong with a slit on my woolly aperture; and my
love slipped comfortably in . . . his halberd slightly irritating my
entry—he was biting my ear, uttering the most salacious dreams in
all of the Western empire. In "my tenth orifice," we traveled the
world. He was the tour guide, whispering in my ear, in French and
Hebrew and various hybrid argots, offering all kinds of delectable
treats—half-naked mulatto boys on the beach of Pago Pago, in and
out and astride the Leaning Tower of Pisa, in and out and astride
the capsule of Gemini—betwixt and between the coffins of that
gilded boy Tut and Chin Shih Huangti; OOOOOhhhh baby, he

murmured; OOhh Bathsheba, OOhh Lesbia, OOhh Mary Magda-
lene, Oohh the tundras, the prairies, Ohhh, the furrows of the Dead
Sea. How he plowed me backward and forward, until I couldn't
remember my race, my color, my destiny . . . "Gender Studies"
now rendered moot or just the name of some dusty journal printed
in Indiana. My postcolonial "position" in the world at this moment
was "prone." And now as his finger was focusing on my ninth
aperture, his penis was fulfilling my tenth, and his tongue was
deeply spelunking in my fifth and most cavernous enterprise . . .

Suddenly, he said something terribly appalling: "I am fucking you
now in the bathroom of your grandmother's Hong Kong flat." I
finally balked. Now there are forbidden avenues—fruits that should
be left unplucked, frocks to be left unsullied. "Oh, all right, all
right, forget that last narrative about the bathroom of your grandmother's Hong Kong flat. How about in the callaloo of your father's
giant wok? Yes, that is wonderful, that is a way to get back at him,
for abandoning your mother, for making you peel ten thousand
shrimps in his restaurant in the summer of 1969." We know it is
the end of Confucian world order when filial piety meets the eroge-
nous zone:

Then, he whispered, "In the heavens. We are now fucking in
the heavens." I said, "I can't. I just happened to be a leftist, radical,
feminist, Marxist, Chinese-American separatist who believed in
God. SHE would not approve." He continued, rocking me back and
forth, in and out; the metal desk under my ass felt cold. The
friction: the metal against my thigh against the plaster wall. The
cultural anthropologist next door pounded. "Hey, hey, what in hell
are you doing? Hanging pictures? Fucking again, Ms. Asian American Poet!" And I let Charles harpoon me as I howled my humpback
whale mating call.

Against our throbbing and pounding and the abstract melody

of a busy campus in rain. Against the murmuring of our most
verboten fantasies. Against the Zen of willful subversion, we fucked.
A distant telephone rang in the dark corridor. Nearby, my colleague, Dr. So-and-so Smith, was having a loud confrontation with
an enraged Pocahontas. "You gave me a B, you pig," we heard her
say. And suddenly, in slow motion, the giant metal shelf cradling
the A through Z of major and minor female literary geniuses
started toppling: Alcott, Aidoo, Bradstreet, Aphra Behn (sadly un-
opened) and two Brontës as stout bookends, Browning (Liz and not
Bob), Bishop (collected) and Mama Gwendolyn Brooks (fraught
with Christmas greetings), Cather and Cixous, Chopin (Kate, not
the pianist), Dickinson, Doolittle, Eliot (George and not Tom),
hooks and Hurston and Hong-Kingston, Jordan (O sister river!), Li
(not Po but Ch'ing Chao), Lessing (lots of her), Lowell (Amy's
embarrassing Chinoiserie . . . well, better than Robert's iambic
doldrums) Minh-Ha, and Mew, McCullers poised with cigarette,
Rhys, Rossetti, Rich (lots of her) Gerty, Gerty . . . down to Stein
and Sojourner: Truth is truth is truth . . . Silko and Mary Shelley
rolled off the shelves like tongues of the twisted sea . . . down
past Wheatley, Wordsworth (a small pamphlet of Dorothy's) . . .
down to Untermeyer (ughh, how did that mangy anthology get
there?) . . . down to yet another misplaced minor male poet
named Zukofsky (got that for Christmas from some pedantic L-A-N-
G-U-A-G-E poet). The shelves came tumbling down. O Mother
Jericho, what a historical occasion; how appropriately synchronized
with our orgasmic paroxysms! The walls waved. The earth grimaced
a giant gaping chasm. We stayed attached, cock and cunt, two
multilimbed creatures, fucking for dear life.

Let me hereby issue "Mei Ling's Manifesto"—I am the fiercest
radical Feminist Asian-American Separatist vigilante. But at rest, I
am that primitive beast of the village: love and work—and an

occasional feast and epithalamium; the sound of roosters crowing in the morning; the breeze off a good sunset; a guffaw of a good story from a neighbor:

> *The lathe-turner is in love with the silk merchant.*
> *They lie happily under a banyan; the cool breeze grazing*
> *their lovely bodies just so.*

I called Charles on the telephone. "What epicurean treat are you brewing on the stove, my little lamb, my little sweetmeat?" He lamented in his coy, paltry way. "Darling, I ruined the tomato sauce." "So, ruin it," I said. "You're a ruined man, don't you know?" Yes, indeed, his beautiful ruin. At the end of the twentieth century, apocalypse has taken hold. This is a world where all preconceived notions of race and gender roles have faltered. Charles is possible because I am possible. Hate, fear, rape, murder is possible; so is full-bodied love, marital bliss, world peace and harmony possible.

Such sweet ruins: as we fucked, angel hair pasta flattened into bails of icky mush, white butter sauce dried to powder; his favorite Caphalon pan burned so black he wept. "I'll buy you a new one, baby," only to violate it again, again in future romping.

This is what you call Coitus Interruptus of the culinary type. Many of his best dishes never reached orgasmic completion. Meanwhile, we swoon in the caldron of forgetfulness. In the life of the heart, there are no hierarchical distinctions, our skins are the same slickness under the rivulets of sweat. His milk that I drink, my milk that he drinks, placate the dearth of the ages.

Freedom is the celebration of all things—so vast its music, so intense its ardor, so blind its love. The white horse is not a horse; it is the paradoxical other. And I yearn to ride him with all my might. He is all sinew and flesh and bone delivered from the gods.

Tonight, we shall assume the missionary position, and we shall proselytize each other all over again. You can play Christ to my Buddha; your Mohammed to my Shiva. Plunder my primal civilization, force your almighty god, threaten hell and damnation . . . I am not afraid of you.

I like this "position," I, on top, where I can "really" see you . . . your face contorted in love, in pain, in angst, in the final letting go; and I shall eat you and drink you. Together we shall invent a vast new lascivious literature.

Our civilization is not toppling. Life is short, experience is long and love, love is our sweet nation.

The Poet Welcomes His Male Muse

REGIE CABICO

At four in the morning, my apartment buzzer rings.
I recognize his voice. He looks like Montgomery Clift
before the accident. Closer to a Tom Cruise—
but with brains. He throws his duffel bag
on my sofa, then eats everything in my fridge—
including the leftover chicken & finishes the rest
of my Sapporo. Where did you go?
I was taking a bus ride with dysfunctional
families and screaming kids, he says—looking
through my closet—tossing empty cardboard
boxes out. Why didn't you leave? I say to him
as I watch him shed his 501s on the floor.
He lights a cigarette and lets the ashes fall
on the wooden tile and smiles at me for a long time.
I thought the view would be worth the ride—
now I'm here. He still smiles at me and removes his
T-shirt. I can tell he hasn't showered for days.
Without his shirt, he looks like the guy in
Betty Blue. In a suit, he looks like Harry Connick.
He chooses to wear my striped nightshirt. The one
he gave me last Xmas. He drops his cigarette butt

in the sink of dishes, kisses me on the cheek
and whispers in my ear, You don't realize
how far you've come until you leave.
He smiles again. Do you know what I mean?—
I don't say anything but remove the nightshirt
he just put on. My lips don't let go of him.
After we're through making love, I watch him fall
asleep and leave the door ajar.

Potato Eater

EULALIO YERRO IBARRA

I must admit, I am a potato eater. That's what they call me. Even back home. In gay Filipino-speak, this means that I am a *baklâ* who shuns rice and chomps on white meat instead. Almost exclusively interested in a *Kanô,* a white foreigner. Given a choice, I would rather go out with a white man, or at least a *mestizo,* a half-breed, or someone who looks like a white man.

My preference for Kanos has always been a source of much discomfort. To my politically correct colleagues, I am perpetuating a stereotype, one that they have been trying to smash. Even back in the Philippines, just because I was always seen in the company of white men, I would always be branded as *Amboy,* an American boy, afflicted with colonial mentality. And when I would be in the tourist belt cruising for an *afám* (as a white man is also called in Filipino *sward*-speak), people would automatically brand me a call boy, a hustler, a *civam,* a *shaolin,* or whatever term was fashionable at that time, leeching money off some rich old Kanô. Intellectually, I know that I am maintaining some form of imperialist ideal here, something like the rich-white-man-exploiting-a-third-world-boy syndrome that activists in the streets chirp about so much. But ideology has nothing to do with my sexual proclivities. It's my dick that knows what's better.

I don't know why I became a potato eater. But ever since I was a kid, I had always dreamed that some white knight in shining armor would someday sweep me off my feet and carry me to a faraway land. During my high school years in Manila, while I would emulate my classmates in their lusting for the voluptuous sister of Denise Clyde, our homely American classmate, inside I wished that Denise had a brother instead. Someone I fantasized about, who, like the sister, put out with Filipinos, and had eyes as blue as the November sky, and hair as fair as the color of corn during harvest time—just like Mr. Sean Marvin, the American Peace Corps volunteer in my hometown who adopted me as his little brown brother when I was in Grade IV.

When I was at the University of the Philippines wrestling with my sexuality, I witnessed an incident that became a turning point in my peripatetic life. Just before I turned eighteen, Mother's, a sauna and massage parlor with a beer garden featuring a live band and topless dancing girls, opened near our house in Quezon City. Because of its novelty and for want of better things to do, I frequented the bar with my classmates after school, to drink beer and flirt with skimpily clad waitresses who were mostly young Visayan women fresh off the boat from Samar and Leyte.

We also sometimes patronized the massage parlor, which in the macho society of the Philippines generally meant screwing the attendants. I would always choose an older woman (No. 69, what else?), for I felt that I would be safe with her. From what, I had no idea. She always started our session with the question, "Powder, lotion, rubbing alcohol, or *derecho na?*" I would, however, decline her invitation for the derecho na part, not because I did not like her, but I was too afraid of getting the *tulò,* a form of gonorrhea which is hard to treat.

The attendant would always feel slighted by my rejection, saying that I insulted her beauty. I wished I could tell her the truth. With her age and experience, she probably was good, but the thought of having sex, especially with her, horrified me. I was there only because my friends were there. I was saving myself for something better, for what, I didn't know yet. So to appease her, I would let her demonstrate her abilities on me—full-body massage capped by her jacking me off with her adroit hands. I would always pretend to enjoy her ministrations, which actually felt wonderful but left me unsatisfied, and afterward I would brag to my friends how terrific a lay No. 69 was. "You guys should try her," I would say to them, as they always picked sweet young things for their partners. "She isn't the favorite of General Olivas for nothing."

I did not indulge myself in the sauna that often, though, for it was beyond my student budget. But I always was in the bar, especially toward closing time, when they had a show that featured girls performing incredible tricks with their vaginas—demonstrating their famed muscle control, like the simple tasks of smoking a cigarette or picking up coins on the floor and putting them inside beer bottles or the more amazing feats of spinning a web made of string on the floor or stringing Gillette blades together with a piece of thread.

Friday nights were special nights, when the bar had an extended fuck show with audience participation, with the promise, as announced by the DJ with a fake American accent, that all drinks ordered at the participant's table would be on the house if the guy didn't reach orgasm in twenty minutes.

"So come one, come all, come up the stage and enjoy!"

I was never absent from Mother's on Friday nights. In fact, I was always there early, as there was this military man, a Metropolitan Command colonel, a big and burly muscular lout with a dick like a horse's, who always participated in the show and whose performance I always enjoyed, especially in my rich fantasy life. He would be the first to go up on stage ("Ha! It's better to be first, when their cunts are still fresh!"), his big but flaccid dick already protruding out of his fly, to screw the same plain-looking young girl, the one with the underdeveloped tits and a twat that could pick up a peeled hard-boiled egg and lay it on stage, sliced.

On stage, he would strip out of his fatigues, showing his dark muscular trunk, while fondling himself to erection and walking toward the girls, who were in a chorus line. He would yank out his favorite girl from the line, unceremoniously push her down onto the narrow bench that served as the bed, and screw her without preliminaries, without even taking her bikini pants off. While pumping the girl, the army man would be lip-synching Frank Sinatra's "My Way," which the DJ always played for him. His singing would graduate to loud moans and groans while he thrashed about, the flimsy wooden stage creaking and the hapless girl lying impassively on the bench biting her lower lip, crushed by his bulk. Sometimes the army man pointed his .38 service revolver to her head while plunging his purple dick deep into her vigorously, but without coming.

At about the last minute, the girl would start to grunt and moan just like the army man, sometimes even squealing like a pig in heat. She would lick his throat and lock her legs around his waist, while her hands clung to his ass, kneading his muscular cheeks like dough. She would rub her crotch to his and, contracting her powerful pelvic muscles, finally milk him just before the twenty allotted minutes was up. She would push him off her while he was still spurting like the Taal Volcano, to show the audience that he'd failed. Amid the applause, she would leave the stage, wiping his come off her crotch with her hands and flicking it toward the army man. The army man would be left slouched on the bench, spent, with a smirk on his face.

Every Friday night it was like this, a ritual for both of them, and for me too—for the army man to screw his girl and try to resist her cunning ways, and for me, to watch him lose. I hated him. He was the same man in uniform who ransacked my room when the Metrocom came to our house in the middle of the night, to "invite" my father to spend a month in the dreaded stockade in Camp Crame just a few months after Marcos declared martial law in 1972.

Our house was surrounded by a battalion of soldiers bearing

U.S.-made armalites, and several of them went inside and turned the house inside out searching for whatever. Then they took my father away. They said he needed re-education. They said he had been writing subversive poems that were inimical to the goals of the New Society. The following days, my brother and I combed the various detention centers in Manila to look for *Tatay*. We bribed guards with crisp twenty-peso bills so we could go in and check if our diabetic university professor father was among the common criminals who were incarcerated in the stockades. Thanks to his fraternity brother, who was a ranking officer in Marcos's elite presidential guard, we found Tatay in Crame three days later, just in time, because he would have died in the military's custody, unknown, for he ran out of medications.

I was very young then. I did not know what was wrong with my father's poems. He wrote poems about life during World War II as a guerrilla and their hope for freedom and liberation from the Japanese occupation, but the Marcos government said his poems could be interpreted as inciting revolution. My father's poems did not mean anything to me. It was not until my whole family came to America as political refugees several years after my father was freed that I learned the true meaning of his writings. Freedom and liberation; those are such heady words. Back in the Philippines, I had never experienced how it was to be truly free. It is true, though, that back there one is free to be born, and to die in the hands of the military. Life is that cheap.

But I surely knew what the face of tyranny looked like. To this day, whenever I see uniformed military men, even in the streets of Smalltown, U.S.A., I freeze in terror. Because they remind me of the soldiers who came to my room and pointed their guns at me while they searched my belongings. They remind me of the soldier who struck my mother with the butt of his armalite as she tried to rush to my father's side when he was being taken away, precipitating her miscarriage. And one of them was the army man, the notorious torturer of political prisoners, Colonel Mariano Abadilla, whom I enjoyed watching being outwitted by an ordinary-looking *probinsiyana* at Mother's.

One particular Friday, I had a double treat watching the fuck show; not only was my favorite man in uniform there, but after him, there was this Kanô, a student from a nearby university who was egged on by his friends to go up the stage and join in the fun. He was a new Kanô to the bar; I had never seen him there before. Three of the girls on stage picked up his friends' cue, so they came down and pulled the Kanô from the table. He did not offer much resistance. He looked like he was too drunk to fight.

The Kanos had been a fixture at Mother's since it opened, but they had almost always kept to themselves, except of course when they were flirting with the girls. They were mostly medical and veterinary students from nearby universities, and the girls were always coming on to them, asking them to participate in the show.

There was much anticipation in the mostly male audience when the Kanô mounted the makeshift stage to join the girls in the limelight. Suddenly, a mass of humanity came into the bar and surrounded the stage, some pouring in from the sauna next door still wearing towels wrapped around their middles, and some from outside, hangers-on, like the peanut and cigarette vendors, security guards, and watch-your-car boys. They all moved toward the front of the stage, jostling and pushing each other to have a better view. Those who were far from the stage stood on chairs or, like me, on tables, so we could have a better vantage point to what went on with the Kanô and the four women who were lasciviously dancing around him. Colonel Abadilla, of course, got the best view in the house—as he was putting his clothes on, he placed his chair right in front of the platform so he could see the action up close.

There was a general murmur of agreement in the audience when the girls started to strip the Kanô out of his school uniform. He probably didn't have any idea what was about to transpire, for he hesitated a moment and tried to leave the stage when the girls ripped his shirt off. But the crowd jeered and cheered him to have a go at it. He didn't have any choice. Either perform or face the mob. There was a big hurrah when the girls finally undressed him to his shorts. For he was transformed into a god.

The Kanô stood on stage, tall and proud, and worshiped by all —he was more than six feet tall, massively built, with a smooth body, large chest, muscular torso, washboard stomach, narrow waist, full buns, tree-trunk-like legs, dark curly hair, pouty lips, and blue eyes accentuated by his golden tan. Even his friends back at his table—all Kano themselves, except for one Filipino runt who spoke in a clearly studied American accent—were clapping and hooting in obvious appreciation. The Kanô on stage seemed to have jumped out of one of those SoloFlex advertisements from the pages of the imported American *GQ* magazine.

It was obvious that the Kanô knew he looked good, because he started to pose like a body builder with a wide grin on his face, lapping up the accolades. He even invited the adventurous ones from the audience to feel his well-developed biceps while he was flexing. And when the girls ripped his white boxer shorts off, there was even wilder applause, well, more of a gasp really, for the Kanô was hung like a *burro,* bigger than Colonel Abadilla, and he was already semi-erect!

It looked to me at least like the Kanô had a dick about a foot and a half long, as round as a San Miguel beer bottle, but with a ridiculously small knob, and balls as huge as Bangkok *santól* fruit hanging low to his thighs. And pink! Baby blush pink!

Two of the girls with him on stage fled, shrieking and running away after they saw the Kanô's monster dick. They complained to the manager, shouting hysterically that they didn't want to partici-pate. They were afraid they would get hurt handling the Kanô's giant *tarugô.* But Colonel Abadilla waved his gun to the girls, ordering them to come back. The colonel was like a madman, clapping and shouting in his chair and directing the girls what to do with the Kanô up there in the spotlight.

The Kanô wasn't there for long though, not even five minutes. For the manager called out his secret weapon—No. 69, who else! As soon as the older woman worked vigorously on the Kanô with her expert mouth, using the Kanô's *titî* like a toothbrush, he came right away. Just like that. Poor woman, the Kanô came in gallons, and he held her head against his crotch, not letting go of her before he finished. She gagged and was flailing her arms about while her face was impaled on the Kanô's front. She could have drowned in his come! When he released her, she cleared her throat loudly and spat toward the audience, which stampeded, laughing while they ran out of the line of fire.

The Kanô's performance was so anticlimactic the audience felt they'd been robbed of something. Some actually booed the Kanô for his dismal showing, because they were expecting a wild show and wanted to see him work the girls, just like, as one of them said, what he saw in an American porno Betamax tape.

The audience saw more of the Kanô just the same though, because one of the girls, No. 69 of course, hid his clothes, and he had to sit down back at his table stark naked. He didn't seem to care.

The whole spectacle left me with a feeling of excitement, an excitement I was sure I had experienced before, but just refused to remember. But in that bar that night with the Kanô god on stage, it came to me in a flash, jolting me, the remembrance of the first time that I had this kind of sensation, a remembrance that I had been suppressing all my life. It was when I was still a kid in the province, maybe five or six years old.

My teenage *yaya,* Vital, who was also our *lavandera,* our washer-woman, brought me along with her to the river to wash clothes together with other *lavanderas* of other families. While my yaya and her young friends were gossiping about their respective households, a *gravasán,* one of those large trucks that haul gravel from the river to wherever it is needed, thunderously announced its arrival. It stopped near where we were, and its crew, instead of commencing to load their truck with gravel and sand, decided to wash in the river, stripping themselves naked in front of us.

The men, there must have been eight of them—probably teenagers like the lavanderas, but they looked like big men to me—were all lean, dark, and muscular, except for their *mestizo* foreman, who was fat and pale, and who just sat on a huge rock, fanning himself in the shadow of the rickety *gravasán*. His crew were happily playing and splashing like children in the water, displaying their nudity without shame in front of the girls.

I noticed that the men had hair on their crotches, which looked odd to me, because I had none and wanted very much to have some, right at that moment. All of them had skin extensions over their *potóy*, rather, their *botô*, which also looked odd to me, for my potóy was *palták*, and I did not understand why.

The men started to tease the girls, holding and pointing their botô at them, asking the girls to join them in the water. In response, the girls giggled and screamed, pointing to the men's botô, acting as if they were shocked, telling them they weren't big enough, and also taunting them to come near them in return, while at the same time holding their *palo-palô*, the piece of wood which they used to pound clothes to extract dirt.

One girl, whose name was Venid, pretended to want to go and join the men in the water. Her friends mockingly restrained her, and then they all collapsed in laughter, their legs kicking in air, showing their naked buttocks to the men in the water. (My yaya actually pushed Venid into the water. Vital hated Venid. She said she slept around with the *señoritos* from all the families in town and told everybody about it. This was true, for I saw her and my cousin Nong Junior coupling like dogs under the big *sampalok* tree behind our house.) It was all good-natured banter, and everybody was laughing and having a good time.

I, on the other hand, was having sensations at the pit of my stomach, from looking at the naked men with their botos surrounded with hair, flopping in the wind. I was particularly enthralled by the half-breed foreman, who had now since joined his minions in the water. From the neck up, he looked like Ben Hur. *Ben Hur* was the first movie I had ever seen; it was scary and exciting and Ben Hur was the first Kanô whose face had stuck in my mind. Unlike Ben Hur though, the supervisor was stripped bare-assed. I had never seen Ben Hur naked in the *cine*. I sure wished I had.

Mr. Bisû, as the supervisor was known, had a hairy body and an exceptionally large botô compared to those of his men, and his huge balls were *eakgak,* hanging low to his thighs. His botô then started to get *otóg* while he was playing and wrestling with the others. This excited me and also elicited nervous squeals from my yaya and her friends. The other men, probably out of sympathy with their boss, were getting otóg too. The girls got quieter, their laughter became stifled, and soon they remained silent, except for a few muffled giggles here and there.

I had difficulty breathing as I watched the naked men dancing in the water with their proud botô all standing in the air. I kept beating on my chest because I thought I was going to die, for my heart was racing to the winds. And to my astonishment, my potóy also stood proud, the proudest of them all. I tried hard to hide my excitement from yaya Vital, but she was too busy to notice, for she too was having her silent scream, probably the quietest scream of her life.

But that was a long time ago, and those memories came back to me in the shabby bar where the Kanô was being stripped on stage. Watching the Kanô being peeled of his clothes piece by piece, I felt my throat become dry, my heart palpitating really fast, sometimes missing a beat here and there. I thought I was going to die. I couldn't breathe! I was scared, really scared, for I noticed that I wet my pants, just from looking at the naked white boy with the muscular body and the big dick. I felt so disturbed by it that that night, I must have downed more than a case of San Miguel beer, to drown that exciting but unpleasant feeling.

Later, back at his table after things had settled down, the Kanô looked a bit subdued in his chair, perhaps ashamed to have lost in a game that was always interpreted in the bar as a small battle between the sexes. He looked so pathetic in his chair, like a lost wet fledgling. The Filipino in his group, the runt, tried to console him in his best American accent, but to no avail. The Kanô looked very down, his ego obviously hurt.

Colonel Abadilla came up to him to commiserate. "God dang those women," he said like a Texan. "When we think that we figured everything out, they have another trick up their boxes, don't they? We just can't win, can't we?" He tapped the Kanô on the shoulder and winked at him. The Kanô, having heard this, cheered up a little bit. After all, he wasn't alone in the boat; the army man lost every week!

Without waiting for an invitation, Colonel Abadilla pulled up a chair and sat down beside the Kanô. He was quite gallant to the white man and his friends, even ordering several rounds of beer for them. And while he was sitting next to the naked white boy, he joked a lot with him, telling him stories of his stay in Fort Bragg, sometimes slapping the Kanô's bare back, or gripping parts of his naked thighs, or brushing the Kanô's dick with his hands. The Filipino runt's face looked sour upon seeing all the attention the colonel was paying to his friend.

Colonel Abadilla plied the Kanô with so many drinks that the young man passed out, slumped on his chair. Everybody at his table tried to revive him, but he just groaned. At closing time, the other Kanos tried to wake him again, but no dice. Finally, the colonel just hoisted him on his shoulder and carried him singlehandedly to his jeep. He said that he would bring the Kanô home himself after he finished with him, if that was okay with them—and drove off with the Kanô dead drunk in the vehicle, naked as a newborn babe. The Filipino friend who remained behind looked like he'd been robbed of something, he looked so pathetic in his chair.

I surely had my fill of amusement that night. My head was

light from too much excitement, and my stomach was queasy from too much beer. Walking home, I puked several times in the streets and one more time, very violently, in front of our gate, retching slime and my guts out. I swore I would never drink that much again.

I knew that my father was furious at me when I came into the house reeking of alcohol and vomit. He was still up, waiting for me. But he really didn't say anything. In the morning, at breakfast, he said something in Spanish to me, that old harsh language that he failed to teach me, and to which he always retreated when he was upset or angry.

I understood what he said. I had two years of Spanish in high school and was taking an advanced course in the university at that time, perhaps because I wanted to capture the glory of my Spanish-speaking ancestry that my father always reminisced about but deprived me of. In front of his *chorizo de Bilbao, estrellado, champurado,* and *chocolate e,* he said something to the effect that maybe if I had been born a girl, I would have already become a *puta* by that time.

In my mind, I agreed with him, for I needed some kind of escape. Or maybe some attention and a little bit of love.

My dreams that night were full of images of the Kanô god from the bar—that he was Bruce, the secret Kanô pal of my childhood, named after Bruce Wayne of Batman fame, and I was his Robin, always ready to be by his side. Or he was turned into an Alexander the Great, and I was Bagoas, his page boy, schooled in the art of love, giving him soothing massages after a hard day in the fields of battle, or that he was a General Douglas MacArthur and I was his Filipino aide or . . . I would have many dreams like these with the Kanô transformed into many forms and guises. In time, my life became a relentless search for the perfect Kanô, a search which dictated my life, eventually bringing me to the hustling bars in many cities, first Manila, and now San Francisco, Chicago, New Orleans, and New York. I'm a fool I guess, for my dreams, well, they are only real when they are raging inside my head.

Poet's Café

MEENA ALEXANDER

I needed to talk to Rinaldo, bad, bad. He was the only home I had. My head was filled with babble I couldn't unsnarl. Italian? I thought. Basque? He was out of town, selling Fiats. There was an ache in my calf muscles, a heat in my head I couldn't control. I stood for long periods staring out my window. Rough sky and water entered my soul.

I breathed hard, trying to conceive the atmosphere Melville breathed in, letting Ahab take shape in his brain, the monumental whale of desire sharpening its teeth. I exiled myself in thoughts of a man racked by a dream of islands, chartless longing, where trees with live heads of women sway in the wind, where men in concupiscent camaraderie chuck each other under the chin, then swarm into oily piles of ambergris in celebration of the all-American thing. I wanted to be free of longing.

I made notes: O America, my new-found land, I sang, but still my legs hurt and something aside from my bowels seemed a stirring in me.

I'll Rollerblade, I swore, right past the financial district, Twin Towers swaying in the wind, Dow Jones Average quivering as Tokyo turns or London, Rome, Paris, unreal all. Only roll, roll woman I whispered to myself. The way to keep breath blossoming, the burden out of your legs.

Then I thought, Maybe in a room on Avenue B set up with a bar and all, I can catch hold of myself again, grow into freedom. But the chairs and tables at the Poet's Café grew dark. Heavy the counter where Manuel stood with his back to me, saying, "You next, Dottie, you next, why so out of breath, gal?"

What could I say to Manuel? I had wound myself tight in a skin-hugging thing, black and blue, hair poking out of a turban and perched atop it a whale I cut out from the *National Geographic.* I was trying for a picture of Krishna but no such luck, so the whale became my totem, a silvery thing in heavy paper pinned atop my turban. An Indian sign I would say if anyone asked me. Images transact their own gravity. I meant to have Kaliya, I would add. Don't you see, he's the Leviathan on whose snout Krishna danced, feet tapping the wet hide, cleansing the seas of poison.

I race up the stairs at Poet's Café. Sounds shoot out of my head, heavenward. Anthony stares, dreadlocks askew, mike in his hand, then wipes his eyes. Mago with his Bwango Band: "New York Salsified," he cries in delight. The Fifth Avenue matron brought in by her gigolo screams as Anthony, squinting to see if Mago's microphone's in place, trips over her knee, his *Free South Africa* shirt tight over his chest, poised for war—"Go Dam, Go Dam em all." She does not hear. "I am dirt, I am dirt," she whispers to the lapdog tucked in her hair. Her hair sprouts over Mago's mouth.

The crooner with the hennaed hair and jet-blue art silk, they brought her in from Arthur Avenue where the Mafioso rove. "Ah, ah pre-tend," she sings. She cries in me without stopping,

> Draupadi, O Draupadi, syncretic buhuhu
> Where have all the maidens guhuhu

Stopping up my mouth my ears, I leave my soul sisters up there to sing "Dottie and Her Sisters all Exiles with Their Heads Flaming."

I performed for all of them, Simon Escobar and Juan and the woman from the literacy program and the Fifth Avenue matron and Anthony and the bunch of kids from the South Bronx who were turning themselves into a Unit for the Propagation of Poetry in Our Streets. I performed for the lovers twined around each other, men whose mouths sprouted perfect mustaches. For others whose lips were turned the color of ripe pomegranate with kisses, such as Cavafy might have showered in secret on the body of his love as he lay in a darkened room, in a side street in Alexandria, candles at his head and feet.

"Father," cried the young man of Constantin Cavafy's dream. "Father I am burning." And his dead father heard him and, rising out of the Levant, which is where the sun is, rushed in and put out the flames that were eating the young man's legs, his thighs, the purple blotches from the HIV turned malignant that hurt him too, too terribly. This too entered Cavafy's poetry. So for those afflicted lovers—male with male, female with female, male with female—I performed my piece. I black queen not yet under the hill.

"Gimme, gimme, gimme gogo," Dotty cries at the shelter door—
I shall live in Paradise House forever more.
"Gimme, gimme, gimme gogo," Dottie cries at the shelter door.

I crooned to myself to soften it up, figuring it out as I went.
Music thickens and Mago with his Bwango show croons, "Congo Boys, Congo," and then turns to the girls.

"Say Pwango girls, say Pwango." The two girls, one touching fifty, lean up, wiggling their breasts, their shirts decked out in squares of red and blue. They grind their hips and put out their hands and the marimba calls.

Anthony's eyes screw my back so hot I walk upright. I know through the muscles in my back—it's a wise muscle that knows—he's trying to straighten himself up and get off the lapdog's leash.

"Come, come tonight," I heard him hiss, a little earlier. To who? Then the wind blew the door open. The wind blew as a man walked in the door. The wind's son, son of the black Manhattan wind. My flesh is burned inside me, don't you know?

Suddenly I wanted Rinaldo. His arm against mine, his thigh so firm to keep me from this surge of flesh as the wind blew the door open. Where was Rinaldo now? In what high-rise glass Mecca, sipping Sanka, delicately tasting grilled quail, pheasant under glass, oysters in cherry sauce. His mind roaming free. O Rinaldo!

It was time for the impromptu performance. They brought in the mad guy, the ex-Vietnam vet. He stood outside the cage I had leaped into. He stuck his fist out. He offered me an orange.

"Who are you?"

"Who?"

"I said you. Hear me, girl?"

"Draupadi."

"Dropti!" He starts laughing at that.

"Funny name that for a gal with black hair. Come over here, Dopti, Dopti."

Again he beckoned me. Suddenly I was glad I was in a cage.

"Bette," he called me, changing my name. "Bette, you Asian cunt, come, come slow over here." I held myself straight in the cell.

Slowly I raised myself. I have nothing in my pockets, I

thought. I must survive. Sail the black waters. I faced him, the blond one with glittering blue eyes.

"Draupadi," I said, "that's my name. Call me Draupadi."

Later, much, much later, I found my way back to Poet's Café. I squatted on the floor, my back against the metal cage I had put myself in. They had kept it on as part of the decor. I sat back, stretched out my feet, picked paper and pen I had carefully brought with me. I was very still, very clear. Then I wrote Rinaldo a letter. "Poet's Café, Avenue B," I wrote at the top so he would know where I was. Not Perugia or Paris or Bruges.

Dear Rinaldo—

You told me that your reading of Nabokov drew you to America. Not irrelevant perhaps is that the nimble genius of butterflies, White Russian fallen from grace, confessed in print he had to invent America in order to make *Lolita* that artwork you so admire.

Did you have to invent me in order to live here, Rinaldo? I need to know. Let me tell you this: I, a young Asian-African-American, much influenced by all the colored aesthetics of the tail end of this century, have a Fuck the Fathers program in my head. I will make new friends. I will love my life.

Later I thought of tearing the letter into little bits. Smearing lipstick on the bits. Instead, then and there I found a scrap of wall to write on, right next to the cage I had put myself in. I was all alone in the Poet's Café, a lean thing dressed in black, scrawling with black-cased Revlon:

Rinaldo,

Lest we forget: You picked me up when I was just a young thing and then got me into the Paradise House program. You are an old man with a hot cock, spit on you. Signed, Draupadi.

Dear Rinaldo,

Down with sorrow. Up with fucking. We are all we are now in the present. I should not be addressing myself to you anymore. My thumb up your . . .

Signed, Your Beloved

(She who has no name, whose skin is no color, queen under each hill you ride your super special Fiat over.)

Draupadi.

·

I felt little pulses, little jabs of electricity. Weak as if something cold had bitten in. I tried to move to the stove, but couldn't. The next day it was the same thing.

Ping, ping, right by the stove, I sensed something strumming. Mama with the knife in her hand so the blade slid onto gas flame; the handle started smoking. My period just starting. The heavy pad between my legs. Warm stuff go whoosh, whoosh, an ocean starting up. Warm waves of Montauk, as if a whale had been spiked, all ready to spill over my thighs, except for that pad Mama had readied, belt and all.

"Mama, Mama," I called. "What is it, Mama, Mama?" But she was dying already, my mama in the hospital in Gingee.

First I thought what I felt was heat from the fire. But there was no fire. When I moved onto the blue stool, I sat down heavily, I felt I would faint. Dragged the stool toward the window. My legs felt as if they were stuffed with lead.

Staring out of my high window at gray water did not calm me nor lull the stirring. A pot with black and blue stripes. Something

Rinaldo got in Florence. I picked it up, smashed it against the wall. Crawled to the corner where the bits lay. Set my lips there, head down, a dog, a goat, a she-cow. Wept into the broken bits.

At that point I knew nothing about the abyss of transition. Nor about the crying out into the abyss, that the Draupadi dancers did, invoking in their souls, both Shiva and Ogun, invoking the fragments of iron ore that had splintered from the great god Orisa-nla.

Started talking in my head:

"Rinaldo darling I am not a child.

"A little thing, a jot, a scrap of flesh and blood and air, a slight blessedness is stirring in me.

"Rinaldo I am going to have this child."

He was there in front of me. He had returned from Saudi Arabia. He stood against my fridge. Nothing. Said absolutely nothing.

"Rinaldo, this could be our new life, our life together. Make a choice."

Nothing, he said nothing.

Because of Laura in her blue silken gown, you do not want this child. Laura who lives in Perugia, who's been married to you for thirty years, would know about us and your lovely son Mario who's all set to work for Fiat, hot, axe and all against the Red Brigade, having seen their terrorist work close at hand.

But no, it's not Laura. It's the color thing, no?

Who wants a mongrel African-American-Asian child, by a woman who strolls through Harlem on full moon nights?

Harlem's an oyster, Rinaldo.

Glows in the night. The crack lights it up, the crack in the earth. Did you know about that? It runs down 135th all the way from the Hudson.

I shall go, my belly huge, and stand by the Korean grocery store. Look, look at my unborn child. I shall front the black men and women pouring in, I shall front the Asians. I shall paint a placard and hold it up.

"Gaze. Gaze."

I shall stand there, a living testimony. When the beer bottles fall, when the cops rise and batter our young men, I shall stand there.

I shall not enter Bellevue. No, no. Nor leave Columbus Circle nor Tompkins Square.

Look at all the cardboard I have packed in. I shall lift my skirts.

DO NOT BEWARE I shall make out in sign language.

The nuns in Nyack taught me sign language. Did you know that, Rinaldo? We have nuns in Nyack, too.

Lookie, sir, it's cardboard not flesh, not my small stirring blessedness.

She it is, queen under the hill, mound of flesh and blood and skin you kissed.

A woman with one breast and no eyes, chin packed with hairs, stares back at me in the mirror.

Mama Marya, she cries, all lips and thighs, how shall I enter the kingdom of heaven?

Will the black virgin of Westbeth, she who is covered with condoms . . .

Will the red virgin of this native soil, bleeding with shrapnel, intercede for me?

Scissors in hand, Frida Kahlo turns in her grave toward Ana Mendiata. They wave crisp ribbons of flesh. I am their sister. Crying's not the thing to be done. Frida cries, though, lying through her teeth to Diego.

Crying. Amor amor and all that.

I tore the bit about the mother who killed her dearly beloved child from the genius black sister's novel I was reading. Tore it out and stuck it in my dress.

O ghostly flesh of my foremothers. The slave ships are still in port. Did you know that? Docked right by the *Intrepid* where they take the schoolchildren to teach them the glories of America.

O ghostly flesh of my black mothers, crying in me.

I stuck the bit from that book in my dress. At the abortion clinic I lifted up the dress. I took it off. I hung it on a hook.

Amor, amor, she cried and all that. Swallowing her sobs.

I felt nothing. I swear I felt nothing.

*L*et our bodies be our playgrounds. You said that to me, two weeks after I told you about our child. You chucked me under my chin.

"A child needs a home, Dotti. I have no home for you."

I hung my dress, with the bit of paper in it, on a hook in the changing room. Wanted to hold the paper in my hand.

*N*o dearie, no, they said. No, no.

Saw the metal bucket at the foot of the bed.

Metal lined with plastic the color of a cloud over the Hudson. A cloud filled with semen.

R, can you hear? I felt nothing.

They tied my legs. Parted my sweet soft center.

Slide down, slide down, dearie. Lower, lower.

Put out his hands with the rubber gloves, slid them in.

You'll fall asleep. I promise.

Slid the skin-thin gloves up, up as the barbiturates strummed.

Of course it was my choice.

Later I recovered my dress.

I love you, he said, long distance from São Paulo, Dotti darling, my poor America.

────────

She beats her head in the metal chamber of the new subway cars imported from Japan. Against the shining metal she beats her head, over and over again. A stick-thin figure racing from the exit signs.

She claps her face against the sign that says EMERGENCY EVACUATION PROCEDURES. *Las vias del tren son peligrosas.*

A week later she stands on the subway platform at Union Square, by the garbage dump.

Gazes there for her flesh. Her sweet, stirring blessedness.

Stories to Read Aloud: No. VI

ALLAN DESOUZA

HOT AISHUN HUNNY
AND THE FRENDLI COKAYSHUN

*i*s it troo wot they say abowt oryentls my new frend aast me that if
you eet one you want anuther an owur latur smyling inscrootably i
sed lets find owt the aishan hunnypot btween my legs wuz boyling
wit desiyer but furst i wantd to taist his corcayshun cok mmmm
nice i coudent get enuf of dat wunnerful sweet taisting cok of his
my huneypot craivd sturing and i new just wat hard rod was
avalible for the job i climed on hees lap and pushd my berning
croch down on hiz throbbing prong i luv the adoring look on
cawcaishun mails faises wile they humping me it maik the sex eevn
moor enjoibal i lyke a man hoo can fuk me from ani an evry angl he
enjoi it too becoz he getz a very seenic vuw all aroun my senshuos
yet innicent look and my slim yootful boddy freekwently dryve
dem wiled witt deesier duz it do anithing to yu the feel of his big
meet in my littel pot taek my breth away the moor hiz rod stird my
hunnypot the hotta it got an the joosyur suddnly he gasp i want to
taist yore hunnypot his tung eegerly lapt up the flowing streem of
hot ashun joos sweeping it into his greedi mowth it felt sowwww
good he luvd the eerotik flaiva of my sweet an sowr hoal but his cok
was hungery too he ramd it into my boddy with firm steddy stroaks

i skwirmd and skweeld as I ett him again maiking shuwer his rod staid stif for moor fukking i had anudder orgasum letting my voalcanic jooses berst free an still his hard cok skweezd and skwishd into my hot wet tite orrientle hole he gaspd and groned reddy for an orgasum of his oan he turnd me ova saying he wantd to see my fais when he caim all ovur my belli he gruntd and puld his hard rod sending streems of jizum over my boddy i luvd the look of ekstassy on his fais givving his kok a frendly pull i ast want me agane in an ower he shuk his hed i cunt wate an ower lets do it agane rite now

A Yin and Her Man

RUSSELL LEONG

"Where did you put that goddammed Buddha!" she quipped on my answering machine. She was three thousand miles away. That Sunday she had gone to the Isamu Noguchi Sculpture Garden, in Long Island City, with her new boyfriend. I told her that when I was there, a few weeks before, I had hidden a small bronze Buddha in the grass near the plaque carved with Noguchi's name.

After I returned to LA, they went to visit that granite sculpture garden, and searched for the inch-tall figurine I had left behind. The garden, I was told, closed to the public from October through April. Whether it rained or snowed, I would not be able to see the sculptures. So the Buddha would be my surrogate, taking my place there.

But the two could not find it. Either the caretaker had discovered it, weeds had grown over it, or it had been swallowed by the ground below.

I remember the last meal she and I had together at the Chiuchow café off Mulberry Street. How, after each bite of meat or vegetable doused in shrimp paste, curry sauce, or garlic, she wiped her mouth, daintily, with the corner of the paper napkin. She devoured the fishhead quickly. Ditto the slivers of green onion. There were no bones around her bowl or plate; mine was littered with them.

We went to her room, a four-story walk-up studio fifteen blocks north of her haunt, the Strand Bookstore. It was emptier than the week before, minimal, except for her books, pens, albums of scrawled and blank paper, and a clear jelly glass with weedy-looking purple flowers on her desk. Her gamine smile and the way she lifted her feet out of her shoes and set those perfectly flat arches onto the rug provoked me. Maybe it was her wide-set eyes that could take in a whole garden, stones and me, at a glance. She let me unbutton the back of her summer dress; orange-colored, it slid quickly to the floor. She was not like Noguchi at all, as pensive, as weighed down by granite. She was lighter, a pale limestone that left powder on my flesh. Though she shared her body with me willingly, she always kept something secret for herself.

When she lifted her elbow, the bend of her arm showed the untanned skin, pale until my tongue reached the aureole of her right breast, where I felt its surprising pinkness on my lips.

"Tell me," I said, "how your new boyfriend enters this room."

"On wall-to-wall raggedy carpet. This is our last night," she said. "Why spoil things?"

"No, tell me, as if I were gone, how you would make love to him."

"Why?"

"Because when I'm not around, I'd like to imagine you making love to his body. That's the most I can have, can't I?" I laid my head between the smooth lines of her back and held her closer to me, my teeth in her hair, which seemed to have grown an inch since last week.

"Okay," she said, flatly. "If it turns you on to hear about another Asian man fucking me, I'll tell you."

"I don't want to force you."

"Then I'll tell you everything. But don't use it against me, betray me like the others. Promise?"

"Promise."

"Well, he walks in the door, dragging his feet. Maybe he was used to doing this as a child. I look at his shoes, usually scuffed, and at his hands, his clean nails as he takes his shoes off. He doesn't usually wear socks."

I pressed her breasts against the palms of my hands, and she moved closer, almost whispering what she had to tell me about him.

"His lips are full, and beautiful for a man's. But he doesn't say much, you know."

"Not a word?" With my fingers, I silently traced the letters for w-o-r-d around one breast, with the o encircling her erect nipple.

"He brings flowers instead. Those purple ones, there, on the table, he brought me."

"I brought them."

"No, yours died already. He brought those after you left, almost the same color, but deeper."

"I see."

"He likes to walk around in his white Jockey shorts that he irons himself, I believe."

"Strange fellow. What do you think of my shorts?" I asked, tugging at my waistband.

"I bet you paid retail for those."

"Ironing's for immigrants."

"A Chinese custom, I heard. He has nice short legs. Thick, muscular, with the calves and thighs all out of proportion to his long torso, chest, and arms."

"A native. Go on."

"And a nice behind, the kind I can run my hands over. Almost stick my favorite cards—an ace, a king of spades and a queen of hearts—between his crack."

I began to massage the small of her back, my fingers making small concentric circles. "So you and him play cards?"

"Yes, naked, and with a full deck. But never for money, only for love."

"And what about his . . ."

"There's always a bulge in his shorts when he sees me. In fact, men go crazy over that and his behind too. When we're in the Village or SoHo I see them looking."

"Is he gay or bi?"

"I don't know. I don't care. We use condoms, Mr. Interrogator."

"Does he take off his shirt when he makes love to you?"

"Eventually, after tea, or after I've read my latest poem to him."

"Read me a poem."

"Oh, I've memorized my last lines for you. They go like this: 'Ploppy floppy it falls to the ground / Floppy ploppy all good things must end.' "

My penis went limp for a second, because as she spoke she was smiling right through me. But I caught myself before she caught me.

"This person, do I know him?"

"You may have met him. Remember when we were marching in the rally downtown to City Hall? Protesting the visit of the Japanese Emperor?"

"Oh, you mean the rape of Nanking, the Korean comfort women . . ."

"I think we were all marching. He had scrawled 'Down with Japanese Militarism' on his cardboard sign, and was waving his hands. It was drizzling, and the words were running like blood. Like during my bloody period. Don't you remember? But I guess his face is ordinary in the daylight. Unlike yours."

"And at night?"

"It absorbs darkness, takes on angles and caves. Each feature becomes fuller and darker. His lips, lashes, the blackness of his hair."

"He's a chameleon?"

"No, he's Asian."

"Born here?"

"Unfair question."

"In that case, your honor, let me have some pussy." I went down between her legs and worked my tongue in her until I could taste her sticky sex juice, our thrashing wrinkling the new pages of sonnets she had written, smearing them with my sweat and her scent. She was pulling at my hair, and I thought I felt the strands snap in her hands.

"Does my description of him turn you on?"

I pulled my tongue out, tasting her tartness between my teeth. "I'm hard, but for you, not for him."

"I don't believe you. I get turned on by a pretty woman. Don't you get turned on by a good-looking man?"

"No. Have you ever made love to a woman?"

"Once."

"Was it good?"

"Like incest without any bad blood between us."

"So, what does she, or he, do for you that I don't?"

"He likes to dip a small white towel in warm water, and bathe me first. Kind of like a dry-wet bath."

"You can't clean yourself off?"

"He says my skin is dry, and since I come from the tropics, a bit more humidity in my skin makes it glow."

"He is strange."

"He's sensitive. Politically conscious. Knows how to make money and eat well. Then I pull down his shorts."

"What about you?"

"I usually wear one of his shirts and I'm already naked underneath. I slide right out."

"So, who's on top?"

"Usually me. I'm so pale against his tan. Against his muscles."

"I know I'm better."

"Who says? He can wrap his legs around me and I can feel his thighs and butt and toes against mine. Not all bony kneecaps."

I began to straddle her but something made me pull it out.

"So fast, dear? Full moon. And we have until morning, you know."

Maybe she had been faking it all along. How does she really like it, I asked myself. "Does he fuck from front or back?"

"Does your kitchen have a back door? Silly. I do everything with him that I do with you."

"Why is this our last night then?"

"Because your mind is not with me when I am with you. Because you, you're a goddammed Shanghainese aesthete who puts more energy into lifting weights than in lifting my spirits." She laughed.

I flexed my biceps and shrugged. "Feel this."

With her fingers she pinched her own left nipple. "Here, feel this."

"Enough of that—now back to him. He must be from Asia, those stubby little legs and all."

With anger flashing across her face, she got up from the futon and walked to the window, her back toward me. "So, you think you American-born milk-fed cows with your Reeboks, long legs, and Acuras are better?"

"So you like 'em?"

She turned, a delicate ironic smile on her lips. "Them? I'm one of them, remember. Brandeis gave me a B.A. in East Asian history. But I'm still that country girl who uses wooden combs to comb out her hair. The insects and lice that used to get into my hair when I was a child in Penang."

"And he likes that—affectation—I suppose?"

"He doesn't talk much, really. Curses or smiles. He uses his lips and his tongue and his legs and butt. He uses up his body, all the rounds and squares of it, on me. Sometimes I'm bathed in his saliva, from my toes to my brow."

"I think I need a drink, babe."

"Help yourself to the diet Coke in the fridge." She pointed in the direction of the kitchen.

"Later. I wanna know, do you really like spit?"

"I really like spit. And he really drinks lots of tea, okay? I'll lay it out for you. He's the manager of a Szechwan restaurant on the Upper West Side. Shitwan chop goey, he tells me. He only eats Cantonese food—he likes his eel thrown live on top of the rice, then steamed."

"A diehard nationalist. You've met your match."

"Match? He's just a stocky Cantonese who drags his feet and presses his Jockey shorts at midnight when he gets off work. An ordinary yang man who has made peace with his yin—and with me. So I tease him. I love him."

"What's his name?"

"I call him Mat. Short for Maitreya. Buddha of the future. If he doesn't stop eating Chinese pastries and beer, he'll get fat. But his mind is as pure as geyser water."

"I'm the Buddhist, remember?"

"You do the rituals and chant the mantras—so you got the incense and knickknacks. But I'm not convinced."

"Hush." I put my fingers over her lips to silence her. Instantly, she set her teeth on my forefinger, drawing blood as I pulled away, stumbling to the bathroom.

She followed me and we made love on the floor without another word between us. The tile floor shone with sweat and saliva. Both of us, separately and for different reasons, were imagining *his* arms and legs wrapped around our own.

Excerpts:

From the Diary of Bu Yau Shu Cai

OR, A Translation from the Ancient Secrets

of Forbidden Fruits BY I QI XIAO JIE*

CAROLYN LEI-LANILAU

*W*ell, I never had sex with an Asian American and *Tian ah,* heaven forbid that ever happens! I'm old-fashioned Chinese woman. I like to hear my lovers swoon bits of opera in Chinese. I don't want to hear "Oh baby, it feels soo good." I demand stones move in battles. I treasure galloping horses and chariots with whips—gimme a Chinese man with a title. Butcher is good. Cadre is common. A watchmaker can promise an orgasm every day at five o'clock after he closes the shop. A paleontologist can promise romance into the past, but if he urges you to square off on the grid lines so he can measure your mouth or tail, you'd better be the type that enjoys eating bitter melon. Once I had a semiotician for a lover. Oh, he was so jealous. I couldn't powder my skin or twirl my neck in the breeze without him interpreting my gestures as erotic or perverse. And I was forced to speak in English to him. When it was time for us to challenge our wits skin to skin, I refused to roll out the golden carpet for him. I screamed in Chinese. I never said "Fuck me, baby" in English. No, I was nuts with him. He liked the calamity. He was so skinny and

---

* *Note:* I Qi Xiao Jie is the name of a Good Chinese Wife.

nearly blind that till this day, I'm amazed how crazy I was for his
tin cannon, but he was smart. Really, I didn't need anyone else to
talk with. He was so smart and could reference everything in at
least four languages. That was scholar Deng.

Before my husband, I used to believe that I loved dreaming about
the paleontologist the most. Just dropping his title as director of
the *bo wu guan* raised my position. How many people know a
"paleontologist" and can be linked with one in a tragic and romantic way? I remember requesting a photo of him properly smoking a
cigarette when he was out doing field work in the dry grasses of
Yuanmou. What I didn't know—and probably didn't care about—
was that he didn't smoke. Worst (and better!) the fire hazard was
risky the day when he posed for his beloved (*shi wo:* me) thousands
of miles away. Nonetheless, as a dutiful Chinese scholar, he lit up
nested in the high and very papery grasses. When my colleagues in
America saw this virile and Clark Gable-ish jock, pronto they
dubbed him the "Marlboro Man." His friend the taxi driver recited
great poetry and gave me splendid gifts. Oh, yes, and the zookeeper
smelled marvelous but I loved dreaming about the paleontologist
shamefully, *the most:* God, he was good-looking. Tall, confident—
the mustache is what hooked me. None of these Americanized
versions of yellow Ken, partner to Barbie. Couldn't speak a word of
English, thank God! High forehead, cheekbones like guarding
lions; could travel abroad easily; many keys and special privileges;
plus, the wormiest cannon in four thousand years of Chinese
history. No problem with *kou jiao,* therefore as well, no challenge.

Ai ya, we all shrivel and fade as we get old, don't we? Crags and
rivers as he was when I last saw him during Mid-Autumn Festival,
he looked like a has-been *and* had the nerve to convince himself that

I still was the foolish girl that he was introduced to by nature. No, just because my husband was not visiting the capital with me did not mean that my legs were fast noodles ready to be boiled. *Tai tsou le,* it was over.

Speaking of *kou jiao,* it is engraved on the ancient family's female seal that "to eat persimmon is like eating woman." *"Chi qi si xiang chi nu zi."* The other saying goes "A mouthful of *won ton* or *shui jiao* is good eating cunt." I cannot provide the translation for that in English because this original family saying is still banned in China. My male cousin is a female partner to a very high official and the official could lose face if a translation is produced. Never mind, I was relieved for the deliverance of that raindrop of a cannon because I have a classic beauty's mouth: a red dot, no more. And my gatekeeper whom I dearly miss created the smallest and most delicious *jiao zi* on earth for my mouth so that it need not stretch or shove or shift to accommodate the delicacy. One day, when I was swallowing herbs for my well-known charm, it occurred to me that I had a difficulty swallowing the potions. Well, lightning struck my intellect and I resolved that how could I swallow my young husband's too big cannon if I could barely swallow the smooth capsules of charm? This was a question for my mother, my soul's inspiration.

When my mother was visiting a month ago and I was in the East Wing taking my charm potions, as usual the discomfort of taking the herbs forced me to complain.

"These big chucks are hard to swallow. It's like having oral sex." My mother slapped her knee and frowned. Then, I began to choke and burp.

"What's your problem?" she remarked.

"I told you. This medicine is like oral sex."

Again, she slapped her knee indignantly. But when I continued to burp, she curiously turned and whispered: "What's matter, mouth too small?"

My mother has a special language with my Chinaspecial: she is constantly reminding me that I don't appreciate Him, Mr. Big and Yummy Cannon, my husband.

"Look at the new roof. Twenty double-paned new windows. You don't appreciate anything."

I swooned; "I did appreciate them in December. I don't appreciate them now. He's so firm. He's so tall. He's so bad. He's so cute, I want him to love me."

"The problem with you is that you're just itchy down there all the time." Yup, that's what my mama told me.

When the government requested that I write a special article on the Education of Youth Regarding *Kou Jiao,* I was so alarmed. Such responsibility, such a privilege! What research it would entail and what nightmare experiences I only had. It was time to consult Ah Fut. Poor scholar Fut. A long-time companion who had practiced English with me for many many years, he knew all the secrets. In Chinese, he was known as a Piggyback, also known as a Crossover. Born in Kaifeng to a Jewish mother and a Chinese father, he was raised in Shanghai in the Jewish concession after his mother was forced to seek refuge from his father, who required that his mother perform the famous ancient Animal Acts named after a monkey master. Then, it was still common practice among scholars to insist that their wives devote their bodies to the Art of the Oyster or the very tragic Art of the Anteater. The Art of the Frog was most humorous, but it was the Art of the Turtle that shocked scholar Fut's talkative mother into silence. Gossip believed that the old man planned it that way so that he could then practice Traveling Lotus and Dangling Cold without question or correction by his loving but not exactly erotic wife. There is an old Chinese saying,

"A son's cannon is stretched by his father's digging." Of course, this does not travel well once transferred into English, but scholar Fut and I sobbed many evenings into the next sunrise desperate to rearrange the gamut of his metal cannon. Disguised as monks we ransacked all the best gardens for panda eyedrops, wisteria pollen and royal peanut jelly. In those days, I was a slave to any human failure, and scholar Fut was an embarrassment. Fast with words, bald, big eyes, he sometimes snorted but he could never produce an heir. One day while dredging his bad luck over noodles, I overheard some foreigners brag about the benefits of something called oral sex! On fire with the danger of these new thrills, I conveyed the concept to Ah Fut, who nearly fainted. Upon finishing our order, we rushed out of the noodle house to strategize how we might locate the candidate who could most flatter Ah Fut with this new trick. If he wasn't so picky, I would have tried to be the first myself, but deprived as he was, recovering from his long attachment to his former mistress Lady Mangoes, and given his talent for biting, I offered the occasion to another beauty. *Ai ya!* When it was over, he told me in detail how much oral sex rescued his soul and that rather than pursue the production of an heir, he preferred to spread his thighs like a walrus and forget he was human!

Poi! My daughters and I had very long chats about the subject and while squatting in the public toilets one afternoon, my younger daughter Lightning Intellect clued me in that just because I supposedly have a difficult time with oral sex I was not the universal measurement: that every woman in the universe did not encounter chaos when challenged with the near occasion of oral sex. Another time, my older daughter offered that my own saintly mother probably did it with my father because he was from Xinjiang and it's well known that the Chinese from Xinjiang are really Turks. Peony Eyes also remarked that probably her grandmother didn't initiate anything but that she probably went along because grandfather seduced her analytic mind with some powerful delivery of forbidden fruits.

———————

With that ammunition, I was determined that when my mother next came to visit, I would kindly inquire, but when I tried she stamped her tiny foot onto the floor. At the very last opportunity, while accompanying Mother to the city gate, I tried once more, only to miss the right road and wind up in a narrow alley. Undaunted, mother rolled her eyeballs as though pleading for Father to release her from my taunts. Then we patted each other's back, kissed and turned.

When my husband returned from the capital, I wanted to fill his ear with my silly wisdom, but no. I boiled the corn that he had brought as gifts. We ate the flame-white peaches without skins. We sat side by side not quite knowing what to say to each other. It was so long since I had last smelled the corners of his body in his clothes or seen the thickness of his wrists. His fingernails needed to be clipped. He was as handsome as ever. Bold and as deep in his pain as when I first felt his presence. He was still sick, coughing and sneezing. One day he was home; the next day he was off to another city. Today, he was home to look at me and not touch. And then, briefly, he angled his arm like a hook through my neck. All I needed. My raw and clever man. I took a deep breath and swore loyalty to him.

Politely, in the classic Chinese way, not looking at him, I praise him saying: "I love you."

"I love you," says my China husband. "You don't know how painful it is." And he's right, I don't. As for oral sex, someday I will embroider the pleasures of Nine Mountains and Snow Rivers in order that the government may have their auspicious report on reference. Meanwhile, I am refining some aspects of the policy. Soon, though, soon, the report shall be in order.

Desire as the Gesture Between Us

TIMOTHY LIU

One moment we lie in a meadow
listening to the wind, and the next
    we are lost in a forest

of fallen needles. Even when birds
are out of sight, I cannot stop
    the singing. It's late summer

and I walk into the coldest room
of the house. You wait in the garden,
    break an iris off its stalk

then set it in a bowl of water.
In that quiet, the space between us
    changes into music. An ant

emerges from the flower's chamber,
inching its way to the petal's edge
    then turns back. You look at me

but I no longer can hear your voice
as I take the flower and thrust it
    all the way into my mouth.

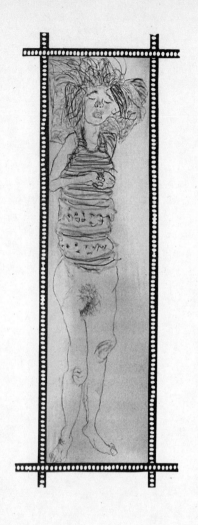

Betrayal and Infidelities

VII

Fried Yams

BARBARA TRAN

My cousin writes
of his new love,
a Viet kieu—one who has returned.
She asks, he says,
How long was her hair,
how soft were the soles of her feet,
what was the condition of her hands
Who has left you difficult as bamboo?
He says nothing of the sheets
we once strung up
in our one-room bungalow
to keep our cries from Grandmother's ears,
nothing of our wall-less outhouse.
He knows she is made jealous
simply by the faceless girl
bent over a hot pan,
selling fried yams
and sugar on the street.

Onofre's Happy Romance

JEFF TAGAMI

Onofre waited in the parking garage of Ford's Department Store for his lover to arrive. He had been waiting a long time. He had loved many women in his lifetime, but never a married one. Josie was special. She was a Filipina, and he considered himself lucky, though he had to share her with another man. He sat in his black Buick Riviera near the edge of the open-sided garage where there was a good view of some children at the playground across the street. He thought any one of those half-breed children could be his. It was very possible. Anything was possible in a small town like Watsonville.

There had been that blonde he took in the back seat of her daddy's car at the Starlite Drive-in in 1942. She had worked with him, packing zucchini in a shed in Corralitos. She was from Oklahoma. At lunchtime they snuck out and ate together on a nearby hill. He spread out a blanket as if they were having a picnic. She talked about the movies, so he asked her if she would like to go out some time. He arranged to meet her on a side street downtown where he left his car, and they drove off in hers. Somewhere along the line, they decided it wasn't such a good idea for a white woman to be seen driving up to the ticket box with a Filipino, so she suggested that he hide in the trunk. It was musky in there, and it smelled of rubber and spilled oil. He felt like a fool, but he convinced himself that it would be worth it in the end.

She parked in the back near the fence so that no one noticed when she opened the trunk to let him out. They sat in the front like husband and wife. She had fried some chicken and put it in a paper sack which had begun to show grease stains. They ate the chicken and poured coffee from a thermos.

"You're not that dark," she told him. "You're kind of chocolate-colored." She liked to think of him the way she thought of food.

"Do you like me?" he asked.

"My daddy says Filipinos are one step up from a nigger."

He was taken aback then. He felt a tightness in his stomach. He thought it might be the cold grease from the chicken. He was beginning to lose his desire for her.

"What do *you* think?" he asked her.

"When I was ten," she said, "my momma baked me a chocolate cake for my birthday, and I'll be danged if I didn't eat the whole thing. Chocolate is my favorite."

He didn't remember exactly when they moved to the back seat or the exact moment when he unhooked her brassiere. It had started to rain, and the windows were fogged up. Some of the people in their cars had begun to leave, and the few who remained were not watching the movie; it was obvious in the downpour. Certain no one could see them, she became bold and sat on his lap with her dress still on. He held the front of her neckline down with both hands and sucked on her breasts while he thrust as deep as he could inside her. Her breasts were large, and when he squeezed them together, he could get both nipples into his mouth. This excited her, and she squirmed, changing the rhythm of their thrusting so that he was afraid he was going to slip out of her. She moved her hips in a circular motion, bending his penis side to side, but he was rock-hard and wouldn't bend. He was in a little pain. She was much bigger than him, and he felt like a little boy beneath her. It all happened too easy, he thought. She was too easy. As he rolled the tip of his tongue around her nipple, he imagined how pink it must be. He knew her lips down there where he was entering with his dark member must also be pink. He wished he could see her pink- ness, but it was too dark. He felt cheated. He began to think of those pink frosted flowers jutting out of the center of white cup- cakes that he had seen behind the glass cases of Bake-rite Bakery. Then he started to come.

He became aroused again when he remembered the white woman, and he shifted his prick under his trousers until it pointed twelve o'clock toward his belly, feeling more comfortable that way. He looked out the windshield, and the sight of the children playing across the street made his hard-on recede. He had been waiting for almost an hour when Josie finally arrived, parking her car next to his. She brought the two youngest boys. They waved at him. He felt for the paper bag full of penny candy under the seat, then opened the door, motioning them inside with a nod.

The older boy was seven and dark-skinned. It was almost eight years since they had started their affair. She had named the boy after him, Ono. She hadn't even tried to hide it. Her husband was a son- of-a-bitch, really. He was a handsome man, but a braggart, and he chased every woman he could, even Josie's best friends. Onofre had bunked with him once when they both worked in the lettuce in the Imperial Valley. There had been these two white runaway teenage girls. Her husband had made love to both of them and offered them to the other men in the bunkhouse. It had made Onofre sick. Everywhere her husband went, following the crops, there had been women. One pregnant Eskimo woman had even followed him from Alaska, showing up at Josie's door. She had had enough of it. He was a cheat and would never change. She would leave him someday, but not now, because of the children. There were eight altogether. She would wait until they were grown.

Onofre remembered when he first saw Josie. It was at a Filipino Sweetheart Dance in Stockton. She was one of only a handful of American-born daughters on the West Coast, and all the single *Pinoy* men came in throngs to remember what a *Pinay* woman looked like. Yet, she was—at least for him—untouchable. She was born in Honolulu, the beautiful daughter of Visayans. The dance was part of a contest in which the young women were running for Stockton Filipino Beauty Queen. Josie was the best-looking, and many men crowded around her, trying to outbid each other with money to keep dancing with her. They didn't care that half of the money went to the organization sponsoring the dance. It was a courting ritual, because the parents of one of the daughters would feel obligated to the highest bidder. Then he came out from where he was waiting under a doorway, handsome with a square jaw, and bid five hundred dollars. Where he got that kind of money, no one knew. He and Josie glided across the floor to a slow waltz. They might as well have been dancing in an empty hall. Onofre's heart sank.

Josie slipped into the front seat with Onofre, and the two boys sat in the back. He kissed her openly on the lips in front of the children.

"Hello, sweetheart," she said.

"Hello, love," he called her. "And where is he today?"

"He went to the cockfights. I told him I was going shopping. He said to bring the little ones with me."

"Today's Daddy's birthday," little Ono said. "We bought him a birthday present."

He looked at the boy and saw his own frightening resemblance, the dark skin, the thick lips, the flat nose and the wavy hair.

"What did you buy him?" He asked the boy.

"I can't tell. It's a secret. Right, Mommy?"

"That's right," she said and turning to the younger boy, "Don't tell Daddy, Jerry, okay?"

Little Jerry was six. He was pouting in the back seat. He had a toy pistol that he pointed at the back of the seat where Onofre was sitting and pulled the trigger again and again.

"Stop that," his mother told him.

"Mommy, when are we going home?" Jerry asked.

"We're going for a ride," she said.

"Yeah, we're going for a ride," his brother said.

They drove toward the mountains, past the apple orchards of Salsipuedes and the wild mustard with its yellow blossoms laid out like thick carpet under the trees. They passed an apple-drying shed named Buac with a realistic painting of a gigantic red Delicious apple on the side of the building. The road narrowed as they entered a forest of towering redwood trees, and it suddenly became darker.

"Ooooh," said little Ono, grinning.

"Let's go home," little Jerry said under his breath.

Onofre turned off on a dirt road that led to a small clearing hidden by a circle of trees. There were already two other cars parked there, but it looked as if no one was in them. He chose a spot on the far side.

"Not here again!" Jerry said. "There's nothing to do here!"

"How would you two like to play in the front seat?" their mother asked.

"Okay," little Ono said.

The two boys climbed over the front seat while Onofre and Josie opened the doors and switched to the back. Ono played with the steering wheel, and Jerry fiddled with the chrome-plated knobs on the dashboard. Onofre and Josie took their shoes off and lay down on the back seat, her back to him. She turned her head to him and let him kiss her with long lingering kisses. She let him put his tongue in her mouth. She was contented to cuddle like that for a long time. He stroked her legs and buttocks from outside her skirt, and she murmured softly.

"What are you doing back there?" Jerry asked.

"We're just taking a nap," she said. "Why don't you and Ono lie down and take a nap, too?"

"We're not sleepy," Jerry said.

"Yeah, we want to play," his brother said.

"Okay then, play, but don't turn around. Keep looking forward."

"Look straight ahead, boys," Onofre said.

She just wanted to kiss and cuddle, but he already had slipped his hand under her skirt and was feeling her thighs. He liked her thighs because they were smooth and hairless. He had never known anything so silky. With one finger he softly traced the outside of her panties where her mound was.

"No," she whispered. "Not with the kids."

He withdrew his hand and placed it on her breast. He covered her mouth with his, sucking her tongue out of her mouth with such force that she tightened her body. He kneaded her breast from outside her blouse until he felt her nipple harden under his palm, and she slackened her body a bit. He fumbled with the buttons until he managed to free one of her breasts from her bra. Moving deftly, he moved his mouth to her breast before she could say anything. Her nipples were brown and long like blackberries, and the skin of her breasts was light-colored. When he moved his mouth to the other breast, she was already so lost to the sensation that she hardly noticed his hand pulling her panties halfway down her hips and his fingers probing the wet folds between her legs. She bolted suddenly and, reaching over the front seat, she shoved first one boy's head, then the other's down onto the seat roughly.

"Take a nap, now!" she told them, her voice shaky.

"Hey!" the boys said, startled.

She was surprised at her own roughness and said, in a much

sweeter voice, "You had a long day and you have to take a nap. Just lie down and don't get up until I tell you, okay?"

"There's candy under the seat," Onofre said.

Little Ono reached under the front seat and pulled out the bag. He spilled the candy onto the seat, and the boys began to divide them. By the time Onofre pulled Josie beside him again, he had undone the front of his trousers. He sucked on her breasts some more and placed his penis between her legs from behind and was fucking her smooth thighs. He remembered how she had looked when he first saw her at the dance in Stockton years before, how pristine, how untouchable she was to him. And now here he was, rubbing his dick against her, and she wanted it. She grabbed the tip and placed it in her. She kept her legs clamped shut so that only the head entered her, and the shaft moved between her closed thighs. Her wetness and the tip of his penis moving in and out of her made a slurping noise.

"What's that?" Jerry asked.

"Nothing," she said, drawing her knees up to stop the sound.

Soon the inside of the car began to reek of sex, but they couldn't stop.

"What stinks?" Jerry asked.

She didn't answer him. The pressure of the head of his cock rubbing against her clitoris brought her to orgasm, her body convulsing, and she couldn't stifle a small cry.

"What did you say?" Jerry asked. Then he said under his breath, "I don't want this candy."

Onofre, his arms wrapped around her waist, tried to hold her still as he started to come, but she bucked, and his penis popped out of her. He ejaculated up the front of her blouse and hair. He reached by the rear window for some Kleenex.

Josie, with her blouse neatly tucked back into her skirt, stepped out of the car, brushing her hair and stood in the sunlight, drying the small wet spots on her blouse. She leaned into the front window and said, "Don't tell Daddy where we went today. It's a secret."

After he dropped them off again at the department store parking lot, Onofre drove home. As he reached the boarding house that he shared with four other bachelors on Bridge Street, something made him pass it up. Maybe it was the hot, dry day or the boredom of his simple room that he didn't want to go back to, or the mindless chatter of his compatriots talking about cockfights, or prostitutes, or going home to the islands someday to marry a young school-teacher or even a doctor. He was tired of it all. He kept driving in the bright sunlight past acres and acres of row crops. He pulled over beside a field of lettuce and got out and started to walk. He was tired of being in a car all day and wanted to stretch his legs.

He walked along the side of the road. The lettuce had just begun to sprout in the fields, and the leaves looked like crumpled dollar bills. He thought how unchanged the fields really were. It had been a lettuce field for as long as he could remember—the sprouting, the harvesting, the turning over of soil. It was all the same. Year after year. He remembered when he was younger and had worked this field. He knew somebody got rich from this field, but he had nothing to show for it. He realized he could never go back to the Philippines.

He thought of Josie. He loved her. He hadn't done so bad, he thought. At one time she was desired by every Filipino man. Stock-ton beauty queen. And she said she loved him. She would leave her husband, she told him, and they would live together, grow old together, and his own son would know something about the truth and call him *father*. Everything would work out. All he had to do was wait.

He remembered the joke that the old Chinese men used to tell about Pinoys when he first came to America. "The Filipinos are like fairies. They masturbate and blow away in the wind." At first he didn't understand it. Then he got angry. Goddamn Chinamen, he thought. He had promised himself that he would never be without a woman. Yes, he had done all right for himself. He didn't spend nights gambling and getting drunk. He didn't have to come home to his dingy room with a whore and listen to her lies. Whores didn't count.

The sound of a car horn made Onofre turn around. It was his boarding house compatriots.

"Compadre," one called, "did your car break down? Where are you going? Town is the other way."

The others in the car laughed.

"I'm just counting my money," he said, pointing to the lettuce.

"Come on. We're going to a cockfight in San Juan Bautista."

"No, I'm tired."

"Come on," they called. "There's plenty of *blondies!*"

The car door swung open. Onofre hesitated. He grinned slightly and stepped in, shutting the door behind him. The car wheels spun in the dirt before they found the paved surface of the road, sending a small cloud of dust in the air.

At Josie's house a small group of friends gathered around the birthday cake at the kitchen table. Though it was only three o'clock, they were already half drunk, and the women were smoking cigarettes. One of the women went to sit on Josie's husband's lap.

"You're getting too old," she told him. "You need help to blow out these candles."

Everyone laughed.

Then she opened her eyes wide in mock surprise and said, "Wait! What is this hard thing I'm sitting on?"

Everyone shrieked.

While Josie's husband started to open the present she and the boys bought him, he asked little Jerry, "What's inside, son?"

Little Jerry, caught up in the laughter of the grownups, blurted out, "I know, it's a tie!"

"You stupid," little Ono said.

Josie bent over Jerry and in her whiskey breath whispered in his ear, "Jerry! I told you it was a secret!"

Little Jerry's ears turned red from embarrassment, and he started to cry. In his confusion he thought he had told the other secret.

from

Inday

Cecilia Manguerra Brainard

*H*e tastes of the
sea, this man. He is like a god risen from the sea. I like to cup his
face in my palms, touch his neck, his arm, feel his skin against
mine. He is always warm, warmer than me: he says it's from desire.
In the semidarkness, I stand against him and lick his neck—first
the one side, then the other. The smoothness of his skin, that slight
salty taste amazes me. Sometimes I bite him gently, and I leave
love-marks on his chest and neck, as if to brand him. He tries to do
the same, but I shake my head. A part of me fears Victor may return
and find these marks, and know what I've done.

I am unfaithful, and so we do not speak. It is as if we are other
people in another place. In the beginning, he would talk and tell
me how beautiful I am, how desirable. But his words would jar me,
make thoughts flow through my mind, and I knew I did not belong
in that cabaña with him, that I should leave, and I was filled with
great confusion. It is better when we are silent. The moment I enter
his room and close the door, we do not exchange a word. There is
always something frightening when I lock that door. It is forbidden. I hold my breath, but my heart pounds. I fear someone will
barge in—the servants, or Victor himself. After the metallic click of
the latch, we hear only the crickets outside and the rhythmic
pounding sea. I put my finger on his lips to silence him. He kisses

my fingertips, my hand, my arm, my neck. It is as if he and I are riding an enormous wave. Every cell of our bodies awakens and we can feel the coolness of the breeze, the warmth of the other. We melt, he and I, in a sea of desire that laps back and forth, this enormous ocean on which we flounder, working hard to satisfy that desire, end that palpable, palpitating wanting. Fingers touching, lips kissing, tongues probing. Once, in the semidarkness I saw sparks from our fingers when they touched. Could that be so? I wanted to ask but could not break our unspoken promise of silence. We float, he and I, on this wave of desire, rising higher and higher. Sometimes to torture him, I pull away and walk around the room naked, knowing he is desiring me. And once, when the moon was full and moonlight streamed into a window, I stood by the window so the rays fell on my breasts, the curve of my neck, my waist, my sex, and I knew I glowed like some moon goddess. He from the sea, I from the moon.

He likes to watch me. From the moment I enter, he observes me, noticing everything about me, a new hairdo, new nail polish, a little scratch on my arm. He likes to see me desire him. This is what he sometimes does: he kisses me, his mouth sucking my lower lip, and when I kiss back, he pulls away to look at me. My face is tilted upward, eyes closed, lost in the sensation of his soft mouth on mine. When I open my eyes slowly, as if waking from some wonderful dream, he is staring at me, then he kisses me again. This time he runs his tongue into my mouth, and just when I start to suck his tongue, he pulls away again just to watch me. He does this several times, until I feel I am going mad, then he pulls me up and holds me tight so I can feel his body, feel his hardness. I think surely he will take me now. But he walks back into the shadows while I stand in the middle of the room, expectant, full of desire, until I approach him and touch his hardness, pull him toward me. And then comes the breathing and skin rubbing skin, and moisture and sweat and the rhythmic sounds of the bed rocking. Those are the only sounds.

———

On the beach, away from our sanctuary of silence, he asked me about the first time I made love. I shouldn't have but I told him anyway. It was with Victor, after a party, and we had driven up to the hills. There he had kissed my mouth and touched my breasts, and kissed my nipples, then he slid his hand under my skirt and began touching me there until I grew moist and lost all sense of time, of place, of decency. We tried to do it there, but Victor had a difficult time. I was too tight. He said we'd go someplace private; and so we went to Stardust Motel, drove into a garage and walked up to a room. I did not know what to expect, and I was frightened. I told Victor this, and he kissed my hand and said we didn't have to do anything, we could just talk if that was what I wanted. I felt safer, more relaxed. We sat side by side on the bed for a while, my head resting on his shoulder, he stroking my hair. Then he started kissing me once again and touching me, gently, softly, always pulling back when I became agitated. When he started kissing my breasts through my blouse, I didn't even realize that I was the one who unbuttoned my top. I wanted him that much. He repeated that we didn't have to do it, that his rubbing against me would feel good. We were now in bed, without any clothes on. He was on top of me; instead of touching me there with his hand, he used his manhood—rubbing me there back and forth in a rhythm that was mesmerizing. Suddenly I felt a sharp sensation of pleasure; it happened when he rubbed me in a certain place; and he did this over and over until my breathing grew rapid and my body quivered. "You came," he said. I didn't know what that meant, I only knew I wanted him to enter me. It was difficult and there was much pain and blood. But later, when he entered me again, it was better. Victor was a good lover; he knew how to wait until I was the one begging him to do things to me.

I did not tell him everything but my sea god became jealous. He walked toward the sea and threw a stone into the water. He stood there for a long time, studying the bay. Then he turned to me. "You love him," he said.

"I *loved* him. I married him," I said, as if that absolved everything.

"How can you continue to love him after all he's done to you?"

"I said, 'I loved him.' I was young then. I am no longer so young."

Still my sea god remained distant until I went to him and stroked his hair and caressed his cheek, and he kissed the palm of my hand, and I felt his warm breath.

"I love you," he said, and the most frightening thought entered my mind: I could love this man.

The Lover

David Mura

The other day I received a letter from an old lover.

She has two children now, she lives in Boston. One of the children has a disease which she does not specify. It is, she says, the tragedy of her life. Nothing in her life now seems what she expected. She has lost contact with all her former friends in the city where she used to live and where we met. She says that at times she sits in her kitchen, at some quiet hour, the children at day care or asleep, her husband at work or at sleep, and she stares at the swing set which only one of the children can use, at the long, drooping branches of the weeping willow in her yard, and she thinks about her life and wonders how she got to this point. I don't know if her marriage is happy or not. I know such tragedies like spina bifida or autism can place such strains on a couple, and for some couples, this is too much. What would have been a satisfactory marriage if nothing untoward had ever happened in their family becomes a marriage whose very foundation seems to be disappointment and depression.

She writes that of all the people she knew before she moved, I was the one she remembered. She quotes from some poem: "They come, they go. They change you more than they know." Or maybe it's "you know." She sent that on a card to me nearly twenty years ago, when she was nineteen and I was twenty-three. I was in graduate school and living with the woman who was to become my wife. That was the way I did things then. I have no defense for it.

In the letter, Michelle says that she saw *The Lover* a week ago, the film of the Marguerite Duras novel about an affair between a young Chinese banker and a French schoolgirl in colonial Vietnam. The script wasn't written by Duras, but it retains enough of the book to become the vibrant-hued echo of the black-and-white film *Hiroshima Mon Amour,* a film written by Duras about an affair between a Japanese architect and a French actress in the city of Hiroshima. For me these films and the novel *The Lover* are talismans, the only echoes in a media-saturated world where I find anything resembling the sexual relationships I have had. My lovers have always been American women, not French, but with the exception of a Vietnamese-American student, they have all been white. I know this seems a rather generic connection, but in the vague desperation of the Chinese banker or the Japanese architect, in the way they seem to pursue their French lovers, in the ways the issues of race and colonialism filter the vision of their affair, as if peering upon figures grappling in a bed through the cover of netting, in all these slippages, I feel something in my own psyche responding. I know those men, they are inside me. I know that bed.

Michelle writes that she thought of me after seeing that movie. Not in a romantic way, she says, but in some sentimental, some nostalgic way, some place where she was free from the burdens or responsibilities, the trappings of her present life; some place where all was possibility, where there was this young graduate student who read Shakespeare with her and helped her with her papers, who took her to the best restaurants he could afford and then dancing, who changed her in ways he did not know. Reading this, it occurred to me that for her our affair somehow retained a nobility, a purity of emotion and care that I did not feel. My interpretation of what our affair had been was only half of the story, was only my interpretation.

She ended by remarking that I had not answered a couple cards she had written in the last few years. She assumed that my not writing said more about the business of my life than my feelings about her. On the surface, she was right in this. I am a poor correspondent in regard to personal letters. They are just something I do not do. Is this the male inability to retain connections, to keep contact with the past? No, it's more complicated than that. The emotions I feel are too confused and shameful, too difficult to reconcile.

I had a linguistics class just before hers. After the tedious task of diagramming sentences or investigating the structural semantics of Chomsky, I'd see her smiling at me as I left the classroom. She wore a flower print blouse, cutoffs that showed tanned legs, toned by lengths and lengths of swimming. Despite this lean muscularity, there was a fleshiness to her body that would have hinted of something more zaftig if she hadn't been in such great shape. And that was what attracted me to her. That and her hair, which was carefully curled and flipped off her face in generous waves. As my wife has often said, "You like women with large hair."

My wife, I should point out, has never had large hair. Large hair and what would be called a classically voluptuous body demarcate for me those women who excite me sexually, who elicit my lust. I see these women in the light of my sexual fantasies, in the role of an affair. In appearance, they seem to have bought into a certain feminine ideal that smacks of fifties foldouts or country western singers or actresses in grade B sorority flicks. Not women you take to poetry readings. Not intellectuals.

The way this demarcation works is simple and twisted—those women whom one could not imagine having an Asiatic lover and those whom one could. I was attracted most to the former. To what I thought would deny me, to what was most forbidden.

As it turns out, Michelle would eventually go on to become a stellar student in the English Department. But I don't think that changed the way I saw her sexually, the way I felt about how she looked, about her body.

And the fact that she was attracted to me?

That was a sign that I was special. I was not like other Asian men. I was sexual in the way most of them could never be.

But whatever I did as an individual did not change the stereotype of the asexual Asian man or prevent new examples from cropping up in the media. Nor could I change what I imagined was the way most whites looked at me. I constantly suspected those women who were attracted to me were exceptions; living as I did in the Midwest, I almost never saw an Asian man with a white woman, though I'd certainly seen examples of a white man with an Asian woman. Even if I might be different from other Asian men, I wasn't that different.

There were other reactions I could have had. I could have chosen to ignore the stereotype; I could have dated only women of color or Asian women; I could have tried to be less self-conscious about my sexuality (though, in reality, I was unconscious of much that was driving my behavior). There are those who accept the world and the limitations they are surrounded with, who find a sense a peace in not trying to fight or change the world around them; perhaps this is a better way. I don't think it's my way. Even if I've come to see the falseness, the sexism, in the ways I measured myself against the racial grid of sexuality, how much I was searching for some validation of myself from something outside rather than within, I still believe that racism does help form our sexual desires in this society and that such desires ought to change.

I take her to Magic Pan or Chez Collette, the North Star Inn, a young man's images of sophistication. I spend as much as I can, given my stipend as a graduate assistant. Crepes begnet, Beef Wellington, coq au vin. The waiter is elderly, suspicious. I pay in cash.

We go dancing at discos, the awful and tasteless music of the times. I wear a three-piece suit and am a good dancer. My hair stylishly long, I look like a Hong Kong playboy.

She lives in a sorority, and this excites me. When I visit her, there are always other attractive women around. I play piano for her in the lounge. She asks if there is nothing I cannot do. I smile and say nothing.

We make love on our second date. She comes back with me to the apartment I share with Laura, the woman who will become my wife. It is in the basement of a three-story complex; the bedroom window faces the parking lot. White plaster walls, used furniture. Cheap student housing. I have arranged for Laura to be elsewhere. Michelle knows about her; I have hidden nothing. It is almost like dating a married man. She doesn't care. Later she told me she had forced herself to wait for our second date.

In the bedroom, we smoke from a bong. Disco music again on the stereo, the Average White Band, Earth Wind and Fire. A dense cloud begins to hover above the bed. My movements are slow, deliberate. Tense. I do not always perform well the first time, and this worries me. My worries are unfounded. After I kiss her, she pulls back, asks me to wait. She goes to the washroom. When the door opens again, she stands before me naked. Her body blinds me, moves me with its power. I take a long time preparing her, my tongue patient, probing. I love the smell of her, of women; it intoxicates me, a rush of adrenaline, an instant high.

I am floating above her. Her legs are powerful, a counterweight to my motions. It is as if I were rowing in violent oceanic waters, the current strong, the groundswells large, the whitecaps churning into foam beneath the bow of the boat. I am afraid she will thrust me off of her. I push down. We sprawl about the futon, turning in a circle, tangled amid the sheets. We spill out onto the floor, in a slipstream of movement. Back onto the bed. She is moaning beneath me. I want it to go on forever. I am weakening, I cannot stop.

It will get even better than this. Always I will recall the tremendous push of her thighs, the way our bodies circle the bed. The blue panties I uncover when she allows me to undress her. How she tells me there is no one like me, the other men she has been with are nothing.

We do not talk of the woman I live with. That is a zone of silence. A place we pretend does not exist. This is one of the lies I use to satisfy my desires, and if there's a sense of shame in this lie, there's also a sense of power, a feeling that I'm getting away with something, that I'm entitled to do this.

She talks of her high school years, how she ran away from home often. Hitched from her small town to the city. To Colorado and ski country. She took acid, smoked dope, drank herself into a stupor. Was absent from school for weeks at a time. Her father had died when she was fourteen. She warred with her mother. Her boyfriends were drug dealers, petty thieves, ski bums. Older than her. Her father had been an insurance salesman, had left the family enough money when he died. Her mother remarried. A car dealer. Her stepfather was a stranger, someone she had no attachment to, not even anger or resentment. She hated her small town, its quaint ways. Had she made it all the way to California as she had planned one summer hitching, who knows what would have happened.

And then in the last semester of her senior year, something changed. She started attending school, quit the boyfriends, the running away from home. While the other kids circled the main street in the cars and pickups, she spent her weekends writing in her diary. She read fashion magazines, *Jane Eyre, Pride and Prejudice.* She said nothing still to her mother, but they had stopped their war. She even regretted the trouble she had given her. She stopped the drugs except for the marijuana. She was going to college next year; she would join a sorority.

At first I think she is not intelligent. After all she is a sorority girl. She asks me for help on her papers, which ramble and then trail off into confusion. I sit with her at a desk in the basement of the sorority, the complete works of Shakespeare open before us. Othello. The attributes of the tragic hero. I explain to her Eliot's essay on Shakespeare and Seneca, on the self-dramatics of Othello as he makes his last confession, as he tries to put the mess he has made of things in the best light. I do not note the line about the "black sheep tupping the white ewe" or the issues of miscegenation that hover within the text. What I know are the classic readings, the criticism of Traversi and Harrison. That is what I am trying to teach her.

Gradually she begins to get A's on her papers. I tell myself I am responsible for her success. It keeps me from thinking about other aspects of the relationship. Occasionally she will make remarks about blacks, how she cannot imagine making love to one. I am different from them, though she does not say exactly how. I would like to chastise her for her prejudice, but keep silent. It's useless; what good would it do? Besides, I like the fact that she thinks of me as different from blacks and yet, at the same time, somehow more romantic, more exotic, more of a lover than the white men she has known. She admires my brilliance, or what she takes for my brilliance, my knowledge of literature, which is not vast yet considerably vaster than hers at this point.

Once I show her my poetry. Lines about my grandfather, a stroke which kept him from writing haiku, how he cried when this happened and went upstairs and stayed in bed for a week, how this story seemed a paradigm for me of all my father is not. My father works in public relations for Blue Shield, talks like a character from an Andrew Carnegie seminar; his passion is golf, his politics Republican; he lives in a white brick colonial in a suburb of doctors and lawyers. My grandfather is a figure of romance, of escape. The father a figure of repression, a Nobodaddy of darkness and anger, a finger pointing at me to work harder, to buckle down. I seldom talk to my parents. They are a source of guilt, remorse, shame, but exactly why I cannot say. I prefer not to think of them.

She gives me a record of John Klemmer, the jazz saxophonist. It is the music we make love to. When I put it on the stereo, it is like a Pavlovian bell. That and the bong we smoke. More than our conversations, what I will remember is our lovemaking. How she straddled me once, how it felt inside her, how her long dark hair hung down over me and then whipped back with a fling of her hand. Her breasts rising and falling above me. Her muffled moans, tiny whimpers like the concentric circles that ripple outward from a stone flung into a pool, each echoing the one before, setting the random world in a design of delight.

I will think of her as the perfect body. And how she preferred to appear before me, suddenly undressed. Her delight in that. Her utter delight.

It ends several times. One takes place in a high-rise apartment, when she talks of dating an airline pilot, her boredom with him, her suspicions that all men want from her is sex. It shames me, this talk, since this is what I am thinking of. I try to be sympathetic. We have not gone out together for months. We are and are not like strangers. She rambles on about the pilot. I look down through the picture window at the highway streaming below, at the lights of the city. A curving snake of darkness that is the river, dotted with reflective lights. She shares the apartment with two other women who are gone for the summer months. She will be a senior, is planning to go to graduate school in library sciences. I have met her again taking out a book of poetry from the college library. She smiled at me the way she first smiled when I emerged from the linguistic class. I could not resist her.

And then we are grappling together on the couch. I am kneeling before her on the floor, bending over her. I hear a slight rip in my pants. I ignore it. We kiss for a long time. Then she pulls back. We go to the bedroom. I wait on the bed in darkness. And then there is her naked shadow at the door. She slides up to me.

I have to tell her. I don't want to, but I know I should. We cannot have intercourse tonight; I have just been to a clinic. No, it is not a venereal disease, but warts. I am embarrassed. She is clearly disappointed.

Our movements now are awkward, tentative. I feel I should not have told her. When she comes beneath my mouth, her body jack-knifes off the bed, in violent strokes. My orgasm is smaller, by hand, too mechanical for her to lose herself in the act. Afterward we stare forward in the dark, without speaking, as if waiting for someone else to appear.

In the morning she is cheerful but rushed. I do not see her again till spring. We take a long walk. She talks of visiting New York with her current boyfriend, of seeing down near the docks rats as large as dogs. For some reason, she intimates that her boyfriend's family is not only rich but somehow has ties with organized crime. Or is this only because of his name? She talks of wild parties with cocaine, how it feels to put cocaine on her clitoris and then make love. I'm not shocked at this, but envious. A graduate student, I don't have the money for such use of cocaine, though I have used it while making love. I wonder why she is telling me all this.

At her apartment, in her bedroom, I have my face buried in her breasts, mouthing them beneath her silk blouse, when she stops me. She cannot do anything. She has a streptococci infection. She tells me how angry she was at the nurse who told her only those with poor hygiene contract such infections. Her boyfriend had this sore throat, that was all. I release her, let out a deep breath, sit back down on the bed.

And then, as she stands before me, looking toward me but not at my face, she tells me that she still loves me, that perhaps she will always love me. She says this without great emotion, calmly, though with a certain warmth, like a doctor pronouncing a grave illness to a patient. She says this without any expectation that I will do anything about this. And perhaps even without a hope that I will do anything. She knows whom I am tied to. And it is not her.

After we break up for good, her new boyfriend will go out East to get his MBA. She will get her degree in library science and then move with him to Boston. They will get married, have a daughter, and then another, who will bring her own tragedy into their lives. Later, she will call me, when she sees my name in the *New York Times* for winning a grant. Then a Christmas card a year later with a photo of her daughters. Another card the next year. And then the cards stop. And then, upon seeing the film *The Lover,* her letter.

In me the letter evokes sadness and sympathy, a bewilderment at how my own vision of our affair must not coincide in many ways with hers. The events were the same, but what we were feeling, what we remember is different. That we see things differently is not in itself odd. It seems odd to me that I somehow come out better in her mind than I do in mine. Part of me wants to attribute this to her being taken in by my façade, the wonderful face I tried to put on for her. But perhaps it's more complex than that; whether good or bad, rarely do others view us exactly as we view ourselves, and there is truth in each of those views, including our own; they exist, they are real, and we don't necessarily get any closer to the truth by finding some median between conflicting views or some point where they merge. That divergence is our reality.

I have no idea what she made of my being Japanese American. At the time I made little of it myself. My brief consciousness of my ethnicity was restricted to a few poems and a generalized resentment, which I never vocalized out loud, that white women were not as attracted to Asian men as to white men. Or black men.

At the time I was beginning to plunge into pornography—x-rated magazines and picture books, movies, strip shows, even beginning to see an occasional prostitute. All the while I was living with Laura. I felt I was living double, triple lives of degradation and deceit, of searching for what I thought were pleasures I could not live without, could not get enough of, trying to focus on those places which resembled what I thought could be conceived of as normal or within the purview of the ordinary. I saw my affair with Michelle mostly in this way. Compared to the pornography or the prostitutes or the casual one-night stands, it was not so shameful. Only I knew I did not love her, and she loved me, that what attracted me most to her was her beauty and her body.

What did she see in me? I know I was smart, I was a good lover. But there were obvious limits to what I could offer her, limits I don't think in retrospect she should have accepted. Affairs with men like the man I was, in situations like that, are doomed to failure. They echo some need in the woman for her own self-loathing and wish to be abandoned. Or so I now believe.

But this is not how she chooses to see our affair in her letter. In her letter we are something other than what I have believed.

In *The North China Lover,* her film treatment of *The Lover,* Duras writes the following notes to the first meeting of the two lovers, the Chinese banker and the French colonial schoolgirl:

> The man who gets out of the black limousine is other than the one in the book, but still Manchurian. He is a little different from the one in the book: he's a little more solid than the other, less frightened than the other, bolder. He is better looking, more robust. He is more "cinematic" than the one in the book. And he's also less timid facing the child.

Am I the lover in the book or in the movie version in Michelle's eyes? Both are like me. It depends on your angle of vision.

Michelle, of course, is nothing like the young Duras, except perhaps for a certain sense of abandonment and defiance.

> She, she has stayed the way she was in the book, small, skinny, tough, hard to get a sense of, hard to label, less pretty

than she looks, poor, the daughter of poor people, poor ancestors, farmers, cobblers, always first in French at all her
schools, yet disgusted by France, and mourning the country of
her birth and youth, spitting out the red meat of Western
steaks, with a taste for weak men, and sexy like you've never
seen before. Wild about reading, seeing—fresh free.

What I constantly forget in this recounting is that she did love
me, and what she loved in me was something I did not or chose not
to see in myself. Or she saw in me the specialness I wanted to
project but did not believe in, the singular lover who was like no
other, that would leave his print indelibly etched in her psyche,
unerasable by husband or child or tragedy, by distance or time.
Who has gone on to write more poems about his Issei grandfather,
about his parents, about love affairs between Japanese-American
men and white women, who returned to Japan and wrote a book
about it, chronicling among other things an aborted affair with a
German artist. Who writes essays and speaks on college campuses
about race and multiculturalism, about identity, about raising his
happa-eyed daughter. Who would write a monograph repudiating
pornography, arguing the harm it does to men as well as women.
Who would seem in his books a more puritanical, less romantic
figure, a bit too filled with resentment and self-preoccupation.

And still for her there is this connection. A mother and house-
wife in Boston, who, in some ways, lives a life not very different
from my own (so domestic and child-centered these days, I surprise
myself). She emerges from the movie theater with her husband, the
images of the young Chinese lover and the lithe French schoolgirl
reverberating in her mind's eye, the undulating motion of their
bodies, the contrast of the darker skin against the lighter, the
Chinese restaurant where he unpeels from a roll of bills and pays the
tab, dapper in his white silk tussore suit, his face vibrant and
unretractably sad. And this mother, this wife, thinks of herself as a
young girl, in bed with a man who did not resemble this Chinese

lover, who is too sleek, too hollow and slight, too beautiful, yet who is brought to mind by the appearance of the Chinese lover on the screen, rolling about the floor, making love to a white woman. Such a thin and obvious connection. In the parking lot this mother, this wife, enters their Lexus quietly, saying nothing, absorbed in meditation. Or perhaps this reflects the distance they have come to feel between them, a distance that has grown since the birth of their second daughter, since the onset of unfamiliar burdens, too numerous to mention. They drive home through the summer suburban streets, the lawns where sprinklers jet through the darkness and air conditioners hum in metal cases in between the houses, where the streetlight catches a few moths fluttering about but no pedestrians below. It is like a ghost town they are driving through, some pneumatic tube, encased within the air conditioning of the car, the soft rock on the stereo, singing a song about old Mexico. She turns to look at this man, her husband, a broker, a father who loves his children and is good to them, though hampered by his distance as a man, as the one who must work to support them. He is still good-looking, attractive to the secretaries at work. She doesn't wonder if he has a lover; that is not part of the equation. She is wondering what it would have been like if she had made other choices. No, that's only speculation on my part. She is simply remembering, knowing what she remembers cannot be shared, cannot be explained. All the husband knows is that she once dated this man when she was in college, a Japanese-American writer. She has not spoken of him more than that. She thinks of how they are approaching forty, of the years of childraising she has ahead. She thinks of the paper on Othello, of a spinning ball of lights above a dance floor, of someone playing piano in a darkened room. She closes her eyes, falls briefly asleep, only to waken as they come up the drive. She tries to recall if she has change for the baby sitter. She looks at her husband as he gets out of the car, his hair thinning, his neck reddened by last weekend on the golf course. He stops, tells her he'll wait in the car for the baby sitter. She opens the garage door into the house, hears the hum of the refrigerator, the sounds of the television in the living room. She feels blinded by the ordinariness of her life, she feels an acceptance that is by now as familiar to her as this sadness that sits within the concavity of her chest, and moves almost like breath, rising and falling moment after moment, day after day. She imagines her children asleep upstairs. And then she sees the lover on the screen, and then she recalls herself standing naked in a doorway, approaching a man who does not love her, whom she will never forget. "How were the kids?" she says as she enters the room. The baby sitter looks up, bleary-eyed. She had fallen asleep. On the television screen the audience titters and the host smirks. The mother turns the television off and opens her purse. From the corner of the room, the cat purrs.

Two days later, she will write a letter. When she is finished, she will stare out the back window for a long time. The letter will bear a faint hint of her perfume. She doesn't expect an answer.

The Orange

TONY OSUMI

She's not supposed to be here
A few years ago—yes, but not now—not tonight
But for the moment, this is exactly where I want her to be
Immorality proves itself an effective aphrodisiac

Her cheekbones have moved up and her hips have widened
Still wearing her thick mane cut far below her shoulders
Snaking down the small of her back when wet, I remember its
herbal essence and those silky translucent
hairs behind her neck:
always hiding, yet always wanting to be found

Small talk mixes with the television
"How's your parents?"
"Guess who's getting married?"

Tonight, she thumbs through my sketchbook
I confront a large navel orange
It puts up a fight before surrendering its ripe heart
Offering the first of my spoils, her tongue greets it
lips pulling lightly

Dragging her brown eyes up my arm, she pauses to savor the
ends of my fingertips

I'm encouraged as she shifts to face me square

Tearing off a small piece,
I hold it in my mouth and move toward her
gingerly
fighting to move smoothly
   Our heads tilt
   Our eyes lock
   Her breath; my want
   Darkness . . .

Two auras fuse in fleshy union
Pulp and saliva mix slowly
A tang of sweetness; a baritone giggle; a streak down her chin

The volume fades on the television

Pieces get smaller—the feedings longer, deeper, more frenzied
She slides off her shoes; I pull at my shirt
Buttons manipulated and zippers set free
Clasped like fingers we wrap and entwine the other
twisting and turning . . .

Somewhere, half an orange gets lost in the sheets.

Defection

CHRISTINA YAO

Only one of us could attend the annual cancer genetics meeting in Paris. My boss, Franklin Richard, picked me because he thought I needed a vacation. My friend and colleague, Nancy, was happy I could leave my family and work. "Ping, you don't have a life." She has been telling me this for four years. "Do all Chinese people work so hard?" she asked, and I would answer, "Yes."

In the cab from the airport to my hotel, I looked out the taxi window and saw beautiful Parisian greenery everywhere. I realized green was something missing in New York City. Was that why New Yorkers looked so pale? I had become paler every day. I spent most of time in the office, kitchen, and subway stations. I had finished my Ph.D. at Johns Hopkins, then did a postdoc at Yale. Afterward, I moved to New York to work for a medical center. Realizing the only way to get respect was to excel in my work, I hadn't seen a movie in four years. Even so, when Nancy had asked me whether I had a life, I was upset.

"Where are you from?" the driver suddenly asked me.

"China." Even after I got U.S. citizenship, I still had trouble claiming myself as an American. I was afraid to be asked, "Why don't you go back to China?" Xue-Fei, my husband, wanted to go back because he was not happy in the United States. He was getting more and more upset that our daughter, Xiao-Jie, spoke perfect English but very little Chinese.

"China? My wife, Chinese, too." The driver stared at me for a few minutes then commented, "Chinese women are beautiful. They cook good too." Right, we looked good and cooked good food. Was that why men wanted to marry us?

Xue-Fei and I met at Beijing Medical University. I was eighteen, he was nineteen. The first time I saw Xue-Fei, I was attracted to his black eyes, which were so deep I could never see through them. I waited for a message from him but it never came. Xue-Fei was too shy to say anything, because I was the best student and class monitor. Then I organized a trip to Xiang-Shen Park to see its famous maple trees. Xue-Fei and his friends refused to go. I went to his dormitory and demanded, "Xue-Fei, why don't you want to go? Don't you like our class?"

"I have something else to do," Xue-Fei answered in a low voice. "Plus, why do we always have to do things with our classmates?"

"If I invite you as a friend, would you go?" I asked.

"A friend?" Xue-Fei looked into my eyes for the first time. "Are you serious?"

"Yes," I said, and Xue-Fei smiled.

We went to the park and saw the autumn maple trees. Xue-Fei asked me whether I thought the leaves looked like blood, fire, or sunsets. I did not like any of his metaphors. Leaves are simply the symbols of love because they are warm, strong, and irresistible. When it was time to go home, Xue-Fei put me on the back of his bike. No words could describe my happiness. It had been my dream to be close to him. As Xue-Fei made a left turn, I put my hands on his waist. "That is the way it should be," he said. Encouraged, I asked him to go to a movie with me. We watched *Not for Love's Sake.* It was the first Chinese movie since the end of the Cultural Revolution with a scene of a man and woman kissing passionately. During that scene, Xue-Fei started breathing hard and my heart beat fast. That night, in my diary, I claimed I was in love.

What happened to Xue-Fei? Was this overweight, middle-aged man who drank and watched TV most of the time the same boy I fell in love with fifteen years ago? Xue-Fei was annoyed that our daughter, Xiao-Jie, was growing up as an American-born Chinese. Xiao-Jie did well in school but refused to learn Chinese culture. She never did any housework, because I did not let her. I said Xiao-Jie would go to Harvard after she graduated from high school. She had no time for those things. Just to get back at me, Xue-Fei wanted Xiao-Jie to play Chinese folk music during her piano lessons. "You always want her to be an American. She is my daughter too. She has to learn Chinese culture." We argued about this many times. Xiao-Jie was born in the United States. We had no right to force her to be Chinese. At the end of our arguments, Xue-Fei always concluded we should send Xiao-Jie back to China.

"Madame, here is your hotel," the driver informed me. He said goodbye and warned, "Be careful, young lady. French men are all bad. Don't believe them."

French men are all bad? What about Chinese men? What about Xue-Fei? He came to the United States for my sake, but he refused to adapt. He had no friends and wished me to have no friends as well. Had he ever known how disappointed I felt about our marriage? For a long time, I had no desire for sex. Xue-Fei usually ended his orgasm in a minute or two and then asked, "Are you done?" I always lied to him. I had known we were not doing it right ever since we were married. I thought that was because I was insensitive to sex. Who would put up with me, such a cold-blooded woman? When Nancy talked about her sex life, I was painfully jealous. I could not admit this to Xue-Fei.

In my room, during my bath, I continued thinking about my life. I had always thought Xue-Fei was smart and able to achieve anything he wanted, but he dropped out of the Ph.D. program. "Ping, I don't like to write papers. My brain hurts when I sit in a seminar. Isn't this a good enough reason?" Xue-Fei got mad when I called him a quitter. He refused to learn how to cook. He got mad when he had to do dishes. He gradually lost the ability to understand me. He was happy with football, broken English and being a good lab technician. Deep down, he was terrified that I was more successful than he was.

Xue-Fei, I know you stopped loving me a long time ago, but why should I look at your unhappy face every day? Should I divorce you? Or should I lie to Xiao-Jie, telling her I still love her dad? Last Valentine's Day, when Xiao-Jie bought a card with two pink hearts on it and asked me to give it to you, tears rolled down my cheeks. How could I betray our daughter?

The next morning, I woke up late. I jumped out of bed and ran to the Métro station half a block away. Following the map, I had no trouble transferring between trains. The trouble arrived when I realized I misplaced my ticket. I was searching for it when I heard someone speaking to me in French. Looking up, I saw a youthful-looking guy. I told him that I could not speak French and didn't have a ticket. He gave me his and showed me how to insert it into the slot. I used his ticket, then worried about how he would get out. He simply jumped over the turnstile, then helped me find the conference center. He even got me an updated program. The first lecture had been postponed, so we chatted. I briefly explained my work in cancer genetics. He was a medical student. He planned on doing clinical research for a year or two, then becoming a surgeon. After half an hour, he said, "Have we been formally introduced?" I started to laugh. His name was Tahar. How interesting! It sounded like HE in Chinese. He was amused by my name. "Ping? Do you hit your hand against wall, ping-ping?"

I went to my lecture; then, coming out, saw Tahar still standing there. Holding a program up, he called out, "Dr. Ping Wu." I asked, "Did you register for the conference?" He said yes, and invited me to lunch. While we ate, he asked me if I had any other plans in Paris. I told him I wanted to visit the Louvre. "Of course," he said. "We can do that this weekend." He presumed he was invited. Then in a tone so much like Xiao-Jie's when she wanted to sleep with me, Tahar asked me to meet him for dinner. I hated to refuse him. "Maybe."

"I'll wait for you at the front door."

"Listen, you're acting like my daughter."

"Your daughter? Are you married?"

"Yes, I'm an old woman. We should only have lunch! Please, find someone younger for dinner."

Tahar was astonished. "Ping, aren't we still friends? Can't we still have dinner? Just dinner?"

That night, I followed him to a French restaurant in the Latin Quarter. We sat at his favorite table outside the restaurant. Tahar liked to watch people pass. He would approach those he found interesting. "I have always learned and made many friends this way. What about you? Do you have many friends?"

"No, I had close friends in China. After we moved, I could not afford the long-distance phone calls. I have been lonely for many years, but I do not know how to make friends."

I told him about my work and my daughter. I also told him I had difficulty calling myself an American. Tahar told me that he was born in Paris but his parents were from Nigeria. Tahar told me that he had to face discrimination ever since he was a child. Even though he was born in France, he is not a citizen. He said, "I do not feel home here. Maybe I will move to America. Maybe I will feel home there."

When Tahar took me back to the hotel, it was almost one o'clock. He kissed on my cheek. "Thank you for a wonderful evening, Ping. I am glad that I met you." I could not fall asleep. I liked Tahar because he was blunt, warm and intelligent. He was young but I felt he understood me. How did Tahar feel about me? He was ten years younger. I was afraid to think about him any further.

After the third day's program, Tahar took me on a dinner

cruise. Unfortunately, it was raining. We were not able to see anything from the cruise window, which was okay, because most of the evening, we were staring at each other. Finally, Tahar broke the silence by saying he was falling in love. I told him, "I do not believe in love. I loved one man a long time ago and I lost it. It is not something reliable."

"How sad you don't believe in love. How sad you live with someone you don't love."

"It is sad, but I am Chinese. We are not supposed to be happy. I know that we have suffered generation after generation. We are too practical. My mother never had good sex with my father because of his impotency. They have been married for thirty-seven years. We have always lived as if living was a habit."

Tahar thought about this, then asked, "Do you have good sex with your husband?"

Offended, I jumped back. "Stop that! Who do you think you are?"

He apologized. Deeply ashamed of myself, I started to cry. He did not know what to do. He just patted my back. Surprising myself, I admitted my lack of sensitivity to him. Tahar was silent. Then he said, "I don't believe it."

At my hotel, Tahar kissed me on my lips. "Ping, would you give me a chance to make you happy?"

That night, I discovered I was not insensitive. How ironic—I had been a medical student, then earned a Ph.D. in science, but I knew nothing about sex! Deprived of pleasure, I felt Xue-Fei mistreated me. Wasn't it a big loss in my life? I had never had an orgasm. But weren't there many Chinese women who had suffered such losses?

I felt as if I was in a dream. We skipped the conference closing sessions and went to the Louvre. When we sat by the Rodin sculptures, Tahar asked me to move to Paris. I told him that I needed time to think. "Is it because of your daughter?" he asked.

"Yes, I don't want to break her heart."

"But you can easily break my heart," Tahar said. He became angry. "I never heard of people who can't fall in love because of their children. You may be Chinese, but you're still human."

"Tahar . . ." I said his name for the first time. That name sounded so special to me. Would I ever be able to forget him?

"Listen," he said excitedly, "you can bring her with you. I'll be her friend. But if you do not want to move, I'll move to New York."

Monday came too soon. He borrowed a car and drove me to the airport. We watched each other in the driver's mirror. Before I boarded the plane, Tahar asked, "Will I have a chance?" I hesitated. I was tempted, but could I take a chance? Was I in love with Tahar? How would I face Xiao-Jie? What about Xue-Fei? Would I ever be able to forget my past? Even though I was puzzled and scared, I told Tahar, "I will call you tomorrow." I saw hope in his eyes.

"Tomorrow?"

"Yes, tomorrow," I promised.

from

Year of the Dog

Henry Chang

NIGHTRIDER

Johnny Wong pulled the black Lincoln over, onto the sidewalk halfway down the narrow Hip Ching street. It was nine in the evening, and before he could kill the engine they appeared, the stocky mustached man they called Uncle Four and the fragile Hong Kong lady Mona. They were in the car before he could get out and open the door, the man motioning to him with a hard gesture.

"Lotus Blossom Club," said Uncle Four. The lady was silent as Johnny drove off, wondering about her passing the nine neon blocks through the rainy Chinatown night.

Uncle Four never said another word until they arrived.

"Come back eleven," he said. Mona followed him out, then down into the karaoke nightclub, never glancing back. When they were out of view Johnny slammed the steering wheel, hard, pausing for a long moment before urging the car away.

"Dew nei louh mou hei," he hissed, and soon enough the chopping sound of windshield wipers brought him around to East Broadway, the lower part of town, where the radio car boys gathered and gossiped away the dead-ends of their evenings.

Their vocabulary was limited. Every other Chinese phrase rang out "motherfucker this—motherfucker that." Johnny felt he was above them, yet he felt comfortable among them. He enjoyed their camaraderie, the spirit they generously shared with him. But he wasn't like them, and he knew it. They drove their cars because it was easy enough to fall into, and they found satisfaction in being their own bosses. They refused to wait tables for the long hours, sucking up to the white tourists. They disdained the misery of the market workers, and the hard labor of the construction cowboy gangs. Their destinations were the racetracks and the gaming parlors, karaoke clubs and airports, nightclubs and whorehouses, glamorous hideaway places where they chauffeured their shady clients of the night.

The tips were always better at night, bigger dollars from men who gambled with their lives. But Johnny saw beyond jockeying the radio car. He imagined he was going to make his money and get out, put his cash in other directions.

"Wong Jai," they called him, Kid Wong. "What's with this piece of pussy you keep telling us about?"

Johnny never elaborated, but he couldn't keep Mona off his mind. The others knew this and always teased him, knowing he'd only clam up, change the subject.

Almost four months now he'd been picking her up, since the end of the fierce New York City winter. Four nights a week, three or four stops a night. They hardly spoke the first two months, and never in front of Uncle Four.

Gradually she opened up to him, and now he wished she hadn't. The money and tips were good, and he didn't like to get involved with the customers, but what she'd confided in him was like a throbbing in his brain, a dull and bothersome headache.

The month before, after they had been speaking regularly, she gave him a fearful look, and quietly said some nasty things about Uncle Four. He wished he hadn't heard it, wished he could do something about it.

She said Uncle Four beat her and raped her, and that he did this regularly.

What the fuck, he thought. She's his mistress. What the fuck does she expect? Why stay with him then?

When he asked her why she didn't leave, she only cried. They didn't speak for weeks after that, but he knew that she had given him part of her pain, and he was suffering along with her. She didn't have to speak. He saw it in her eyes every time they stole glances at each other, every time she touched his hand, every time she walked away behind the Mustache, never glancing back.

"Fuckin' bitches," the other drivers said, "play you for a sucker."

"Don't let them use you," they warned.

"Money talks, bullshit walks. That's what those *hei* care about."

He was trying to control the fever slowly warming in his brain. He had two hours before he'd pick her up, until he'd face her eyes asking a hundred questions. He glanced at his wristwatch, tossed his bet money pooling with the other drivers. Two hours. He invested twenty dollars at Yonkers. Snappin Dragon in the fourth. Samurai Warrior in the eleventh. What the hell, he thought, and closed his eyes.

But eleven o'clock came around faster than he expected.

DESTINY

Despite the fact that she depended on them, Mona had given birth to a hatred for men, all men. Except for Johnny, who had asked for nothing and expected nothing. All the other men in her life had purchased her time, bought her body, played with her mind.

Nothing for nothing; that was the lesson she learned a lifetime ago halfway around the world in Hong Kong, when the Triads had forced her, at fourteen years old, to sell her body to repay her father's gambling debts. When her mother found out, she cursed her husband, then immediately suffered a heart attack. Mona never forgot that extra week in the seedy brothel, on her back to pay for the funeral.

Her mother's curse came true. In the end they killed her father anyway, those evil men with snake tattoos and black hearts.

The tears welled up quickly in her almond eyes.

"Men have hurt me tonight, again," Mona whispered.

Johnny stood quietly and wrapped his arms around her until there were no more words. That's how it was with Mona. Her words came infrequently, and then only wrapped in precise phrases full with poignancy and passion. But it was the heartbreak in her face, the tears spilling from her eyes, the quiver of her lips, the shiver of her body when he pulled her close; that was how she expressed herself.

There was no escape from these images, Johnny knew. They wrenched your heart and shredded your toughness. She made you as vulnerable as you thought she was, and then she'd nail you.

You couldn't say no to anything she desired.

Later, when they lay together in his tenement flat, there was no need for words, the only sounds coming from the slap and pull of their bodies against each other, the soft clutching groans and whispers leading to hard fast breathing and the sharp anguished cry of desperate pleasure.

ALBATROSS

When Uncle Four came to Hong Kong almost three years ago, Mona had been promoted to China City, the big nightclub on Kowloon where hundreds of *siu jeer,* young ladies, sold themselves while seeking overseas American Chinese with the promise of green cards. She and Uncle Four discovered they had roots in the same province in China, and that had served as a convenient enough excuse for her to follow him to New York City, overstay her visa, and disappear underground.

At first, all had gone well with this older man, at fifty-nine some thirty years her senior. Although he was married, Uncle Four provided her with a clean co-op apartment, food, money for clothes and personal expenses. In return, she accompanied him only at night, a decoration on his arm that he liked to show off in the gambling houses and karaoke nightclubs.

All types of men ogled her wherever they went, raping her with their eyes as she passed, hungry-looking men with furtive stares. None of this went unnoticed by Uncle Four, but he gave big face to the club owners and didn't bring trouble to their places.

As time went by he accused Mona of looking back at some of the younger men, suspected her of harboring other desires, which could cause him big loss of face. This was unacceptable. He was, after all, an elder man of respect. Gradually, he became abusive and violent, always threatening her with deportation, or even death, if she ever tried to leave him. As leader of the Hip Chings, who sponsored the Black Dragons, his people were everywhere, and she feared she would never escape.

Jing deng, she cried secretly. It was destiny, her Fate.

But Johnny Wong had given her hope. Not that he promised her anything. In fact, he coolly offered no suggestions. But he was there to comfort her, and although he tried to keep a distance between them, she sensed that he did care for her. In their intimate moments she found the tender, soft side of him, a side she knew she could exploit.

Johnny would be useful when she decided to exact her revenge on Uncle Four.

Eye of the Storm

After Uncle Four had unsuccessfully mounted her with his horny drunk erection, then finally rolled his fat weight off of her, she lay in bed quiet. She was pretending to be asleep.

Uncle Four was at her desk now, drinking again and talking on the phone, with the night light on. When he was drunk this way he talked a lot, bragging about his deals.

Mona lay quiet, heard about the six diamonds, the forty thousand, something about washing money and a silent partner.

"October tenth," she heard, the day of the Double Ten celebration, two weeks away. Her eyes open in the dark, she heard: "The lawyer's office, on Hester, at noon." Uncle Four was slugging down the XO now. Bragging, laughing. Then he hung up the phone, grunted, headed back toward the bed, toward Mona.

He rolled in next to her, his hands already on her body, squeezing her breasts, her nipples, his fat fingers sliding down to her soft downy triangle, poking, violating her. He rubbed his flaccid flesh against her backside, licked his tongue on her neck, the stench of liquor on his breath.

She kept from recoiling, as she always did, even as he turned her face toward him. The six diamonds, she thought, as he pushed her head lower. The forty thousand. Her head was on his stomach. She opened her mouth.

Then she closed her mind.

Titan

"Cost ya fourteen hundred," Bags said quietly.

Cheen say, thought Johnny, the Chinese words sounding vaguely like "a thousand deaths."

"I need it," Johnny said.

"You got it, cuz," said Bags.

"You need some cash now?"

Bags just smiled and said, "Pay me later. Gotta make sure I get the piece first. Know what I'm saying?"

"Cool, man," Johnny said, in his Hong Kong voice. "You find me."

Bags grinned. "You got that right," he said.

She counted out the wad of crisp new hundreds, twenty of them, crinkling each one slightly so they wouldn't stick.

Johnny didn't want to know, didn't ask who or when, and didn't need to ask why. He simply agreed to run the errand, to buy the merchandise, knowing he'd clear six hundred in the exchange. A gun, with a silencer, she said.

The risk of his getting caught was his unspoken contribution to their relationship. He couldn't say no, and, in an odd way, he was impressed that she was finally taking action.

A gun, she had said, with a silencer.

He scooped the money off the table. She leaned in and kissed him on the soft part of his throat, gathered in the fleshiness with her lips, bit him. He gave her a hard and long hug, then turned abruptly out the door, thinking of Bags.

And the gun, with the silencer.

The way Johnny unpeeled the Ben Franklins from the wad Mona had given him impressed Tony Bags. Bags opened his lips enough to hiss smoke, working the cigarette over to one corner of his mouth, speaking through the other side.

"It's a Titan twenny-five caliber, six shots. Less than a pound wit the silencer. And I got you an extra magazine clip." He ran his finger over the ivory grips, the blue metal finish, the knurled steel silencer. Not that any of it made any difference to Johnny, as long as it worked.

"Good up to fiteen, twenny feet." Bags grinned. He pointed it in Johnny's direction a second, then aimed it out the window and squeezed the trigger.

Johnny heard the compressed suppressed explosion—poof!—at the same time the fluorescent sign shattered, leaving jagged plastic hanging above the take-out shop.

"It's clean right now, but it's probably got bodies on it, know what I'm saying?"

Johnny nodded. "I didn't plan on keeping it."

She peered down the barrel and silencer, squinted and imagined the mustached head in her sights. She took a breath and squeezed the trigger, heard the hammer snapping down on the unloaded pistol.

"Don't worry," Johnny said. "You won't be shooting far and there's no kick."

Mona watched as Johnny chambered a round for her, flicking on the safety, then ejecting the round, explaining the slide action to her. He passed the bedsheet over the Titan in a cursory wiping, careful to take his prints off it.

Mona turned off the light on the night table, leaving the bedroom with only the moonlight that came in through the window. She climbed on top of him and worked her body until he was hard, inside her. Almost a half hour passed before she rolled off him.

"Will you load those extra bullets, my love," her lips demanded just before sliding over the head of his hardness.

In the dim light he groped for and found the extra six-shot magazine, never taking his eyes off her head, then felt again for the small box of bullets, spilling them across the night table. He was in ecstasy, his mind drifting, with clammy hands slipping the little bullets into the magazine.

Her head was bobbing, eyes open watching him, her tongue twisting inside her mouth. He tossed the loaded clip onto the night table as her lips tightened on him, her fingernails fluttering, closing on his testes. He was ready to explode, to blast himself away from Chinatown, to a sunny place far from the reaches of the dark and dirty city.

PAYBACK

The news item appeared in the *New York Post* on October eleventh, a two-inch column in the Metro section sandwiched between a photo of an auto accident and a piece on condoms in schools. The headline read "Man Shot In Chinatown."

A man believed to be the undersecretary of the Hip Ching Good Association, a Chinatown Tong, was shot as he left his lawyer's office, police said yesterday. Wah Yee Tam, 59, was shot once in the head, execution style, as he left his lawyer's office at 444 Hester Street about 1:30 P.M. Police have no suspects and could not comment on motive, only fearing that the shooting signals a resumption of local gang warfare. Anyone with information is urged to call (212) 555-0711. All calls will be kept confidential.

Night Sweats

for Jose Rivera, my first great love

JOËL B. TAN

*E*ven now, I remember the sweat between us. I can smell our love-making, a mixture of cologne, lube, saliva and sweat. I can feel the heavy weight of him on my chest. I look up, and I can still see him rubbing, beating his hard throbbing cock on my face. I can taste the lubricant, his kisses, our perspiration and the sharp taste of his semen. I can see all this today. He was my first love.

Watching Lazarus move was like watching soft-core porn. From the moment I saw him, I knew fucking was inevitable. It was something about the way we danced together. I've always believed that you can tell how a person fucks by the way they dance. Half-jokingly, we attributed our dancing skills to our equatorial ancestry. We were both island men. Lazarus was Puerto Rican. I am Filipino. Given all the Roman Catholic, Spanish-colonized baggage we both carried, we were doomed. Nevertheless, we fell in love.

We were extreme opposites. I was openly gay. Lazarus got off on fronting the straight, macho role. I aspired to become a writer. Lazarus was barely literate. He was a troubled but practicing Catholic. I meditated. I firmly believed in communication, expression and articulation. He rarely broke his vow of silence. He took great interest in possessions (video gadgetry, stereo equipment, TVs, me) and I was a hopeless romantic who also took interests in possessions (commitment, passion, reciprocation, him). Our union depended on our differences. Our differences added to desire. Common ground was rare and we learned to find our commonalities in each other's flesh.

Lazarus and I fucked a lot. We fucked even more when we were angry. We never really learned how to talk to one another. We never found a common vernacular. Instead, we articulated feelings with our kisses. We listened with our tongues. We expressed joy with our fingers. We connected with our cocks. We gave with our asses. We could express grief, sorrow, anger, fraternity, empathy, sympathy, any and every feeling in our love-making. At the end of our heavy breathing, we were always silent. In the dark, we would lie on our sweat-soaked sheets, sexually satiated, equally understanding of the other's thoughts and feelings. We developed a language of our own.

Our bodies fit together perfectly. A brush of the hand would lead to a soft caress. The soft caress would quickly turn into fingers pinching nipples. Twisted nipples would turn into wide canyon kisses. Zippers would fly open, shirts flung. Waistbands of boxers yanked down, knife-like tongue on Adam's apple, teeth gnashing delicate corners, ring fingers probing, cocks hard and ready, drooling thick liquid ooze.

The only time Lazarus could come was when he was fucking me. His favorite position was when we were face to face. He said he loved the pained look in my eyes when he entered me. He told me that my expression matched that of his protective saint, San Martin de Porres, the black saint. He didn't like to fuck me doggy-style. He believed that two people in love should look each other in the eye during their love-making. We weren't much for slow, gentle exchanges. In fact, he plowed in and out of me ruthlessly. He pushed and I pushed back harder. Lazarus cursed in Spanish when he fucked. On the verge of his orgasm, he would yell, "I love you" or *"Te amo,"* as if surrendering. When he milked his last drop, he would engulf my body with tender kisses. I too would think, *Mahal kita,* I love you, Lazarus. *Mahal kita.*

I believed him when he told me he loved me. It wasn't easy establishing trust with him. See, Lazarus had a problem with lying. His sister confided that his lying started when he was young. Apparently, Lazarus Sr., Lazarus's father, had a drinking problem. They say that he died with a bottle in his right hand and a gun in the left. Lazarus Santo, Sr., left Lazarus Santo, Jr., his mother and his sisters a legacy of violence, disappointment and brutality, nothing more. Shortly after his death, Lazarus's mother medicated her pain with extravagant doses of cocaine. What was left of their family disintegrated. Lazarus was left to raise himself. Lazarus never could accept reality, so he created his own. The first time he told me he was falling in love with me was after I read him a short story I wrote about my guardian angel. He told me that he believed that I was his guardian angel. I wanted to believe that was true.

Our beginning was magical. We were both young and handsome. We needed to be needed. We thrived on hearing love songs and dedicating them to each other. We proudly declared to all of our friends that we were officially "boyfriends." Lazarus made me proud to be with him. Women and men alike were drawn to his raw sexiness. He had dark curly hair and slanted eyes. His goatee framed his pretty but masculine face. His body was in peak form at twenty-four. He was five feet nine inches tall, with a stocky, boxer's build. I was slightly taller, with a bigger build. We were the same cocoa brown. He cut his hair into a military-style flattop to match mine. We wanted to let the world know we were together. We moved into a three-bedroom apartment after only a few months of dating.

We created a beautiful home on credit and silences. We littered the house with tasteful antiques, paintings by contemporary Puerto Rican artists, native Filipino art and small talk. We adopted possessions as if they were children. We created a perfect environment to deter the inevitable. We talked less. We made love less. We fucked more. We fucked in every corner of our large apartment. We christened three bedrooms, two-and-a-half baths, an outdoor patio, a fully equipped kitchen, a formal dining room and a sunken den with our sweat and semen. We played house, knowing that we couldn't possibly pay back the debt we'd incurred. We were young and had no regard for consequences or tomorrows. When the last stick of furniture was bought, we knew it was over.

In retrospect, I realize that my decision to leave Lazarus was inevitable. Nevertheless, the pain of walking away from us was excruciating. He was the one man on earth that made me feel needed. He made me feel loved. A void grew between my legs in his absence. During the first year of our separation, I tried to replace him with drunken Friday nights. I became an indiscriminating receptacle for anyone's attention or affection. I searched for men who resembled him, no matter how slightly. I sought refuge from one bedroom to another. I was barely breathing.

Through mutual friends, I tracked his moves. Lazarus sought to be comforted between sheets. He also numbed himself with booze and crystal meth. He used crystal to bring him up, make him happy. He needed booze to bring him down. He countered his pain with chemicals and the illusion of "the glamorous life." He blamed me for abandoning him. He said that he couldn't understand why I left. He thought we were perfect. After all, we never once fought.

Ironically, the vices he once rebuked became his salvation. The addicted parents he once disowned came back to haunt him through his own reflection. Lazarus's habit altered his lifestyle to the point where he couldn't maintain legitimate employment. So he got involved in credit scams. He hocked and sold jewelry he claimed he "traded" or "found." His amateurish criminal activity increased to meet the needs of his quickly growing appetite. Crystal and booze slowly devoured him. His once heavily muscled frame caved in, giving way to a thin, jackal-like shadow with sharp teeth and sad eyes. When he had nothing left to sell, he gladly traded his mouth, his cock, his ass for another hit of the "glamorous life."

I saw him once at a burger shack on Santa Monica and Virgil. He was facing the street, smoking, hunting for prey. He looked into the intersection and recognized me. We made eye contact. I was tempted to pull over. He quickly turned away. The light turned green. I sped off.

After that incident, I didn't hear from him for another six years. One day, I received a call at work. It was Lazarus. He was calling to invite me to his graduation from a drug rehabilitation program. Proudly, he told me that he finally completed six months of abstinence and sobriety from crystal and alcohol. This was his fourth attempt in this particular program. His counselors were placing him in a halfway house with other recovering addicts so that he could gradually integrate back into society. In great detail, he told me his story. He recounted the past six years—needles, fat lines on slick mirrors, dollar wine, more lies, hooking, loan sharks, the old men, jail, rape, the police, suicide attempts, the program, back to selling drugs, doing drugs, five-dollar tricks, robbing, being robbed, the program again, back out, the habit again, hotels, a drug bust, conviction, sentencing, the pen, parole, rehab and finally, graduation.

I came to his graduation. I was his only guest. He looked older and slightly weathered. He was stockier; his bulky muscles threatened to tear the thin fabric of his shirt. He had a trim beard that accentuated his maturity. He wore a flattop, reminding me of days long gone. He was darker, even more alluring than I remembered. His exposed neck, his forearms revealed tattoos that weren't there in our youth. To my surprise, he broke from his fellow graduates to hug me. Unabashedly, he planted a wet kiss on my lips. I froze, shocked by his spontaneous display of affection. He drew back, eyes down, apologizing. Before I could react, a group of his friends came over to introduce themselves.

"So you're the famous Lorenzo. You're right, bro. He *is* all that!" they said teasingly.

Lazarus was embarrassed. After a few handshakes, hellos and nice-to-meet-you's, I offered Lazarus a ride to his new home. We had quite a ways to go. He was relocating to Oceanside—a two-hour drive from Los Angeles.

We took the ocean-view route along the Pacific. I skimmed over the dull events of the last four years and recounted one failed relationship after another. Mario, Greg, Arnel, another Greg, Alejandro, Dartanian, Enrique, Mario *again,* and now, single. I failed in marriage after marriage, which said nothing about my writing career. My art succeeded where my marriages failed. My third book of poetry was finally picked up by a major publisher. A play I had written had finished its final run. And finally, despite never having been academically trained, I was offered a teaching position at a small college. Lazarus seemed genuinely happy for me.

Lazarus flatly announced that he had recently tested HIV positive. He told me he tested a year ago after experiencing flulike symptoms and night sweats. He said he had under two hundred T cells, which qualified as an official diagnosis of AIDS. He was starting to experience HIV-related symptoms. He told me he doesn't know when he became infected nor does he care, but he suspected that he may have been infected for some time. No one knew, not his family nor his friends. With tears in his voice, he confessed that he hadn't been able to touch anybody since his diagnosis. He was afraid of infecting them. He felt like a leper. After a millennium of silence, he placed his hand over mine and asked me if I were HIV negative or positive.

I told him that I was negative and that I tested every six months. I also told him that I was no stranger to HIV or AIDS. The past few years had taught me how to accept the reality of AIDS in our lives—the lives of gay men, the lives of men of color. Many of my friends, my past lovers, have lived with and have died from AIDS. Impulsively, I pulled off the freeway and drove into a motel.

I parked my car, headed toward the office and asked them for a room with a large bed. Lazarus seemed confused. In the dark motel room, I removed my clothes. Slowly, I undressed him. His burly brown torso was a map of tattoos. A thin film of sweat that covered his body glistened silver-blue in the dim light. I got on my knees until I was eye-level with his half-hard cock. The dark sticky head was already starting to shyly peek out from his uncircumcised sheath. Without hesitation, I swallowed his quickly stiffening member in my mouth.

"Lorenzo, please! Don't," he begged.

I ignored his pleas and brought his fat monster to life. Surrendering, he gripped my bobbing head and started to fuck my mouth. I slid to the floor. He sat down, bringing his whole weight down on my chest. Hypnotically, he started to rub and grind his saliva-wet prick all over my face. His hairy thighs scraped roughly under my arms. His cock blocked my airways. I struggled to breathe. Sweat poured like rain. The air was pungent with our union. Releasing myself from his grasp, I climbed aboard the creaky motel bed. I grabbed my ankles, spread them from east to west and demanded, "Lazarus, you gonna slip that jimmy on and you gonna fuck me till I faint!"

Excitedly, he rolled a latex sheath over his throbbing tool. He then gently pushed a liberal amount of lube into the tight recesses of my asshole. In one confident stroke, he pushed his steely, throbbing prick into my tortured chasm, forcing my tight muscle ring to accommodate his fevered thrusts. Waves of pain washed across the length of my body. I was drowning in acid sweat and tears. Instinctively, I remembered our rhythm. I looked up to see Lazarus intently studying my face. I remembered his fascination with my labored expressions. We were dancing again. At the end of our brutal joust, "I love you," *"Te amo,"* and *"Mahal kita"* were exchanged.

We called on our lost language of love-making to communicate what we weren't able to articulate to each other in the past seven years. It became clear to me then. When we were young, we were both unwilling and incapable of articulating our emotions. Fate, maturity, recovery, shared pain and the reality of our impending mortalities afforded us this opportunity to establish resolution. We did it in the best way we knew how.

He called room service to send up more sheets; the damage we created was irreparable. We took a shower together. The hot water, his odor mingled with mine, the gentle kisses, the aftermath of our ferocious melee brought back happy young memories of matrimony. Like children, we washed each other's back and laughed.

That was the last time I saw Lazarus healthy. He landed a job at a local rehab program in San Diego. My writing career demanded more time. He found his niche peer-counseling other HIV-positive addicts. Life events were traded via letters and long-distance calls. Months melted into years and Lazarus evolved from childhood lover memory to an occasional hello on late nights, funny birthday cards, religious Christmas cards and, oddly enough, anniversary cards. He addressed each letter with *"Mi Vida"* (My Life), and ended each conversation, each written correspondence with *"Te Amo"* (I Love You).

One Sunday, Pedro, one of Lazarus's co-workers, called. He asked me to come to San Diego as soon as possible, Lazarus was dying. Lazarus never once hinted how serious his condition was. He downplayed all his symptoms over the phone. In fact, colds were really bouts of pneumocystis, (a type of pneumonia, lethal to those who are immunally suppressed). He was also battling a variety of other opportunistic infections. Lazarus had lied to me again. I was furious.

Sadly, Pedro informed me that Lazarus had slipped into a coma two weeks ago. I was speechless. We arrived at the hospital, and his caseworker and doctor officially declared his condition terminal. His caseworker outlined the terms of his living will. According to his wishes, Lazarus was to be taken off life-support systems at eight o'clock the next morning. He requested that no one was to be contacted but me. His savings covered his crematorial expenses. Finally, his caseworker handed me a white envelope. The contents read:

Mi Vida,
Please don't be mad. I know you are, but I didn't want to worry you. I guess you wouldn't be surprised if I told you I couldn't find words to tell you about my condition. Forgive me, for everything. Mijo, I will always love you. I will always be with you. Take this humble amount and buy you something in black. You always had a way of making the color black, well, beautiful. Until next time . . .

Te Amo,
Lazarus
Santo

That night, the nurses, the doctors, the caseworkers left me alone with Lazarus. AIDS had destroyed his Herculean body. There was nothing left of him but a bare skeletal frame. His breathing was labored, heavy, monitored. His hair clung in thin patches. A thick, scraggly beard covered his hollow visage. His body was a highway of wires and thick plastic tubes. The air-conditioned cold room beeped and pulsed with the sounds of technology and its cruel miracles. A small dim light came under the crack of the room's closed door. It illuminated his chemotherapy-tanned face, now angelic and grotesque at the same time.

In the darkness of the hospital room, I removed my clothes and headed toward matrimony. I untied the gown that fell easily from my lover's body. He was curled in a fetal position. With great care, I maneuvered my body under the wires, under the tubes, and lay spoon-style with my dying Lazarus. My arm slipped easily under his featherweight body as I placed my hand over his weakly beating heart. I protectively wrapped my fleshy legs around his bony, jutting hips, burying my face in the wispy patches of his hair. Painstakingly, I pushed his catheter aside and gripped his flaccid penis with my other hand. In the dark, I rocked him. His body gave off a cold night sweat, our final baptismal. This would be the last time. My erect penis moved bitterly along his sagging buttocks. That night, I spoke to him. Words were insufficient, so I spoke to him in our primary tongue. I held him tighter, making love to his hollow shell. That night, I buried prayers in his hair. I hid blessings in his mouth. He drank from my tears. That night, with one orgasmic thrust, I bade Lazarus farewell.

When it was over, I dressed him. I took my razor and shaved his beautiful countenance for the last time. I washed his feet and combed his hair. At 8 A.M., his doctor and his caseworker arrived, with long, regretful faces. I insisted on hitting the last switch. I was barely breathing.

Even now, I remember the sweat between us. I can smell our love-making, a mixture of cologne, lube, saliva and sweat. I can feel the heavy weight of him on my chest. I look up, and I can still see him rubbing, grinding his hard throbbing cock on my face. I can taste the lubricant, his kisses, our perspiration and the sweet taste of his semen. I can see all this today. I guess I've never stopped looking for him. Lazarus was my first love.

Rain

Ameena Meer

Crossing the street on a steamy gray day in September, Zerina feels like she's walked into a memory of last summer in Delhi, the last few days before the monsoon. When the air was thick and hot, tension building in the clouds and in her forehead, where the humidity made her sinuses swell and block so that she could barely see a few feet ahead of her.

Still the grumbling clouds hold back, occasionally letting go a thunderclap or a flash of lightning like a stinging slap across someone's cheek, a sharp insult that cuts through the skin. There is no release, just a regathering of explosive anger, like a madwoman screaming down a carpeted hallway.

The sweat gathers on the back of her neck, under her thick black hair, steaming her face, each wiry hair sticking to her fingers when she tries to brush it off.

On the subway, she has the bad luck of getting into a non-air-conditioned car, and the air is more suffocating than ever, the heat holding the smells of the bodies around her: sweat, deodorant, stale cigarette smoke, old hamburgers. Someone stands up as she gets in and she squeezes in between an old Chinese man, curled like shrimp over the shopping bag he clutches in his tiny hands, and a hugely fat woman, her body overflowing into the seats beside her. No one ever rushes at rush hour.

Zerina presses her fingers into her forehead, wonders if Gianlucca is going to call her. Wonders if she should call him. Wonders why all the men she gets involved with lately are married, or have relationships that date back more than half the length of her life. As she squeezes herself back up to get off the train, her elbow digs into the soft breast of the fat woman and Zerina turns, as well as she can in the throngs of people, and says, "Sorry, I'm really sorry."

And the woman says, "It's all right, it's all right. We're all stuck here." Her West Indian accent is like molasses poured over the words.

The humidity makes the lock stick on the door of her apartment. The key won't turn at all. She tries to force it, but her wrist aches, evidence of what a bad typist she is. Four hours on the computer and she can't unlock her door, all the veins are blue and bulging on her hand. The phone starts ringing inside. She drops her bag and all her books on the doormat and uses both hands and the force in both arms to twist and pull at the same time. She stops struggling for a minute, realizing the futility of her efforts and strains her ears to hear the muffled voice on the answering machine. "Zerina, this is Gianlucca." She shakes the door violently and it pops open like a vacuum lid. "Madonna, I'm sorry you're not at home. I forgot—I told Melissa that I'd take her to a movie tonight. So we meet tomorrow, all right? Tomorrow night at seven." Zerina stands in the doorway, thinking how bloody liberated she is. The answering machine clicks off, beeps, rewinds.

The apartment is hot, stifling with smell of cooking—oil, garlic, cumin and onions from last night's curry. Zerina picks up her stuff and dumps it all on the floor on the other side of the door. The smell is unbearable. She runs to the windows, throwing them open with the strength she lacked earlier. One crashes against the other, a sharp crack cutting down the center of the glass. "Cheap glass." She turns the fan on. She spins the faucets to full blast so water ricochets off the dirty dishes and sprays greasy yellow spots all over her white T-shirt. "Goddamn it!" She gulps the water. It's still lukewarm.

Zerina spreads the newspaper out on the table and tries to read about the Middle East. Instead, she keeps seeing Prashant's face from last summer. The way he looked lying on his back, his big belly spreading and rising like a loaf of bread as she sat on top of him.

She stroked his stomach in smooth little circles, following the pale brown hairs around his nipples. Eventually, she'd slide off onto the bed and he'd roll over on his side, his stomach spilling forward and his long hair draping his round shoulders and his beard covering his chest. With one arm under his head, the other tapping the bedcover and his chubby legs curled underneath him, he looked like a cartoon of a fat little sultan by a perverse Orientalist. She'd get up and smile at him as she threw her kurta on in a careless, swinging movement that was unfamiliar. She suddenly felt a strange narcissistic pleasure in her own young body, pleased with her hard breasts and strong arms. She'd worked hard on her body this summer. As the hem of the kurta dropped down over her stomach, lightly tanned from mornings at the beach, she'd walk slowly across the room, each step stretching and coiling the muscles from her feet to her buttocks, like a cat.

"Mm," he'd say, stroking his hair, "this is perfect."

And outside in the garden, through a crack in the window, she'd hear the sound of the sparrows and pigeons and the breeze ruffling the leaves of the trees. She could almost feel the sunlight warming the top of her head even in the curtained bedroom. She'd laugh and say, "Of course it is." And she realized that she always liked a scene best if she could make it into a tableau she understood, if she could step outside and see how it looked. How she looked standing there in the doorway, the light seeping through her tissue-thin shirt: the pretty young woman and the decadent old man, wished for a minute that she was really young enough and stupid enough to believe the fantasies he'd spin out, pretty enough to make it last.

And then, faster than she can sort out—trains, planes and buses blurring into a smear of prepackaged meals and uncomfortable nights—bang, she is back in New York, the summer drawing to a hot, cloudy close. Prashant seems to have already lost interest in her, all his plans for their future obviously forgotten—she's more stupid than she guessed—he's brusque and rude on the phone. She can imagine his eyes blank and still beneath the thick eyelashes, his fingers drumming again, hard against the table, an impatient tattoo. The only thing making the painfully long days at her temp job bearable is the air conditioning.

The sweat on her hands is making the newspaper pages stick to them. She peels the paper off her palm and takes another gulp of water. Her fingers leave inky prints on the glass. She picks up the telephone, presses two digits and puts it down. "Not yet," she warns herself. She rubs the fingerprints off the receiver with the edge of her T-shirt. Then she picks it up again.

Her mother's voice on the line, warm and fragrant even five thousand miles away, says, "Hello, darling, why do you sound so unhappy?"

Zerina tries to stop herself. She says, "Oh, it's the weather . . ."

But her mother is already off, saying, "I just wish you would stop wasting your life and come home. Of course you're unhappy. Living on your own like that. Why don't you get married? You know, your reputation is going to be completely spoiled."

Zerina stares at her blank white walls. A little rivulet of sweat drips down her back, tickling her spine like the feet of an insect. A cockroach drops off the ceiling and hits the table with a click.

Her mother is saying, "And if you keep refusing proposals like this, people are just going to say you're too fussy. Look, there's this young economist, Ayesha's brother, he's very, very bright, from what I've been told. He's doing well, he's the top of his group, one of the rising stars in the development organization. Don't you want to get married?"

"Okay, I'll meet him." Zerina smashes the cockroach between the pages of the newspaper.

"But are you serious? You can't just keep meeting them. You've got to take it seriously."

"If you mean, do I want to marry him without meeting him, then, no." She massages her forehead again. "I can't meet someone twice or three times and be able to marry him. I just can't do it."

"Well, how do you think arranged marriages work?" Something tickles: a cockroach is climbing through the hair on her forearm. Zerina flicks it off, shuddering. She jumps up and crushes the roach with her shoe as it tries to scurry across the floor. "What are you doing? Aren't you listening to me?"

"All right, okay, I'll do it," Zerina says. She has another sip of water and pulls up her T-shirt and wipes the perspiration off her upper lip. "How are you?"

"I'm fine. We went to a dinner at the Australian Embassy last night. Everyone was asking about you. I missed you so much. Why don't you just come home? Isn't it nicer to be with us?"

"I miss you, too, Mum. And I love you." Zerina thinks of the electricity around her mother, like the smell of her red lipstick, as she's getting dressed to go out at night and then of Gianlucca's kisses, which are hard. His teeth bite into her lips and the skin around her mouth, leaving red marks on her face and the salty taste of blood on her tongue. The receiver slides smoothly into its holder.

The loose tiles in the bathroom crack under the heels of her shoes. Zerina wipes a layer of white plaster dust off the toilet seat. Two more days for the sink. One more day until she has a working shower. Only one more slow thick day, the sweat shining like polish on her forehead. Her shorts drop around her ankles and she steps out of them, leaving her shoes underneath. She lets her T-shirt fall beside the shorts, enjoying the cushion of soft cotton against the soles of her feet before they touch the gritty floor.

Naked in the kitchen, Zerina washes all the pots and pans. The soapy, greasy water splashes her chest and stomach. When she's finished, she scrubs herself. On full blast for twenty minutes and the water's still not cold, but with the fan blowing across her back, her skin feels almost cool, a slight shiver on the back of her neck. She pours dripping handfuls of water over herself. She wiggles her toes in the puddles they make around her feet. When she stops, the wooden floorboards are soft and swollen with water. She opens the refrigerator, the blast of cold air making goosebumps rise on her wet skin. Standing there, her back against the eggs and the butter tray, she drinks the milk straight out of the carton in long gulps that seem to rise from her fingertips to her forehead.

Zerina lies in the middle of the living room carpet. The fan whirls. Its head turns back and forth, sweeping air in sheets across her body. She closes her eyes.

She wakes to the sound of the phone ringing. In the darkness, she thinks it's her alarm clock. She jumps up, trying to silence it. The receiver bumps off. "Hello? Hello?" says a tiny voice.

"Hi," croaks Zerina, the heat making it almost impossible for her to move. Her body is slippery with sweat.

"Madonna, you were sleeping . . ."

"Mm." Zerina rubs her eyes. Bits of dirt and hair from the carpet stick to her arms and shoulders, sprinkling her face as she moves.

"Were you dreaming about me?" The room is alternately pink and green from the flashing neon lights across the street.

"I don't remember."

"Listen, Zerina, I want to see you."

"Tomorrow. At seven." She stretches and rolls on to her stomach, brushes the fuzz off her bottom. A sudden breeze blows the newspaper across the room.

"Now, baby. I want to see you now. Melissa and I—I don't know, I'm crazy."

"Oh." Zerina's pulse thumps in her wrist, her breath quickens. "What happened?" She imagines her fingers digging into the muscles on his shoulders, his neck, feels his tongue in her ear. Her skin tingles. She wishes he were here already. A page of newspaper flies over her leg. She holds her breath.

"She's jealous. She's always jealous, always thinking I'm betraying her with every woman I know. Forget it, Zerina. I just want to see you."

"She's got good reason to be."

"She doesn't understand me like you—I'm at a pay phone, Zerina—I'll be there in twenty minutes." A lightning bolt illuminates the room like an electric light, the crash of thunder like the switch clicking off.

"You just had a fight with your fiancée and you're coming over here?"

"We'll just talk," pleads Gianlucca.

"Gianlucca, I'm tired and—no. I'm not dressed."

"That's how I like you."

"I'll see you tomorrow, all right? Don't worry, it'll work out. Okay. Sleep well." The newspapers thrash around the room. Zerina remembers the heart-shaped face of Prashant's wife smiling out of a photograph on his desk.

The phone starts ringing again, making the floorboards vibrate. Three loud blasts through the room, then a pause. The code she and Prashant made up for each other. It rings again. Zerina picks up the receiver and twists the cord around her hand. One quick snap. Tiny sparks hiss off the colored wires.

Suddenly, the room rings with silence. The apartment feels remote and abandoned. Prashant's fading voice echoes, bounces from the corners to the high ceilings.

Zerina takes a breath and the gulp of air washes into her, fresh and cool.

She hears the clicking on the fire escape. First, small, hesitant taps. Then the wind slows, sucking in a long deep breath, before letting go. Torrents of rain pour down like overturned buckets. The water hits the metal, hanging on the railings like strips of torn cloth, before splashing down on to the sidewalk below.

Zerina gets up and climbs out the window.

to Women Who Sleep Alone

AMY UYEMATSU

my mother doesn't understand a world with no man in it
tells me I waste too much time
forgets I used to spend hours playing by myself.

I don't tell her what sleeping alone is really like
the sweet oils no one but me can rub into my skin.
I look at my body again
no longer as pretty
all the young men I've sent away
will not be coming back.

lately my body's scent fills every room to smother me
I wonder if any man can still enjoy its taste
a darker odor.
every month my blood flows harder
an ache building within my thighs
a real part of me dying—
I want to let in the smell of trees and wind after it's
rained

there's a small gray bird outside my house
who keeps building
her nest with pine needles.
every evening the wind scatters her work
but she returns the next day with new twigs
determined to make a home here.

I'm not one of those women
who can make up their minds
just like that
to find a man again—
something my mother never taught me.
men have always come to me
asked me to dance
I'm not sure how to bring them back in.

sometimes I take a small branch of asparagus fern
twirl it around and around—
a light green fuzz powdering my arms.
then I curl my hands under my breasts
reassured by the softness of skin
remind myself this is enough for now—
my thin hand pausing on the shoji door
running my fingers along rice paper and wood—
a woman opening to the sound of rain.

Mind Sex

VIII

Pearl Diver

Cecilia Tan

I breathe. As I lie
still in the bottom of the boat, the sea breathes with me, rising and
falling. There is just enough room for me in my little wooden shell,
the oars tucked against each side. Droplets of seawater glisten on
my bare, brown skin, and I watch my own chest as I breathe, touch
my stomach with my hands. The time is coming, and I am almost
ready. The moon is still climbing up the sky, and I wait for it to
reach its peak. It must, because that is the way things are and have
always been, the moon and sun circling forever above without cease,
just as the waves must rise and fall, and the rains to follow the dry
time. Tonight is not just any moonrise, though, not just any night
upon the water. Tonight is the night of the pearls.

I sit up in the boat and peer over the edge. The water is dark,
but the sand and stones are almost white. Below me the silvery flash
of fish in the moonlight catches my eye—but I know it is just fish,
not pearls. I will know the pearls when I see them, when the moon
is at its height. I have been prepared for this moment since my
breasts first began to swell; for years I have prepared my body for
this, to be a pearl diver.

The elders in the village say the pearls fell down from the skies;
some say they are stars out of the heavens; some say *we* came down
from the heavens, that we came long ago from another place where

we were not the only people, where there were people with pink skin and yellow hair, that we traveled on the water in boats like my little shell, and lived on islands in the water just like we do now; some say that when we die we will go back to that place and others say that when we are born that is where we come from, and in any case the only thing we do all agree on is that the pearls are magic and precious, and if there is a link to our ancestors, gods, or afterlife, it is through them. And so we dive, on the night of the pearls, to see what we can learn.

I lie back down in the boat. The moon is taking its time. I let my feet hang over the edge on either side, warm water touching my toes as the shell rocks into a small swell. The night breeze rustles the dark cluster of hair between my legs and the lips sigh open. As they taught me to prepare myself, I lick my finger and let it rest there, rocking my hips as each wave passes, slow as a sleeper's breath. Just as I had been taught, I gather the magic around me, and I can almost see myself beginning to glow as I resist the urge to press my finger harder and let the energy burst and dissipate. It surges through me as I go on touching what we call the *woman's pearl,* the nub of flesh now grown hard like the treasures I will be seeking.

My eyes have slipped closed but I must keep watching the moon. I open them to find it is almost above me, looking down on me like an eager lover, who will now finally be allowed into my virgin flesh. I slip over the side of the boat and into the warm embrace of the sea. Bubbles rise up and catch between my legs, and I want to keep my hand there, but I will need both hands to swim. I lower myself under the surface of the water, and as sounds grow dim, my vision grows sharp. I am a pearl diver and I know how to see through the shadows and murk. But there is nothing to see, yet. I let go of the boat and float face down on the surface, my legs hanging free below me and open. I tense the muscles inside me, and feel the energy shoot through me again. Soon those muscles will do what I have practiced so long to do. The elders chose me out of all

the others to do this task. All the girls of my age had been taken
aside and trained, the old women rubbing our women's pearls with
oil until we learned to do it ourselves, reaching fingers inside of us,
first one, then, two, then three, as they exercised us until we had the
strength that was needed, and holding our breaths until sometimes
it seemed we did not need to breathe at all . . .

And now I see why. The moon must be over my head as the
shadows have all shrunk as small as they can be, and I see them—at
first faint but then as bright as the nighttime stars, the pearls.
Glowing from the bottom. They are invisible and dead as rocks at
any other time, but now they glow. Maybe, I think to myself, they
fell not from the stars but from the moon itself, and they glow only
when the moon draws so near. I take the last breath that I will ever
draw as a girl and with wide strokes I dive toward my womanhood.

The first pearl I find is small, no bigger than the end of my
thumb, and I lift it from its bed of sand and turn it in my fingers to
convince myself that what they told me is true. It is smoother than
anything I have ever felt, much smoother than the wooden beads we
used for practice. Curling myself into a ball with my head between
my knees, I open myself with one hand and slide the pearl inside
me, using my muscles to draw it as far up inside as it will go . . .

The shock of the first vision almost makes me lose my air; a
tiny silver bubble rises toward the moon as I see in my mind's eye
the moon, the stars, not spread out above me like a roof but hanging all around me like a school of fish in the water, and I know that
I feel my place among them, one glistening point in the web of the
universe.

My legs together, I stroke with my arms to the next glowing
spot, and lift out of the sand a pearl the size of my eye. It feels
warm, warmer than the blood-warm seawater, and with one hand I
slip it inside.

This time I am ready when the vision comes: I am moving
through space like a swimmer, circling down toward a planet blue
with oceans, and thinking *Home! Home!* and already I am spiraling

toward the next pearl, this one bright as it protrudes above the sand, almost too large to fit in my closed hand. I press it against my opening, but it does not slide in like the others. I cannot breathe to help me relax, and I do not have time to waste with only one breath of air inside me. While I take the time to do this I float toward the surface and it will be more work to get back to the bottom. As my hands work at my opening, they brush my woman's pearl and I feel something inside me blossom open like a flower, and take the white orb in.

I am swimming, turning and tumbling, as the planet below revolves in its dance around the sun, the moon its partner swinging round, and all the close family of others moving stately through the sky, and beyond, and beyond, and beyond . . . and a voice, not my own, in my head, saying "the seeds of life, scattered."

I realize my vision is getting darker and my air is almost done but I make for one more pearl nearby. This one I lift in two hands; it is the size of my fist. Some part of me thinks I cannot hope to take it in, but one hand is already rubbing hard at my own pearl while the other is pushing the huge thing against me. It goes partway in and then slips back out and if I could, I would be gasping for breath, but there is only water all around me as I thrash. I need this last pearl more than all the others, I am hungry for it, the energy and magic flowing in and out of it as I push my fingers inside myself, trying to open the way wide enough, and then it is going in, it moves in my hand into me bit by bit, up to its widest point, and then, as my other hand presses hard on my woman's pearl, I swallow it whole.

The universe breathes like giant wings beating. I see people infinitely small in a band across the face of the stars; I see white glowing star stuff spread like webs across the void; I see embryos bursting into life inside mothers' wombs; I see the *man's pearl* dripping from the tip of his finger; I see all of creation. I cry out as the magic bursts through me and my bubbles race out of me like a flight of startled birds. My hands are between my legs, one keeping the pearls in place and the other holding my own pearl, which throbs and ebbs, and my head breaks the surface . . .

And I breathe. I lie on my back in the water with the moon shining upon my breasts and I cannot take my hands from between my legs as I burst the bubble again and again, fingers furiously working as the sensations wash over me, and under the moon's watchful eye I return to the shore, bearing the wisdom of ages.

Dream Journal

Minh Duc Nguyen

*W*hile riding with Son on his red scooter to the flea market, we ran out of things to talk about, so Son asked me if I had any interesting dreams. I said no. I explained to him that I can't remember any of my dreams, including those wet dreams which I'm sure I have had. Otherwise, I wouldn't be the kind of guy I am right now. Son said he records all his dreams in a journal. He said he benefits a lot from his dreams because they reveal his weaknesses. For example, he once saw a brand-new shining Harley-Davidson motorcycle in front of Safeway in his dream, and he was so turned on by it that he started masturbating. After he came, he woke up all sweaty, frightened and worried about what the dream meant. Man, I think Son has one major weakness to fix. After I heard that sick dream, I almost jumped off his shitty scooter.

Son gave me some tips on how to remember my dreams and I tried them. But it was tough to wake up in the middle of the night and say to myself, "Wow, that dream was deep, so I better get up and write it down before I forget." But one night I did manage to a few times. Strangely, they were all nightmares.

Nightmare #1. I was Cary Grant, or at least I saw myself as him, on an impossible mission in Vietnam to rescue an American woman. My partner was a short Vietnamese man with a peasant's brown skin and small bones. Throughout the whole mission, he kept asking me annoying questions like, "Of all the women that you have slept with, which one made your toes curl?"; "Were you and Alfred Hitchcock good friends?"; or this stupid one—"Do you really have a British accent?" I ignored him. Soon we found the American woman. I sent a code out on the radio, and an American helicopter flew into the jungle to pick us up. Unable to land because of all the tall rubber trees around us, the pilot threw down a ladder made of rope. The American woman climbed up. I followed right behind her. My partner, however, remained on the ground.

Nightmare #2 was somewhat the opposite of #1. Throughout the whole dream, I was chased by these naked athletic men—each a clone of the other. I mean, all these men looked alike. They had the same roundness on their bald heads, the exact long noses, the right angle of their square jaws, the similar muscular frames; even their large penises were the same. Finally, they caught me and dragged me to a green swamp. They threw me in the cold water. I sank and couldn't see anything, not even the bubbles that I coughed out. But my body rose by itself and soon my head was above water. I looked down and saw the reflection of my face on the water's surface. My features were transforming. My black hair was falling out. My small nose was stretching. My jaw was growing. My eyebrows had turned blond. And next, I immediately checked my penis.

Nightmare #3 was quite enjoyable, until the dramatic ending. I categorized it as a semiwet dream. I described it semiwet because I didn't actually get wet, but would of if my pride didn't get in the way. I was in this nightclub loaded with people dancing like crazy. Then I spotted a gorgeous Asian girl, who was also checking me out. I slid toward her, and she slid toward me. When we met, everybody around us just cleared away and then they shone the spotlight on us. So we made love. Sure, what else could we do? Everything went swell until all of a sudden, she said, "That's it?" And the music died out. And I woke up. And I was pissed. I rolled back and forth on my mattress, forcing my eyes to stay closed so I could go back to sleep and, hopefully, fall back in the same dream. I wanted another chance.

Instead of falling back into Nightmare #3, I landed in Nightmare #4, which was a continuation of Nightmare #1. The American soldier pulled the American woman inside the helicopter. I climbed up quickly and extended my arm to grab his hand, but the soldier pulled out a Rambo knife and cut the ladder. "What the hell are you doing? I'm Cary Grant!" I cried out like a wounded hawk. As I fell down, still hanging on to the ladder, I heard the American soldier say, "Stay in your own country, big shot!" My partner caught me in his small arms. A mother, he was, holding a giant child. In his arms, I looked beyond his round chin, edged by a muddy sky. I watched the metal bird fly away. At that moment, I answered one of my partner's questions: "Of all my lovers, the one that made my toes curl was not a woman, but a man."

from

The Dodo Vaccine

A Solo Multimedia Performance About AIDS and Asian Americana

Dan Kwong

*P*reviously I had never done a performance which dealt explicitly with my sexuality, and for good reason. I felt it was a mess. What clarity, what illumination, what inspiration could I possibly offer people on this subject without feeling like a fraud? Then I was commissioned by Panchayat Arts Resource Unit of London to create a performance as part of "Extreme Unction," an exhibition of Asian-American artists responding to AIDS—a perspective never before presented in the United Kingdom.

This opportunity became a challenge to finally open up a very particular can of worms in a very public manner. I felt obliged to forge onward into these areas despite massive feelings of despair, shame, powerlessness and self-hate. Because silence equals you-know-what. Because with the presence of AIDS, the inner battle between compulsion/obsession and rational behavior takes on immediate life and death implications. And this is a battle waged in the arena of sex, where rationality rarely prevails.

As a heterosexual Asian-American male, I have not yet had to watch many of my friends slowly dying before their time, nor witness an ongoing procession of loved ones' funerals. I do not live with the fear of HIV/AIDS in quite the same way I imagine a gay man does. In general, my sexuality has been expressed in blithe disregard of a global epidemic. My history of compulsive sexual behavior is also a statement of denial, the heterosexual denial that HIV is an issue for me as a straight man. AIDS has been mythologized in the public mind as a gay disease when in fact the World Health Organization estimates that by the year 2000, HIV will be transmitted worldwide primarily through heterosexual contact. It is very much a heterosexual issue, more so than some may want to acknowledge.

Welcome to the new millennium. Bring your sense of humor—you'll need it here . . .

The following occurs in roughly the middle of the performance, preceded and followed by lots of other stuff . . .

IN THE DARK WE HEAR VOICE ON TAPE:

My friend Alan is a veteran actor in Hollywood who happens to be gay. He started getting sick last winter, and one day he called me up to cancel an appointment. And then he said, "Listen, I'm not telling people about this, but I'm HIV positive. So please keep it to yourself. I'm being real 'Japanese' about it . . ."

(MORE VOICES ON TAPE:) JAPANESE NEWS ANNOUNCER; JAPANESE CHILD RECITING NURSERY RHYME (PROJECTED TEXT SLIDES OVER VOICES:)

Gaman shite kudasai.
One must endure suffering
in silence and isolation.
This is strength of spirit.

AIDS means "gay"—
We don't have homosexuals
in our communities, in our families.

. . . DAN ENTERS SLOWLY, CEREMONIALLY DRESSED IN FUNDOSHI LOIN-
CLOTH & CARRYING A KNIFE. HE STANDS IN A POOL OF RED LIGHT AT
CENTER STAGE, MOTIONLESS, HEAD DOWN, BACK TO THE AUDIENCE. HE IS
FACING A WALL OF SHEER NETTING STRETCHED ACROSS THE STAGE. WE HEAR
VOICES ON TAPE:

"So—have you had any unprotected sexual contact over the last
six months?"
"Uh, yes, actually I have. Uh, mostly oral sex with women."
"Now, you do realize that that is risky behavior?"
"Uh, yeah. Yeah, I know. I know that . . ."

AS VOICES SPEAK, DAN CUTS A LONG VERTICAL SLASH IN WALL OF NETTING,
CLIMBS THROUGH INTO SPACE FILLED WITH 100 HANGING INFLATED CLEAR
BALLOONS CONTAINING 500 COLORED PING-PONG BALLS REPRESENTING
INFECTED T-CELLS AND HIV PARTICLES. SUDDENLY WE HEAR:

MUSIC—VERY LOUD, FAST, VIOLENT, THRASH ROCK WITH SCREAMING, WAIL-
ING VOCALS (NIRVANA: "TERRITORIAL PISSINGS").

DAN DOES WILD THRASH DANCE, KNIFE FLAILING, BURSTING BALLOONS,
PING-PONG BALLS FLYING. HIS MOVEMENT HAS SUICIDAL OVERTONES. END
OF SONG, HE COLLAPSES ON FLOOR. SILENCE. THEN WE HEAR:

A SOLO CLARINET SOFTLY PLAYS A GENTLE LULLABYE (RICHARD STOLTZMAN:
"EVERYWHERE").

SLOWLY, PAINFULLY, DAN CRAWLS BACK THRU SLASH IN NETTING TO A
DOWNSTAGE MICROPHONE SET ON A LOW ALTAR TABLE. EN ROUTE HE IS
PROFUSELY APOLOGIZING UNDER HIS BREATH, GASPING FOR AIR.

I'm sorry. Sorry. Please. I'm so sorry. I didn't mean it. I didn't
mean it. I'm so sorry. Please. I'm sorry . . .
(on hands and knees at mic, still gasping:)

When I have had unsafe sex, it wasn't because of ignorance or defying authority or proving my manhood. It was about *compulsion*. Mouth-watering, loin-quivering, low-moaning compulsion. I could not help myself. I would not help myself. Gazing into the eye of yoni sex, I abandoned all reason. Surrendering to sweet sucking, licking and stroking of my beloved or belusted. I fondly recall each unprotected act, performed with full knowledge that it could be lethal. But I just had to take her in my mouth, as if my lips and tongue swimming in her slippery sex could reach the most sacred chambers of her heart and speak to her very soul and with exquisite tenderness, with divine desire—hold her, adore her, show her that I feel—*(leaps up)*

FUCKING STUPID DUMBSHIT IDIOT! *(drops to knees before mic)*

—Oh but I couldn't help it. How can I look at such beauty, feel such heavenly touch and not do that? It's just too much for me to resist. After all, I'm only—*(leaps up)*

A GODDAM STUPID FUCKING ASSHOLE IDIOT! *(drops to knees)*

—And yes, I entered her too. And yeah, it felt good. In fact, it was incredible. It was like, we were *coupled*. Mated. Locked together like two writhing leopards, two golden panthers, two wet seals clinging and grinding together slowly, mingling our juices. It was heaven, it was perfection, it was—*(leaps up)*

STUPID! STUPID!—*(slowly dropping to knees, voice despairing)* Stupid, idiot . . . *(he is near tears)*

—I know all the facts, all the statistics, all the risks, all the consequences, I have all the information—and still I do these things. It drives me nuts. There is no other place in my life where I am so consistently—stupid. I tried using a dental dam once. I didn't give it much of a chance and my girlfriend wouldn't stop laughing. Another woman told me Saran Wrap works better, but I haven't tried it yet. *(he brightens)* Research! Yes, back to the lab!

(leaps up) I'll need a volunteer! It's all in the name of science, you know!—

SUDDENLY WE HEAR A TELEPHONE RING.

(MUSIC—A TACKY MADONNA SONG BEGINS PLAYING IN BACKGROUND. IT RUNS CONTINUOUSLY. DAN PICKS UP A TINY TOY CELLULAR TELEPHONE. THE FOLLOWING SECTION ALTERNATES BETWEEN DAN SPEAKING LIVE AND HEARING HIS VOICE ON TAPE)

DAN: Hello? Oh hi! How are you? You got my message? Oh good . . .

DAN'S VOICE ON TAPE: The Asian Pacific AIDS Intervention Team describes "phone sex" as one of the unquestionably safe practices. This was my first time. She was an old lover of mine from art school days, and she was—open-minded.

DAN: Uh, well, I'm trying to expand my repertoire of safe sex practices so I thought I'd ask you to try this with me . . . Yeah, I'm serious . . . Yeah! . . . Really? Great! Okay, let me get ready . . . Yeah, now! *(Dan climbs under a bedsheet with microphone. He is lying in a dark blue pool of light amidst the burst balloons, completely hidden under the sheet)* You too? Okay! So—

DAN'S VOICE ON TAPE: I was too embarrassed to discuss any preliminary strategy. My guess was that it would be somewhere between a love poem and an obscene phone call . . .

DAN: Uh, what are you wearing? Ooh, I like that. Ooh, that gets me horny already. Well, first I would—first I'd like to—uh, imagine I'm—I'm—

DAN'S VOICE ON TAPE: My first dilemma—which verb tense to use? Present? Present perfect? Suggestive? How do you do this? Just keep going!

DAN: —caressing, you all over, all the softest, smoothest places of your body; your cheeks, along your neck, around your breasts, your inner thighs, all over your ass. Mmm . . .

DAN'S VOICE ON TAPE: I could hear her breathing shift. She moaned softly. All right! She was actually getting excited . . .

DAN: —then I'd bring my mouth to all the same places, kissing you, softly but firmly holding you between my lips. Mm-hm. Yeah. Then I'd do a little wet sucking on the side of your breast, moving my mouth over to dance lightly around your left nipple . . .

DAN'S VOICE ON TAPE: Ooh, very poetic, Dan. She was really getting turned on now, moaning louder, in a rather plaintive manner . . .

DAN: —then I'd start flicking my tongue lightly around your nipple, sucking and licking stronger and stronger, until finally I'd just —oh shit. Is that you? Okay, lemme just see who it is. *(brusquely)* Hello? Oh hi. Yeah. Yeah. Uh-huh. Okay. Sure. Okay, bye. *(sweetly)* Hi I'm back, sorry . . .

DAN'S VOICE ON TAPE: Now she took over, telling me in detail what she would do to various parts of me with various parts of her . . .

DAN: Ooh yeah. Mmm, I like that. Oooooh. Oh yeah do it!

DAN'S VOICE ON TAPE: Hey, this works pretty good! I was imagining our bodies together, in all the different positions and configurations she described. We spontaneously exchanged turns talking in a lovely symbiotic sort of way. This went on for quite some time . . .

DAN: *(much thrashing under sheet)* OHHH! Oh yeah I love that! Oh! **OH GOD! OH DO IT HARD!**

DAN'S VOICE ON TAPE: After a while, my left arm started getting tired. Normally this was not a problem. I switched.

DAN: *(slightly less enthusiastic)* Oh. Uh-huh. Mm.

DAN'S VOICE ON TAPE: After a while my right arm was wearing out too.

DAN: *(even less)* Uh-huh. Oh yeah.

DAN'S VOICE ON TAPE: After a while more, my imagination was wearing out.

DAN: *(sigh)* Well. Did you come? You did? Oh. How nice. When? You should have let me know, I would've—oh, can you hold on a second? I'll be right back—Hello? *(he sits up quickly)* Oh hi, Mom. Oh nothing much, just kinda relaxing. Listen, can I call you right back? OK, bye—Hello? . . . Hello? . . . Hel—

ON TAPE: (Dial tone . . .)

—AS DIAL TONE FADES OUT, LIGHTS FADE TO BLACK . . .

Live Life Empirically

A Comedy Performance

Joyce Nako

He was a bass player and I liked the way he played. He was easy enough to pick out, the only white boy in a sea of black faces, a band that played at a club I'd been going to with a friend recently met who sang back-up for a man who weirdly enough did a mildly good representation of Aretha. I rather liked the club, though I couldn't tell you why now—it's defunct so all I have is a memory of it being an interesting place where I'd met and went home with a white boy. Does this reference to white boys always make me a racist? Probably.

You know, I'm not usually. I mean some of them are my best friends, really, in truth. And they'd probably describe me as a close Japanese friend they know if the subject of sushi ever came up. Fair enough. I can call them white.

What about the boy part? Well. It's strange but I tend to think all blond blue-eyed types that act blond and blue-eyed, even the old ones, are boys. To a Japanese, even a JA, the kind of personality considered open, highly prized American outgoing personality, you know the kind; in any case, to this JA, in comparison to the JA men I know, they, white men, behave like boys. I can't help it. Now hear me out: practically *all* men, in my humble opinion, behave like boys. And I've watched, been with (fucked, if you must know the truth) and have loved as deeply as I was capable of doing in my not too distant past, quite a few of them, and for the most part, with very few exceptions, men are largely untalented, dysfunctional (not necessarily sexually but that sometimes too) boys.

So he happened to be white. And rather good-looking, very passionate (at least he played with a good deal of unexpected soul for a white boy, you know), and I wanted to meet him. My friend said, "Oh, he's a sweetie. Yes, I'd like to hook you up. There's a bitch that's always after him. I'll fix her." Friends are nice to have.

In between sets, he came by with her and she said blah-blah, this is blah-blah, and then left us to our own devices. We barely exchanged greetings, but he reacted to meeting me with the proper amount of enthusiasm, so I did the same. We promised to talk outside at the next break, which occurred, and it was pleasant enough, so I went home pleased.

I didn't go back for quite a while. I suppose I was busy, but when I went back again the next time, I went by myself to the appointment made a couple of months previous. Yes, he remembered me and we were both determined, I think, to match fates. I was probably dating someone, or my house was dirty or something, but I only remember that I didn't want him over at my place. He suggested his own and I said okay. He ended up living so damn far away it took forty minutes by freeway; but it was far enough away that the area was rustic, and I felt as though I was on vacation, as indeed it turned out to be.

Now lest you get me very, very wrong, I usually don't do this kind of picking up—oh, about six or seven times in my life, not too often I should say, but you may think differently. Well, it is *my* story after all. You are welcome to write one yourself.

He lived in a cute little house surrounded by a wood kind of fence, not picket but the kind they have sometimes—uh, split-log, I think it's called; kinda crooked, grayish-looking pieces of wood, long and stuck on Y-looking crosspieces. For a carpenter's daughter, I sure don't know much. In any case, there were lots of windows and a cozy fireplace in which a cozy little fire was soon lit as he chatted away about liking his place a lot, etc., etc. I gingerly glanced around. It was so very cozy, a very nice warm feel, exceedingly neat except for a shitload of dishes in the sink, about three days' worth, I figured.

He told me about his music and I really dug the guy a lot. He also told me about his girlfriend, who was in the hospital getting something or the other removed, how he was really worried about her, and how they were gonna get married, and how I was a final fling. Fair enough. I like negotiations straight and honest. He would have a final fling that he would remember always; hey, this would be fun, I promised myself.

I told him nothing about myself in return for all this intimate talk because I couldn't discuss myself then. Self-revelation was a private thing in those days, and I would normally sit and hear people out, listening to sometimes interesting stories, sometimes whining ones, sometimes heartbreaking ones, but always listening. Picture "The Thinker," you know, the statue? Well, that's sorta like how I can sometimes get but with more clothes on and not quite as muscular.

He asked if I could give massages and I said that I could, that I liked giving them, instructing him to remove his shirt and lie flat, head facing the floor, in front of the fire now blazing chirpily, the only source of light in the darkened house. The outside was casting weird shadows throughout the place but they were friendly ones, not icky. And I competently worked medium-hard muscles only slightly tensed from a night's work and was silent. His was an appreciative body soon moaning slightly, and he'd try to talk and I would hush him because I didn't want to hear it.

I took off the rest of his clothes and worked the entire body to where it was relaxed and pretty. My favorite massage spots are the face and head for some reason, and I particularly enjoy doing the hard ridges around the eyes and nose, opening up the nasal passages, and the hard skull areas, always thinking it opens up thoughts. I stopped when my fingers got tired and dropped away from him lying there facing upward now, hopefully feeling utterly content with the world.

I know we made love. I was in a passionate mood. I usually am the first time out with someone, and we fit well together, anatomically speaking. He said so, too. And he turned out to be a Jesus freak, thanking Jesus for me; it was strange. We also discussed my sexual problem. I didn't come—nonorgasmic—and I told him I often had that problem and I do. Not always, and perhaps that's what I was seeking from a specific encounter. You know, an ultimate fix. Do people write this stuff outside of manuals, I wonder. Well, Masters and Johnson, it's okay. Nothing humanly felt, properly addressed can be far away from connections to any of us.

In any case, during that period, see, I was also taking a sex class. When I work on a problem, I tackle it head-on, American style—take a class. Do we Americans think that solves anything? Mentally speaking, I've known for a long time that I can comprehend anything and everything, given enough time to study, but actual practice—making a thing in reality yours—is field work empirically undertaken. That, I found, is what really sinks in, affecting you all the way down to the place that knows and knows it knows.

The class was actually pretty good, in Beverly Hills, don't you know, costing some bucks, of course, but I figured it would be worth it and it was. There were seven of us with stuff wrong and two female facilitators. We looked at nasty movies, educationally, of course. We read porn and were sent on outside class excursions to those toy shops in Hollywood with instructions to buy whatever tools necessary to feed our fancy, our fantasies. I bought a vibrator, orange plastic with special attachments, a black negligée, slut-looking type, and a molded plastic wanger, a dildo as long as your arm—I do exaggerate!

So I was telling my friend this stuff, in parts and pieces, and he liked the vibrator part, saying it would help me the most, he thought. He was into exercising currently and was fascinated that you could do it anywhere, that gyms weren't necessary, you could run or walk or hop around, that sort of stuff. I smiled.

He was into thanking Jesus, and I was into being grateful I guess in my own way, so I suggested a bath. Hmmm. I like them. We filled the tub and I plopped him into it, all six-odd feet of him, and washed him down like a child, though I imagined a geisha. Why not? No one here to challenge my politics, and I felt like indulging myself, him. There are glad moments, you know, and to remember them as part of your own history is one exquisite aspect of living. For me, this ritual of care has left an indelible impression. It spoke to a sense I've developed, never regretted, and that sense of being with someone without affectation, without fear, without the obligations of tomorrow, but to be exceedingly kind, really caring for today, has helped me. Empirically learned, remember?

Well, he went to sleep. I mean, a massage, great sex, intimate conversation, a hot bath, nothing else left, I'd say.

I washed three days' worth of dishes happily humming to myself, looking out the kitchen window at great woodsy scenery, wiped my hands off on a towel, kissed him goodbye, and drove home forty minutes by freeway and continued to live life.

A Tale of Flesh in Three Parts

Judy Fei Fei Weng

Part I: Ro (Flesh)

"Hi. It's me. I was wondering if you'd like to have dinner some-time this week. I'd like to . . . get to know you better." Beep.

Dinner was uneventful. She laughed too much, hands reflexively fluttering to her throat as if she were trying to hide something. She wanted him. Not sex, or comfort, or companionship. She just wanted to be held. She had a simple burning need to know what his hands would feel like around her body. She recalled the first time she saw him performing in the café. He was playing the guitar, sweat beading on his brow, eyes shut tight, lips pursed, fingers flying. Later that night, she saw him running through the park, his thick calves bulging. Would he bulge like that when she made love to him? She wanted the musician, not the man. The man was boring, vain, anal, a name dropper, and he made an irritating noise when he drank water.

After dinner, they went to his apartment for coffee. His cat hid under the bed, its traffic-light green eyes flashing steadily. His apartment was meticulous. The CD's, tapes, albums and books were all alphabetized, color-coordinated like prisms of the rainbow. His prized Ibanez stood in the corner, next to his Fender bass.

She sat on the futon with a steaming cup of coffee. He was taking a long time in the bathroom. Probably flossing, she mused. He finally came out smelling of Listerine and wearing glasses. He noticed her staring and quickly explained his contacts were bothering him.

She rose to her feet and they embraced. He put his fingers under her chin to lift her face, to kiss her, but she reached up, took his hand and then she kissed every line on his palm. He was biting her neck, her earlobes, tongue venturing into her ear. Much to his delight, she moaned, but it was because she found a tiny callus on the tip of his finger. She now understood what it was like to be a string on his guitar—to be controlled by him, to sing sad as the blues, hard as rock, soulful as gospel, sassy as jazz. He was behind her, unhooking her bra, hands cupping her breasts. An unspeakable beauty consoled her, like a chord expanding into a dimension, suspended fourth, added ninth, an eleventh, a descending bridge slipping into a chorus of music. His hands, his hands. She wanted his hands.

PART II: RO PU TUAN
(FLESH ON A PILLOW)

Neon lights from the In-and-Out Inn sign flashed into their room. She walked to the window and yanked the curtains shut. Then she inspected the bathroom and came back with a mischievous smile.

"The shower rod looks strong enough. Do you have the rope?"

———

The rod, unfortunately, wasn't as strong as it appeared—but then James was tall. When he hung from his ankle, his head kept bumping against the floor, which made it difficult for him to concentrate on his erection.

She was disappointed, so they gave up and sat on the bed naked. The motel room was curiously silent except for the "whoosh" of her exhaling her Churchill-sized Cuban cigar.

He stroked her thigh suggestively, but she remained sullen. He finally spoke: "Do you want to make . . ."

"Ssshhh," she said, then leaned over to seductively cover his mouth with her breast.

He was annoyed at her sudden shift of mood and pushed her small tit out of the way. "I was going to say . . ."

She interrupted again, "I know what you were going to say. Don't say it. Besides, you're still thinking of HER."

"NO! Not at all!" he scoffed. "What makes you think . . . dammit, I drank too much and that silly ginseng-rhino powder didn't work. Besides—I DON'T LOVE HER!"

She burst out laughing. "Oh, please! Who are you kidding? Look, can't we just fuck without all the excuses?"

He frowned. "I really hate that word. It's ugly. Can't you say . . ."

"YOUR word is uglier. It's duplicitous." She snuffed her cigar.

He shook his head. "You are irreparably crude."

She shook his limp cock and mimicked his inflections, saying, "You are sooo genteel . . ."

He tried to suppress his anger. "Well, do you want to make . . ."

"Fuck," she sneered.

"Love," he insisted.

"FUCK."

"LOVE."

"FUCK YOU."

"That's not fair."

"You're cute when you're angry."

"Bitch!"

"You want me?"

"Yes, you fucking cunt!"

With surprising speed he flipped her onto her stomach roughly and shoved his hard cock into her anus, making her scream out in pain and shock. He thrust hard, deep, clawing at her breasts, pinching her nipples. Despite the tears streaming down her face and her pleas begging for him to stop, her hands were behind her, clasping onto his hips, making him thrust deeper, her buttocks rearing until he finally shot his cum down her warm passage and smiled sheepishly. "Sorry I came so fast."

"Don't ever apologize for cumming," she said sweetly, kissing him on the cheek. As she rubbed her toe against his muscular calves, his voice deepened. "You know, I could fall in love with you."

She pulled away to look at him, eyes serious, narrowed. "Yes, you could," she said matter-of-factly.

He waited.

She nodded. "Oh. You want me to say something in response. All right. Yes, I could fall in love too, but being in love would be a distraction, which at this point in my career I couldn't afford, so I'd have to kill you."

He smiled weakly. "Couldn't you just fall out of love?"

"No."

"Hmm . . . could I move to another country?"

She sipped her Scotch thoughtfully. "I would be consumed with imaginary scenarios of you fucking beautiful, exotic women. No. I'd have to find you, and kill you."

She smiled apologetically as he rose out of bed mumbling, trying to sound calm, "Well, it was . . . interesting."

He grabbed his pants and walked into the bathroom. She called out, "Don't take the rope."

PART III: RO BU DUAN
(THE FLESH NOT BROKEN)

"*P*ositive. That's what the nurse said." As he slept that night, she fondled parts of his body, trying to decide what cuts would be prepared, marinated, or aged.

"I'm a dead man. Eat me."

3 P.M.: James was a runner so that his calves would be muscular and chewy. She would take the tubular cuts whole and cook them for eight hours immersed in water, brown sugar, anise, soy, ginger, whole peppercorns and whole cardamom. Chill the meat, slice it into paper-thin rounds, then add a piece of shiitake marinated in balsamic vinegar, roll it with minced cilantro—it'll look like confetti . . . She checked her watch and hastened to the market. He would be expecting her soon and she was always punctual.

5 P.M.: She straddled him—one hand spreading her swollen lips and the other hand guiding his engorged cock into her warm walls of flesh. They simultaneously moaned at the first thrust. She fell forward, mouth seeking mouth, tongues darting past salty fingers, hips pounding with a bone-crunching intensity. With one hand behind his head, she pulled him into a sitting position. He sucked on her left breast as she rode him silently, right hand cupping his testicles. They were tightening. He was close. His lips pulled away from her hard nipple. She slid off him and pushed him against the pillows. Taking his cock into her mouth, tongue gliding along the smooth slick surface, guiding it into the pocket of her cheek, teeth clenched, one side smooth but textured, the other side soft-giving.

It was too much for him. He felt himself start to give, his hands clutched at her back, drawing blood that splashed onto her heaving breasts as she quickly inserted his penis into her deceptively delicate orifice again. Her tight walls pumping him hard. He cried out —a deep bestial strangulated scream as he gave himself over to the long spasms of tumultuous ecstasy bursting into her with the force of a tsunami as she felt her walls breaking, sliding, dissolving, careening around sharp curves then flinging herself off the precipice of orgasm . . . After he stopped twitching, she removed the plastic garment bag from around his head, kissed his puffy purple lips, put on her apron and went to the kitchen to prepare the funeral repast.

9 p.m.: The guests started arriving. They gaily exchanged salutations—women kissing each other on the cheek, men doing the hand-shake-half-hug-thump-on-the-back. She passed around snifters of a rare liqueur made by Burmese monks. The label was handwritten in Mon-Khmer so that no one could tell when it was bottled, but T. Pendleton guessed from the level of tannin it must have been 1948. Henri L. commented on the delightful aromas wafting from the kitchen, to which Elisa L. gently chided, "Of course darling, it's James!"

It was time to eat. The soup, salad, and appetizers were all fabulous—light but substantial, an honest tribute to James's personality. The piece de résistance was astounding. Slender shavings of deep-fried cartilage sprinkled onto a terrine of liver pâté. The cartilage was a crunchy contrast to the creamy terrine. A 1987 Tokay accompanied the meal and a late harvest Riesling was served in place of dessert. Ying W. passed around Sobranie Black Russian cigarettes, and Diana W. couldn't stop giggling as everyone lit up. Then, they lifted their glasses. "To James. Thanks for dinner."

Seeds of Betrayal

Yuri Kageyama

Since our move to Japan, you have gotten to digging in the yard, the black, fungus-like earth. It's a neurotic habit. Our neighbors must wonder how many aborted babies, or stolen ones, we have buried. You have planted an avocado sapling, gladiolus bulbs. There is no order to the arrangement, as though a schizophrenic has been hard at work.

A pumpkin vine sprouts. Undoubtedly, a castaway of leftovers from our pungent kitchen sink included seeds gouged out from orange flesh. Under the lazy sun, the tentacles grow, gripping innocent stems, shadowing bushes with its huge drooping leaves.

Our Japanese neighbors clip and water their tiny lawns, plant pansies in neat, polite rows on both sides of their gate.

In our garden, the jungle stirs and spreads, all-knowing, pulsating a force so bizarre any garden keeper would turn away in shame.

"*I* can't stand it anymore. I have to tell you," he says, a scrunched up boy-look in his flushed face. "I have to tell you because I am scared. They're after me, and I need your help."

It takes a while to sink in.

For the past several months, he has been slipping out at night on his bicycle, roaming the streets, "talking to anything that moved." Most of the women ran away.

One laughed when he offered to give her a ride home. He spoke to her in his broken Japanese, she in her broken English. They walked, hand in hand, in the moonlight, a married man pushing a bicycle, and a woman, who, as it turned out, was also married.

She was flattered. She was flirting, maybe hoping to tell her husband and watch his jealousy.

They paused, and he kissed her hand, then he kissed her mouth.

She had the red painted mouth most Japanese women had, swimming listlessly in a masklike ivory face. She was skinny, waist pinched, frail shoulders caved in, perfect for draping a kimono.

She was like the others. They swore to a conformity that made them predictable and reassuring. If ankle boots were in, they all wore ankle boots. They all dutifully carried Louis Vuitton bags. They kept hemlines high, barely missing their asses, as though God had created them for a lifetime of squeaky clean prostitution.

"All this time, I was into you, too," he says.

"Did you want to have sex with them?" I ask.

"Yes," he replies, probably wishing he hadn't as soon as he said it.

After that encounter, he really couldn't stop. He kept going out, pedaling fiercely, searching for that stranger who'd lust for him at first sight. While he pedaled, the humid wind brushing against his cheek, he felt free.

Now, he believes she was a setup by the police. The word is out and they're investigating, possibly trying to pin a murder, a rape, or worse, on him.

"I may be stupid, but I'm not a rapist. I don't eat children," he says over and over.

At first, I was surprisingly calm. I had expected the worst after his introduction. He was a serial killer. He wanted a divorce. He wasn't who I thought he was all this time.

We sit in our moldy-smelling kitchen, facing each other across the table.

You didn't break any laws, I assured him. You're just imagining things. Maybe it's just the local right-wing gangsters who're peeved you've harassed their bar girls. If you feel like people are staring, well, Japanese society is small, everyone knows everyone's business. But at this point, it's all hearsay. It's not against the law to ride around in a bicycle, even at three in the morning. And if you approached women and they ran away, well, you could have been asking for directions.

He wants us to move into the bedroom and turn on the radio. He believes the house is bugged. They're listening to our conversation.

"People have been coming into our house. They have our keys. I've set up traps for them so I know. The Kanezakis, their son has been following me. They have this light shining right toward our door, every night. They're spying on me. I've gone out toward the back, and I know they're listening. They're spreading rumors about me, that I kidnap kids and molest them. You know those signs about beware of 'chikan'—that was me."

The Japanese have a word for sexual harassers, "chikan," those dirty old men who can't resist their hands on crowded trains, those men who stop their cars and offer a ride.

"Don't heed sweet words on dark streets," the signs on the telephone poles warned.

He got a sense of power out of parading around wearing shorts without underwear, believing that his phallic organ dangled in a daring exhibitionism. All the women he approached, he had lost count. He returned over and over to talk to one with dyed hair in an all-night coffee shop because she didn't act scared and he believed she was a prostitute.

Why? He doesn't know why. Perhaps if he went to a shrink, he or she would explain why. He would like to know.

Perhaps it was because too many Japanese had asked him where he worked. And he didn't have the right answers, like Mitsubishi or Toyota. If he was unemployed and just teaching English at home while taking care of the house, he might as well be a criminal, child molester, or worse.

Perhaps it just got to be too much, separating the garbage between burnable and nonburnable, putting them out on specific corners on specific days.

Tokyo streets were parodies, right off "Blade Runner." Surreal, without angst, without pathos. The salarymen with greasy hair and Armani suits all had breaths that stank of fermented rice. They would totter through train station platforms, stoop over a bench, and puke.

It was easy for him to look down upon Japanese men. But he looked down on Japanese women with a vengeance. They giggled coquettishly, served food they had cooked, waiting wide-eyed for approval. And, because he was gaijin, a foreigner, he thought he could get away with anything. They seemed so in awe of him, the casual way he dressed, his defiant mannerisms, his carefree lifestyle, his unconventional marriage.

Of course, he knows now, he was wrong. He believes arrest is imminent. Sweat breaks out on his palms. He hears helicopters. Now, I am beginning to hear them, flapping over our roof. We see dark-suited mustached men following us, swishing by on their cars, almost running us over.

We talk into the night about possible fabricated evidence, pore over the newspaper crime pages to second-guess what he is being suspected of. We shudder at those famous frame-ups in Japan, like Mr. Menda, whose death-row case turned out to be a mistake.

I can barely keep my eyes open. I can no longer add the simplest numbers. I can barely stand. Nothing is ever what you think it is.

———

The Kabuki play was directed by and starred Ennosuke Ichikawa III. Like most Kabuki plays, it made no pretense at realism. But it made a great story.

A loving young couple gets separated when the man is tricked into borrowing money and ends up killing the villain in a fit of rage. The man's life is spared, but he is exiled. The man and his beautiful wife send each other long letters on rice-paper scrolls.

Many, many years later, he returns, a hobbling old man. He is to meet his wife at their old home at a certain time. He shows up early. So does she. They both look at the cherry tree they had planted years ago, a mere twig of a tree now heavy with blossoms. They write poems on pieces of paper and hang them from the tree.

The audience laughs because the two keep bowing to each other but don't recognize each other—until the old man starts rubbing his nose, a habit he had since his youth.

"Oh, it is you," she cries out.

The audience fights back tears.

We are sitting side by side, staring at the painted faces. His hand reaches over my shoulder, tugging it.

"We'll be just like that when we get older," he whispers into my ear.

Was it Shuntaro Tanikawa who observed that married couples have the most perverse sex? It's the comfort of knowing, years of knowing, even the exact words you mumble in your sleep.

You know the precise spots in my body that scream for your reptile tongue, your strong callused fingers, your penis. You knead with knowing hands the pale doughy folds of my stomach that still remember, with fading translucent stretch marks, housing your fetus.

We know what to do. How to exactly time our moves, a ritual numbing in its pleasurable sameness. I know how you prefer your penis licked, where it must lodge in the throat, while I slither my tongue busily, till you moan like a woman. How my nipples must brush against your thighs as I suck, till you arch your back or hold my head still to thrust.

In your weathered age, you know how to use the wooden phallic instrument, shaking it wildly in time to frantic agitation, so that by the time your penis enters, my brain has soared, seeping, my nipples are erect, reaching, my legs are spread wide, not caring how those less knowing may be aghast at such whorish joy.

"I just want you to come a lot," you whisper. "I love you. Come, come."

And there's no time, then or later, to ask why you believe this so passionately, or whether this is love or a delusion of trapped dependence, why it seems more a ritual, as though you are my partner, not in life, but in this moment.

He would masturbate, fantasizing about the Japanese women.

The one woman he was genuinely attracted to was a religion student. He had coffee with her once.

"But I was real cool," he explained.

She was petite and had chiseled features. More important, she was smarter than the rest.

But, now, he thinks she was a setup, too. She had been too aggressive, talking about J. D. Salinger and claiming to be a Jimi Hendrix fan. Obviously, the police had done their homework. But when he'd mention a tune or an album title, he drew only blank stares. Her paper in English on *Catcher in the Rye* made no sense.

For a while, he had gladly answered her phone calls. "Hello, Yumiko," he would say with a cheerful ring in his voice. They all had those names that ended in "ko," which means "child." He was beginning to giggle, like them.

Even after he grew to cowering in the house, worrying about the police, we got letters from the women.

"She is worried about you. Please telephone my friend," one

woman wrote in round ink handwriting. "Why do you stop teaching English? I enjoy speaking English."

*O*ur bedtime ritual always crescendos in violence. There is no whip, no dripping candle, no fists, no gun, no calls to the police. One's motive is to hurt, while the other's is to endure. Till the hurting and the enduring can't last. The one intent on hurting is spent. The enduring one is silent, having begged too long for forgiveness.

You remember those times we talked about a separation.

You held a hand over your face, muttering, "You're going to suck on some other guy's dick." Yet, other times, you said you enjoyed imagining my sleeping with someone else. You would play voyeur, you said, peeking through the keyhole.

When I imagined a separation, my vagina would get wet. After you had ejaculated, I would beg you to use your fingers so that I would know that you were always there.

I lie awake, my body blending into the cold sheets, floating weightless. The darkness stretches, a liquid universe where gnarled octopi and swaying anemones dwell.

I squeeze my legs, letting my vagina tighten against nothing, stirring like an ember into a warm spot inside of me, a numbness trickling up my crotch until it fills my womb with blood and joy. My hairs stretch, slithering through follicles, creatures with their own lives planted by an unknown hand.

I pull on my breasts, pinching my nipples, and imagine a love that never fails.

from

Come

DAVID HENRY HWANG AND PRINCE

Since I first heard the music of the artist formerly known as Prince, I have admired him as the only genius currently working in pop music. In 1989 I heard he had come to see M. Butterfly. *In 1993, after my bound-for-Broadway comedy* Face Value *closed in previews, I got two phone calls, first from Prince's office, then from the Symbol himself.*

A month later we met in a New York hotel room. He gave me a cassette of new songs. Then he told me a story about the relationship between a rock star and a fan, an intense erotic affair conducted through letters, spinning off into exercises of fantasy and dominance. Sex between lovers who never met in the flesh.

From this premise I wrote the libretto for a musical, Come, *which incorporates the songs on his cassette. The first fruit of our collaboration to reach the public was the song "Solo," on Prince's 1994 album,* Come. *This is our second exposure. More to Come*

D.H.H.

(SETTING: ACTION FUNCTIONS ON TWO LEVELS, OFTEN SIMULTANEOUSLY: ONSTAGE: SETS COME ON AND OFF VIA A REVOLVING TURNTABLE. ABOVE THE STAGE HANGS A HI-DEF VIDEO MONITOR, WHICH SERVES OUR STORY BY VISUALLY ILLUSTRATING THE VIRTUAL REALITIES OUR ONSTAGE PERFORMERS WILL ENTER.)

(ONSTAGE: ORLANDO CARRIES A VIDEO-SPHERE UPSTAGE TOWARD A COMPUTER, SLIPS ON VIRTUAL REALITY EQUIPMENT. BEHIND A DOWNSTAGE SCRIM, THE SILHOUETTE OF MARIE-ANNE SITS AT HER COMPUTER.)

(THE MONITOR TAKES ON ORLANDO'S REALITY: THE FACES OF DIFFERENT WOMEN, ONE MORPHING INTO ANOTHER, ALL SPEAKING IN HER VOICE.)

MARIE-ANNE (on monitor): I spend a lot of time alone, you see. I read. I imagine. I have a very good imagination. So fine, in fact, that I've always believed it to be my secret treasure, to be hidden and protected from the world outside.

ORLANDO: You think pretty highly of yourself.

MARIE-ANNE: Maybe you're thinking I'm arrogant. All I can say is, I can be so bold because, in this form, it's only our minds that are meeting. Believe me, were I with you in person right now, I would go completely tongue-tied, I'd be afraid to show my face.

ORLANDO: How come? What's wrong with it?

MARIE-ANNE: Don't be rude. Many people have a secret self they shield from the eyes of others. I think I do, too. But it's always frightened me, I've been so afraid of my dirty mind . . . that I've tried to bury it away, to live in ignorance. Yet every morning, when I awaken from my dreams and feel my heart beating . . . beating all through my body . . . I know there's another girl . . . deep inside me.

(ONSTAGE: UNDERSCORING MOVES TOWARD A MORE BUMP-AND-GRIND GROOVE. ON THE MONITOR, SCENE DISSOLVES TO A LUSH GARDEN. WE SEE THE *BACK* OF A NAKED WOMAN APPROACHING A FRUIT TREE. *NOTE:* THE IMAGES OF EDEN AND LATER OF BABYLON SHOULD NOT BE REALISTIC. THEY MIGHT LOOK LIKE KLIMT OR PRE-RAPHAELITE PAINTINGS COME TO LIFE.)

MARIE-ANNE: You, you're the Serpent who crept into my garden. You make me brave . . . to find the girl in my dreams . . . and expose her to you.

(MONITOR: ON A *SNAKE*, WRITHING ABOUT THE FRUIT TREE.)

MARIE-ANNE: I want to pluck the fruit of knowledge from my tree . . . and take a long, luscious bite.

(MONITOR: ON A DROP OF FRUIT JUICE, AS IT RUNS FROM A WOMAN'S FULL LOWER LIP, DOWN HER CHIN, BETWEEN HER BOSOMS, DOWNWARD.)

MARIE-ANNE: Would you like to taste my dreams?

(ONSTAGE, THE SILHOUETTE OF MARIE-ANNE RISES TO HER FEET, STRETCHES LANGUOROUSLY; STILL UPSTAGE OF SCRIM, THE SHADOWS OF FLATS AND DANCERS ENTER TO POPULATE A STREET SCENE.)
(MONITOR: DISSOLVE FROM FRUIT JUICE TO ORLANDO, TRANSPORTED TO THE STREETS OF A MYTHICAL BABYLON, DOWN WHICH HE WALKS AT NIGHT.)

MARIE-ANNE: I was born a princess in the ancient empire of Babylon. It's now called Iraq and has become a very sad place. But in my day, all the wonders of the world were encompassed within our borders and the Hanging Gardens brought pilgrims from the farthest corners of the globe to fall to their knees in my own backyard. I would look down at night, from the secret window in my bedroom wall, and spy lovers meeting secretly beneath the brushing vines, and I would note their many positions and how each altered the look on their faces.

(ONSTAGE: UPSTAGE OF THE SCRIM, SHADOWS JOIN TOGETHER IN VARIOUS SEXUAL ARRANGEMENTS, STRAIGHT AND GAY AND GROUP. MARIE-ANNE WATCHES FROM A PERCH ABOVE.)

(MONITOR: ORLANDO SPIES A GARDEN POPULATED WITH DEEPLY SHADOWED FIGURES WRITHING IN VARIOUS UNIONS. CLOSE-UPS ON RANDOM CURVES, MOUTHS, FINGERS ON FLESH, THIGHS SLAPPING AGAINST ONE ANOTHER.)

MARIE-ANNE: It became a magnificent hunt, with my eyes the deadly arrows. Who would I spot tonight, how much of themselves would they reveal to me? I was only fifteen years old, but my mind was filled with the memories of a precious harlot.

(MONITOR: ORLANDO NOW APPEARS IN THE GARDEN, BUT HIS IMAGE ON-SCREEN IS THAT OF A BABYLONIAN NOBLEMAN, HOLDING THE HAND OF A YOUNG GIRL.)

MARIE-ANNE: One night, a well-dressed man came into the garden and parked himself on the stone bench directly beneath my secret window. He had in his arms a girl from the streets, a piece of trash, really, little more than a beggar.

(ONSTAGE: UPSTAGE OF THE SCRIM, THE SHADOW OF A MAN RESEMBLING ORLANDO'S MONITOR IMAGE ENTERS WITH A GIRL. HIS MOVEMENTS ARE SYNCHED TO MATCH PERFECTLY THOSE OF ORLANDO ONSCREEN.)

MAN: (on monitor, to girl) Precious . . . like a jewel . . . purity . . . without blemish . . . the pride of the kingdom . . .

(MONITOR: DURING THE FOLLOWING SPEECH, CUT BETWEEN A MONTAGE OF IMAGES AND IMPRESSIONS ONE EXPERIENCES DURING THE ACT OF LOVE AND THE EYES OF A YOUNG GIRL, WATCHING THROUGH A CRACK IN A WALL.)

MARIE-ANNE: He touched her so gently, with so much care, pausing to bless every inch of her flesh, this thing from the gutter, that from above, it looked almost like love. And as I watched them, my hips started to tremble uncontrollably, sending shock waves out the soles of my feet, my fingertips, between my parched and burning lips. My breathing . . . was no longer my own . . . I was possessed . . . by his movement . . . in her unworthy body. (pause) As their animal noises . . . assaulted my white-hot ears . . . I felt my insides exploding. At that moment, I knew my world was disappearing forever. I knew . . . that I was dying.

(ONSTAGE: UPSTAGE OF SCRIM, LIGHTS GO OUT ON THE LOVE-MAKING COUPLE, AS MARIE-ANNE COLLAPSES. OTHER LOVERS SPLIT UP.)

(MONITOR: ORLANDO (AS THE BABYLONIAN MAN) STARES AT THE HORIZON AS THE SUN RISES AND SETS ONCE MORE OVER THE KINGDOM.)

MARIE-ANNE: I slept all through the next day. By the time I awoke, I knew I'd been right—I *had* died the night before. So I slipped on my robe—

(ONSTAGE: HER SHADOW SLIPS ON A TRANSPARENT GOWN.)

MARIE-ANNE: And went out into the garden. And every night, from that day onward, I have returned to my garden.

(ONSTAGE: DANCERS OF BOTH SEXES NOW GATHER AROUND HER, FONDLING HER, SUCKLING HER, MOUNTING HER IN VARIOUS POSITIONS.)

(MONITOR: CLOSE-UPS ON DIFFERENT HANDS AND LIPS TOUCHING DIFFERENT PARTS OF HER BODY.)

MARIE-ANNE: Where I float like an angel, beneath the hanging vines, now knowing, seeing, feeling all things, meeting all the needs of hungry mortals. And as I minister to the beings of flesh, I keep always one eye peeled, in hope that I will one day see that man again, who ravished the filthy slave girl with such emotion. (pause) And he will say to me, "Princess?" And I will reply, "Yes, father."

And he will answer, "Come, sit with me on the stone bench, my dear Jezebel."

(ONSTAGE AND ONSCREEN: MUSIC AND LIGHTS FADE SLOWLY ON THE IMAGE OF MARIE-ANNE, RAVISHED BY A LARGE GROUP OF STRANGERS. FADE DOWN TO A SINGLE SPOT ON THE LIVE ORLANDO'S FACE AS HE SLOWLY REMOVES THE VIRTUAL REALITY SHADES.)

Chui Chai

S. P. Somtow

*T*he living dead are not as you imagine them. There are no dangling innards, no dripping slime. They carry their guts and gore inside them, as do you and I. In the right light they can be beautiful, as when they stand in a doorway caught between cross-shafts of contrasting neon. Fueled by the right fantasy, they become indistinguishable from us. Listen. I know. I've touched them.

In the eighties I used to go to Bangkok a lot. The brokerage I worked for had a lot of business there, some of it shady, some not. The flight of money from Hong Kong had begun, and our company, vulture that it was, was staking out its share of the loot. Bangkok was booming like there was no tomorrow. It made Los Angeles seem like Peoria. It was wild and fast and frantic and frustrating. It had temples and buildings shaped like giant robots. Its skyline was a cross between Shangri-La and Manhattan. For a dapper yuppie executive like me there were always meetings to be taken, faxes to fax, traffic to be sat in, credit cards to burn. There was also sex.

There was Patpong.

I was addicted. Days, after hours of high-level talks and poring over papers and banquets that lasted from the close of business until midnight, I stalked the crammed alleys of Patpong. The night smelled of sewage and jasmine. The heat seeped into everything. Each step I took was colored by a different neon sign. From half-open nightclub doorways buttocks bounced to jaunty soulless synthrock. Everything was for sale: the women, the boys, the pirated software, the fake Rolexes. Everything sweated. I stalked the streets and sometimes at random took an entrance, took in a live show, women propelling Ping-Pong balls from their pussies, boys buttfucking on motorbikes. I was addicted. There were other entrances where I sat in waiting rooms, watched women with numbers around their necks through the one-way glass, soft, slender brown women. Picked a number. Fingered the American-made condoms in my pocket. Never buy the local ones, brother; they leak like a sieve.

I was addicted. I didn't know what I was looking for. But I knew it wasn't something you could find in Encino. I was a knight on a quest, but I didn't know that to find the holy grail is the worst thing that can possibly happen.

I first got a glimpse of the grail at Club Pagoda, which was near my hotel and which is where we often liked to take our clients. The club was on the very edge of Patpong, but it was respectable—the kind of place the serves up a plastic imitation of *The King and I,* which is, of course, a plastic imitation of life in ancient Siam . . . artifice imitating artifice, you see. Waiters crawled around in mediaeval uniforms, the guests sat on the floor, except there was a well under the table to accommodate the dangling legs of lumbering white people. The floor show was eminently sober . . . it was all classical Thai dances, women wearing those pagoda-shaped hats moving with painstaking grace and slowness to a tinkling, alien music. A good place to interview prospective grant recipients, because it tended to make them very nervous.

Dr. Frances Stone wasn't at all nervous, though. She was already there when I arrived. She was preoccupied with picking the peanuts out of her *gaeng massaman* and arranging them over her rice plate in such a way that they looked like little eyes, a nose, and a mouth.

"You like to play with your food?" I said, taking my shoes off at the edge of our private booth and sliding my legs under the table across from her.

"No," she said, "I just prefer them crushed rather than whole. The peanuts, I mean. You must be Mr. Leibowitz."

"Russell."

"The man I'm supposed to charm out of a few million dollars." She was doing a sort of coquettish pout, not really the sort of thing I expected from someone in medical research. Her face was ravaged, but the way she smiled kindled the memory of youthful beauty. I wondered what had happened to change her so much; according to her dossier, she was only in her mid-forties.

"Mostly we're in town to take," I said, "not to give. R and D is not one of our strengths. You might want to go to Hoechst or Berli Jucker, Frances."

"But Russell . . ." She had not touched her curry, but the peanuts on the rice were now formed into a perfect human face, with a few strands of sauce for hair. "This is not exactly R and D. This is a discovery that's been around for almost a century and a half. My great-grandfather's paper—"

"For which he was booted out of the Austrian Academy? Yes, my dossier is pretty thorough, Dr. Stone; I know all about how he fled to America and changed his name."

She smiled. "And my dossier on you, Mr. Leibowitz, is pretty thorough too," she said, as she began removing a number of compromising photographs from her purse.

A gong sounded to announce the next dance. It was a solo. Fog roiled across the stage, and from it a woman emerged. Her clothes glittered with crystal beadwork, but her eyes outshone the yards of cubic zirconia. She looked at me and I felt the pangs of the addiction. She smiled and her lips seemed to glisten with lubricious moisture.

"You like what you see," Frances said softly.

"I—"

"The dance is called Chui Chai, the dance of transformation. In every Thai classical drama, there are transformations—a woman transforming herself into a rose, a spirit transforming itself into a human. After the character's metamorphosis, he performs a Chui Chai dance, exulting in the completeness and beauty of his transformed self."

I wasn't interested, but for some reason she insisted on giving me the entire story behind the dance. "This particular Chui Chai is called Chui Chai Benjakai . . . the demoness Benjakai has been dispatched by the demon king, Thotsakanth, to seduce the hero Rama. Disguised as the beautiful Sita, she will float down the river toward Rama's camp, trying to convince him that his beloved has died . . . only when she is placed on a funeral pyre, woken from her death trance by the flames, will she take on her demonic shape once more and fly away toward the dark kingdom of Lanka. But you're not listening."

How could I listen? She was the kind of woman that existed only in dreams, in poems. Slowly she moved against the tawdry backdrop, a faded painting of a palace with pointed eaves. Her feet barely touched the floor. Her arms undulated. And always her eyes held me. As though she were looking at me alone. Thai women can do things with their eyes that no other women can do. Their eyes have a secret language.

"Why are you looking at her so much?" said Frances. "She's just a Patpong bar girl . . . she moonlights here . . . classics in the evening, pussy after midnight."

"You know her?" I said.

"I have had some . . . dealings with her."

"Just what is it that you're doing research into, Dr. Stone?"

"The boundary between life and death," she said. She pointed to the photographs. Next to them was a contract, an R and D grant agreement of some kind. The print was blurry. "Oh, don't worry, it's only a couple of million dollars . . . your company won't even miss it . . . and you'll own the greatest secret of all . . . the tree of life and death . . . the apples of Eve. Besides, I know your price, and I can meet it." And she looked at the dancing girl. "Her name is Keo. I don't mind procuring if it's in the name of science."

Suddenly I realized that Dr. Stone and I were the only customers in the Club Pagoda. Somehow I had been set up.

The woman continued to dance, faster now, her hands sweeping through the air in mysterious gestures. She never stopped looking at me. She *was* the character she was playing, seductive and diabolical. There was darkness in every look, every hand movement. I downed the rest of my Kloster lager and beckoned for another. An erection strained against my pants.

The dance ended and she prostrated herself before the audience of two, pressing her palms together in a graceful *wai*. Her eyes downcast, she left the stage. I had signed the grant papers without even knowing it.

Dr. Stone said, "On your way to the upstairs toilet, take the second door on the left. She'll be waiting for you."

I drank another beer, and when I looked up, she was gone. She hadn't eaten one bite. But the food on her plate had been sculpted into the face of a beautiful woman. It was so lifelike that . . . but no. It wasn't alive. It wasn't breathing.

She was still in her dancing clothes when I went in. A little girl was carefully taking out the stitches with a seamripper. There was a pile of garments on the floor. In the glare of a naked bulb, the vestments of the goddess had little glamor. "They no have buttons on classical dance clothes," she said. "They just sew us into them. Cannot go pipi!" She giggled.

The little girl scooped up the pile and slipped away.

"You're . . . very beautiful," I said. "I don't understand why . . . I mean, why you *need* to . . ."

"I have problem," she said. "Expensive problem. Dr. Stone no tell you?"

"No." Her hands were coyly clasped across her bosom. Gently I pried them away.

"You want I dance for you?"

"Dance," I said. She was naked. The way she smelled was different from other women. It was like crushed flowers. Maybe a hint of decay in them. She shook her hair and it coiled across her breasts like a nest of black serpents. When I'd seen her on stage I'd been entertaining some kind of rape fantasy about her, but now I wanted to string it out for as long as I could. God, she was driving me mad.

"I see big emptiness inside you. Come to me. I fill you. We both empty people. Need filling up."

I started to protest. But I knew she had seen me for what I was. I had money coming out my ass, but I was one fucked-up yuppie. That was the root of my addiction.

Again she danced the dance of transforming, this time for me alone. Really for me alone. I mean, all the girls in Patpong have this way of making you think they love you. It's what gets you addicted. It's the only street in the world where you *can* buy love. But that's not how she was. When she touched me it was as though she reached out to me across an invisible barrier, an unbreachable gulf. Even when I entered her she was untouchable. We were from different worlds and neither of us ever left our private hells.

Not that there wasn't passion. She knew every position in the book. She knew them backward and forward. She kept me there all night, and each act seemed as though it been freshly invented for the two of us. It was the last time I came that I felt I had glimpsed the grail. Her eyes, staring up into the naked bulb, brimmed with some remembered sadness. I loved her with all my might. Then I was seized with terror. She was a demon. Yellow-eyed, dragon-clawed. She was me, she was my insatiable hunger. I was fucking my own addiction. I think I sobbed. I accused her of lacing my drink with hallucinogens. I cried myself to sleep and then she left me.

I didn't notice the lumpy mattress or the peeling walls or the way the light bulb jiggled to the music from downstairs. I didn't notice the cockroaches.

I didn't notice until morning that I had forgotten to use my condoms.

It was a productive trip, but I didn't go back to Thailand for another two years. I was promoted off the traveling circuit, moved from Encino to Beverly Hills, got myself a newer, late-model wife, packed my kids off to a Swiss boarding school. I also found a new therapist and a new support group. I smothered the addiction in new addictions. My old therapist had been a strict Freudian. He'd tried to root out the cause from some childhood trauma—molestation, potty training, Oedipal games—he'd never been able to find anything. I'm good at blocking out memories. To the best of my knowledge, I popped into being around age eight or nine. My parents were dead, but I had a trust fund.

My best friends in the support group were Janine, who'd had eight husbands, and Mike, a transvestite with a spectacular 'fro. The clinic was in Malibu, so we could do the beach in between bouts of tearing ourselves apart. One day Thailand came up.

Mike said, "I knew this woman in Thailand. I had fun in Thailand, you know? R and R. Lot of transvestites there, hon. I'm not a fag; I just like lingerie. I met this girl." He rarely stuck to the point because he was always stoned. Our therapist, Glen, had passed out in the redwood tub. The beach was deserted. "I knew this girl in Thailand, a dancer. She would change when she danced.

I mean *change.* You shoulda seen her skin. Translucent. And she smelled different. Smelled of strange drugs."

You know, I started shaking when he said that, because I'd tried not to think of her all this time even though she came to me in dreams. Even before I'd start to dream, when I'd just closed my eyes, I'd hear the hollow tinkle of marimbas and see her eyes floating in the darkness.

"Sounds familiar," I said.

"Nah. There was nobody like this girl, hon, nobody. She danced in a classical dance show *and* she worked the whorehouses . . . had a day job too, working for a nutty professor woman . . . honky woman, withered face, glasses. Some kind of doctor, I think. Sleazy office in Patpong, gave the girls free VD drugs."

"Dr. Frances Stone." Was the company paying for a free VD clinic? What about the research into the secrets of the universe?

"Hey, how'd you know her name?"

"Did you have sex with her?" Suddenly I was trembling with rage. I don't know why. I mean, I knew what she did for a living.

"Did you?" Mike said. He was all nervous. He inched away from me, rolling a joint with one hand and scootching along the redwood deck with the other.

"I asked first!" I shouted, thinking, Jesus, I sound like a ten-year-old kid.

"Of *course* not! She had problems, all right? Expensive problems. But she was beautiful, mm-mm, good enough to eat."

I looked wildly around. Mr. Therapist was still dozing—fabulous way to earn a thousand bucks an hour—and the others had broken up into little groups. Janine was sort of listening, but she was more interested in getting her suntan lotion on evenly.

"I want to go back," I said. "I want to see Keo again."

"Totally, like, bullshit," she said, sidling up to me. "You're just, like, externalizing the interior hurt onto a fantasy object. Like, you need to be in touch with your child, know what I mean?"

"You're getting your support groups muddled up, hon," Mike said edgily.

"Hey, Russ, instead of, like, projecting on some past-forgettable female two years back and ten thousand miles away, why don't you, like, fixate on someone a little closer to home? I mean, I've been *looking* at you. I only joined this support group 'cause, like, support groups are the only place you can find like *sensitive* guys."

"Janine, I'm married."

"So let's have an affair."

I liked the idea. My marriage to Trisha had mostly been a joke; I'd needed a fresh ornament for cocktail parties and openings; she needed security. We hadn't had much sex; how could we? I was hooked on memory. Perhaps this woman would cure me. And I wanted to be cured so badly because Mike's story had jolted me out of the fantasy that Keo had existed only for me.

By now it was the nineties, so Janine insisted on a blood test before we did anything. I tested positive. I was scared shitless. Because the only time I'd ever been so careless as to forget to use a condom was . . . that night. And we'd done everything. Plumbed every orifice. Shared every fluid.

It had been a dance of transformation, all right.

I had nothing to lose. I divorced my wife and sent my kids to an even more expensive school in Connecticut. I was feeling fine. Maybe I'd never come down with anything. I read all the books and articles about it. I didn't tell anyone. I packed a couple of suits and some casual clothes and a supply of bootleg AZT. I was feeling fine. Fine, I told myself. Fine.

I took the next flight to Bangkok.

The company was surprised to see me, but I was such a big executive by now they assumed I was doing some kind of internal troubleshooting. They put me up at the Oriental. They gave me a 10,000 baht per diem. In Bangkok you can buy a lot for four hundred bucks. I told them to leave me alone. The investigation didn't concern them. They didn't know what I was investigating, so they feared the worst.

I went to Silom Road, where Club Pagoda had stood. It was gone. In its stead stood a brand-new McDonald's and an airline ticket office. Perhaps Keo was already dead. Wasn't that what I had smelled on her? The odor of crushed flowers, wilting . . . the smell of coming death? And the passion with which she had made love. I understood it now. It was the passion of the damned. She had reached out to me from a place between life and death. She had sucked the life from me and given me the virus as a gift of love.

I strolled through Patpong. Hustlers tugged at my elbows. Fake Rolexes were flashed in my face. It was useless to ask for Keo. There are a million women named Keo. Keo means jewel. It also means glass. In Thai there are many words that are used indiscriminately for reality and artifice. I didn't have a photograph, and Keo's beauty was hard to describe. And every girl in Patpong is beautiful. Every night, parading before me in the neon labyrinth, a thousand pairs of lips and eyes, sensuous and infinitely giving. The wrong lips, the wrong eyes.

There are only a few city blocks in Patpong, but to trudge up and down them in the searing heat, questioning, observing every face for a trace of the remembered grail . . . it can age you. I stopped shaving and took recreational drugs. What did it matter anyway?

But I was still fine; I wasn't coming down with anything.

I was fine. Fine!

And then, one day, while paying for a Big Mac, I saw her hands. I was looking down at the counter counting out the money. I heard the computer beep of the cash register and then I saw them: proffering the hamburger in both hands, palms up, like an offering to the gods. The fingers arched upward, just so, with delicacy and hidden strength. God, I knew those hands. Their delicacy as they skimmed my shoulder blades, as they glided across my testicles just a hair's breadth away from touching. Their strength when she balled up her fist and shoved it into my rectum. Jesus, we'd done everything that night. I dropped my wallet on the counter, I seized those hands and gripped them, burger and all, and I felt the familiar response. Oh, God, I ached.

"Mister, you want a blowjob?"

It wasn't her voice. I looked up. It wasn't even a woman.

I looked back down at the hands. I looked up at the face. They didn't even belong together. It was a pockmarked boy and when he talked to me he stared off into space. There was no relation between the vacuity of his expression and the passion with which those hands caressed my hands.

"I don't like to do such thing," he said, "but I'm a poor college student and I needing money. So you can come back after five P.M. You not be disappointed."

The fingers kneaded my wrists with the familiarity of one who has touched every part of your body, who has memorized the varicose veins in your left leg and the mole on your right testicle.

It was obscene. I wrenched my own hands free. I barely remembered to retrieve my wallet before I ran out into the street.

I had been trying to find Dr. Frances Stone since I arrived, looking through the files at the corporate headquarters, screaming at secretaries. Although the corporation had funded Dr. Stone's project, the records seemed to have been spirited away.

At last I realized that that was the wrong way to go about it. I remembered what Mike had told me, so the day after the encounter with Keo's hands, I was back in Patpong, asking around for a good VD clinic. The most highly regarded one of all turned out to be at the corner of Patpong and Soi Cowboy, above a store that sold pirated software and videotapes.

I walked up a steep staircase into a tiny room without windows, with a ceiling fan moving the same sweaty air around and around. A receptionist smiled at me. Her eyes had the same vacuity that the boy at McDonald's had possessed. I sat in an unraveling rattan chair and waited, and Dr. Stone summoned me into her office.

"You've done something with her," I said.

"Yes." She was shuffling a stack of papers. She had a window; she had an air conditioner blasting away in the direction of all the computers. I was still drenched with sweat.

The phone rang and she had a brief conversation in Thai that I couldn't catch. "You're angry, of course," she said, putting down the phone. "But it was better than nothing. Better than the cold emptiness of the earth. And she had nothing to lose."

"She was dying of AIDS! And now *I* have it!" It was the first time I'd allowed the word to cross my lips. "You *killed* me!"

Frances laughed. "My," she said, "aren't we being a little melo-dramatic? You have the virus, but you haven't actually come down with anything."

"I'm fine. Fine."

"Well, why don't you sit down. I'll order up some food. We'll talk."

She had really gone native. In Thailand it's rude to talk busi-ness without ordering up food. Sullenly I sat down while she opened a window and yelled out an order to one of the street vendors.

"To be honest, Mr. Leibowitz," she said, "we really could use another grant. We had to spend *so* much of the last one on cloak-and-dagger nonsense, security, bribes, and so on; so little could be spared for research itself . . . I mean, look around you . . . I'm not exactly wasting money on luxurious office space, am I?"

"I saw her hands."

"Very effective, wasn't it?" The food arrived. It was some kind of noodle thing wrapped in banana leaves and groaning from the weight of chili peppers. She did not eat; instead, she amused her-self by rearranging the peppers in the shape of . . . "The hands, I mean. Beautiful as ever. Vibrant. Sensual. My first break-through."

I started shaking again. I'd read about Dr. Stone's great-grand-father and his graverobbing experiments. Jigsaw corpses brought to life with bolts of lightning. Not life. A simulacrum of life. Could this have happened to Keo? But she was dying. Perhaps it was better than nothing. Perhaps . . .

"Anyhow. I was hoping you'd arrive soon, Mr. Leibowitz. Be-cause we've made up another grant proposal. I have the papers here. I know that you've become so important now that your signature alone will suffice to bring us ten times the amount you authorized two years ago."

"I want to see her."

"Would you like to dance with her? Would you like to see her in the Chui Chai one more time?"

She led me down a different stairwell. Many flights. I was sure we were below ground level. I knew we were getting nearer to Keo, because there was a hint of that rotting flower fragrance in the air. We descended. There was an unnatural chill.

And then, at last, we reached the laboratory. No shambling Igors or bubbling retorts. Just a clean, well-lit basement room. Cold, like the vault of a morgue. Walls of white tile; ceiling of stucco; fluorescent lamps; the pervasive smell of the not-quite-dead.

Perspex tanks lined the walls. They were full of fluid and body parts. Arms and legs floating past me. Torsos twirled. A woman's breast peered from between a child's thighs. In another tank, hu-man hearts swirled, each neatly severed at the aorta. There was a tank of eyes. Another of genitalia. A necklace of tongues hung suspended in a third. A mass of intestines writhed in a fourth. Computers drew intricate charts on a bank of monitors. Oscillo-scopes beeped. A pet gibbon was chained to a post topped by a human skull. There was something so outlandishly antiseptic about this spectacle that I couldn't feel the horror.

"I'm sorry about the décor, Russell, but you see, we've had to forgo the usual decoration allowance." The one attempt at dressing up the place was a frayed poster of *Young Frankenstein* tacked to the far wall. "Please don't be upset at all the body parts," she added. "It's all very macabre, but one gets inured to it in med school; if you feel like losing your lunch, there's a small restroom on your left . . . yes, between the eyes and the tongues." I did not feel sick. I was feeling . . . excited. It was the odor. I knew I was getting closer to Keo.

She unlocked another door. We stepped into an inner room.

Keo was there. A cloth was draped over her, but seeing her face after all these years made my heart almost stop beating. The eyes. The parted lips. The hair, streaming upward toward a source of blue light . . . although I felt no wind in the room. "It is an electron wind," said Dr. Stone. "No more waiting for the monsoon lightning. We can get more power from a wall socket than Great-grandfather Victor could ever dream of stealing from the sky."

And she laughed the laughter of mad scientists.

I saw the boy from McDonald's sitting in a chair. The hands reached out toward me. There were electrodes fastened to his temples. He was naked now, and I saw the scars where the hands had been joined at the wrists to someone else's arms. I saw a woman with Keo's breasts, wired to a pillar of glass, straining, heaving while jags of blue lightning danced about her bonds. I saw her vagina stitched onto the pubis of a dwarf, who lay twitching at the foot of the pillar. Her feet were fastened to the body of a five-year-old boy, transforming their grace to ungainliness as he stomped in circles around the pillar.

"Jigsaw people!" I said.

"Of course!" said Dr. Stone. "Do you think I would be so foolish as to bring back people whole? Do you not realize what the

consequences would be? The legal redefinition of life and death
. . . wills declared void, humans made subservient to walking
corpses . . . I'm a scientist, not a philosopher."

"But who are they now?"

"They were nobody before. Street kids. Prostitutes. They were
dying, Mr. Leibowitz, dying! They were glad to will their bodies to
me. And now they're more than human. They're many persons in
many bodies. A gestalt. I can shuffle them and put them back
together, oh, so many different ways . . . and the beautiful Keo.
Oh, she wept when she came to me. When she found out she had
given you the virus. She loved you. You were the last person she
ever loved. I saved her for you. She's been sleeping here, waiting to
dance for you, since the day she died. Oh, let us not say *died.* The
day she . . . she . . . I am no poet, Mr. Leibowitz. Just a scientist."

I didn't want to listen to her. All I could see was Keo's face. It
all came back to me. Everything we had done. I wanted to relive it.
I didn't care if she was dead or undead. I wanted to seize the grail
and clutch it in my hands and own it.

Frances threw a switch. The music started. The shrilling of the
pinai, the pounding of the *taphon,* the tinkling of marimbas and
xylophones rang in the Chui Chai music. Then she slipped away
unobtrusively. I heard a key turn in a lock. She had left the grant
contract lying on the floor. I was alone with all the parts of the
woman I'd loved. Slowly I walked toward the draped head. The
electron wind surged; the cold blue light intensified. Her eyes
opened. Her lips moved as though discovering speech for the first
time . . .

"Rus . . . sell."

On the pizza-faced boy, the hands stirred of their own accord.
He turned his head from side to side and the hands groped the air,
straining to touch my face. Keo's lips were dry. I put my arms
around the drape-shrouded body and kissed the dead mouth. I
could feel my hair stand on end.

"I see big emptiness inside you. Come to me. I fill you. We both empty people. Need filling up."

"Yes. Jesus, yes."

I hugged her to me. What I embraced was cold and prickly. I whisked away the drape. There was no body. Only a framework of wires and transistors and circuit boards and tubes that fed flasks of flaming reagents.

"I dance for you now."

I turned. The hands of the McDonald's boy twisted into graceful patterns. The feet of the child moved in syncopation to the music, dragging the rest of the body with them. The breasts of the chained woman stood firm, waiting for my touch. The music welled up. A contralto voice spun plaintive melismas over the interlocking rhythms of wood and metal. I kissed her. I kissed that severed head and lent my warmth to the cold tongue, awakened passion in her. I kissed her. I could hear chains breaking and wires slithering along the floor tiles. There were hands pressed into my spine, rubbing my neck, unfastening my belt. A breast touched my left buttock and a foot trod lightly on my right. I didn't care that these parts were attached to other bodies. They were hers. She was loving me all over. The dwarf that wore her pudenda was climbing up my leg. Every part of her was in love with me. Oh, she danced. We danced together. I was the epicenter of their passion. We were empty people but now we drank our fill. Oh, God, we danced. Oh, it was a grave music, but it contented us.

And I signed everything, even the codicil.

Today I am in the AIDS ward of a Beverly Hills hospital. I don't have long to wait. Soon the codicil will come into effect, and my body will be preserved in liquid nitrogen and shipped to Patpong.

The nurses hate to look at me. They come at me with rubber gloves on so that I won't contaminate them, even though they should know better. My insurance policy has disowned me. My children no longer write me letters, though I've paid for them to go to Ivy League colleges. Trisha comes by sometimes. She is happy that we rarely made love.

One day I will close my eyes and wake up in a dozen other bodies. I will be closer to her than I could ever be in life. In life we are all islands. Only in Dr. Stone's laboratory can we know true intimacy, the mind of one commanding the muscles of another and causing the nerves of a third to tingle with unnameable desires. I hope I shall die soon.

The living dead are not as you imagine them. There are no dangling innards, no dripping slime. They carry their guts and gore inside them, as do you and I. In the right light they can be beautiful, as when they stand in the cold luminescence of a basement laboratory, waiting for an electron stream to lend them the illusion of life. Fueled by the right fantasy, they become indistinguishable from us.

Listen. I know. I've loved them.

Contributors' Biographies

The following biographies use slash marks to indicate contributors' parents and hyphens for parental mixtures. Generations are: first (immigrant), second (United States as contributor's birthplace), and third (United States as birthplace of contributor and one parent or both parents).

Ai

Amerasian of Japanese/African American–Choctaw–Dutch–Irish descent, Ai is author of five books of poetry (*Cruelty, Killing Floor, Sin, Fate,* and *Greed*) and a novel (*Blackout,* Norton, 1995). Her awards and grants include the Lamont Poetry Award, the Pushcart Prize, the Before Columbus Foundation's American Book Award, and the Floralia Prize, as well as a Guggenheim Fellowship, an NEA Fellowship, and an Ingram Merrill Fellowship. Ai lives in Tucson, Arizona, where she grew up.

Ahn, Eugene

Born in Cold Springs, New York, and raised in San Jose, California, Korean American Ahn studied Creative Writing at UCLA. Ahn's photography has appeared in various publications, including *Amerasia Journal, The Anchorage Daily News, Los Angeles Times Magazine, Muae,* and other periodicals and books. Ahn lives in Los Angeles.

Alexander, Meena

Born in 1951 in India, Alexander was raised in North Africa and Great Britain. First generation, she has lived in New York for the last twenty years. She is the author of a novel (*Nampally Road*), two books of criticism, a memoir (*Fault Lines,* Feminist Press, 1991), and six books of poetry (including *House of a Thousand Doors*). Mena is Professor of English and Creative Writing at Hunter College and the Graduate Center of the City University of New York.

Ancheta, Shirley

Second-generation Filipino American Ancheta was born and raised in Watsonville, California. She co-edited *Without Names: A Filipino American Poetry Anthology*

(Kearny Street Press, 1985). Her work has appeared in *Quarry West*. The mother of two sons, Miles and Travis, Ancheta lives in Watsonville.

Au, Wagner Wai Jim

Born in 1967 in New Mexico, Chinese/British-Irish-German American Au grew up in Kailua, Hawaii. He received his B.A. in Philosophy from the University of Hawaii, and has been published in *Future Sex* and *Harper's* magazines. Au currently lives in San Francisco.

Brainard, Cecilia Manguerra

Born and raised in the Philippines, Brainard received a Communication Arts degree from Maryknoll College, then did her graduate work at UCLA. First generation, she has written and edited five books, including *When the Rainbow Goddess Wept* (E. P. Dutton, 1994). The recipient of several literary awards, Brainard teaches Creative Writing at the Writers' Program, UCLA Extension. She lives in Southern California with her husband and three sons.

Cabico, Regie

Born in Baltimore and raised in Clinton, Maryland, second-generation Filipino American Cabico received his B.F.A. in Acting and East Asian Studies from New York University, and studied poetry at The Writer's Voice. MTV Spoken Word Champion, he was the winner of the 1993 New York Poetry Slam and was Lollapalooza Road Poet in 1994. His works are featured on compact disc as well as in the anthologies *Aloud: Voices from the Nuyorican Poets Cafe* (Henry Holt, 1994) and *The Name of Love* (St. Martin's, 1995).

Chan, Gaye

Born in Hong Kong, Chan immigrated to the United States when she was twelve, and eventually received her M.F.A. from the San Francisco Art Institute. She has had solo exhibitions at the Center for Photography in Woodstock, the Contemporary Museum in Honolulu, and the North Fort Gallery, in Osaka. She has participated in numerous group exhibitions and is currently Assistant Professor in the Art Department at the University of Hawaii.

Chandra, G. S. Sharat

Born in 1938 in India, Chandra grew up there and in England and America. After receiving two law degrees, he abandoned the legal profession to study at the Iowa Writers' Workshop. He is the author of six books of poetry. His recent *Family of Mirrors* was nominated for the Pulitzer Prize, and his *Immigrants of Loss* (London, 1994) was nominated for both the T. S. Eliot Prize and the Commonwealth Poetry Prize. He teaches at the University of Missouri, Kansas City.

Chang, Diana

Born in New York City, third-generation Chinese American Chang spent part of her childhood in China. She received her B.A. from Barnard College and studied at the Sorbonne on a Fulbright Scholarship. The author of six novels, including *The Frontiers of Love,* she has also published three poetry chapbooks and edited PEN's literary quarterly, *The American Pen.* Her awards include the John Hay Whitney Opportunity Fellowship and the Mademoiselle Woman of the Year Award.

Chang, Henry

Chinese American Chang was born in New York City's Chinatown and raised on the Lower East Side. He studied English at the City College of New York. He has been published in *Yellow Pearl* and *Bridge* magazine. He is presently completing a detective novel, *Year of the Dog.* His greatest achievement is his "recent plunge into fatherhood and the joys thereof."

Chin, Charlie

Born in 1944 in New York City, third-generation Chinese American Chin grew up on Manhattan's Lower East Side. Musician, singer, writer, playwright, and actor, Chin has work experience that includes sixteen years of bartending, two years as a health inspector, and four years as a Chinatown tour guide. He was the 1993 National Spokesperson for La Choy/Chun King Products.

Chin, Frank

Born in 1940 in Berkeley, California, Chinese American Chin studied at the Iowa Writers' Workshop and graduated from the University of California at Santa Barbara. His plays are *Chickencoop Chairman* and *The Year of the Dragon.* Co-editor of *Aiiieeeee!* and *The Big Aiiieeeee!*, he is the author of a collection of short fiction, *Chinaman Pacific & Frisco R.R. Co.*, and two novels: *Donald Duk* (Coffee House Press, 1991) and *Gunga Din Highway* (Coffee House Press, 1994).

Chin, Marilyn

Born in 1955 in Hong Kong and raised in Portland, Oregon, Chinese American Chin received a B.A. in Classical Chinese Literature, an M.F.A. from the University of Iowa, and a Stegner Fellowship at Stanford. She has published two books of poetry: *The Terrace Empty* (Milkweed) and *Dwarf Bamboo* (Greenfield Review Press). Recipient of two NEA Poetry Fellowships, Chin is Associate Professor in the Creative Writing Program at San Diego State University.

Chin, Woon Ping

Born and raised in Malayasia, Chin received her Ph.D. from the University of Toledo. She was a Fulbright Lecturer at the University of Indonesia and the Shanghai Foreign Language Institute. She is the author of *The Naturalization of Camellia Song & Details Cannot Body Wants* and co-authored *Tales of Shaman: Collection of Jah Hut Aboriginal Malaysian Myths.* She is on the faculty of Swarthmore College.

Cobb, Nora Okja

Born in 1965 in Seoul, Korea, Korean/Euro-American Cobb grew up in Honolulu, Hawaii. She received an M.A. in American Literature, with an emphasis on Asian American Literature, from the University of California at Santa Cruz. A free-lance writer and journalist, Cobb has had her work published in *Bamboo Ridge, Hawaii Review, Melus, Making Face, Making Soul,* and *New Visions.* She has taught at Santa Cruz and at the University of Hawaii at Manoa.

deSouza, Allan

Born in 1958 in Kenya, South Asian mixed-media artist deSouza grew up in England. He had exhibited extensively (Great Britain, United States, Canada, Germany, Cuba, and the Philippines) before turning to fiction. Author of *The Sikhs in Britain* (Batsford, 1986), he has seen his critical writing and artwork appear in *Tracing Cultures* (Whitney Museum, 1994), *Ecstatic Antibodies* (Rivers Oram Press, 1989), and various journals, including *Third Text, Rungh,* and *Bazaar.*

Divakaruni, Chitra

Born in 1956 in India, Divakaruni has written three books of poetry, including *The Reason for Nasturtiums* (Berkeley Poets Press, 1990) and *Black Candle* (Calyx Books, 1991). Editor of *Multitude* (McGraw-Hill, 1992), she is author of the short-story collection *Arranged Marriage* (Anchor Books, 1995). Her awards include the Gerbode Foundation Award, the Pushcart Prize, and two PEN Syndicated Fiction Project Awards. She teaches at Foothill College in Los Altos Hills, California, and is President of MAITRI, a helpline for South Asian women.

Fuentes, Marlon

Born and raised in Manila, Fuentes is a filmmaker, photographer, and conceptual artist who, since 1981, has exhibited nationally in group and individual shows. His work is in the collection of the Library of Congress, the National Museum of American art, and the Corcoran Gallery—all in Washington, D.C.—and the Houston Museum of Fine Art. He is completing his experimental documentary, *Bontoc Eulogy,* about the Filipino experience in the St. Louis World's Fair of 1904.

Goto, L. T.

Born and raised in Seattle, Washington, third-generation Japanese American Goto double-majored in English and Psychology at Washington State University at Pullman. He studied with David Henry Hwang at the Writers' Institute, and he has published in various magazines and journals, including sexually oriented feature articles in *Yolk* magazine. Goto lives in Los Angeles.

Hahn, Kimiko

Born in 1955 in Pleasantville, New York, Japanese American Hahn received her B.A. from the University of Iowa and her M.A. in Japanese Literature from Columbia University. She is the author of three books of poetry: *Air Pocket* and *Earshot* (Hanging Loose Press, 1989 and 1992) as well as *The Unbearable Heart* (Kaya Press, 1995). She is a recipient of an NEA Fellowship in Poetry, and her work has been published in numerous magazines and anthologies, including *Charlie Chan Is Dead* (Penguin, 1993).

Hill, Amy

Born in South Dakota and raised in Seattle, Washington, Japanese/Finnish American Hill studied at the University of Washington and Sophia International University in Tokyo. A second-generation actress and performance artist, she has a regular role on ABC's *All American Girl* and has performed her solo trilogy (*Tokyo Bound, Beside Myself,* and *Reunion*) across the country.

Hongo, Garrett

Born in Volcano, Hawaii, third-generation Japanese American Hongo received an M.F.A. in English from the University of California at Irvine. Author of *Yellow Light* (Wesleyan, 1982) and *The River of Heaven* (Knopf, 1988), which was the Lamont Poetry Selection and a finalist for the Pulitzer Prize, he also edited *The Open Boat: Poems from Asian America* (Anchor Books, 1993), Wakako Yamauchi's

Songs My Mother Taught Me (Feminist Press, 1994), and *Under Western Eyes* (Anchor Books, 1995). His recently completed memoir is *Volcano* (Knopf, 1995).

Hwang, David Henry

Born in 1957 in Los Angeles, second-generation Chinese American Hwang studied at Stanford and the Yale School of Drama. His works include seven plays (*FOB, The Dance and the Railroad, Family Devotions, The House of Sleeping Beauties & the Sound of a Voice, M. Butterfly, Bondage,* and *Face Value*), librettos for Philip Glass and Prince, and two screenplays (*M. Butterfly* and *Golden Gate*). His awards include the Obie, Drama-Logue Award, Tony, and Drama Desk Award.

Ibarra, Eulalio Yerro

Born in 1956 in the Philippines, Ibarra was trained in Manila as a veterinarian. He received his master's degree in Anatomy in New Zealand and his Ph.D. in Male Reproductive Biology from the University of Illinois. First generation, he is currently a postdoctoral fellow at a large Chicago teaching hospital. *Potato Eater* is his first publication.

Ishima, Zio

Born and raised in Los Angeles, third-generation Japanese American Ishima is a self-taught artist who has exhibited his photographs and paintings across the United States. He won the outstanding Achievement Award for nude photography, in the Artitudes International Competition in 1989, and his work has appeared in *Paramour, Transpacific/XO,* and *Yolk* magazines. His work is included in American, European, and Asian art collections.

Kageyama, Yuri

Born in 1953 in Japan, Kageyama grew up in Japan and the United States. She graduated magna cum laude from Cornell and has an M.A. in Sociology from the University of California at Berkeley. A poet, journalist, and translator, she wrote *Peeling—Poems by Yuri Kageyama* (I. Reed Books, 1988) and co-authored *Picking a Fight with Japanese Companies* (Tokyo: OS Publishers, 1993). She works as a reporter in Detroit.

Kamani, Ginu

Born in Bombay, India, Kamani moved to the United States with her family at the age of fourteen. She received a B.A. in Linguistics and an M.A. in Creative Writing from the University of Colorado at Boulder. Her writing has appeared in *Our Feet Walk the Sky: Women of the South Asian Diaspora* (Aunt Lute Books, 1993). She has recently published a collection of short stories, *Junglee Girl* (Aunt Lute Books, 1995). Kamani lives in Northern California with her husband.

Kaneko, Lonny

Born in 1939 in Seattle, Washington, third-generation Japanese American Kaneko has contributed to a number of anthologies, including *The Big Aiiieeeee!, Ear to the Ground,* and *Breaking Silence.* The author of a collection of poems, *Coming Home from Camp* (Brooding Heron Press), he has also co-authored the play *Lady Is Dying,* which was performed in San Francisco and Seattle in the 1970s and early 1980s.

Kashiwagi, Hiroshi

Born in 1922 in Sacramento, California, second-generation Japanese American Kashiwagi grew up in nearby Loomis. He received a B.A. in Oriental Languages from UCLA and an M.L.S. from the University of California at Berkeley. He worked as the San Francisco Public Library's Reference Librarian for twenty years. His work has appeared in *Ayumi* (Japanese American Anthology Committee, 1980) and *The Big Aiiieeeee!* (Penguin, 1991).

Kogawa, Joy

Born in 1935 in Vancouver, British Columbia, Japanese Canadian Kogawa and her family were interned during World War II. She is the author of two novels, *Obasan* and *Itsuka* (Anchor Books, 1992), and four books of petry: *The Splintered Moon, A Choice of Dreams, Jericho Road,* and *Woman in the Woods.* Kogawa has worked as a schoolteacher and as a writer for the Canadian Prime Minister's office, and she is a member of the Order of Canada.

Kono, Juliet S.

Born and raised in Hilo, Hawaii, third-generation Japanese American Kono received both her B.A. and M.A. in English Literature from the University of Hawaii at Manoa. She is the author of two poetry books, *Hilo Rains* (Bamboo Ridge Press, 1988) and *Tsunami Years* (Bamboo Ridge Press, 1995). In 1991, Kono received the American Japanese National Literary Award.

Koyama, Tina

Born in 1958 in Seattle, Washington, third-generation Japanese American Koyama received her M.A. in Creative Writing from the University of Washington. Her work has appeared in numerous publications, including *Breaking Silence: An Anthology of Asian American Poets* (Greenfield Review Press, 1983).

Kudaka, Geraldine

Born in Maui, Hawaii, third-generation Okinawan American Kudaka studied at San Jose State University and UCLA's School of Theater, Film, and Television, and is recipient of an NEA Fellowship in film studies. Her poetry has appeared in numerous publications, including *New Letters, Tokyo Literary Review, Califia, Time to Greez!, Breaking Silence,* and *Under Western Eyes* (Anchor Books, 1995). Editor of *The Third World Women's Book* (Third World Communications, 1972) and *Beyond Rice: A Broadside Series* (Noro Press, 1978), she is story editor for Lumière Films.

Kumar, Mina

Born in Madras, India, Kumar lives in New York, where she is attending Columbia University. Her work has appeared in various publications, including *Hanging Loose* and *Turnstile,* and she writes for *Sojourner* and *Rungh.*

Kwong, Dan

Born and raised in Los Angeles, third-generation Chinese/Japanese American Kwong studied Fine Arts at the University of Southern California, as well as Video and Sound at the School of the Art Institute of Chicago. A performance artist, he has received grants from the Rockefeller Foundation, the NEA, the Los Angeles Cultural Affairs Department, and Art Matters Inc. He was a 1995 Alpert Award nominee.

Lau, Alan

Born in 1948 in Oroville, California, third-generation Chinese American Lau was raised in Paradise, California. A painter and poet, he received the American Book Award for his *Songs for Jadina* (Greenfield Review Press, 1980). As an artist, Lau has exhibited his work in the United States, England, and Japan. He is represented by the Francine Seders Gallery in Seattle, where he also coordinates the *International Examiner*'s "Pacific Reader: An Asian Pacific American Review of Books."

Lau, Evelyn

Born in 1971 in Vancouver, Chinese Canadian Lau saw her first book, *Runaway: Diary of a Street Kid,* become a 1989 bestseller—one that was adapted into a CBC-TV movie. Her poetry books are *You Are Not Who You Claim* (Coach House, 1990), winner of the Milton Acorn People's Poetry Award; *Oedipal Dreams* (Coach House, 1992), which was short-listed for Canada's prestigious Governor General's Award; and *In the House of Slaves* (Coach House, 1994). The youngest Canadian to receive such acclaim, she is author of *Fresh Girls and Other Stories* (Hyperion, 1995).

Lee, Chang-rae

Born in 1967 in South Korea, Lee immigrated to the United States with his family when he was three. He graduated from Phillips Exeter Academy and Yale University, and he received his M.F.A. from the University of Oregon, where he is currently an Assistant Professor in the Program in Creative Writing. *Native Speaker* (Riverhead Books, 1995) is his first novel.

Lei-lanilau, Carolyn

Born in 1946 and raised in Honolulu, Chinese/Hawaiian Lei-lanilau's first poetry book, *Wode Shuofa* (*My Way of Speaking*), received the 1989 American Book Award for Poetry. Her second book is *The Marginalia on Gorilla/Bird.* She has lectured on translation and literary criticism in the United States and China, particularly on Nu Shu, the Secret Women's Language of Hunan Province, and is Director of a Native Hawaiian oral history project, Ha'ina Mai Ana Ka Puana (Tell the Story).

Leong, Russell

Born in 1950 in San Francisco, third-generation Chinese American Leong received an M.F.A. in Film from UCLA. His book of poetry *The Country of Dreams and Dust* (West End Press, 1993) won PEN's Josephine Miles Literature Award. Leong is the editor of *Amerasia Journal* (UCLA Asian American Studies Center), *Moving the Image: Independent Asian Pacific American Media Arts* (Visual Communications and UCLA Asian American Studies Center, 1991), and *Asian American Sexualities* (Routledge, 1995).

Liu, Timothy

Born in 1965 and raised in San Jose, California, second-generation Chinese American Liu received his M.A. in English from the University of Houston. His book of poetry *Vox Angelica* (Alice James Books) received the 1992 Norma Farber First Book Award from the Poetry Society of America. Recipient of the 1993 John Ciardi Fellowship at the Breadloaf Writers' Conference, Liu is an Assistant Professor at Cornell University.

Louie, David Wong
Born in 1954 in Rockville Center, New York, Chinese American Louie attended Vassar College and the University of Iowa. His collection of short stories *Pangs of Love* (Plume, 1991) won both the *Los Angeles Times*'s Art Seidenbaum Award and *Ploughshares'* John C. Zacharis First Book Award. His work has appeared in numerous anthologies, including *The Best American Short Stories, 1989*. He now teaches in the English Department at UCLA.

Meer, Ameena
Born in 1964 in Boston, Massachusetts, Indian American Meer studied Postcolonial Literature at Delhi University in India and received her B.A. in Creative Writing from the University of California at Santa Cruz. Editor of *Big* magazine, Meer has had her work published in *The Flaming Spirit: The Asian Women Writers Collective* (Virago, U.K.) and *Low Low Rent* (Grove Press, 1994). Meer's first novel is *Bombay Talkie* (High Risk/Serpent's Tail Books, 1994).

Monji, Jana J.
Born in San Diego, California, third-generation Japanese American Monji received a B.A. in both Studio Arts and Asian Studies from the University of California at Santa Barbara and an M.A. in East Asian Languages and Cultures from UCLA. She is a theater critic for the *L.A. Weekly,* and her essays on race issues have appeared in the *Los Angeles Times.* Her photography has been published in *Rafu Shimpo* and *Transpacific,* as well as exhibited in Southern California.

Mukherjee, Bharati
Born in Calcutta, India, Mukherjee received her M.A. in English and Ancient Indian Culture at the Universities of Calcutta and Baroda. She came to the United States in 1961, receiving her M.F.A. and Ph.D. in English from the University of Iowa. She is the author of five books, *The Tiger's Daughter, Wife, Darkness, Jasmine,* and *The Middleman and Other Stories.* Mukherjee is Professor of English at the University of California at Berkeley.

Mura, David
Born in 1952 in Great Lakes, Illinois, Sansei Mura received his B.A. from Grinnell College and his M.F.A. from Vermont College. Writer and performance artist, he is the author of *Turning Japanese: Memoirs of a Sansei* (Anchor Books, 1992), *The Colors of Desire* (Anchor Books, 1995), and the forthcoming *Where the Body Meets Memory: An Odyssey of Race, Sexuality, and Identity* (Anchor Books). He has received the Lila Wallace Reader's Digest Award and two NEA Fellowships.

Nako, Joyce
Born in 1948 in Maui, Hawaii, third-generation Okinawan American Nako received her education in Los Angeles. She is currently editing an anthology for Pacific Asian American Women Writers West (PAAWWW), of which she is a founding member, and *Imaging: A Century of Asian Women in Film* for Visual Communications. She lives in Los Angeles with her husband and dog.

Nguyen, Minh Duc
Born in 1972 in Nha Trang, Vietnam, Nguyen was raised in San Jose, California. He received his B.S. in Molecular Cell Biology from the University of California at

Berkeley. His short fiction was awarded second place in both *A Magazine*'s First Annual Asian American Literary Contest (1994) and the Shrout Short Fiction Contest at the University of California at Berkeley (also 1994). His work is also included in the anthology *American Eyes* (Henry Holt, 1994).

Osumi, Tony

Born in 1967 in Culver City, California, Amerasian Osumi received a B.A. from California State University at Northridge and an M.A. in Asian American Studies from UCLA. His poetry has appeared in *Dis.Orient Journalzine.* A kindergarten teacher and community artist, he has collaborated on murals for the University of California at Riverside and in Los Angeles's Koreatown.

Ping, Wang

Born in Shanghai, since 1985 Ping has lived in New York, where she is currently enrolled in the Comparative Literature Ph.D. Program at New York University. Her work has appeared in numerous publications, including *The Literary Review, The Portable Lower East Side, Chicago Review,* and *West Coast Line.* Her poem "Of Flesh and Spirit" was included in *The Best of American Poetry, 1993.* She is the author of *American Visa* (Coffee House Press, 1994).

Posey, Sandra Mizumoto

Born in 1966 and raised in California, Japanese/Euro-American Posey received her B.A., magna cum laude, in Comparative Literature from California State University at Long Beach, and an M.A. in Folklore and Mythology from UCLA. Her work has appeared in the *Los Angeles Times, Mid-American Review,* and *Art Spiral.* Posey's nonfiction book on stamp and mail art is *God Spoke and He Said Rubber Stamp* (University Press of Mississippi, 1996).

Shigekuni, Julie

Born in 1962 in Panorama City, California, fifty-generation Japanese American Shigekuni received her B.A. from New York's Hunter College and her M.F.A. from Sarah Lawrence College, Bronxville, N.Y. She is the author of *A Bridge Between Us* (Anchor Books, 1995) and recipient of both the Henfield Award and the American Japanese National Literary Award. She is Professor of Creative Writing at the Institute of American Indian Arts in Santa Fe, New Mexico.

Shin, Ann

Born in 1968 in London, Ontario, Korean Canadian Shin received her M.A. in English from the University of Toronto. Her work has appeared in various Canadian publications and journals such as *Canadian Forum* and *Fireweed.* She performs poetry with sampled sound and music and, as a member of the Collective Public Things International, staged an on-line installation piece on telecommunications, *Communication Park.*

Somtow, S. P.

Born in Bangkok and educated at Eton College and Cambridge, noted science fiction/fantasy, and horror author S. P. Somtow has been nominated for the Hugo Award, the John W. Campbell Award, and the American Horror Award. He has won the Locus Award, and the Edmond Hamilton Memorial Award. A prolific writer with thirty-one books to his credit, he is also an accomplished composer and filmmaker. *Jasmine Nights* (St. Martin's Press, 1995), a satire of Thai high society, is his first "semiautobiographical" novel.

Tagami, Jeff

Born in 1954 and raised in Watsonville, California, third-generation Filipino American Tagami attended San Francisco State University. He is the author of a book of poetry, *October Light* (Kearny Street Workshop Press). His work has also appeared in *The Open Boat: Poems from Asian America* (Anchor Books, 1993). After fourteen years of living in San Francisco, Tagami has returned to his hometown of Watsonville.

Tan, Cecilia

Born in 1967 in New York, Chinese-Filipina/Irish-Welsh American Tan received an M.A. in Professional Writing and Publishing from Boston's Emerson College. She is the author of a collection of erotic science fiction short stories, *Telepaths Don't Need Safewords,* and her fiction has also appeared in *Penthouse* magazine and *Herotica 3* (Plume, 1994). A member of the National Leather Association, Tan is active in bisexual politics.

tan, joël b.

Born in 1968 in Manila, Filipino American joël tan is a poet and performance artist. His work has appeared in *Amerasia Journal, Blood Whispers,* and *Dis.Orient Journalzine.* His performances include *Mama's Boy, Life on the Runway,* and *Queer N'Asian.* Co-founder of Barangay (a Filipino gay men's group) and founder of Colors United Action Coalition (a gay and lesbian political action collective), he is an AIDS activist.

Tran, Barbara

Born in New York, second-generation Vietnamese American Tran received her M.F.A. in Poetry from Columbia University. She has received the Van Lier Fellowship from the Asian American Writer's Workshop, and her work has appeared in *Premonitions: The Kaya Anthology of New Asian North American Poetry* (Kaya Press), as well as *The Asian Pacific American Journal, Antioch Review, Pequod,* and *The Southern Poetry Review.* Tran works at the Joseph Papp Public Theater in New York City.

Tsui, Kitty

Born in 1952 in Hong Kong, Chinese American Tsui attended San Francisco State University. She is the author of *The Words of a Woman Who Breathes Fire* (Spinster's Ink, 1983) and has been included in over thirty-five anthologies, including *Lesbian Erotics* (NYU Press, 1995), *Cloe Plus Olivia* (Viking, 1994), and *Pearls of Passion* (Sister Vision, 1994). A member of the editorial board of the *Lesbian Review of Books,* Tsui has just completed a historical novel, *Bak Sze, White Snake.*

Tyrr, Tanith

Born and raised in the Los Angeles area, Amerasian (Japanese/American) Tyrr received a B.A. in Business and Marketing from California State University at Northridge. Tyrr resides in Northern California, where she owns and manages the Pleasure Chamber, an adult virtual reality studio "on the cutting edge of cybersensuality. I live on the Internet, where I continue causing controversies at an alarming rate."

Uyematsu, Amy
Born in Pasadena, California, third-generation Japanese American Uyematsu received her B.S. in Mathematics from UCLA. Her first book, *30 Miles from J-town* (Story Line Press, 1992), won the 1992 Nicholas Roerich Poetry Prize. She was one of the early staff members of the UCLA Asian American Studies Center and co-edited *Roots: An Asian American Reader* (UCLA, 1971).

Wat, Eric C.
Born in 1970 in Hong Kong, Chinese American Wat immigrated to Los Angeles when he was twelve. He received his B.A. in Communication Studies at UCLA and is a graduate student in American Studies at California State University at Fullerton. A member of Queer and the Asian Writers' Collective, he works for the UCLA Asian American Studies Center.

Weng, Judy Fei Fei
Born in 1970 in Taipei, Chinese/Japanese Weng was raised in New York City and San Francisco. She studied at San Francisco's American Conservatory Theater and is director-writer for Actors Anonymous, a sketch comedy troupe. Her sketch work has been seen on MTV and on *In Living Color* and *America's Funniest People.* This is her first publication.

Wong, Hsu Tzi
Born in Tien Hao Monastery in Singapore, Hsu Tzi grew up in Southeast Asia devoutly religious. She received her B.A. in Hong Kong, then received her master's degree in Electrical Engineering from the Massachusetts Institute of Technology. She works as a systems designer for a Southern California computer manufacturer and writers in her spare time.

Wong, Shawn
Born in 1949 in Oakland, California, Wong is second-generation Chinese American. He is co-editor of the anthologies *Before Columbus Foundation Fiction/Poetry, Aiiieeeee!,* and *The Big Aiiieeeee!* His novels are *Homebase* (Reed and Cannon, 1979; reprinted Plume/American Library, 1990) and *American Knees* (Simon & Schuster, 1995). He is Professor of English at the University of Washington, Seattle.

Yamanaka, Lois Ann
Born in Ho'olehua, Molokai, Hawaii, Japanese American Lois received her B.A. and M.A. in Education from the University of Hawaii at Manoa. She has been named the National Book Award Winner of the Association for Asian American Studies and won the Pushcart Prize XVIII 1993 for *Saturday Night at the Pahala Theatre* (Bamboo Ridge Press, 1993), as well as the Pushcart Prize XIX 1994 for *Yam Wig.* Her first novel is *Wild Meat and the Bully Burgers* (Farrar Straus & Giroux).

Yao, Christina
Born in Shanghai, Yao was raised in mainland China, where she started publishing stories at the age of sixteen. She has received an M.Phil., is a Ph.D. candidate at Columbia University in New York, and is a member of the European Human Genetics Society. Her work has appeared in *Medical Genetics* and *Journal of American Human Genetics.*

Yau, John
Born in 1950 in Lynn, Massachusetts, second-generation Chinese American Yau received his B.A. in Literature from Bard College and his M.F.A. in Creative Writing from Brooklyn College. He has published a dozen books of poetry, including *Edificio Sayonara,* (Black Sparrow, 1992) and *Berlin Diptychon* (Timken Publishers, 1995); short stories: *Hawaiian Cowboys* (Black Sparrow, 1994); and criticism: *In the Realm of Appearances: The Art of Andy Warhol* (Ecco Press, 1993).

Yee, Marian
Yee graduated from Rutgers University and has published in *The Forbidden Stitch: An Asian American Women's Anthology* (Calyx Books, 1989).

He was smaller than any
man she'd been w/ B4...
& how must she seem to
him?